W9-BOD-778

PLAINCLOTHES NaKED

also by jerry stahl

Permanent Midnight
Perv—A Love Story

Jerry Stahl

PLAINCLOTHES

NAKED

wm WILLIAM MORROW   75 YEARS OF PUBLISHING

An Imprint of HarperCollins*Publishers*

PLAINCLOTHES NAKED. Copyright © 2001 by Jerry
Stahl. All rights reserved. Printed in the United
States of America. No part of this book may be
used or reproduced in any manner whatsoever
without written permission except in the case of
brief quotations embodied in critical articles and
reviews. For information address HarperCollins
Publishers Inc., 10 East 53rd Street, New York, NY
10022.

HarperCollins books may be purchased for
educational, business, or sales promotional use.
For information please write: Special Markets
Department, HarperCollins Publishers Inc.,
10 East 53rd Street, New York, NY 10022.

FIRST EDITION

Designed by Nicola Ferguson

Printed on acid-free paper

Library of Congress Cataloging-in-Publication Data
Stahl, Jerry.
Plainclothes naked / by Jerry Stahl.— 1st ed.
p.   cm.
ISBN 0-06-018556-2 (acid-free paper)
I. Title.
PS3569. T3125 P58 2001
813'.54—dc21   2001030293

01 02 03 04 05 QW 10 9 8 7 6 5 4 3 2 1

For the anonymous, in all their demented splendor

Do you vow to keep your wits among the witless? Do you commit yourself
to pondering ceaselessly the uselessness of caring, the uselessness of love,
that great reality for which all else must be abandoned?

—Joy Williams

Hey Man, let's dress up like cops and see what we could do . . .

—Tom Verlaine

PLAINCLOTHES NaKED

PROLOGUE

Spongy buttocks exposed and wobbling, Tony Zank's mother piled down the rest home corridor, screaming "Help me!" and "Stop the monster!"

Her walker clattered off the floor and her Seventh Heaven gown clung half-on, half-off, as though she'd run through a backyard clothesline and the paper-thin garment had caught an arm.

"Pretty good pipes for an oldster," said McCardle, Zank's sullen partner, a Dean Martin look-alike, if Dean Martin had been African-American. He added, when Zank gave him a stare, "I mean, she seems pretty upset."

Zank burped beef jerky fumes into his fist and shrugged. "She's always upset. That's her job. She's been upset for fifty years."

Zank realized, with a sinking twinge, that hiding the key to his happy tomorrow in his mother's bed, wedged between the plastic protecto-pad and the mattress beneath, had not been the brightest idea he'd ever had. But this was no time for regrets. He had to get in there and slip the envelope out before the authorities—some breed of rest home police, if there was such a thing—showed up and asked what all the shrieks were about. Asked him why, if the morning went really south, he had decided to visit his mom with a two-time loser who'd showed up on *America's Most Wanted* the week before, wanted for a gay shovel murder.

"Mac, reach in and grab the thing," Zank snapped. "I'll cover the door."

In passive-aggressive splendor, McCardle made drama of clamping his jaw and squinting as though into a strong gale.

"What?" Zank hissed at him from the doorway.

"I'm not gonna go in there and touch bedding, Tony. You can catch all kinds of stuff, reaching in old people's beds."

Zank threw the punch before he knew he was going to, then pushed past his partner and began to tackle the mattress himself. His mother's screams had faded, but some kind of other business was going on down the hall.

"That wasn't necessary," McCardle mumbled. He tugged his soul patch and worked his lower lip indignantly. "I wasn't dissing your moms. It's just, I got a phobia, on account of after her stroke my Auntie Big'n went incontinental. I used to have to tidy up and it gave me a condition. My hands swelled up like catcher's mitts. It was like havin' paws, and all the kids used to make fun. I loved my auntie, even though she beat me with rolled-up magazines, but her bed gave me some kind of mitt disease."

Zank pounded the nearest wall with his fist. "Jesus Christ, enough! That's not something I need to hear about right now, okay? That's not something I ever need to hear about!"

"Okay! Down Simba. . . . Maybe you should lighten up on the rock, Cuz. You're getting cranky."

McCardle shook his head and pinched the tiny bulb of his button nose, which looked like it had been ordered from a Make-Me-White catalogue, though he swore his entire family had been born with them.

That tiny nose, and his cocoa hue, were the only things that kept Mac's Martin resemblance from being freakish. This added to Tony's suspicion that his partner in crime had had some nasal work to keep from being stopped on the street and forced to sing "That's Amore."

"I'm only trying to tell you," McCardle persisted, "bed stuff gets me tweaked, on account of my childhood abuse. It upsets my little McCardle. I figured it out in therapy, when I was inside."

By now, however, Zank had stopped listening. He'd stopped hearing altogether, busy as he was peeling off Mom's Seventh Heaven bedspread, followed by her blankets, her sheets, and her plastic pad in a frantic effort to retrieve the envelope he'd stashed. The envelope that was going to change everything.

The envelope, he realized as the sound of clicking heels and agitated female voices drew nearer, that wasn't there anymore.

ONE

Tina couldn't decide between ground glass and Drano.

She'd already sprinkled a pinch of smashed-up light-bulb—an easy-reading 40-watter—in Marvin's Lucky Charms, when she started thinking maybe drain cleaner was the way to go.

One of the old Jews at the home, Mister Cornfeld, came down with the blood-squirts for a week and finally died after somebody put Liquid-Plumr in his prune juice. Old Jews were always drinking prune juice, always talking about what was going on in their pants. Either their constipation or their prostates or something skanky like that. At least her granddaddy, whatever his other faults, had not spent a whole lot of time boring her with what was happening downstairs. Till he bought the mall at ninety, Pop Lee snored like an idling diesel and still liked to grab ass and talk nasty. When she found the trunk full of *Moppets* and *Barely Legals* after the funeral, she wasn't exactly surprised. But at least the old skeek didn't discuss his plumbing.

Tina could hear Marvin doing his prosperity chants from the bedroom and knew she had to make up her mind. Since he'd redirected his energy from day trading—which had cost them their condo—to developing and selling his new "Millionaire Mantra," Marv had been experimenting with the perfect brand of *satsang* to put up on the Web. He was convinced there was an untapped pool of desperate New Agers who wanted to be rich and cosmic at the same time. His goal was to create the perfect quarter hour chant—ten minutes for Personal Prosperity, five for World Peace and Feeding the Children—then get himself up and streaming so folks could vocalize along with him, and send away for his line of videos, audiocassettes, and the ever-popular BUDDHA WANTS YOU TO HAVE IT ALL! T-shirts.

Unfortunately, with each minute of spiritual honking, Tina's determination to kill Marvin, sell his computers, and quit her job at Seventh Heaven was given renewed impetus. Mostly she just wanted to shut him up.

"Hungh-uh, hungh-uh, *HUNGH-UH,*" came the turbulent sounds from their bedroom. "Hungh-uh, hungh-uh, hungh hungh *HUNGH!*"

No doubt he was taping himself, too. Marv had the vid-cam on a tripod in front of the bed. Which was another thing. . . .

Marvin wasn't a petite man. In fact he was husky. Husky and soft, with a shaved head, no chest hair, and a little red moustache. Just the thought of him in there, cross-legged on a throw pillow, wearing the Gunga Din loincloth he thought made him look guruesque, was enough to set Tina crunching another pinch of glass and dipping into her bag for the industrial-strength Drano she'd pilfered from the rest home janitor's closet.

"Oh God, shut *up!*" Tina yelled to no one but herself. No way Marvin could hear over the din of his chants. By now he'd shifted to nose-hums, which really drove her off a cliff. It was hard to describe the sound he produced. The odd *Om* alternated with guttural blasts of ersatz Sanskrit and quick, bleated syllables like *sneep* or *snerm,* the kind of noise a goat might make if it tried to speak English and suffered from a cleft palate.

Marvin was always a big planner. After his Chant for Prosperity site was up and running, he told her, it was on to the next big plum: Eternal Life. If he could just cook up the right pitch, maybe mock up some phony interviews with people who looked 120 but healthy, he could charge aspiring eternal lifers fifty bucks a pop for tapes, books, and videocassettes explaining his discovery that certain sound vibrations could keep you young, possibly even ensure immortality.

"You can't prove they *don't*," he explained to Tina one morning, sitting at the kitchen table slathered in Indoor Sun, his artificial tan lotion, wearing the turban he'd fashioned from a floral dish towel. "As long as I'm still up on my hind legs, who's to say I'm not the one guy on earth who's gonna be here for the Trilennium, or whatever comes next?"

It was Marvin's belief that Indian heritage, *India* Indian—curry, turban, *memsahib*—made for an effective sales tool. But lately, for Tina's money, he'd gone too far. These days he went straight from flossing his teeth in the morning to lounging around in turban and loincloth, inventing new and different chants and mantras. A necessary lifestyle, he'd tell her, if you wanted to turn yourself into the first big On-line Money Swami. Every day the cosmos blessed him with another sanctified cash concept.

Recalling all this made Tina wince. The idea of eternity spent listening to Marvin hum through his nose was so awful that she pulled out the Drano and poured a shot in his cereal before she remembered the envelope. Plenty of residents slid valuables of one kind or another under their mattresses, and the one perk of sheet-and-blanket duty was getting first crack at whatever treasures Seventh Heaven-ites saw fit to hide. Her first week on the job, she'd retrieved a sandwich bag stuffed with clipped-out cake recipes, an autographed photo of Frank Sinatra Junior, and sixteen crisp one-hundred-dollar bills wedged in a tattered paperback of Conrad Hilton's autobiography, *Be My Guest*.

What with Alzheimer's, general forgetfulness, and the simple fact that people who moved into rest homes rarely moved out alive, mattress stashes made for a steady and occasionally fascinating second income.

Not wanting to miss a chance to poison her husband, but anxious to check out her booty, Tina hollered that breakfast was ready. She pulled the envelope out of her purse and ripped it open. Then she tapped the contents onto the kitchen table, stared at it, and screamed for a solid twenty seconds. It was that kind of day.

She didn't even hear Marvin when he stepped behind her.

"My God, you're a *natural!*"

Delighted, he had flown in from the bedroom at the sound of his wife's sudden demo of vocal skills. "Put a little more sinus in it and you're right on target."

In jubilation—for his next *next* project, Marv had his heart set on "His'n'Her Love Chants," so Tina's outburst was pretty much an answered prayer—he snatched the bowl of Lucky Charms off the table with both hands, then leaned back and tipped the contents down his gullet in two enormous, chomping gulps.

"Still crunchy," he observed happily. "I hate when they sog up."

Until he said it, Tina'd all but forgotten about the Drano and glass. It wasn't the first time she'd spiked his food, just the first time she hadn't scraped it into the trash at the last minute. Before this, it had been a tease, something she'd done to entertain herself. A little ant killer here, a dollop of furniture polish there. All in nuptial fun. . . .

Tina was about to say something when Marv dropped on all fours and started frothing. What looked like dirty yogurt bubbled between his lips. It gushed out in a steady splurge, reminding her of the foam they sprayed on downed passenger planes. Tina'd never told anyone, but she always got weirdly excited by footage of houses with jets sticking out of them. Burning metal on lawns. The way the news cameras honed in on a single purse or tennis shoe. It did something to her. All those burly firemen with no faces wielding giant, spewing hoses. . . .

When the foam-splats stopped, Marv grabbed a table leg and heaved himself to his knees. He began to claw at his throat, craning his head sideways like the RCA dog. His eyes met hers bulging with questions.

"I better shower," Tina said, to the room at large, as she slid the item back in the envelope. It hit her, with the kind of wanton clarity the Almighty grants in moments of high emergency, that when the paramedics came, she wanted to look like she hadn't even been in the kitchen. Like she'd been showering and had padded out, dewy fresh, to find her husband dead from a toxic breakfast.

"Howg gum?" Marv managed to sputter, a far cry from the disciplined mantras he'd perfected in the past few weeks.

"Accident." Tina shrugged, feeling she owed him an explanation, however insincere.

But Marv was beyond replying. The convulsions had knocked his turban off, and Tina could see his artificial tan line, a complete circle around his skull where his headgear started and the application of Indoor Sun had stopped. He was perfectly two-toned: toasty brown below and mottled pink above. The line cut just over his ears, lending his head a peculiar, makeshift quality, as if the top screwed off.

"I'm going to miss you," Tina said, and almost meant it. If she hadn't bothered to pilfer Mrs. Zank's mattress, things might have turned out differently. But it didn't matter now. Marvin's tongue had swelled up like a purple sock with a foot in it, and he seemed to be chewing. Blood leaked out of his mouth onto the linoleum.

It was Marvin who'd selected—without consulting her—a cow-jumping-over-the-moon pattern for the kitchen floor. The cows had polka-dot pants on. And from the moment Marv worked the first self-adhesive tile out of the Home Depot box, she'd hated the sight of them.

So it was with a certain satisfaction that Tina realized a sea of clothed and smiling linoleum cows might well be the last sight her husband ever enjoyed on earth.

"Say good-bye to your friends," she said.

TWO

Detective Manny Rubert hated the idea of policemen almost as much as he hated himself for being one. He always figured there were people who chose their fate, and people who had a fate they'd more or less ended up with. He thought of himself as the "ending up" type.

Scant as it was, his early interaction with law enforcement had been uniformly grim. When he was little the cops would break up Wiffle ball games in the street and keep the bat. Later on, security guards would twist his collar or smack him when they caught him shoplifting. Still later the police were back, knocking on his parents' door to warn them that their pride-and-joy was jail-bound. Once inside, they'd hand his nervous mother and defeated little dad some Polaroids of him smoking dope with the other losers in the Marilyn High parking lot. To this day he'd never discovered the narc, though the cop who'd come to his house, Officer Chatlak, was still on the squad at seventy-something.

The worst part, for Manny, was that Chatlak never actually arrested him. He seemed to prefer keeping him out of jail so he could continue hassling him. Things were more touchy-feely in the late seventies. The public hadn't yet developed a taste for sending boys with no armpit hair to San Quentin.

After the dozenth time Officer Chatlak took it upon himself to tell Manny's father, man-to-man, that his only son had the makings of a "drug-addled degenerate," the old mill-hunk showed some tough love and threw him out of the house. He was seventeen, and thrilled. It wasn't like *nothing* positive had ever come out of his mild police problem. He got to leave home and move in with a dope fiend named Harvey he met at the Greyhound station.

Why Manny became a cop he didn't know—or maybe he did and didn't want to think about it. Near as he could figure, on those rare occasions when he bothered to try, it broke down to two possibilities, equally pathetic. First, being a policeman gave him a reason to feel as badly about himself as he tended to feel anyway. At twenty-two, and coming off his season on heroin, happiness was not part of the package. Being a junkie, when you broke it down, was nothing more than a crazed day job. (Though, oddly, in that capacity, the police never seemed to hassle him at all. He became a daily shooter, thanks to his bus station roomie, and never once got so much as a parking ticket.) On some level, he believed, he needed a life that offered as much borderline insanity as the one he'd left behind. . . .

The second possibility was more cut and dry. Excluding food service, being a cop was the one job you could get without a college education that did not involve heavy lifting. The last thing he wanted was to join his father at J & L. But even if he'd been dying to spend his days breathing fumes from a blast furnace, the steel mills were expiring faster than World War Two vets with emphysema and Pall Mall habits.

The academy was no picnic, and most of the recruits were assholes. But the brass were overjoyed to get a rookie whose test scores qualified him for more than reminding folks that, for fifty cents more, they could get a medium Coke and free refill with their cheeseburger.

"Ruby, you're dozing again," an old cop named Merch, Manny's ex-partner, barked from his desk by the candy machine. The candy desk was a coveted slot at the station, since whoever got it could just lean over, bang on the sweet spot by the machine's change dispenser, and knock out a free candy bar whenever he wanted. You never knew what you were going to get, but still. . . .

"You're dozing," Merch repeated, unpeeling a fresh Fifth Avenue. Since sliding onto desk duty, he'd packed on an easy fifty pounds. "I'm trying to tell you you're supposed to go to Carmichael Street. Guy splarked on his kitchen floor. Name's Podolsky. *Marvin*. They said he was all foamed up. Could be rabies."

Manny hated being called Ruby, but didn't mention it since Merch, and everybody else, knew it already. Instead, he replied mildly to the overweight quill-driver. "If it's rabies, that's Animal Rescue. We don't do dog calls."

"Hardy-har," said Merch. "I wrote down the address."

THREE

Upper Marilyn maintained a five-man police force, if you counted the chief. The town had begun life as an unincorporated area, a hodgepodge batch of neighborhoods plunked due southwest of Pittsburgh. When the mall craze first kicked in, developers realized that owning their own city would mean heftier tax breaks than even the sweetest deal Pittsburgh could cut them. So Upper Marilyn was born. As conceived, the fledgling burg was supposed to come with a sister municipality, Lower Marilyn.

All of this took place when J.F.K. was in office, in the heyday of Marilyn Monroe, and certain financially involved Methodists thought that "Lower Marilyn" sent the wrong message. No God-fearing soul would put down roots in a place named for an actress's nether parts. Why Upper was okay but Lower taboo was a question that engendered decades of obscene and inflammatory lore.

Old-timers dubbed the two regions "Tit-ville" and "Butt-burg." And, in certain shot-and-Iron City bars, "Meet me at the Bentelbo, up in Tits" or "Uncle Slats got drunk and lost his Buick down in Butt" were still perfectly acceptable locutions.

An Uppy by birth, Manny now boasted a pad in the heart of Butt-burg. As it turned out, the dead foamer's place squatted no more than three blocks from Manny's own half-a-rowhouse. He didn't need the number to locate Chez Marvin. A black-and-white—the town's only one—had already pulled into the front yard, where its tires left three-foot ruts in the dirt. If five years on the force had taught him nothing else, it was that cops didn't pull onto the lawns in Upper Marilyn. They didn't kick down doors, roust teens on the street, or drag drivers out of their cars at random up in Tit-ville, either.

After pulling into the driveway—it never hurt to block a perp's car, even if somebody'd already cashed his Lotto—Manny slapped and shoved his way through the sight-seers milling around the yard like guests at a summer wedding. About the only officially sanctioned police violence left was the pummeling of "necks," as the souls who flocked to crime scenes were called. What moved these humans to drop what they were doing so they could loiter within sniffing distance of death was anybody's guess. Manny wasn't the kind of cop who needed to blow off steam doing some honest "neck-deckin'." But he understood guys who did.

Right away, he made a note of the house: a nondescript brown brick on a street of nondescript brown bricks. This stretch of non–Upper Marilyn had seen swankier times. At one point the people who lived here actually had jobs. Some still boasted little lawns, but the deceased's featured only mud. There was nothing else notable, except for the paramedics at either end of the empty gurney being hauled through the front door. Both, for some strange reason, were giggling.

Tina slouched at the kitchen table, absently tapping the stubby toe of her tennis shoe a few inches from her husband's white-sheeted head. A pair of "evidence technicians" (plump chemistry profs from Pitt who moonlighted scooping hairs into tiny sandwich bags) knee-walked around Marvin's body, occasionally "oohing" and "aahing" at a partic-ularly intriguing spray of fiber. They'd already bagged his hands, and spoke in meaningful whispers. Manny had a theory that they dumped the stuff in the nearest Dumpster, and billed the P.D. for lifting the lid.

Tina did not know what to feel. She plucked tissues from a Kleenex Junior box one of the social workers had left, dabbing her eyes and puffing on a Viceroy with the filter ripped off. It was the first thing Manny noticed, that little mountain of cast-off filters in the middle of the table. You could still see the fan pattern where someone had recently sponged the pink Formica.

Manny liked to arrive on the scene a little late, when whoever he was chatting up was already tired and pissed off from talking and being talked at by half a dozen other nightmares with faces. All detectives had their specialty—reading the scene, turning snitches, following leads. But Manny's was more basic. He had ears. He knew how to listen, could almost taste things in the way people talked. It wasn't about what the pacing neighbor or bottle-blond sister-in-law actually said—or not *just*—but how they picked the lint off their elbows when they said it. How they made sure their eyes drilled into his. (*Look at me, I'm hon-est!*) How an accent thickened up or faded in the course of a five-minute chat.

Much of the time, the people he interviewed didn't believe he was a cop. He was too upset with himself. He kept sighing. He stared at the ceiling a lot. Which unnerved them even more. This was *their* drama—and here was this unhappy weirdo clearly struggling to forget his own problems long enough to do his job. *"I'm sorry . . . I had a thing with my wife,"* was one of his standard openers. *"Go ahead, I'm lis-tening. . . ."*

When Tina saw Detective Manny Rubert shuffle in, she threw a balled-up Kleenex on the floor. "Not another one!"

Manny pulled a chair from the table and sat down like an in-law. "I know, it's a drag," he said. "Believe me, I'm not in the mood, either."

He hadn't expected anyone so pretty, and it threw him. Tina had that Faye Dunaway thing. Faye before the surgery, when her cheek-bones were still sharp as can openers and she looked like a feral gazelle.

She was that kind of gorgeous. She didn't look like the wife of a foamer.

"If you think I'm going to answer another fucking question about anything, you better have a hard ass," Tina said.

"Beg pardon?"

Manny had no idea what that meant. Rather, he had a couple of ideas: She was going to kick him, or he was going to have sit there until Christmas. . . .

The meaning didn't matter. Just the *weight* of the sentence, the way it came at him like a rock dropped off a freeway overpass. (*Airmail,* in happy cop lexicon.) Tina hit that tingle in the back of his head, the fuse that usually stayed damp, the one that got lit on those rare occasions when he met a woman who actually scared him. It was sort of like sex, but harder to find.

FOUR

His mother's ankles felt like hot salamis as Tony Zank held her out the rest home window.

"You gonna talk, Ma, or am I gonna have to waggle?"

He was surprised by how tough she was. And he wasn't loving swinging her out the fourth floor of Seventh Heaven, where anyone could look up and see he wasn't exactly running her a sitz bath. The worst part, though, was the view. Mrs. Zank wore nothing under her nightie, and every time Tony looked down he got an eyeful.

"Mom-twat," McCardle said, shaking his Dinoesque head. He'd sidled up to give moral support after tying the ninety-year-old whose room they'd appropriated, a retired osteopath named Fitzer, to the wheelchair bar beside his bathtub. "Not something a boy should ever have to see. My mom used to get drunk and do splits on a pool table, so I oughta know."

"Do I need to hear about this?" snarled Zank. "Right this minute?"

Originally, the idea seemed simple. Once his mom calmed down and crawled back in bed after her trot down the hall, Tony managed to convince the attendants that she'd been having an "episode."

"She imagines things," he'd confided, looking just ashamed enough to make it sound authentic. "It started when my dad hit her with a bowling pin twenty years ago. Today she thought I was trying to steal something from her. That hurts, you know? This is my mother. This lady *raised* me. Plus, and tell me if I'm wrong here, there's nothing in this dump anybody'd want to steal."

Carmella, the big Puerto Rican lady in charge, had cut her teeth in Leisure World and seen it all. Her beehive gave her an extra six inches on top, and her hips, though shapely, could have smothered triplets. She was the sort of large woman who celebrated her largeness, accentuating it with doughnut-size hoop earrings and brash magenta lipstick plumping up her lips. She neither replied to Tony's explanation nor totally ignored him. Not until McCardle popped out of the bathroom waving a jar of thyroid medication, mistaking it for speed, did she slam her palm on the bedpan like a tambourine and pipe up. "You wanna ransack the joint, you gotta pay like everybody else, Gomer."

Carmella whipped her hand out to Tony but her eyes stayed fixed on McCardle, who responded with courtly charm.

"I don't believe anyone has ever called me Gomer before. Not many of us Negro fellows get named that."

Carmella didn't bother to reply, but kept her hand extended until Tony warmed it with a pair of twenties.

"Just don't leave stains," she warned, "and don't put no cigarettes out on the furniture. The inspector from the state board sees burns on the furniture, he's gonna think we're letting residents smoke, which since they tend to nod off—and ain't allowed to have matches—means all kinda bad news. You got me, *hombres?* Behave your ass in here!"

Before Tony could even thank her she turned and hurried out.

"You believe that?" he said, checking to make sure his mother was under control. Carmella either hadn't seen his grip on the old lady's wrist, or hadn't cared. "She thinks we don't know half the staff is bangin' old guys for pin money. That's why they hire 'em so young. A smart chick can mop up. Get one of these bum tickers to smoke out in the sack, it's payday. Any family with dough will cough up. Who wants it gettin' out Gramps bought the farm goin' Tommy Lee on some gash whose last job before this was homework?"

Zank shook his head, then turned on his mother and asked her straight out. "Who's been sniffin' around your bed, Ma?"

"What are you, *jealous?*" she snapped back. "A girl gotta have some fun, even on this crap farm."

His mother didn't talk like this before entering the home. For as long as Zank could remember, she was a mild-mannered, miserable woman who tended to housework and made lunch for the vicious lunk of a husband she'd married at nineteen until he keeled over, under questionable circumstances, when she was forty. Decades later, after a bowling party on her sixty-third birthday, Zank found her passed out on a throw rug with her face in her needlepoint. It turned out she'd been guzzling a quart of gin a day for years and hiding it. The doctor said it was not uncommon. "It's when they don't get the stuff that you notice," he'd explained, before announcing that his mom needed round-the-clock care. He suggested a convalescent home, and the cheapest Tony could find was Seventh Heaven. But since moving in with the other seniors, she'd become a gutter-mouth.

"You think you can put the squeeze on me, you're stupid *and* ugly," she told her son.

"Mom," Zank pleaded, "how come you're talkin' like this? You used to talk nice."

Mrs. Zank snorted. "You had the good sense to bring a bottle when you visit, we wouldn't be in this pickle."

Genuinely distressed, Tony dropped his mom's wrist to tap for the Slim Jim in his jacket pocket. In a second she had her fingers around her ashtray, which she kept in a hollowed-out phone book by the bed. It was a brass replica of William Penn, with grooves in his three-cornered hat for butts. And it made a dent in Tony's forehead like a ball-peen hammer.

"Mom, *Jesus!*" Tony shrieked. But she was up out of her bed before he could grab her. Lunging for the call button, she thumbed it as she scooted past McCardle, who just managed to nab the tail of her gown.

"I could cry rape," the old lady teased. "You've got your paw pretty close to my thingy. They hang your kind for that."

McCardle cringed, but Tony smiled. "Maybe he likes you, Ma."

"His type always do," she said, snatching her walker and whacking the *America's Most Wanted* grad across the shins. She smiled saucily, then threw out one exposed old-lady hip, and spanked herself. "You think your father was the only one who wanted a piece of angel cake?"

Zank was so horrified he zombied up, staring straight ahead in a catatonic daze. McCardle pulled the walker away from his partner's mother, and when she fought him he tried to punch her. He'd never hit a woman this old before. Despite topping off at five four, he could bench-press 375, and there was a chance he could do damage. McCardle was relieved when she dodged the blow, though it meant that now he had to restrain her. After a brief tussle the feisty senior ended up in a headlock. Not sure what to do next, Mac tried to rouse Tony back to life.

"Come on, big guy, don't go Thorazine on me. *Wake up!*"

Nervous lest anyone happen by and see him wrestling an elderly white woman, McCardle edged Tony's mother away from the door. When he tried to force her onto the bed, she screamed "Mandingo!" and bit him.

"Hey, ouch, *shit!*" McCardle cried, trying not to get loud when Mrs. Zank started chewing on his forearm. Her teeth were small but pointy, like a Chihuahua's. He started to pull her hair, but stopped when he saw the frail map of veins under her blue rinse. Her scalp reminded him of his auntie, with her stroke and hygiene problems.

"Tony." Mac tried again, pleading this time, and Zank jerked back to life.

"We gotta split," Tony announced, as if he hadn't just blanked out. "I think the old bitch pressed the call button."

Swinging into action, he scooped his mother under one armpit while McCardle grabbed her under the other.

"Ready?" Tony asked. McCardle grunted and, eyes straight ahead, the two men stepped out of the room and half-marched, half-dragged

Mrs. Zank down the hall. They held their breaths, waiting for her screams. But when they finally dared to look, the old lady was beaming.

"Check me out, I'm double-datin'!" she called to Snooks, the janitor, who happened to be pushing by with a floor waxer. Snooks was rumored to have gang connections and deal a little. Dr. Dre leaked out of his earphones and he pretended not to hear anything. One peek at the purple bruise on Tony Zank's forehead, and the face of the semi-naked crazy lady, and he made a point of waxing fast toward the other end of the corridor.

When Snooks passed, Mrs. Zank waved happily to a well-coifed woman in a wheelchair. She even winked. "Don't wait up, Hilda. Tonight's sandwich night!"

The wheelchair woman just stared, and McCardle and Zank tried hard not to look at each other. A flutey voice on the PA said, "All staff report to Fourth Floor West."

"That's where *we* are," Tony hissed. "Duck in here!"

They tooled into what looked like an empty room, and it wasn't until Mac turned on a lamp that they noticed the unbelievably old man propped on a wicker rocker.

"Have I had the pleasure?" the ancient fellow piped up, his voice a surprising baritone. He managed to look elegant in a pair of shorty pajamas. "Name's Fitzer. In my time, I was known as a first-class osteopath. My motto is 'Bones make the man!'"

"Bathroom," was all Zank said, and McCardle nodded. He had the well-heeled senior tied up and gagged with a fistful of Tucks when Tony hung his mother out the window.

"Mom, you ready to spill?" Tony called to her. He hated the way her ankles felt in his hands and wished he'd thought to bring gloves. Of course, he hadn't known he was going to be dangling his mother upside down. If he had, he would have made her wear underwear. . . .

"I'll spill," she cried up at him. "I'll spill the beans on what a little milk-pussy you were as a boy, that's what I'll spill, you good-for-nothing drug addict."

McCardle fought hard to keep his face in neutral. He was impressed at the way Tony kept his cool. He didn't know what he'd do if his own moms shamed him that way. Happily, she wouldn't be out before 2039, so it wasn't an issue.

"All I want is a name, Ma. I want to know who had access to the bed. That's it. Then I'll let you go."

"Your father never messed around. Did you know that?" his mother shrieked. Not once! *The idiot!*"

Tony's jaw began to twitch. He hadn't had any crack for twenty minutes, and it was killing him. He swung his mom so her head crunched off the ivy crawling up the wall. Then he leaned out the window and called down to her. "I hate when you talk nasty, Ma. You didn't used to do that. You used to whine all the time, but you didn't talk nasty."

"Fell in with the wrong crowd," she yelled. "You dump somebody in this bone factory, they're gonna get wrong pretty fast. Everybody in here's pissed off, 'specially us boozehounds." The effort of speaking upward was taxing, and she let herself sag. "All we got to slurp in here is mouthwash."

By now, people were starting to gather in the plaza under the window. McCardle couldn't watch and decided to check on the osteopath.

"Okay," Mrs. Zank cackled finally. "I saw the girl who took your precious envelope. Her name's Tina, but she'd never go out with *you*. She hates losers. She likes her sugar with class. We talked."

"Mom," Tony sighed, but quieter than before, like he didn't *want* to say what he was about to say, but he just *had* to. He didn't have a choice. It was something he'd once heard on *Dr. Laura.* "Mom, when you hurt me this way, I have to let you go with love. . . ."

McCardle, who'd popped back out of the bathroom after peeking in on Fitzer, could not quite believe what had happened. At first, hearing the screams and shouting from outside, he told himself that maybe a celeb was visiting. Tony had bragged that Joey Bishop sometimes dropped in to Seventh Heaven to visit his older brother, Rummy. But he couldn't imagine the seventy-plus, second-tier Rat Packer getting those kinds of screams.

"We better go," Tony said, slipping a Slim Jim out of his pocket and sniffing it. He had a theory that they made them in batches, like cigars, and some were more vintage than others. "We wanna get painadelic on this Tina chick, we gotta get there before she thinks anybody's comin'."

"Right," said McCardle, but as they were leaving, he kept checking the room. One minute Mrs. Zank's scarlet toenails were poking over the windowsill, the next Tony was walking toward the door, unwrapping a beef stick.

"I wish I hadn't seen between her legs," was all Tony said on the way out.

McCardle didn't mention that he agreed with him. Or that a guy who nibbled Slim Jims after dropping his mother out a fourth-floor window might need a little therapy himself.

FIVE

Manny could not take his eyes off the straw. Tina kept it lodged in the left side of her mouth, between a gap in her teeth. A splotch of chocolate dotted her lip, and he resisted the urge to reach over and wipe it away. Instead, he glanced out the window, fixating on the Golden Arches, which weren't gold at all. Which were, in fact, a vitamin-rich urine yellow.

"McDonald's," Tina said, when she'd sucked her way to the bottom of her shake. "I bet you're a regular charm-pot with the ladies."

"This isn't a date," Manny said, returning her gaze and keeping things bland.

"Oh, it's not!" Tina threw herself back in the booth. "Gee, Mistuh Powiceman, I thought you wiked me."

Manny sighed and pushed the stirrer around in his

coffee. It tasted like watered-down transmission fluid. He hadn't known he was going to ask her out until he did. This raised the eyebrows of the chubby evidence guys, but Manny'd made a show of tapping his nose behind Tina's back, letting the hair-pluckers know he thought she was hinky. Though he wasn't sure he did. In fact, it was just the opposite. There was something about her that made *him* feel guilty. But he didn't need to share that with Tweedledee and Tweedledum. They might not understand existential angst.

"I hate baby talk," Tina blurted suddenly. "Marvin thought it was cute." She plucked the straw from her mouth and threw it at him. "What do you think?"

Manny considered, decided to ignore the question, and waited to see if she'd say more. When she didn't, he leaned toward her over the table. "Nothin' personal, but I don't see you with a Marvin. Not *your* Marvin specifically, just, you know, any Marvin. You don't look like the Marvin type."

"You never know until you get there," she shrugged. "Besides, I'm not gonna tell you I didn't like the guy. He was a train wreck. But he didn't start off that way."

"Do they ever?"

Manny did his staring-off thing, letting his eyes fall on the French Fry boy, a sloe-eyed stringbean named Lance. He'd popped him a few years ago for planting a bug in the women's rest room of an Exxon station. Lance was caught sneaking in to remove the tape. It wasn't the most sophisticated setup: a sound-activated microcassette superglued under the sink. What intrigued Manny was the kind of charge a fourteen-year-old got from listening to strange women relieve themselves. It wasn't until he interviewed the family that he found out the truth. Mommy French Fry had a thing for the station owner, a wiry Egyptian named Haik. She and Haik liked to sneak off for romantic little Exxon trysts. The boy wanted to play the evidence to Daddy, who worked three jobs so his wife could stay home and watch the kids. Unfortunately, by the time Manny'd made his discovery, Lance was already outed. His junior high paper ran a story: POLICE NAB POOPER SCOOPER!—and the scorn was so harsh Lance dropped out. Since then, he'd joined the glamorous world of fast-food preparation. Where he was clearly thriving.

When Manny thought he'd ignored her long enough, he turned back to Tina, who was shaking her head. "My luck," she said, "I get a cop with A.D.D. Does your insurance cover Ritalin, or are we stuck here?"

"I was just thinking," Manny lied.

"Anything good? 'Cause much as I love watching you cogitate, I've got a lot of loose ends to tie up back at my house. My husband just died, in case you forgot."

"I didn't forget. That's what I was thinking about. How whatever happened happened. You realize everybody's gonna pretty much assume you did it, right?"

Tina appeared to size him up for a moment, her face tightening, then did the exact opposite of what he thought she'd do. He expected denials, flight, maybe a milkshake flung at his head. Instead—and now he was really hooked—she laughed in his face.

"What are we, on TV? You think I'm gonna roll over and say 'Please Daddy Cop-man, don't hurt me?' "

"What I think is that a guy who was gonna drink drain cleaner wouldn't bother to pour it over his cereal, you know what I mean? I've seen foamers before. A guy's gonna go out that way, he doesn't get gourmet about it. He just guzzles."

Tina shrugged. "Marvin was kind of a roughage freak. Maybe he wanted to make sure he was regular in the afterlife. Say what you will about Lucky Charms, they go right through you."

"Is that true?"

"Well, I don't know from experience. I don't eat breakfast. I need to be up a while before I can chew and swallow. But from what Marv said, the stuff got the job done." She paused to pull a pack of Viceroys out of her purse. She flipped one out, tore the filter off, and lit up in a single motion.

"You know you can't smoke here," said Manny, though he loved that she'd just gone ahead and fired one up. A family of overweight towheads at the next table was already grumbling "Mickey D's is a wholesome place."

Her response was a smoke ring the size of a Krispy Kreme blown straight at his nose, followed by another that floated through the first. "You're about to bust me for breakfast food murder, and I'm supposed to worry about smoking in public? What's that gonna get me, an extra half hour on top of life?"

Manny smiled and sipped his transmission fluid. He was such a sucker for women with balls.

Tina flicked ash in his coffee. "So you gonna arrest me or what?"

Just then the McDonald's manager, a serious Asian fellow with WING on his nametag, stepped smartly up to their table. He stopped cold when he saw the look on Tina's face. "I'm on medication," she said to him. "If I don't smoke cigarettes I break things." Wing looked at Manny, who busied himself picking ash out of his coffee. The manager remembered him from his uniform days. People were always expecting the police to solve their problems.

"Where were we?" she said, when the young fast-food exec was safely back behind his counter.

"You asked if I was going to arrest you."

It was a question Manny'd been sidestepping since she'd told him he'd better have a hard ass.

"Well are you?"

"That depends," he said, more cautiously than he'd intended.

Tina picked up her shake and tipped the last of it down her throat, tapping the bottom. "On what?"

He didn't have an answer, so he just stared at her, furrowing his brows and squinting as though deeper meaning were just oozing out of him. In his mind he looked like Clint Eastwood, but something told him it stopped there.

Tina fixed him with a mirthless smile. "That something you practice in front of the mirror, or they teach that 'Look at me, I'm deep' look at the academy?"

"Tell you the truth, I forget," he said. "I only went 'cause I couldn't get into Clown College. I'm actually pretty fucking sick of it."

"You lookin' to get out?"

She regarded him as much with curiosity as anything else. If she'd reached under the table and rubbed his thigh, or licked her lips, he'd have pegged her as another perpette trying to slut her way out of a fall. But Tina was different. She was just laying it out. He got that tingle in the back of his head again. Only this time his fear had a friend. A little pal called lust.

. . .

After their snack, Manny steered back to Carmichael Street in a pre-occupied haze. Tina must have been staring at him for a while before he noticed, and when he did, she still didn't speak.

"What?" said Manny finally. They slowed to a stop sign a block from her house.

"I want to show you something, *Detective,* but I don't know if you want to see it."

"Try me."

"I would, but you don't know what it is. Maybe I shouldn't."

"You trying to make me beg?"

Manny sat back in the seat and rubbed his neck. His car, an unmarked Impala the color of mayonnaise, had been issued previously to a Pittsburgh P.D. lieutenant in Vice named Hanes. (Upper Marilyn got most of its equipment, and some its employees, used.) Hanes's claim to fame was a ten-year lawsuit that kept him on the force despite tipping the scales at 390. What the mammoth vice dick's behind had done to the seat of the Impala was fairly predictable. For Manny, it was like riding in a bomb crater, but the seat-back was worse. His spine sort of curved in, where the stuffing had been smashed down to the springs. No amount of adjusting could make it bearable. There wasn't a Comfy Cushion, Sacro-Ease, or inflatable pillow invented that countered the discomfort of sitting in the fat detective's divot.

It was the Hanes seat-crater, as much as anything, that made him say yes—or at least "Why the fuck not?"—when Tina made her proposition. He'd been pleading with the department for a new car for two years.

"Okay, pull over," she said, when the house was in sight. She was already fishing in her purse.

Part of Manny worried someone might see him sitting with a possible perp. But it wasn't like she had her head between his legs—he wasn't the sex-for-favors type. They weren't even touching. Besides which, detectives had a lot of leeway when it came to "freshies," suspects close enough to the crime to still be freaked out about it. (As a rule this meant being caught, if not red-handed, then right after a crime had been discovered, in situations too ludicrous to explain by coincidence: the teen with panties in his pocket, outside the dorm where three cheerleaders had been raped; the lug with the diamond choker in his ashtray, geezing speed in a clunker three blocks from the broken-in jeweler's.) In freshy-state, souls were more likely to spill than they were when they'd had time to mull.

Manny himself was famous for bonding with suspects. He'd once dined at Der Wienerschnitzel with a man found on the scene at a mosque-defacing. Midway through his bratwurst, the fellow confessed that he'd hated Moslems ever since an unscrupulous Armenian sold his ex–father-in-law a bad toupee. Just recounting it got him furious. "The thing slipped off at our wedding dinner, right into the lobster bisque. After that, the whole thing was a joke. Whenever anybody mentions my wedding, they never mention how pretty the bride looked, or the beautiful service. . . . Never! It's always, 'Ha-ha, remember when Mr. Depew's rug slipped in the bisque!' Ha-fucking-ha! I bet we wouldn't even be divorced if that camel-kisser hadn't sold us the crappy rug!"

When Manny pointed out that Armenians weren't actually Arab, that they pretty much hailed from Europe—though, admittedly, some oddball corner of it—Depew's ex–son-in-law dropped his head onto his bratwurst and began to weep. "Now there'll be a jihad. . . ."

Happily, Manny'd got the DA to recommend a psychiatric work-up and community service.

"You sure you're ready?" asked Tina, when he finally finessed the Chevy within shouting distance of the curb. "I always heard cops can't parallel park. I mean, why should they learn? It's not like anybody's gonna give them a ticket, right?"

"That's not true," Manny said. "Sometimes I give them to myself, just to keep me honest."

"Is that right?" Tina had the envelope in her hand, and a look in her eye that said 'Fuck with me now and I'll kill you, too.' In that moment, Manny had to admit, he was so in love it hurt.

"What I'm gonna show you," she began, then stopped and fired up another filter-ripped Viceroy. When she started talking again, she aimed her gaze straight ahead, at the back of the red minivan in front of them. A bumper sticker on the window said I BRAKE FOR JESUS.

"What I'm going to show you, I had *nothing* to do with, okay?" She chose her words carefully, "I found it, but it wasn't something I was supposed to find."

"You mean you stole it," Manny said mildly. Always mildly, when coaching your way through a perp chat. "You didn't *buy* or *create* the thing, you *stole* the thing."

"Technically, yes," said Tina, with new respect. "But I don't know who I stole it from. As long as you understand that."

"I do," he said, and slid the manila envelope out of her hand before she changed her mind. She stayed on him, wide-eyed, itching to see his reaction when he pulled what was inside out. But he didn't want to give her the thrill. Not yet.

"I'm just wondering, did Marvin have anything to do with what I'm about to look at? Was this one of his scams?"

"Marvin?"

Tina rolled down the window and tossed her hardly smoked cigarette onto somebody's lawn. It looked like AstroTurf, with bald spots. "Marvin had nothing to do with this," she said. "Marvin was an accident."

"I've had a few of those," Manny sighed, catching himself when he realized just what she might think he was saying. "I mean, I've been in a relationship with the wrong person, I don't mean I've been in a relationship with them and left them slumped in a bowl of Grape-Nuts."

"Lucky Charms," said Tina, "but I hear what you're saying." She met his gaze in a way that made his brain buzz. "When it comes to romance, you're a fuck-up, too."

Manny hadn't exactly ever looked in the mirror and yelped this at himself, but hearing it now, it sounded true.

"Well," he said, "one divorce, a handful of quasimonogamous nightmares, and here I am, getting cozy with a murder suspect. I'd say my track record speaks for itself."

Tina turned away, and Manny had a feeling she was staring at her own reflection in the passenger window, or staring at his. When she spoke again her voice was flatter, somewhere between weary and serene. "I always start out liking guys for one thing, and when I find out the thing I liked them for isn't real, I sort of hang around pretending it is—or trying to make it that way. Like with Marvin. When I met him, he was this wild-eyed entrepreneur type. The guy had all kinds of ideas. He was making crazy money off them. I thought he was a genius."

"Was he?"

"Sometimes," said Tina. "Other times he was a total Mongoloid. When he made some dough on one crackpot idea, he'd blow it all on three other ones. His new thing, he was an on-line money guru. Literally. He videoed himself in loincloth and turban, like Gandhi with a potbelly, giving financial advice. Then he switched from investment tips to chanting for money. He cooked up these special mantras."

"Om nyoho renge cash?"

"Basically. Except we didn't have any money, which didn't say much for his cash-chanting efficiency. I could never pin him down, though. He was so enthusiastic, you just kind of wanted everything to work. That's what I loved about him. Until . . ."

She faltered, and Manny had to prompt her. "Until?"

"Until he started chanting through his nose, and I had to listen to him snuffle and *Om* all day like a monk with a harelip. That's what put me over the edge. Hangovers are bad enough without Hindu sound effects."

Manny's ears burned, the way they did when people's words slipped into the Red Zone: when they were confessing, whether they knew it or not. The air between them had gone electric.

"There's always something like that," he said, too casually, "something you don't expect that comes along and changes everything."

Tina rested the tip of one forefinger on the back of his wrist. No more than that, and it was more than he could remember feeling since he was thirteen.

"The nose-humming was pretty much out of the blue," she said.

"I rest my case," said Manny, and ripped open the envelope.

SIX

Carmella Dendez looked left and right, then slipped a pudgy forefinger into her cleavage to retrieve the wad of twenties she'd stashed there. A slight drizzle moistened her beehive and made the cars shiny. Nothing would be stupider than letting someone from work spot her counting her cash. But she couldn't resist. Along with the two twenties the *blanco* creep had given her, her count came to $320. But she had to keep checking. That was the fun part. She owed a month-and-a-half to Jenny Craig: $250 right there. And Daisy, the little neighbor girl who cleaned her house, needed a mole removed from her nose. It was sprouting hairs, like an old widow's. Boys were starting to make fun. Carmella'd been promising the child for weeks she'd take her to that nice doctor, Dr. Roos, who'd done so much for her. More than she could tell a living soul. . . .

Riffling the bills under her nose, Carmella stood in front of her Gremlin. If she didn't go back to Jenny Craig, the Gremlin would have to go to. It wasn't dignified, a Big Beautiful Woman having to squidge herself into a tiny hatchback. Carmella did not believe that a bit of heft was necessarily bad. Plenty of men liked a gal who had some stuffing in her seat. But squeezing in and out of the Gremlin was not just unseemly, it was unsafe. She knew this from the Rape Prevention Class she'd taken at the Y. Getting in and out of your vehicle was a TAM—Target Attack Moment—for all women. But it was doubly dangerous for a woman of size, who, if she's unlucky enough to drive a Gremlin, may have a patch of involuntary downtime when she's stuck half-in and half-out of her car, waiting for the strength to make that final *oomph* that will put her inside.

The policeman who taught the class owned just the kind of tight butt and big shoulders Carmella liked. Plus he wasn't too handsome, just *knowing*. As if the ho-hum face under his no-style brown hair had made its way through a lifetime of peculiar situations, and didn't judge. *Officer Manny.* Carmella could never tell if he was smiling at her or not. But she liked it when he picked her to demonstrate the hip-roll. More than one evening, after downing her Slim-Fast, she'd lay on the couch daydreaming about the time she'd thrown the hottie cop over her hip and landed on top of him, the way his eyes went wide when she put just enough push in her pelvis to let him know she didn't mind tossing a guy around a little.

Carmella had her hand in her purse when she heard the voices.

"Hey lady, got a light?"

"Ain't nuthin' light about her."

She knew that nasty tone. Mrs. Zank's boy. That shit. And the Dean Martin–looking *hombre negro* he ran with. Without turning around, Carmella slipped her fingers in her dress, re-stashing her cash, then eased her hand to her purse, deciding between car keys and comb.

"May I help you?" she said, without turning around.

"You can help *you*," Zank said, "if you do what I tell you. We need you to walk your big ass back in the office and get the address of the girl who changed my mother's sheets. That's not such a big deal, is it?"

Thinking, for some reason, of the scene in *Deliverance* where the killer hillbillies ask Ned Beatty to squeal like a pig (another juicy image, along with hip-rolling Officer Manny onto the mat), Carmella took a deep breath and swung around with the comb in her fist. She raked the plastic teeth under Tony's dime-size nostrils, drawing blood before he had a chance to stop smirking.

Tony dropped to one knee, clutching his face. His screams caught McCardle off guard. He made a lunge for Carmella, but she was ready for him. Sidestepping, she jammed a high heel down on the tender bones of his foot, where his Florsheim's loafer stopped and his argyles started. The pain was excruciating.

McCardle looked at Carmella with honest wonder—*Why?*—and his suffering visage was meat to her appetite. She felt her heart racing, in a good way, and took her fingers to his ears, twisting with everything she had while the little muscle man flailed. Then Zank picked himself up and kicked her in the shin, and it was over.

Carmella didn't go down, but she let go. McCardle rubbed his bruised lobes and tried to breathe normally.

"Man!" was all he could say.

Tony told him to shut up and open the trunk. McCardle obliged, looking skeptically from the available volume in the Gremlin to the volume of Carmella in her stretch capris. Most of the available space was taken up with boxes of Jenny Craig's lo-cal snack bars. Chocolate and Banana-Orange. Even empty, it would have been snug for an anorexic.

"Gonna be tight, T."

Zank sneered. "Thanks for the input." An ambulance wailed from blocks away, no doubt racing over to pick up his mother. "This could've been a walk in the park if Miss Porkchop didn't get heroic. All we wanted was an address," he said, grabbing Carmella by her chins. He pinched the extra flesh until her eyes watered. This was indignity beyond indignity. She made a silent vow to wreak revenge on this Anglo asshole, if she had to walk a continent of broken glass in paper slippers to get to him.

When Zank let go, Carmella touched her fingers to her throat flesh, and decided she would pay Jenny Craig the rest of the money she owed. Come her day of revenge, she wanted to be trim and gorgeous.

She wanted this *malo* dog to eat his heart out before he begged for death.

"It's gonna be work getting that ass in this bread box," said Tony. He slapped Carmella hard on her solid behind and McCardle frowned. That kind of talk was uncalled for.

"Nothin' wrong with this lady's ass," Mac said. "Man could take a winter in the North Pole with an ass like that."

Carmella eyed him with gratitude. *This one*, she promised herself, *I pleasure for a while before I castrate.* . . . He had the most adorable little nose she'd ever seen.

"We don't gain nothin' by kidnapping her," McCardle pointed out. "You already bought a murder beef, less'n your moms landed in some soft mud. And we still didn't get what we come for."

Tony slammed the hatchback shut again.

"So what's your idea, Puff Daddy?"

"I say we stick to the plan. Send the lady back into the building to check the files, find us that damn Tina's home address. She's not gonna do nobody any good locked in here. That's on the *real*."

Zank considered, then scanned the parking lot to make sure they were still in the clear. "What makes you think she's not gonna run? Or should I say waddle," he snickered. He reached for her chins again but Carmella slapped his hand.

"If you're worried about that, I'll go with her," McCardle offered. "A thing worth doing is worth doing right."

Tony regarded the pair of them skeptically, then reached in his jacket for a Slim Jim.

"This bitch called me a Gomer," McCardle reminded him as Zank unwrapped his snack. He wanted to sound persuasive, and laid it on thick. "No way I'm lettin' her get away without payin' for that."

"**Man's got** mental problems," whispered McCardle, when they were out of earshot.

He spoke out the side of his mouth, keeping his head straight forward as he limped alongside Carmella through the parking lot, toward the Seventh Heaven employees' entrance.

Carmella spit on the ground and turned to give her handler some full-on stink-eye. Mac melted under her scrutiny. His Auntie Big'n had been a woman of girth. When she wasn't beating him with magazines, or making him clean her, she would let him nuzzle up on her fifty-four-inch bosoms.

"You gay?" Carmella asked him.

"No way! I'm cool," Mac replied, weirded-out by the question but enjoying the nearness of so much flesh. (He could swear, the big woman gave off *heat*.) "I'm just saying, don't let Tony see you talking to me or he'll think something's up. You got him pretty good with that comb."

Carmella stopped and plunked one lethal heel down on the asphalt. "You know I could pick you up and throw you across a room, don't you?"

She could see the effect of her words on the tiny-nosed black man. A glaze came over his eyes. "I didn't mean to call you a bitch," he apologized, gazing up at her with abject emotion. "I *had* to say that. I have to make Tony think I'm that kind of person."

For a little guy, Carmella was thinking, Mac had pretty good muscle. Biceps like baby hams. In spite of herself, she reached out and gave one of his arms a squeeze. McCardle was a small but *muscular* Dean Martin.

"Four-fifty," he lied. "That's how much I bench. I bet I could lift you over my face. How'd you like that?"

"Carmella Dendez does her own lifting, *Meester.*"

"Maybe we could bench each other," he said, heart pounding under well-developed pecs.

Before Carmella could respond to that, McCardle zipped up the wheelchair ramp and threw open the door. *"I'm courting,"* he tittered to himself, waiting with head bowed while his companion stomped past.

Back inside the old age home, McCardle tried to put his arm around Carmella's waist. He barely made it before she swatted his hand away. "Are you on *drugs? Is that* what this is all about?"

"Baby, with you around, I don't *need* drugs," Mac answered, employing his smooth-ass, Barry White voice. "Are you thinkin' what I'm thinkin'?"

"I'm thinking *this,*" said Carmella, and jammed her heel in his foot for the second time. McCardle hopped in a tight circle while she tried to figure things. The hall smelled like Lysol. She knew that Snooks, the janitor, snuck around spraying little scented puffs out of a spray can to make it smell like he'd done some cleaning. Anything to keep from actually taking a mop to anything. If the lazy son of a bitch didn't have a line on diet pills, she'd have fired him at Christmas.

McCardle stopped hopping and checked over his shoulder. Then he turned back to Carmella. "You ever do any wrestling?"

"What?"

"I don't mean professional," Mac exclaimed, as though this misunderstanding was the source of her reaction. "I mean, private-like, just you and . . . a friend. *I* like to wrestle," he added, in case he hadn't dropped enough hints already.

Carmella parked her hands on her hips. "You mean, you think. . . . *You and me?*"

"Darling," McCardle cut in, "we shouldn't stand here like this. We have to look normal."

Carmella flicked his ear, which was still sore from being twisted. "Listen, mango, the people here *know* me, okay?" Her accent thickened the angrier she got. "They see me walking the halls with some *puto* fireplug when I'm supposed to be at home, getting ready for my Weight Watchers meeting, normal is the *last* thing anyone is going to think, *ho-kay?*"

Mac didn't answer right away, but instead took her in—*savored* her while rubbing his foot. She'd mashed the same one twice. "That's not right!" he cried.

This time Carmella ignored him. She brought the keys out of her purse, found the one she wanted, and slipped it in the door of the Administration Office. Again, a layer of honey seemed to glaze McCardle's eyeballs. Breathing heavily, he stared at the exposed flesh between Carmella's capri pants and her sweater as she bent to the lock.

"I'm saying you don't have to do all that," he went on, his voice cracking slightly.

"You know another way to get in, besides unlock it?"

"Not *that*. I'm talking about Weight Watchers. You don't have to lose weight. You're perfect the way you are. I've been wanting to tell you since I saw all those Jenny Craig bars in your trunk."

"You seem to know a lot about the subject."

McCardle dried his palms on his pant legs. "That's because I *care!* I don't think a real woman should have to make herself small. Women, some women, were meant to be *big*. I believe . . ." Here he stopped, grinning shyly, eyes lowered to the unpolished floor. "I believe women like you are the kind of women that God would want if . . . if God messed around with women."

Carmella paused, then hip-bumped the door open. "So you're one of *those*, eh?" She pulled the door shut behind them, careful not to slam, and brought her face very close to his. "Well listen, *maricón*, I don't see you pointing no gun, so don't think Carmella is going along with this 'cause she's scared you know jiujitsu. The only reason I have not splattered you off the wall already is 'cause your boyfriend is out there with my car. I can't afford to have some loco freak who beats his mother in public do something to my car."

McCardle, crestfallen, sulked by the file cabinet while Carmella opened a middle drawer and walked her fingers over the tops of the file folders. "Aha," she sang, plucking out a hazy Xerox of Tina's driver's license. "You're lucky I remembered her last name. *Podolsky*. What kind of a name is that for such a pretty girl? I was her, I'd change it."

Carmella whomped the drawer shut with her buttocks and handed over the paper. Then, with no warning, she grabbed McCardle's face. She jerked it right and left under the light, checking his profile. McCardle continued to pout, but her violent interest, the way she squeezed his cheeks, really *hurting* him, gave him all kinds of hope.

"Do I know you?" she asked suddenly. "I feel like I know you."

McCardle guessed what was coming next. He gazed moistly up at her, resting against a metal desk with a Dilbert cartoon taped to the computer monitor. (He didn't get people who went to work. Why didn't they just steal something expensive and quit?) From this point on, things could go a couple of ways. But if they went the way he wanted, he wondered how much time he'd have alone with Carmella before Tony got antsy and came barging in.

"Oh my God," squealed Carmella, when the synapse she'd been waiting for fired off. "*America's Most Wanted*! You killed that *chavalla* with a shovel."

"It wasn't my fault." McCardle protested. "He tried to brain me with a fire extinguisher."

But Carmella wasn't listening. "There's a reward, right?"

Unconsciously, she fingered the wad between her breasts. She imagined how thick it would feel with a hundred thousand friends folded around it.

"You're *mine* now," she said, which McCardle took as his cue.

The little strong man looked from side to side, then lowered his voice theatrically. "Listen, baby, you want to make some money, I can get you something worth a lot more than *my* black ass."

McCardle slid toward her on the desk, until his bulging thighs grazed her swollen stretch pants. She reached for the phone and he stopped her. His tiny hand clamped hers like a turtle on its mother's back.

Carmella considered an elbow to the neck but held off. "How much more and what I gotta do to get it?"

"That all depends," said McCardle, easing his phone hand free, pirouetting his fingertips off one of Carmella's haunches. It was all he could do not to try and climb her right there. "I'm gonna be conservative and say a million. But, like I say, that's being conservative."

Carmella did some figuring. She sucked on her ring finger and gazed out the window, where her car sat at the far corner of the parking lot. An agitated Zank could be seen pacing in front of it, popping his fist in his hand. If she didn't call *America's Most Wanted* just this minute, McCardle would not be worth any less tomorrow. The reward wouldn't go away unless someone else dialed 1-800-NOCRIME, or he disappeared.

Carmella made up her mind. She whipped sideways and grabbed McCardle's groin. Grunting slightly, making a claw, she hoisted him off the metal desk. Her grasp brought tears to his eyes. For good measure, she wrapped her other hand around the mini muscle man's throat, mashing his face to her massive breasts.

"*Huerco,* pay attention," she snapped, her face no more than an inch from his dainty nostrils. "You try and run some game on Carmella, she'll hurt you so bad you'll think this was foreplay."

McCardle, spotting the lump of cash in her cleavage, smiled dreamily and went limp.

SEVEN

There was a weird intimacy, sitting in a car together. Couples sat in cars. Cops and their partners. Strangers became unstrange, sharing a windshield view of the world. Manny contemplated the sensation, this unforeseen closeness with a woman he barely knew, in front of whose house he was now parked, inside of which he'd found a man he'd never met dead on the kitchen floor. Her husband. . . . But none of it was enough to take his mind off the photograph.

"You have to go?" Tina asked. She sounded more than slightly annoyed. "You have to leave right now?"

Manny was still in overload. He could not stop gawking at that eight-by-ten glossy. "You heard the dispatcher," he said mechanically. "Somebody's being murdered. I'm a policeman, remember? Somebody gets murdered, I have to show up. It's part of the job description."

Despite the speech, he made no move to start the car. All he could do was stare at the picture. The words scribbled across the bottom said MISTER BIOBRAIN. Above that plopped the thing itself, a bulging flesh-tone orb, oblong and veiny, with a peculiar shine. Someone's thumb and forefinger were just visible where they pinched the root, no doubt to make the object in question bulb out that way. To make it . . . *brain*like.

What made this more than just a white man's scrotum was the Happy Face tattooed on top it. A pair of eyes and a smile. The Happy Face lent a festive, wholesome quality to the whole package.

Two human faces also appeared in the picture. Part of a man's and all of a woman's. The features were easier to make out than the distended equipment. They hovered at twelve o'clock and three. Up top, bizarrely enough, was George Bush Jr., beaming and giddy, with that jolly-perplexed expression he wore when asked about foreign-policy issues. Eye level with W's puffed-out testicles, looking equally jaunty, was Margaret Beeman, mayor of Upper Marilyn since 1995.

Manny continued blinking over the photo. "Jesus, check out Marge's expression."

"You call the Mayor *Marge?*"

"Not anymore," he said, sliding the picture back in the envelope. "But I did when we were married."

Tina was stunned by this bit of info. So stunned that she didn't mention that she worked at the very place where the murder-in-progress was progressing. She knew, as soon as the dispatcher barked out the address, that it had something to do with the photograph. Whoever stuffed Mister Biobrain in Mrs. Zank's mattress must have had big plans for it. And she'd fucked them up. . . .

Tina started to speak, but before she could, Manny took her hands. The radio was squawking nonstop, and he killed it. It was plain that he wanted to say something before letting her out. A rookie named Krantz, who fancied himself a rocker, had been dispatched to guard Marv's body until it was time to zip it up. They watched him walk in and out of the front door, as if he couldn't decide what to do with himself. Corpsewise, cops bagged and paramedics carried. It was a union thing.

Krantz wore his hair in a mullet, which he stuffed under his hat on duty and unfurled when he played weekends in his Top Forty cover band. Manny had heard him once, by accident, while staking out the Holiday Inn, and found himself squirming for two hours to Krantz's Madonna medleys. "Like a Virgin" nearly killed him. Manny waved to him now, staying as far across the front seat from Tina as possible. He knew he'd have to explain to the guitar god why it was smart to get chummy with good-looking possible murder suspects. Krantz was always eager for tips, and Manny tried to be nice to him. When he wasn't, the rookie ratted him out to Fayton.

"So you gonna be all right?" said Manny finally. "This picture, it's an intense little item to be walking around with. I mean, W with a smiley-scrote. . . . Not to mention the lovely Marge. I guess you know what certain people would pay for that thing. Or what they'd do to get it."

He let his voice trail off, and Tina nodded. She cast a last, nervous glance at the picture, whispered "Keep it for me," then jumped out of the Impala and ran up the muddy path to her door.

Once he saw her go in, Manny swung the car into a neighbor's driveway, turned around, and sped up the street doing sixty. As he drove, he kept one hand on the envelope. He'd have to find a safe place for it. He'd also have to make a report—leaving out everything—and cook up some version of his interview with Tina that kept her clean. But it was hard keeping his mind off Mister Biobrain. George Bush's *basket,* for Christ's sake! The last thing he thought he was going to see when up woke up that morning was his ex-wife eyeball-to-testicle with the President. The Happy Face was beyond even contemplating. . . . But he loved the fact that Tina wanted him to hold on to it.

Phone poles clicked past as Manny tried to work out fake suicide scenarios for Marvin. What he needed was proof that the faux guru had a history of guzzling drain cleaners, or some similar weirdness. The answer came to him as he swung up the circular ramp to the parking lot that police headquarters shared with a small office building full of lawyers, insurance men, and some kind of vocational college he could never get a handle on. Arby Tech. The "students" all looked like they'd come straight from their methadone clinic by way of Attica. It was the methadone thing that made him think of Dr. Roos, a bent plastic surgeon he'd busted for selling ketamine two years ago. It turned out Special K was the least of it. Gripped by wholly justifiable paranoia, the doctor believed he was being popped for shopping photos of mutant she-males to fetishists on the Net. He confessed before Manny knew what the hell he was talking about.

Dr. Roos hadn't claimed innocence, which always impressed Manny, but he did maintain that no one really got hurt, since you couldn't see anything from the neck up. "Your fetish types don't care about faces," he'd explained. "They all have about one square inch that gets them hot."

It wouldn't take much to get Roos to lie and sign off on Marv's history of medical emergencies. The doctor lived in fear. All Manny had to do was *hint* that the feds were onto him, and he'd do anything for his friend the detective. As if Manny had some kind of federal connections; as if he had any idea what, if anything, they knew about Roos's current racket. But that was the great thing about paranoids: They were easy to impress.

Manny worked out a story on the drive over. If anyone, namely the chief, wondered why a cosmetic surgeon was involved with a dot-commie's suicide attempts, Roos could confess that he was brought in as a "friend of the family." Fayton just liked details. Unless pressed, he didn't ruffle his uniform trying to find out whether they were real or not.

Manny groped in his pocket for a couple of codeine and gulped them as he thought about the plan. It could, he decided, actually work.

In a good week, Manny only had to set foot in the station four or five times. His record low was twice. His high was twenty-nine, but that was around Easter, a traditionally high-crime period, for reasons too mysterious to fathom. Perhaps, Manny'd heard it argued from the dispatcher, a freckled young woman named Mindy, whose father handled snakes at a church in Wheeling, some people lost faith in God when they got to thinking what He did to His Only Son. *Why shouldn't I shoplift a chocolate egg from the A&P,* Mindy posited, by way of example, *when the Lord in Heaven bade His incarnation in flesh to bleed and suffer?* She may have been right.

Manny, in any case, was not having a great week. Before Tina and

Marv's Drano party, he'd been in five times since Monday morning. And it was only Tuesday. The idea was to keep cases working, have a reason to be *out,* wherever out happened to be. The catch was, the more time you spent *out* of the office, the more time you had to spend *in* it, explaining to Chief Fayton exactly what you were doing out there.

Fayton prided himself on being a hands-on kind of boss. This might have had something to do with his background. He came up riding a desk at the State Department of Motor Vehicles before switching to police administration, as Head of Personnel for the Pittsburgh Police Department. After that, of course, came the big leap to Upper Marilyn chief-hood. Never having actually arrested anyone, let alone ever set butt in a squad car, Fayton loved to hear about real police work. *"I want details!"* he'd holler, poised in his immaculate chief's uniform, in his trademark position behind his freshly Lemon Pledged desk: chin propped on his right fist, left hand mysteriously out of view.

Manny and Merch loved to speculate what that left hand was up to when they read aloud from their reports. Fayton insisted on being read to. Which made embellishment pretty much part of the job. It was important to invent an extra suspect or three, to justify floating around the city for days at a time, dreaming up ever more salacious and gripping action to pad the paperwork. How better to account for time spent visiting girlfriends, drinking, reading back issues of *Field and Stream* in the library, or doing whatever else a law enforcement professional did when he was supposed to be working and wasn't?

Fayton had gained his post by securing jobs for friends and family of cops in his capacity as personnel director back in P-burgh. The chief slot in Upper Marilyn was payback. Despite never having cracked a case, let alone gone out and worked one, he always had busloads of ideas on how to help the men beneath him when they came in with their reports.

What made today peculiar was that there actually *was* a ton of salacious details—all real—and this time Manny would have to hide almost all of them. The 10–30, Violent Crime in Progress, had popped up on the radio right after he'd opened Tina's envelope. "All Units to 1660 Bigelow Avenue. Seventh Heaven Senior Village. Repeat. . . ."

He knew Seventh Heaven because his great-uncle Clem had died there. At the end, when Manny was nine, Clem suffered a rare form of senility that made him clap all the time. Every Sunday, when Manny and his brother Stanley went to visit, they'd stand in front of the demented old man and bow, pretending to take curtain calls while he applauded wildly.

By the time Manny stepped in to face the chief, he'd already been to the rest home and had a version of events pretty much straight in his mind—along with a respectable codeine buzz.

"Looks like you got yourself a full platter," Fayton boomed by way of greeting. His uniform looked crisp. His Princeton had been fluffed and blow-dried to Trent Lott–level perfection. The chief propped a hand under his chin and waited.

"Two on the board in one day," said Manny, easing himself into the plain metal chair that faced the desk. "The Seventh Heaven thing was grim. Guy named Tony Zank, a known P.A.T."

"Excuse me?"

"Perp Around Town," said Manny, who knew the chief would file the term away and use it himself. "Apparently, he dropped his mother out the fourth-floor window. It may have been accidental—two sides to every story—but witnesses say he kind of swung her around before he let go. That, and the fact he was holding her by her ankles, screaming at her, could lead a reasonable person to think there was something he wanted from her, and she wasn't giving it up."

"That would be *matricide.*"

Fayton's tone was hushed, as though he'd marched the word out on a velvet cushion and didn't want to get it dirty before he marched it back in again. Manny contemplated the chief's hidden left hand, noting the slight movement of his forearm, and decided to find out once and for all what he was up to.

"Stick 'em up," he said, whipping his .38 out of his shoulder holster.

The chief juked in his chair and brought up both hands. The one he usually hid came up clutching a felt-tip.

"Good reflexes," Manny told him approvingly. "But I didn't mean for you to actually do it. I was just trying to show you what this Zank character pulled on me when I spotted him. Except he had a bigger gun, a real gorilla dick."

Fayton scowled, attempting to remain composed. "Language, Detective. And don't ever do that again. You might get hurt."

"Right," said Manny. "Anyway, I saw Zank coming out of the building with his partner, this really short, really pumped-up African-American male. Looked like Dean Martin in his *Sergeants Three* days."

Snooks, the young rest home janitor, described Tony Zank's partner in exactly these terms after Manny'd found some Dexedrine in his CD case. The shot at a possession beef—his third—rendered him suddenly talkative. ("I'm not just into hip-hop," Snooks boasted, after snitching off Tony Z and pal, "I'm down with the *cinema,* too.") The stuff about Zank packing a hand-cannon was a complete fabrication. Though he probably had one, Manny and Tony Zank had not even crossed paths. Since Manny didn't anticipate Fayton chatting with Tony anytime soon, he figured it was a safe lie. The chief, however, was obsessed by something else entirely.

"Did you say, like Dean Martin, except *colored?*" he asked.

"Actually I said African-American, but yes, that's pretty much what I said." Manny was a fan of political correctness, since it covered so many other sins.

Fayton wriggled excitedly in his chair. "That has to be Mac McCardle. He was on *America's Most Wanted*! Killed that nancy boy right here in town! There's a reward, too. A hundred grand for information leading to his arrest. Those kind always a have a lot of *friends.*"

"Well, I'll be damned," said Manny. In fact, he'd made Zank's pal for the celebrity shovel murderer as soon as he'd heard Snooks's description. But it was always best to let the chief think he was a jump ahead. It made him feel good about himself.

Fayton hid his hand again, and this time Manny leaped up and stepped around the desk. Sure enough, there was a pull-out writing slab between the first and second drawers, and Fayton was busily jotting notes on a pad.

"So *that's* what you do with your missing hand. Some of the fellows were wondering."

Fayton reddened. "For your sake, I'm going to forget you said that, Ruby." Then, unable to hide his pride, he added: "I'm writing a screenplay. About my experiences on the force."

Manny nodded. "Is that right? Well whatever you do, don't leave out the DMV years. That's some damn exciting stuff, you ask me."

Chief Fayton went red again. "Could we just get on with the report? I want to get back to this McCardle situation. This is going to be big."

"Of course, Sir."

Manny returned to his chair and, with a flourish, produced a folded paper and smoothed it on his knee. "If it's all right with you, I'll pick it up at the part where one of the paramedics has an epileptic fit loading Mrs. Zank into the ambulance."

"I can't wait," said the chief.

Manny cleared his throat and considered his "report." It didn't matter that there was nothing on the paper but a list of celebrities with drug problems he'd made while bored out of his mind at the Laundromat. He could type something up later. For now, he had to lay out the story he'd concocted on the drive over. He couldn't very well tell the truth: that he was late to Seventh Heaven because he was pitching woo to a hot murder suspect, let alone that the beauty had flashed him a photo of the President with a smiling nutsack. . . . It was time to improvise.

"While I tended to the old lady, Zank and McCardle must have fled," Manny began. He looked up and pinched the bridge of his nose, as if the strain of reading were really getting to him. "The thing is, I never put anybody in one of these new ambulances, the ones where you have to slide the stretcher onto those tracks so it rolls in and out. I couldn't get the damn thing flush. So there I am trying to secure the old lady, and the ambulance driver's flopping around in the grass like a hooked salmon."

"So you let them get away?" Fayton did not seem angry so much as personally let down, even hurt. "I can't believe this!"

Manny slapped the paper off his thigh. Story time was almost over. "It was tough, Chief! Before the paramedic went epileptic, I was all over those scumbags. I told them I'd shoot, but the truth is there were too many bystanders. Maybe if Krantz had secured the perimeter, instead of jacking off in the day room, jawing with witnesses who can't remember their own names, I could have gotten off a shot. Rookie mistake. The good news is, the fall didn't kill Mrs. Zank. It just broke a bunch of bones and pissed her off."

"So she's not dead?"

"Not yet," said Manny, eyeing the signed photo of his ex-wife and Chief Fayton that graced the wall behind his desk. Flanking it were framed newspaper shots of the chief in all manner of gripping police action. Manny recognized the one of himself slapping handcuffs on Everett Welk, a madman accordionist who claimed to be a distant cousin of Lawrence. Hired to play a Pizza Hut opening, Everett stabbed an insurance man in the cheek for talking during "Beer Barrel Polka." It was one of those joke slayings, though the joke wasn't too funny if you were the guy who got it in the dimple. The chief had shown up ten minutes after Welk was subdued and asked the arresting officer—in this case Manny Rubert—if he'd mind letting him "re-enact" the collar. "Just as a gag," he'd said, though readers of the *Upper Marilyn Trumpet* the next morning wouldn't realize it was Manny who actually tackled the knifer, and not the brave and true Chief of Police, Lyn Fayton.

Beside Everett Welk was a "candid" of the chief at the shooting range, two-handing his Beretta, and another of him crouched behind a black-and-white, wielding a bullhorn during what looked like a hostage situation at a pet hospital. Manny had no recollection of this particular police action, and assumed the chief had hired a photographer and staged it to beef up his two-fisted, crime-fighter image.

Fayton picked a scrap of paper off his desk and studied it importantly. "And what about this Marvin Podolsky thing? Any theories?"

"Straight suicide," said Manny. "I'm still writing up the report, but it looks like our guy took himself out with a slug of Drano in his breakfast cereal. He's got a history of attempts. I tracked down a doctor who treated him. Plus his wife said he'd had some financial setbacks."

"So you're not looking at her for possible homicide?"

"All that broad's guilty of is bad luck in men."

The chief frowned. "You're saying he gave *himself* Drano?"

"For the fourth time," Manny sighed, shaking his head, as if contemplating the depths of hell that lived inside such a soul. "Once he went with lighter fluid. But outside of that, he was strictly a Drano man."

Manny paused while his old nemesis, Officer Chatlak, now in his golden years and semiretired, rattled into the chief's inner sanctum with a tray of coffee and cinnamon buns. Fayton eyed the baked goods with longing as Manny plunged ahead.

"Confidentially, Chief, I wouldn't advise going after the girl. On top of everything else," he lied, gripped by sudden inspiration, "she's pregnant. The papers would crucify us. Police hassling a widowed mom-to-be? Not good. Especially when hubby punched his own ticket."

Fayton harrumphed. "I really don't think bad press should be a consideration." Meaning there wasn't any *other* consideration, but better a lowly dick like Manny Rubert should say it than him. "Detective," he added, "I don't have to tell you, I want those men. Especially McCardle. A hundred thousand dollars would go a long way toward improving the station."

"Amen," said Manny, leaning in to speak man-to-man. "But between us, I'd stay mum about the *AMW* deal. Word gets out Big Mac's on the street, every bo-bo with a phone's gonna be gunnin' for the reward. I say we call the show when we make the collar. It'd look bush-league for a cop to give 'em a tip and have somebody else arrest the guy. You want the cash *and* the glory, right? This could put us on the map."

Chief Fayton puffed himself up in his uniform and fingered his Windsor. "Agreed," he said. "But make sure you bring him to me before you lock him up. I want to get some pictures."

EIGHT

Tina could still smell her dead husband's garlic breath on their telephone. For months, convinced that constant garlic-chewing could boost his sperm count, he had been walking around in a reeking gust. The result, ironically, was that his sperm count became irrelevant. He'd become so saturated his skin began to give off fumes, and Tina had told him, more than once, that the only way she was going make love to him was wearing a gas mask or through a hole in the wall. What she had not told him was that she'd had her tubes tied at nineteen. There was no need to be mean. Next to making a killing in money mantras, squiring a brood of mini-Marvs had been the man in her life's number one dream.

Tina wondered if the people on the other end would ever pick up. When someone finally answered, and said "Good afternoon," her own words came tumbling out. "Is this Martino and Sons Funeral Home? *Hello?* Do I have the right number?"

Tina spoke through a wadded up hanky soaked in Scope, which muffled her voice. The funeral human said a few words, and Tina replied rapidly. "Yes, yes . . . I do have a recently departed. That's why I'm calling."

Oddly, it sounded as if the man at the mortuary was also speaking through a rag. Maybe all those dead people gave off fumes of their own. Maybe talking on mortuary phones was as unpleasant as talking on a receiver marinated in Marv-breath.

"It was all very *sudden,*" said Tina vaguely, after Mister Edward, the "grief representative" handling her call, asked how her husband had "passed." He then asked how she happened to select Martino and Sons. When she told him she remembered their ad from the bus bench by the minimall where she took Jazzercise, he sounded slightly hurt. Still, things didn't get really awkward until the mortician inquired about "transporting the deceased." Tina had to explain that she wasn't sure when that could happen, on account of the police were holding the body.

"The police," Mister Edward repeated, his voice clearing suddenly.

Tina pictured an acned, prematurely bald fellow in pinstripes. She often had these clairvoyant moments, and often as not her creepier premonitions proved accurate.

"To be honest, my husband took his own life."

She let her voice trail off, and Mister Edward seemed relieved, almost upbeat, when he replied.

"We understand! Completely. And we want you to know we can certainly assist you with any . . . *special arrangements.*"

Tina was trying to absorb this—and at the same time suppress the image of Marvin writhing on the floor with bleeding eyeballs and lip foam—when she heard the call-waiting beep. She asked Mister Edward to hang on and hit Flash.

"Tina, it's me," said Manny immediately. "What are you wearing?"

"Manny, really, I'm on the line with the funeral home. Is this one of *those* calls?"

"One of what calls? I just heard there's a reporter coming to your house. I wanted to make sure you look like a grieving widow."

"Well, I usually answer the door in hot pants and a SPANK ME T-shirt, but if you think that's a bad idea, I'll change."

"Change back when I come over. Meanwhile, I'm just telling you, I got the word. A woman from the *Trumpet* is on her way."

"Don't they call first?"

"Not after a death. People might tell them to fuck off. Anyway, you should try and look, I don't know. . . ."

"Sad?"

"Start off sad, then get angry. Those people love it when you throw them out. It shows you're sincere."

He couldn't believe he was having this conversation, and silently thanked himself for making the call from the Thrifty Drugs pay phone. Fayton loved to tape calls from the station, and the transcript of this one would be hard to explain.

"You want," said Tina, "I can throw myself on the floor and rent my hair, then hit her with a table leg. But right now I gotta go."

"No, wait." Manny swallowed and paused. "Just one more thing. I have to ask, what about insurance?"

"What about it?"

"Did Marvin have any? You know, is there anything coming to you?"

"He didn't believe in it," she answered. "His theory was, if you really believed in eternal life, life insurance was a waste of cash."

Manny was beyond relieved. Now there really wasn't any pressing motive. One more reason to let it ride as suicide. *A pregnant widow left with nothing. . . .* Who'd want to make her life any more miserable?

"Wait," Tina said, in a tone he hadn't heard before, something harder and tougher fortifying her words. "Do you remember what I showed you in the car?"

"That's not something you forget."

"Well, that's my insurance."

"I hope you're right," he said, and plunged on before he could summon one of the eight zillion reasons for stopping before things went any further. "You're going to need some."

"Why's that?"

"Because you're pregnant," he told her. "And you're going to name the baby Marvin, in case anybody asks."

"I wanted it to be a surprise," she said choking up on cue. "Now I wish I had told him. Maybe then, he could have found a reason to live."

She sounded so convincing, Manny got a chill. "You're scaring me."

"I scare myself," Tina said.

She clicked off without saying good-bye, and Manny wondered just what it was he thought he was doing. This woman had just murdered her husband, and now he was conspiring with her. *Oh well....* He sighed and checked his watch. Que sera fucking sera.

For an extra second, Manny hunkered in the phone booth and took in his fellow losers milling around the prescription window. He made two home boys for stone dope fiends—the fellas liked to take the edge off with Tussionex, cough syrup of the gods, when smack was scarce—and made a jumpy young skeleton with a boob job as a mommy speed freak, no doubt stealing Ritalin from the hyperactive twins pounding the shit out of each other with Tonka toys while she fine-tuned her eyeliner. Manny's own scrip was under a name he'd momentarily forgotten. He had a few different ones, in different parts of town. If this was Thrifty's, he was Martino. That was it. The name of the mortuary advertising on the bus bench in front of the Thrifty minimall.

"I apologize," Tina was saying to Mister Edward, who'd been on hold, "there are just so many loose ends to tie up. I've forgotten my manners under all this stress."

"That's understandable," he said, a man of studied intonation. "Under the circumstances, I think you're bearing up beautifully."

"Thank you," she said, and announced, by way of trying it out, "I'm actually expecting. This is all such a terrible blow."

Mister Edward said nothing for a moment. Tina pictured him staring in a hand mirror, rubbing ointment on his problem skin. Then he spoke into the phone, if possible, with even more professional sympathy than before. He'd begun to sound like the butler in a thirties movie. "Rest assured, Mrs. . . . ?"

"Podolsky."

"Mrs. Podolsky, yes. Rest assured, Mrs. Podolsky, I will do everything in my power to make the transition process a smooth one. It's never easy, but you have a friend at Martino and Sons."

"Thank you again," said Tina, catching his formality like a bug. She was trying to think of a way of asking how much this bullshit will cost when Mister Edward addressed the issue for her.

"We have a number of burial packages, Mrs. Podolsky. You're welcome to visit us here and select the casket and service you prefer. Or, if you'd like, I or one of my associates can come by for a home consultation. Whatever the method," he continued delicately, "we recommend that the bereaved make arrangements at their earliest convenience. Is there, perhaps, a friend or family member we can contact? We find it wise to establish viewing hours and decide on the type of service that best suits your needs as soon as possible."

"There's just . . . just me," she said, putting some quiver in it.

"I see. And did you and the late Mr. Podolsky have a cemetery you preferred? Have you selected a plot?"

"Not exactly. He was sort of Indian," Tina said, fondling Marv's turban, as if this would somehow explain everything.

Tina was still clutching the turban when the knock came on her door. She peeped through the curtain to see a whip-thin, short-haired woman in a business suit speaking into a cell phone. By now, the new widow had changed into a black skirt and sweater, the closest she had to actual mourning-wear.

Oddly enough, Marvin's face had shown up in the *Trumpet* two weeks ago, in the lifestyle section, as part of a series on Alternative Worship. He'd been interviewed over the phone. The headline read COSMIC CASH-IN. Below that: LOCAL MAN LEADS MOVEMENT TO MONEY MEDITATION. In the story, Marv explained that chanting the proper mantra was a way of not just creating prosperity but establishing a harmony with the cosmos that made possible a life without fear of death overshadowing the joy of living. "If we find the right vibration of joy in the moment," the reporter quoted him, "then we are guaranteed to live forever."

Apparently, he'd been wrong.

Tina thought about that as she opened the door. "I hope this isn't a bad time," said the lady in the business suit, before Tina could get out a hello. "I'm Dee-Dee Walker, from the *Trumpet?*"

The way she left it, like a question, let Tina know she was supposed to recognize her, probably even be impressed. Tina remained noncommittal. She decided to let the reporter do the talking, as though her own grief had rendered her mute.

"Is this," Dee-Dee Walker wondered again, "a bad time?"

Tina thought of a few responses, none polite. But Ms. Walker answered her own question.

"Of *course* it's a bad time! I know how it is. My Buddy died last summer. He was a St. Bernard, but you'd have thought he was human! He was my everything." She sighed, then found the strength to continue. "Since your husband, your late husband, was recently profiled in the paper, my editor thought that we should get a few words, something about what happened. Whether you'll be continuing his work, and so on. It would be, I guess you could say, a way for all of us to get closure."

Tina found herself fascinated by the woman's delivery, the way she kept looking around but pretending not to. Her eyes wandered over Tina's shoulder, into the living room. *Looking for clues.*

"May I come in?" Ms. Walker finally asked. "This won't take more than a *mo,* I promise."

An hour later, having duly recorded the details of Marvin's tragic suicide, Tina's heartbreak, and the difficulty of being left with baby Marvin due in a matter of months, Dee-Dee Walker seemed to expect the sudden mood swing.

"I can't talk about this anymore!" Tina cried. She let her grief metamorphose into rage, just as Manny had advised. "How can you barge into somebody's home and talk to them like this, when they've just lost someone they loved? *And I'm not talking about a fucking dog!*"

Dee-Dee chose this moment to request a picture, and snapped three quick ones with her point-and-shoot before Tina could think about it. With luck, the photo would show a pretty woman crazed by grief. *Either that,* Tina thought, *or I'll look like some heartless bim who pan-fries kittens.* . . .

The whole thing made her so indignant, by the time she showed her uninvited guest the door, she wasn't sure she was acting.

NINE

The Pawnee Lodge was pretty much empty this time of the week, and nobody seemed to notice the trio unloading themselves from Carmella's Gremlin. The motel consisted of a dozen "cottages," each more or less a cinder-block hut with an Indian headdress mounted over the door. Why the Pawnee people had decided to open up on a strip of auto upholstery shops and parts outlets was anybody's guess. But Zank said he'd used the place before and the owner kept his mouth shut.

"Nice place for a honeymoon," McCardle teased, holding the door for Carmella as Zank pushed her through to Number Three.

"Which is exactly what this ain't," Zank said.

The big lady sat on the bed without saying a word. She fixed her gaze on McCardle, who winked at her. Her peach capri pants, he noted happily, matched the bedspread. The walls were the color of ball park mustard. If his plan went the way it did in his head, he'd have her under the blankets and ready to tussle in not too long. That, or she'd be dead. Either way.

"Tony," Mac said to his partner, "we need to talk. Private-ito."

But Zank was in no mood. "Can't it wait?"

McCardle sulked. Tony grabbed him by the arm and moved him to a corner of the room, beside a battered color TV chained to the wall. "What is it? We got business here."

"You got *beez*-iness," Carmella chimed in, "at least let *me* watch the goddamn television."

Tony tossed her the remote, and she clicked on Jerry Springer as the kidnappers huddled. Today's topic was "Women Who Love Men Who Call Them Mommy." McCardle caught a glimpse of a Chinese man in a diaper and had to look away.

"So spill," Zank hissed, giving Mac's shoulder a serious whack to let him know it better be good.

McCardle licked his lips and looked at Carmella. She was so *sexy!* And there was so much of her. . . . *Yum!*

His plan, he knew, could go two ways. That was the genius part. He'd worked it out in the Gremlin while holding Zank's piece on Carmella. The idea was to tell Zank about the money between Carmella's tits, then finagle Tony into going for it himself. Tony didn't know what their hostage was capable of, but McCardle did. All she'd done to Tony was comb his nostrils. What was that? McCardle knew better. And not just because his foot still throbbed where she'd spiked him. *Twice.* No, he'd seen something in her eyes. He knew how to spot a thrill-killer from his stint at Lewisburg. You had to, or you'd end up somebody's thrill.

If Tony tried anything, Carmella would definitely fuck him up. But Tony was his own kind of monster. As soon as Carmella made her move, whatever it was, Tony would go berserk. He couldn't help himself. One time, at a Pirates game, when a blind teenager accidentally bumped him at the water fountain, Tony spun around and punched him in the mouth. Then he pushed the terrified youngster to the ground and yanked his shoes off. The blind boy man kept screaming

"Why?" But Tony didn't care. He threw the kid's Hush Puppies in the trash and started throttling him.

That's how Tony was wired. He was a throttler. Which was perfect. The second Carmella provoked Tony into choking her, Mac would step in and kill him, thereby saving her life and, in his much-mulled-over fantasy, gaining her outsize, willing body in gratitude.

On the other hand—Plan B—if Tony killed Carmella before Mac could intervene, that worked, too. They could share the money. Tony was a maniac, but he was a *fair* maniac. On every job they'd done, he'd split the take a clean sixty–forty.

"How much you say she's holding?" Tony whispered, eyeing the saucy rest home supervisor while Mac explained that he didn't know for sure, but it looked like a tasty wad.

Much to McCardle's disappointment, Tony didn't take the bait. "I don't believe you! We got the chance for serious money, and you're tripping over chump change some pudge stuffed in her boob-wedgie."

"Well . . . yeah," Mac said, a little hurt. "Why not?"

Disgust curled Zank's lips. "You want it, you take it," he said. "I got better fish to fry. You even know why we checked in here?"

"THEY LOVE THEIR MOMS!" Jerry Springer shouted, and Tony ripped the plug out of the wall so hard the TV nearly toppled.

McCardle was stung. Though, come to think of it, he wasn't 100 percent sure what they were doing at the Pawnee. The embarrassing truth showed up on his face.

"The Black Dino doesn't know," Zank mocked, pinching Mac's cheeks and squeezing them until his eyes watered. Zank's voice was getting louder, and McCardle watched Carmella, perched on the edge of the queen-size bed, straining to hear. "The Black Dino thinks we dropped my mother out a fucking window, took off with some fat Spic bitch, and checked into this fleapit so he could pinch a chunk of lunch money. The Black Dino's not too fucking bright is he? *Is he?*" he repeated, louder still, pretend bitch-slapping him as Carmella slipped off the peach bedspread.

She padded forward with the remote held high over her beehive and a look in her eye that stuck McCardle's tongue to the roof of his mouth.

"I can't hear you!" Zank shouted, at the exact second Carmella whipped the remote off his temple. She reared back and banged him again before he could even turn around.

"Spic bitch, huh?"

"Spic bitch," Tony smiled, shaking off the second blow. His temple sprouted a bloodless egg, as if something under the skin had hatched and wanted out.

Carmella was so stunned by his disturbo grin she forgot to hit him again. The remote dangled from her raised hand, neglected.

"You wanna play?" Zank asked her, as happy as McCardle'd ever seen him. "The fat Spic bitch wants to play with a white boy?"

Tony let out a yip, and Carmella dodged his first punch with surprising grace. Ducking under it, she caught Zank on the chin with a punishing uppercut. McCardle had to admit, she fought like a man. He was still thinking about it when he saw the big-barreled .357 in his partner's hand. Tony held the thing like he meant to shoot, but instead he just poked her. He shoved the barrel hard in Carmella's stomach, then giggled and jabbed her in her breast.

"Doughy," he laughed. "We got us the Pillsburita Dough-girl."

Zank eeny-miney-moed Carmella's bosoms with the muzzle. "So where's the dough-girl keep her dough? A dumb-ass black birdy told me there's some dough-re-mi in there somewhere."

Zank turned to McCardle and waggled his eyebrows, sharing the fun, and Carmella made for the gun. She ripped it from Tony's hand, then Tony snatched it back. Carmella slapped at the barrel and for one frantic second, Zank bobbled the weapon, which is when McCardle tried to grab it and fired in his face.

The shot was so loud it left McCardle deaf. When he opened his eyes, Tony was screaming silent movie–style. He must have juked at the last instant because his face was still there, though something was off with the right side of his head. A patch of hair had been blasted down to scalp. The flesh at his temple was scorched, as if he'd napped on a hot radiator. A tarry blotch showed up where his ear used to be.

The ringing in Mac's skull blotted out whatever his partner was screaming. He watched Zank reel in a tight circle, stretching the collar of his Ban-Lon to the side of his head. Tony wore nothing but Ban-

Lon, and now McCardle knew why. In a pinch, it could stretch neatly over a head wound.

The stench of cordite watered McCardle's eyes, and he all but forgot Carmella until he saw her plunge a nail file toward Tony's other ear. Slightly giddy, he heard himself think: *It's Get Tony in the Ear Day!* He felt sad that his good friend only had two ears. Soon the fun would have to stop. He felt worse when he realized she wasn't going for Tony, she was going for *him*. He jerked, and the flimsy metal pierced the skin under his jaw.

"Ow, *shit!*" McCardle cried, barely hearing himself.

By the time he plucked the file out—he closed his eyes and *tugged*—Carmella had the gun on Zank. Mac hadn't seen how she'd gotten ahold of it, but it didn't matter. She had the thing, and she was bug-eyed with fury. With her free hand, she rubbed her breasts where Zank had abused her. McCardle found the gesture spectacularly arousing, despite his injury.

"I *might* not shoot you," Carmella informed them, "but I'm gonna make you wish I did."

Poking Tony with the gun, the exact way he'd gun-poked her, Carmella nudged him to the battered desk by the bed.

"Hands on the chair," she ordered. "I've got to *think*."

Tony's ear bled freely now, and Mac could see that he had not, in fact, shot the whole thing off. Just the top part, drenching the rest in blood. It looked, to McCardle, like Tony was wearing a wet red earmuff. His own wound turned out to be no more than a scratch.

"Tony, you okay?" McCardle squeezed as much genuine concern as he could into his voice. If Tony even suspected he'd meant to shoot him, he knew it was over. On the off chance Carmella spared him, his partner would assassinate him without blinking.

Mac McCardle died in the Pawnee Lodge, McCardle thought to himself, trying the sentence out. He imagined hearing the words in Dan Rather's voice. When he was little, Auntie Big'n always liked to watch the *CBS Evening News* while he tamped her. She left the bathroom door open, so they could catch the TV in the full-length mirror. Thus reflected, Dan Rather had seen him through the most heinous moments of his tender young life. In the full flush of shame, McCardle used to hear Dan talking from the Motorola. "Now Little Tinky's cleaning his auntie's lady-place. . . . Now he's patting her nice and dry. . . ."

Late at night, when Auntie Big'n was sawing logs in her nightie, Dan would talk some more to Little Tinky, which was his special name for him.

"It's okay, Little Tinky," the newsman would reassure him. "You're a fine young man! George Washington Carver had to tamp down his old auntie, too. Same with Bruce Lee and Morley Safer! You're gonna be okay, Champ!"

Hearing Dan's voice in his head, repeating his kindly message, the young McCardle would doze off knowing the closest thing he'd ever known, in his little lifetime, to actual peace.

"I said *BEND OVER*," Carmella barked, bringing Mac violently back to the present. She waved the gun around, pointing first at one man, then the other, a vicious gleam in her eye.

One side of his head sticky with blood, Zank cursed and leaned forward to plant his hands on the back of the desk chair. The bruise on his forehead had morphed to marbly purple, and his nostrils were scabbed. Mac knew Tony sometimes kept a shiv in his sock. But if he was packing now, he was being cagey about it.

Carmella stepped forward and rubbed the .357 through McCardle's chinos, up and down his butt-crack. "Now you, Gomer."

"Oh great," he complained, "I'm Gomer again." Though the truth was, he nearly swooned from her high-caliber caress.

Carmella's heavy face broke into a grin. "You giving me lip? You *disrespecting* me? Just for that I'm gonna ask you to do him."

"Do who?" Zank sounded worried.

"Who you think?" Carmella blew them both a kiss and sat down on the bed, crossing her majestic legs. She sighed deeply and settled back on a pair of pillows against the wall, as though ready for a really good TV show. "You *putos* got a favorite movie? *I* do," she announced. "My favorite movie in the whole world is *Deliverance*. Mmm! That Burt Reynolds is a *real* man. But you know what? That is not even the reason Carmella likes the film. Burt, he's hot in every movie. Even *Cannonball Run.* It's not really about Burt, it's about that one scene. You know the one? *Squeal like a peeg!* Now you're with me, right? Now you know what La Carmella is talking about. . . ."

She leaned forward, pressing the gun to her lips, as if speaking into a blue steel microphone.

"You two *pendejos* have been *muyo* mean to Carmella! But Carmella is going to give you the chance to apologize. In a *special way.* Do you know what that means? Do you, little black man? Eh, *chanate,* what do you say?"

Mac was panicky about giving the wrong answer. "Sq-squeal like a pig?" he stammered. "T-Tony, do you know that scene?"

"Don't talk to me," Zank snapped. "Don't nobody fucking talk to me."

Tony swiveled around, to say more, and Carmella fired again. This time the bullet tore into a wall, shattering plaster and sending the fake oil painting of a rowboat full of happy gypsies tumbling onto the desk.

"Ho-kay, *be* that way?" Carmella shrieked. "You want to have attitude? You want to call Carmella a fat Spic bitch? You want to act like you got some kind of *machismo, Mees-ter Zank?* Thass right, I know your name. Your mama told me everything. And I got news for you, *To*-ny, the more macho you act, the more fun it is for Y-O-*Me.*"

She snorted and turned on McCardle. "Now you, my little black stallion. I want you to cha-cha behind your big white poppa and pull down his *pantalones.*"

Mac swallowed. "You want me to *what?* Hey, Carmella, this wasn't my idea. I just came along to help out. I didn't know nothin', I *swear.*"

"You, shut *up!*" Carmella slapped a hand off her prodigious thigh. "You should say '*Gracias!*' You get to be the *man.* Now drop your fancy little trousers. Show Carmella what you got!"

Keeping his eyes fixed on the fallen gypsy painting, McCardle told himself to be strong. *Look at the little family,* he thought to himself. *They're all alone in a great big ocean! The waves are huge! The sharks are everywhere, but they're SMILING! They're probably singing happy Gypsy songs! They're—*

"NOW!" Carmella shouted. "When Mama wants her hot sauce, Mama doesn't want to wait."

McCardle unbuckled his pants and Zank lashed at him over his shoulder. "You fucking *think* about it, you're dead!"

Mac cast a pleading look at Carmella, who pointed with the gun, indicating his manhood—still covered by his banana-yellow boxers. Why had he chosen those, today of all days? McCardle tried to will Dan Rather back into his head, to get him broadcasting. But the newsman was absent, in the field, tracking down another trouble-spot.

"We don't have all day, *pasmado*."

Trying to remember a prayer—*Now I lay me down to sleep*—McCardle slung his thumbs into the elastic and tugged south. He worked the shorts to his knees and shook them the rest of the way down.

"Mm-hmmm." Carmella cocked her head sideways, like a very large pigeon. "So it's true what they say about you black men."

"What's that?" said Mac, but only because he thought he had to.

"You know," she whispered, "they always lie about how big they are."

"Hey now," McCardle started, then realized he had nothing to say.

Carmella shrugged. "All men are the same, but you *negritos* have more to live up to. It has to be a very, very big disappointment to all the señoritas when you pull down your pants. They must think, 'I was expecting King Kong, and instead I'm getting a *chorizo* like the Curious George.' "

McCardle's face burned in a way it hadn't since his Little Tinky days. "I'm a grower, not a show-er," he said defensively.

Zank turned around to see what Carmella was talking about, and turned back with the ghost of a smirk on his lips. Mac's organ didn't interest him, only the look on his face. Kind of *glazed*. Tony'd had doubts about his partner since he got wind of the shovel thing. Mac's crime went down in a bar Zank knew catered to homoloids. Zank *hated* homos almost as much as he hated Boy Scouts. Your Boy Scouts, especially scoutmasters—those evil *BASTARDS!*—were the biggest homos of all. . . .

McCardle claimed he got blindsided in the Parakeet Lounge when he was in there mugging a guy. In the *bathroom*. But, the way Tony figured, there were plenty of other places to mug somebody. Why a gay *men's room?* Nobody actually went there to pee, did they? Unless it was down some degenerate's throat. Zank once held up a minister in the bathroom at Denny's, but that was different. That was back in his crank days. He was so out of it he had to shade his eyes from the glare off the tile. The methedrine did that, made everything too bright. He thought he'd robbed the guy in an igloo, until he staggered out and saw all these zombies spooning in runny yellow eggs. *Horrible!* It was after that Tony decided to turn his life around, and switched to crack. But a *gay bar!* Any amateur could tell you, thump a chickenhawk and take his wallet, you won't catch a robbery beef, you'll go down for hate crime. There was a big world out there to plunder and rob. You didn't need to hit a joint where slapping someone was a federal case. Unless, of course, you had other reasons for being there.

Now look at him, Zank fumed, about to check my oil in underwear the color of lemon meringue pie. . . .

"You see," Carmella snickered, "even your good friend Tony is disappointed. Even he is wanting more of a man."

"Shut up!" Zank sputtered, and she shifted the gun in his direction.

"Believe me, I'd just as soon kill you as rub my clitty bump. And I *love* to rub my clitty bump."

Again, Mac had to struggle not to get aroused. Just the thought of the hearty Latina, flat on her back on the motel bedspread, legs spread as she pleasured herself with pudgy thumb and forefinger. . . . *No, stop that!* he muttered. To his horror, he found himself stiffening against the cleft of his partner's behind.

"*Caramba,*" Carmella cackled. "Looks like the little lawn jockey is getting ready to gallop."

Zank muttered something, shifting his buttocks, and their hostess bellowed. "No juking, Señor. I got a gun, remember? I got *chor* gun."

She smiled at McCardle and repositioned herself on the bedspread, legs wide apart in her stretch capris. "Now," she purred, "you pull down his pants, and you do him."

"Ex . . . excuse me?"

McCardle closed his eyes and tried not to breathe. Maybe he could make himself pass out. Maybe—

"A señorita is *waiting.*"

When Mac opened his eyes, Carmella was aiming a dildo at him.

She wielded the plastic white missile in one hand, the .357 in other, like an old-time gunslinger. "Bang-bang," she said, and McCardle nearly started to cry. Somewhere Dan Rather was shaking his head.

Carmella winked at him. "You want to spit on your hands, get some lubrication, thass okay. But try anything funny and I shoot you both. I don't care. When the *policia* see what you two tried to do to me, they won't ask questions. They'll send me roses. And hand me that big reward. *Comprendes?* You two are going to give Carmella a pretty little show, or you're going to die. Señor Tony, *los pants,*" she added, blowing another full-lipped kiss as she shimmied her own skin-tight capris a few inches south on her enormous thighs, to the very top of her pubes. Or where her pubes would be if she had any.

"Oh God. . . . *Shaved,*" McCardle gasped, his breath catching in his chest. Now he was helpless. The sight of the colossal beauty's hairless treasure was just *too much.* . . . He was fully erect, and mortified. Feeling him, Zank's face went deep red, then very pale.

"Somebody's ready to rumba," said Carmella huskily. She dropped the gun to her pudendum, but kept the dildo raised to her face. She seemed to be *clicking* it. "You *hombres* want to die to keep your virtue, that's fine by Carmella. Your mommas would be very proud."

"I'll kill you," Zank growled, though whether to his throbbing partner or his jolly audience wasn't clear.

No matter. . . . Carmella eased back on the headboard, smiling happily, and fished in her pocketbook for a Jenny Craig bar.

"*Deliverance,* por favor."

TEN

All the women Manny'd ever really dug had been hugely damaged. All except for his ex-wife, who was confident, adjusted, raised by adoring parents, and responsible for the three most hellish years of his adult life.

Mayor Marge, whose face, in Tina's photo, showed up in sniffing proximity to the commander in chief's distended nates, was the kind of girl he once thought he should love. She attended law school while Manny slogged through the Police Academy. And she had ambitions for both of them. It was easy, young Manny'd thought at the time, to have ambitions when you'd never been within shouting distance of failure. But that bit of insight, steeped in resentment he was barely aware of, did not keep him from pursuing her.

His in-laws' living room—the memory still made

his mouth dry—was dominated by a mahogany breakfront packed two-deep with trophies and plaques, inscribed silver plates and framed certificates, all won by the golden-haired Marge. Archery, debate, swim meets, spelling bees . . . the breakfront was a shrine to the victory. To *winning*. Something Manny had never done once in his entire life. The night of their first date, while her father the snack-cake mogul grilled him about his "career goalposts," Manny could not stop staring at Marge's triumphant booty. He found himself fixated on a big blue ribbon she'd snagged for a "safety slogan" she'd thought up for a contest in second grade. The winning entry was preserved and mounted, in eight-year-old Marge's stellar penmanship. "Don't put yourself in danger, never talk to a stranger!"

All of this, to Manny, was as alien as a tray full of shrunken heads. There was absolutely nothing about Marge he could relate to, so of course he had to have her. His own father, by then a tumor-ridden depressive hunched in his den, bathed in blue TV light around the clock, had given him the one piece of advice he'd ever given after meeting Marge. The old man and the deb had chatted for a tense two minutes after Manny, under pressure from his sweetheart, had run out of excuses for not letting her meet his family.

"Sonny boy, you watch out," his father warned him a week later, speaking over applause for a genius *Jeopardy* guest. "To a girl like that, you're nothing but an exotic dog."

"Meaning what?" Manny asked, all the more outraged because it sounded true.

"Meaning," said his father, fighting off the chemo-heaves, "she'll parade you around for a couple of years to show she's original, but sooner or later, she's gonna want a blue blood. When that happens, kiddo, you'll be lucky if she leaves you lickin' the bowl."

Dad wasn't completely right, Manny thought, pulling in to Marge's mansion to have his little chat. But he wasn't all that wrong, either. She hadn't left him a bowl, she'd just left him. Though technically speaking, that wasn't true, either, since Manny'd moved into the Tit-ville YMCA a month before the official split. Marge's career as attorney-turned-real-estate-mogul was already launching her into the highest strata of Upper Marilyn society. And Manny's status as lowly beat cop, someone she'd see rousting a bus bench drunk while lunching with men who owned office buildings, had become less and less acceptable.

The kicker came at a dinner party Marge dragged him to, a lofty affair hosted by one Melton Heinz, heir to the ketchup throne and a prime mover in the drive to transform the industrially challenged blight they inhabited into a shining city on a hill. Or at least a high-end suburb.

Melton, a thin-faced, silver-haired man with a braying laugh, wore the first ascot Manny'd ever seen outside of *Thin Man* movies. By dessert he was still staring at it, trying to figure out how the burgundy silk stayed puffed out of Melton's collar, defying gravity, when there was a gigantic crash in the kitchen. Manny charged in with the rest of the guests to find the cook, a six-foot-six Swede named Lars, panting by the door with his hand around the neck of a scrawny black kid. The unlucky intruder could not have been more than twelve. He wore a Pirates T-shirt over corduroy pants two sizes too big. And the Mr. Clean–like cook had him hoisted off the ground by his throat.

"I find him in garbage," Lars announced. "Stealing."

As if this news gave him the license he needed, Heinz marched to the door where Lars stood strangling the terrified youth. Ordering his chef to drop him, the condiment heir stepped up and slapped the boy. Hard. Then he snatched a veal chop from a plate on the counter and began wagging it back and forth in the kid's face, baiting him. "Hungry, are you? How about a taste of milk-fed veal? *Well?* How about it? You want a taste?"

When it was clear the captive child was not going to do tricks, Heinz cocked his head of silver hair toward his dinner guests and smiled drolly before turning back to his victim. "We can't have you eating out of my garbage can like an *animal*. I'm a *liberal!* I'll let you eat off my kitchen floor. Better yet, why don't I feed you myself!"

Mister Heinz laughed his braying laugh. Then he stopped laughing and mashed the breaded veal into the boy's mouth.

The boy still didn't react. Only this time, before Heinz could continue playing, Manny was across the room. He planted himself in front of the young man, jacket pulled back so Heinz could see his piece. "I could arrest you right now for assault and battery," he told his startled host, "but it won't stick unless the kid presses charges."

If anything, the twelve-year-old was more alarmed than Heinz. Until something in Manny's eyes let him know it was all right.

"You could, of course, settle out of court," Manny said, keeping it matter-of-fact. "That way you avoid all kinds of hassles."

By now Lars looked ready to shove Manny's face in the grapefruit juicer, but Melton Heinz raised a manicured hand to still him. The guests stayed quiet, no doubt out of respect for all that ketchup money.

"Officer Rubert, you have a point," said Heinz, still trying for droll. Braying only slightly, he turned to his young guest. "Would fifty dollars keep you from siccing Jesse Jackson on me?"

"Five hunnert," the boy countered, without hesitation. His glance flicked from Heinz to Manny, who nodded to let him know it was okay by him.

Heinz produced five bills. The youngster grabbed them, then made a show of counting them. Before he shoved the cash in his pocket, he looked up at the ascot-wearing Heinz and met his smirk with a dead-pan gaze. "I'se lettin' you off easy, bitch."

That got a rise from the dinner guests. And when the newly flush boy from the hood sauntered out the kitchen door, there was no question that Officer Manny Rubert would be right behind him. No question, either, that he'd be sleeping at the YMCA from that night on.

Manny stepped gingerly up the flagstone path from the street to the mayor's residence. The mansion was a glandular Victorian which had been added to over the years. It seemed like every time he drove by, a new cupola had metastasized from the roof, another bay of windows erupted from some second-story balcony or tower. The house kept expanding, though no one officially lived there but Marge and her tiny staff.

"All this could have been yours," cooed a voice from the open front door, and Manny smiled to see Lipton, his ex's *GQ*-handsome, platinum-blond British personal assistant. He was standing astride the welcome mat, arms outstretched. "I look at you, Manny, and I think

Why? You're such a smart, sexy bloke. All this could have been yours, darling!"

The one thing Manny liked about his former wife was that she'd hired Lipton as her assistant. The spritely Brit, who wore nothing but Armani, owned a head of hair he could have sold by the pound. His pompadour was so fluffy and lustrous you wanted to sink your toes in it. The peroxide was a touch only Lipton himself could explain, and nobody asked him to. For years Manny had wondered about the relationship, idly speculating on the arcane combinations the gay fashion plate and Her Honor His Ex might possibly concoct. You never know. . . .

As a lover, Marge had been ardent, if a tad distracted. Manny's dominant erotic memory was a moment when he'd mounted her from behind, pumping frantically while she flicked herself with a buzzing vibrator and barked insults on the speakerphone to a junior realtor who'd let a fixer-upper in Butt-burg go for twenty grand too cheap. "You're in-*COM*-petent!" she'd screamed, her face mashed sideways in the pillow. "You're a *FOOL!* You have no *FEEL* for the *BUS*-iness!" Marge timed every epithet to his thrusts, to the point where Manny felt like stopping just to spare the poor bastard any further abuse.

A year after they split up, it occurred to Manny, out of nowhere, that Marge had actually been talking to *him*. Getting off calling him a *FOOL* and an *ID*-iot and a *TO*-tal *ASS*-hole while writhing beneath him. It was, in retrospect, one of the high points of their union.

"Madame's waiting on the *verahn-dah*," Lipton announced, doing his campy-ironic number, and Manny made his way through the high-ceilinged central hall to the patio in back where Marge sat sipping tea. Her one vice was Celestial Seasons Fast Lane: ginseng and mega-caffeine, two bags at once, sipped from a large white mug with her face and logo on it. "Mayor Marge and Business—The Perfect Blend!"

"You have five minutes," she informed him, without looking up

"Be still my heart," said Manny.

He had to stare, amazed all over again at the choices his ex had made. Marge seemed to be willing herself to Elizabeth Dole-dom, opting for a stiff, camera-ready do and business suits that might as well have had MIDDLE-AGED spray-painted across the back. When they met, she was a fresh-faced, slightly full-of-herself All-American Rich Girl. All perfect skin, pert breasts, and bouncy ponytail. *Now look at her,* he thought. If life was Disneyland, Marge looked like she was standing in line for Menopause Mountain. *Did I do that?* he wondered. In a dishy moment, Lipton confided that milady had a portrait of Margaret Thatcher over her bed.

When he couldn't handle standing anymore, Manny took the liberty of sitting down and saw that the mayor was reading a brochure, "Brink's Home Security—Questions & Answers."

"You're at four-and-a-half," Marge said, still not bothering to raise her eyes. A squirrel stared at him from a bone-dry bird feeder, and a pair of crows Heckled and Jeckled across the manicured lawn. Manny knew better than to wait her out. Marge would just as soon freeze him with silence as grant him a thirty-second conversation. And none of his detective tricks would work, either. She was sharing a bed with him when he'd dreamt them up.

"Having security problems?" he asked, by way of icebreaker. "I hear Brink's does a pretty good job. At least that's what it says on the ads that come on during *Oprah.*"

"You're watching *Oprah* now?"

"Oh constantly," he said. "Is that bad?"

Since the divorce, it was plain his ex found everything about him vaguely nauseating. She could ask him his favorite color, and if he said "green" she'd speak to him in the same tone she was using now. *There's something really unsavory about green,* that tone implied. *Only a deeply disturbed underachiever like you would think green was a decent color. . . .*

"Oprah and I are getting married," he said, just to get her nose out of her Brink's brochure. "She says she wants a man who can eat as much as her and not gain an ounce. I'm one lucky guy."

"Manuel!" Marge sighed, slapping down her pamphlet. She met his eyes with more annoyance than malice. "I'm sure there's a reason you came by, but do you have to do a *routine* before you tell me what it is?"

Manny cranked up a smile. His hunch was that Mister Biobrain had been pinched from the mayor's place, maybe on purpose or maybe—

imagine their surprise!—by some skells who thought they were walking off with cash and Rolexes and ended up with a bonus: a close-up of W blobbing his family jewels in the mayor's face. *Two-for-one day!*

"Okay," he said, leaning forward and reaching for the Brink's brochure, "I'm just wondering if you're checking on extra security because your place got hit."

Marge studied him, crinkling her eyes, and Manny could sense her drive to find out what he knew doing battle with her desire to keep him from knowing anything. She opened her stay-hot teapot and dropped in another Fast Lane, then closed the top with a little *thwop.*

"The thing is, Marge, there's this snitch claims he knows a guy who knows a guy who knocked over the mayor's place. I don't have to tell you, people will spout all kinds of crap to get out of a corner, and since we caught this guy peeping in the window at Immaculate Heart, where the girls change for field hockey, I don't want to waste time tracking this if it's nothing but stay-out-of-jail bullshit. But now that I see you with your shiny Brink's brochure, looking a bit—no offense— less self-assured than usual, I'm wondering if maybe it's true. I'm wondering if this guy with a snitch jacket long as your femur might actually be dealing straight."

Marge opened her teapot and plopped in another bag—that made three—and Manny was reminded of the odd geometry that abides between the formerly married. Much as they may loathe each other, they also *know* each other. So that even the things that drive them craziest are somehow comforting, a source of familiar fury, fermented over time to one of life's most dependable, piquant joys.

"Your instincts are off, as usual," Marge informed him. "If anybody tried to break in here, they'd be caught. But if they did manage"—she smiled her build-a-stadium-in-my-town smile—"I'd report it to the police. So if there's nothing else. . . ."

"Just a little unasked-for advice," said Manny. And, standing up with a pleasant smile, he picked the teapot off the table and peeked inside. "If you really want to make great tea, you might think about adding water. Stuff doesn't taste the same when you drop the bags in dry."

"Very *Columbo,*" said Marge, "but your five minutes are up."

ELEVEN

"Don't talk to me. Not a word. Nothing. Don't even aim your eyeballs in my direction."

"But Tony—"

"I told you, goddamn it! In this car you do not exist!"

Zank slammed his palm off the Gremlin's steering wheel, sending the tiny hatchback into the path of an oncoming tractor trailer. He swerved at the last minute, a frantic move that slammed both men sideways. The Gremlin's front seat was so cramped, McCardle's shoulder brushed Zank's before he could scramble upright.

"DON'T TOUCH ME!" Tony screamed.

"But Tony, I didn't do anything."

Watery blood bubbled from the bruise on Tony' forehead, where his mother had ashtrayed him. A plum-size contusion oozed beside that, and a welt swelled under his nostrils, courtesy of Carmella's comb-slash. Where Mac had accidentally shot the top of Tony's ear off, a clamshell of dried blood gunked the side of his head, flanked by flesh-tone streaks where the hair had been scorched away.

"Tony, I—"

"*NO!*" thundered Zank. "What is *wrong* with you? Shut up! *Stay* shut up!"

"But Tony, come on, man. I didn't *want* to do it. She made me!"

"She made you? She *made* you!"

The madder Tony got, the more weight he put on the gas pedal, until they were zooming down Liberty Boulevard, Upper Marilyn's main drag, swishing by SUVs and pickups that seemed parked doing 35.

"You're sick, you know that?" Tony shouted, pounding the dashboard while McCardle cowered. "And I'll tell you something else, if you ever mention what happened, if you so much as *think* of telling anybody you . . . you. . . ." He couldn't bring himself to continue and bit his lip. "If you do, I'll kill you so fast you won't know you were ever fucking alive. You hear me? I might kill you anyway, just to make sure. I'll rip out your fucking kidneys with a fork."

"You're kidding, right? She had a gun on me. *Your* gun! You saw!"

"I saw," said Zank. "She had a gun. You had a boner. That's what I saw. You weren't some kind of faggot, or half-faggot, or I don't know what, you'd have taken the bullet. You'd have risked it. But you had my ass in your lap, and you were all pudgied up."

McCardle began to sniffle. His lower lip quivered over his soul patch. "C'mon, Dog, it wasn't you. I like fat ladies, okay? My *auntie* was a fat lady."

Zank snorted. "So fucking what?" He rounded a corner with no signal and sent a mail truck screeching out of the way. "My aunt had a fucking moustache. That don't mean I like broads who shave. You had your skink in me!"

McCardle whimpered. "Just an *inch*."

"No, man, you *fucked* me!" Tony cried, his voice beginning to crack. "You fucking *fucked* me!"

"Not technically," McCardle protested. "As soon as you cut her I pulled out."

"Bullshit! You stopped 'cause you thought I was gonna cut *you*. You were afraid I'd cut your plumpy off. I would've, too, you fucking *man-ho!*"

The pair kept squabbling at the red light. The windows of the Gremlin were down, and a swarthy man in a Boy Scout uniform glared at them from the wheel of a minivan. Behind him a dozen Scouts pressed their faces against the glass.

"Damn perverts!" the scoutmaster yelled, waving his cap to get the Gremlin screamers to pipe down.

Zank saw who was yelling and screamed. "Boy Scouts! I fucking *HATE* Boy Scouts! *They should all die!*"

Tony clawed at his seat belt, trying to leap out of the car, but McCardle held him back. "Calm down, Tony, they're kids."

"Get off me, goddamn it! I'll waste 'em all! The little *fuckers!*"

McCardle grabbed him by the shoulder, and Zank threw him off.

"I told you not to touch me!" he roared. "Didn't you hear me? I know about you, man. I know about the Parakeet Lounge!"

Before McCardle could defend his honor, Tony was rolling again. He caught sight of Carmichael Street and swung a hard left. Mac dug his fingers into the seat, to keep from flying sideways and grazing his irate companion a second time.

"You even know why we *went* to that motel with that fat slit?" Zank asked. "You ever figure that out?"

McCardle was busy fighting back sobs and barely heard the question. "I don't know *anything,* Tony!" He buried his face in his hands. "I just know it wasn't you that got me stoked. It was *her,* that Carmella, the way she spread them big legs, the way the inside of her thighs got all sweaty-like, how they touched all the way to her knees, and then, *Sweet Mother of Jesus,* when she pulled out that big vibrator. . . ."

"Enough! You're gonna make me blow chunks." Zank straight-armed McCardle to make him stop. "We went to the motel for insurance, Cocoa Puff. The idea was, one guy stays in the room with the broad, one guy goes out and checks the street and number she gave us, makes sure we're not bein' gamed. I find out Carmella slipped us some phony address, I call you up and you torture the cunt till she coughs up the right info. *Then* you kill her. That's how it's done. Where'd *you* go to school, man?"

McCardle dabbed his eyes with the sleeve of his parka.

"You mean, I could've been *with* her? While you were out check-ing?"

"What'd I just say?"

"But what if she gave us the right address?"

"Then we don't torture her," said Zank. "We just kill her."

McCardle hardly heard. He was still thinking about what could have been: a blissful hour or two, alone with that massive beauty. He could have tied her up, buried his face in her beehive, licked all over her hips. . . . The Big Love opportunity of a lifetime, *gone.* He plunged his face in his hands.

"Get ahold of yourself," Zank growled. "We gotta kamikaze."

Tony shifted on the seat to find a position that didn't ache. He wondered if Mac could tell he wasn't cherry, and quickly blocked the thought with a dozen other ones. But McCardle was somewhere else entirely. In Mac's mind he was tying the bodacious rest home supervi-sor to the bedpost, cinching the rope tight below her belly button, let-ting his fingers linger over that shaved slope down to her no-doubt chubby lovelips. Oh *yeah!* He wanted to leave her hands free, so when he tickled her she could still hit him. He wanted—

"There she is!" Tony cried, gunning the Gremlin up Carmichael just as Dee-Dee Walker stepped out of Tina's house and strode toward the *Trumpet* pool car. He slowed down to check her out and lowered his voice.

"Looks kind of hoity-toity for a fucking old people's nurse. I bet she already got some dough for Mister Biobrain and spent it on clothes, the thieving bitch!"

Tina, meanwhile, watched from behind her living room curtain as the reporter set her camera and notebook on the roof of her Toyota Camry and unlocked the door. She kept watching while her inquisitor picked up her stuff, got in, and started the car. If Tina noticed the avo-cado Gremlin with the bleeding white guy and buff little black man squeezed in front, it didn't register.

She closed the curtain before the two vehicles disappeared around the corner.

TWELVE

Manny had a brother named Stanley he never talked to who went to Penn State and became a stockbroker. Stanley moved to New Jersey, married three shiny blonds in a row, and fathered a pair of children with names like colognes: Artemis and Jade. What made Manny think about Stanley was the stench in the Liver Ward.

Along with cracking her coccyx, breaking some ribs, rupturing her spleen, and shattering both elbows after her rest home plummet, Tony Zank's mom had been diagnosed with acute cirrhosis. So she'd been shipped from Seventh Heaven to Marilyn Charity, where they stuck her in Liver.

Most of the other occupants, walking-dead rummies with distended bellies and tears flowing hepatitic yellow when they begged for a bottle, slumped on the edge of their beds and stared at their hands. An odd fact: Once they stopped seeing giant insects flying out of the walls, dying drunks pretty much stared at their hands all day. But their hands were not what Manny was pondering. It was their stench that grabbed him by the throat, a toxic cocktail of sweat, bile, soaking sheets, and rank desperation that watered the eyes as it keelhauled the stomach. Manny couldn't describe the smell exactly, but there was one thing he was certain of: His brother Stanley would never have to inhale it.

Manny never thought of his brother except in revolting circumstances. Breathing in the hell of a Hefty garbage bag housing an aborted fetus, the stink of a month-dead junkie bloating on a rooftop in July, or the thousand other olfactory treats his job bequeathed him, the same thought always wriggled into Manny's skull: *Fucking Stanley the fucking stockbroker never has to breathe this shit.* Once this bit of psychic self-laceration was over, Detective Rubert could get on with the job, which in this case meant going toe-to-toe with a drying-out hard case named Dolly Zank.

"You the cop?" the old lady whooped the second he stepped toward her bed. "You wanna talk to me, you gotta get me wet—and I don't mean south of the border. I mean in *here*."

Mrs. Zank made a feeble attempt to point down her throat, but so much of her was in traction the effort was doomed. "Don't expect me to rat out Tony," she informed him hoarsely. "You don't pour me a slug of something potent, I'm gonna clam up tighter than the pope's vagina."

She was, clearly, borderline mental. But the part that hadn't crossed the border, Manny figured, would be wondering how big a patsy he was. Manny slid a short dog of Four Roses out of his jacket pocket, unscrewed the top, made a show of checking right and left, then gave her a wink and tipped the bottle into his mouth. He made sure she could see every wriggle in his gullet as he took a long, slow pull. "Hoo-doggy, *that* hits the spot," he said, smacking his lips. He screwed the lid back on the bottle, held it up to the light, and shook it. "Empty," he sighed. "I guess this little soldier's ready to retire."

The old lady stared at the bottle, jowls wobbling. "At least let me lick it," she pleaded. "You can't deny an old girl a little lick."

"No can do." Manny said, "Your doctor said one sip could kill you." He peeked around again and slipped the top of a second bottle out of his other pocket. "Of course, I always travel with reinforcements."

He thought the old alky's eyes were going to crawl out of her face and grab his pant leg. "Mmm," he smiled, going thoughtful on her. "Sometimes I just like to screw the top off real slow and sniff it. You ever do that? I do. I like to take a whiff, then screw the top back on and slip it back in my pocket. Just knowing it's in there makes me happy. Knowing I can take myself a big, fat, kick-in-the-head swallow whenever I want, just *knowing* that makes life pretty damn sweet. Is that crazy?"

Mrs. Zank's tongue lolled out of her mouth, and Manny wondered if he'd laid it on too thick. But her bloodshot eyes packed a mean, hard look that told him otherwise. He hadn't gotten to her. Not completely. Bad as she needed a drink, if she had to choose between killing him or killing her thirst he sensed she'd still have to flip a coin. Clearly, Tony didn't get his sterling personality licking the wallpaper. Mom was tough. Manny tried one more maneuver, pulling the bottle out and kissing it.

"I think I'm in love," he said, and Mrs. Zank finally cracked.

"Okay, okay!" she wailed. "Just tell me what you want to know. I got no reason to protect my boy. He dropped me out the damn window, didn't he?"

"What I want to know," said Manny, "is why would he do something like that?"

"I guess he wanted a bike for Christmas," she said bitterly. "He barreled in ranting about how he hid something under my mattress, but when he came back for it, it wasn't there. I don't know why he was mad at *me*. Only thing I ever tried to hide was a quart of Thunderbird I bought from Snooks the janitor. And that got pinched when I was out doing recreational therapy. They got us makin' moccasins. I look like a Navajo to you?"

She set her ravaged face in profile, and Manny had to look away. "So Tony didn't tell you what he hid?"

"Alls I know is, he said it was gonna get him millions and he lost it all on account of me. Tony's a crap artist. If he asked, I'd've told him it was a stupid place to hide anything. The girls change the damn sheets once a week. Leastways, they're *s'posed to.* But whenever the hell they change 'em, if they find a goddamn prize under the mattress they take it. *I* would, I was making five dollars an hour cleaning up after a bunch of old toads don't have the good sense to be dead."

"What was it?" Manny inquired, more casually this time.

Mrs. Zank treated him to a scowl. "Some kind of envelope, he said. It couldn't have been too bulky or I'd've felt it. Like the princess in 'The Princess and the Pea.' I've always *loved* that story. It's romantic, like. So gimme the juice."

"Not yet." Manny calculated how much longer he could grind her. "Where's Tony now?"

"Someplace stupid," she sneered. "I guarantee, if I know my boy, that's exactly where he is."

Manny stood up, tapped the bottle in his pocket, and gave her a chipper smile. "Sorry, Dolly. Not good enough. Have a nice day."

He bet himself he'd get five steps. The old lady caved on three. "Wait a minute!" she croaked. He turned back and Mama Zank was shaking her head. She sighed dramatically and raised her gaze to the ceiling. Then, going for full-on martyr, she sniffed loudly and squeezed out an off-color tear.

Out of respect, Manny gave her time to perform. He'd had experience with snitches. Like most, Tony's mom was trying hard to convince herself she felt something. Years from now, when she woke up sweating at three in the morning, she'd remember these tears. She'd forget they'd been fake and go back to sleep. Family members always put on the best show.

"Tony's my *son!*" the old woman reminded him, her eyes staying hard and mean beneath the pantomime of anguish. "That should be worth at least . . . three bottles."

"I agree," said Manny. "At *least* three. The bad news is, I've just got the one. Tell you what, though. Give me somethin' that helps, I'll see to it personally you get a whole case of poison under your bed."

Suddenly, Mrs. Zank was all business. "Pawnee Lodge, out on Saw Mill Run. All the rooms got them Indian hats over the door. They call 'em 'cottages.' Ha! Tony gets in trouble, that's his hideout. He thinks I don't know, but seeing as he pays with the Visa he stole outta my purse, it's hard to keep it a secret. God love 'im, he got his late daddy's brain-pan."

Manny nodded thanks. Then he stepped to her bed, lifted a pillow, and slipped in the Four Roses. Before he could move away, she placed a fractured hand on his wrist. With her other one she threw back the blankets, revealing seven decades of thigh.

"I like a man that's not too good-lookin'," she cooed.

"Tempting," Manny said, then backed out of the room before she could show him more.

THIRTEEN

Tina's visit to the funeral home left her in sugar shock. From the outside, the place looked like a supper club, and she'd driven in and out of the lot twice before she noticed the sign, MARTINO AND SONS MORTUARY, between a pair of stunted pines. There was plenty of parking.

Mister Edward, as she'd psychically surmised, was indeed a sallow young gentleman with questionable skin. Along with a bad case of adult acne, he sported a quartet of moles on both cheeks. Tina spent the first moments of their meeting trying to decide whether his right and left mole-squares matched, or if the right was more oblong. His mortuary office was a tasteful imitation mahogany, decorated with numerous renderings of Julius Caesar.

"One of our greatest Italians," he explained, steering Tina to a seat with a hand on the small of her back. "Did you know he had a sweet tooth like a five-year-old? I've done some research. His favorite was marshmallow creams."

The candy thing, apparently, was Mister Ed's way of justifying the half dozen jars of gumdrops, jelly beans, sour balls, and assorted other treats that cluttered his desk between Caesar busts. It was easy to see how he'd gotten his skin problems.

"I never knew the Romans had Mallomars," she said, smiling to let him know she was as fascinated by Caesar's candy habit as he was. She certainly wasn't going to tell Mister Edward that if he cut out sweets, maybe his pimples would clear up. If the police ever asked, she'd need the mortician to recall her as a polite, grief-stricken, and demure-type widow.

Not that Tina didn't think hooking up with Manny could stave off such difficulties. They'd never officially announced, "Well, now we're involved!" But somehow, from the moment they met, it had felt that way. Still, a girl had to take care of herself.

For the appointment, she'd eschewed makeup, going for a tear-streaked *au naturel* look that pretty much screamed *VICTIM*!

"Actually," Mister Edward was saying, "the Romans invented candy bars. They spread honey over blocks of nougat and baked them in clay ovens. They served it at state funerals. I like to think I'm continuing the tradition."

"That *is* lovely," Tina offered, adding shamelessly, "you really seem to care."

Mister Edward blushed, his blemishes glowing a deeper scarlet. He clamped one hand over the other, as if to keep it from hopping up and raiding the gumdrop jar. While her host droned on about the ins and outs of "final care" and "after-life maintenance," Tina found herself popping sweets compulsively. She'd worked her way from gumdrops to jelly beans, on across the desk to the heavy ammo, knuckle-size wrapped caramels and chocolate-covered cherries on a silver platter. Normally she tried not to eat sugar, and the sudden overload made her feel anxious and giddy at the same time, as if she'd IVd bad speed.

"What I'd like," she told him after his spiel, "is a simple cremation."

Mister Edward winced and went for the gumdrops. "Memories,"

he said meaningfully, patting what looked like a soap sculpture of Caesar on the head as he let the word sink in. "What we provide here at Martino and Sons are the final, beautiful memories of your loved one. What we believe, Mrs. Podolsky—"

"Call me Tina, please."

"Tina," he said, flushing again. "What we believe, Tina, is that a life is like a house. A proper funeral is like the roof of that house, the final element that makes the structure complete. If you decide to forego that last—and I believe *necessary*—aspect of your husband's time here with us, you'll have a sense of incompleteness, a lack of closure that, I regret to say, may let the rain in on your peace of mind. . . ."

He stole a glance at the jelly-bean jar, grabbed his left his hand with his right to keep it in line, then gave up and snatched a handful of the little sugar eggs and threw them in his mouth before continuing. "Will you at least consider holding off on the decision for twenty-four hours?"

Tina dabbed at her eyes with a hanky she'd stashed up the sleeve of her dress. "I'd *prefer* a traditional ceremony," she said, "it's just. . . ." She dabbed again and blew her nose, she hoped, with what looked like tragic bravery. "It's just that Marvin left instructions—specific instructions—that he was not to be buried. He was adamant. What *I* want, Mister Edward, doesn't matter. I wouldn't feel right defying his wishes."

"I understand," said the mortician. Tina felt his attitude change, as though a NO SALE sign had popped out of her collar. Or maybe it was something else. "Perhaps we should discuss the service," he went on. "Will family be arriving?"

"No family." Tina shut her eyes and shook her head from side to side. *This is difficult!* she wanted that head-shake to say. *This is sad!* "We met in an orphanage. It was not having a family that brought us together, that made us mean so much to each other." She cupped her hands over her nonexistent belly and tried to look mournful. "That's why I feel so bad for my baby, little Marvin. Now he won't ever get to know his daddy. . . ."

To Tina's horror, Mister Edward smiled. Maybe it sounded as ridiculous to him as it did to her. *Busted,* she thought, and was mentally preparing her escape when he swallowed his jelly beans and announced, in a tone of all new intimacy, "I'm an orphan myself, Tina. Only I never found my little orphan girl."

His smile was so hideous, Tina almost missed the fact that he was hitting on her. She could not stop staring at that smile. His face seemed embalmed. Only the lips moved. Tina could think of absolutely nothing to say, and was hugely relieved when Mister Edward stopped waxing romantic and plunged on with the business at hand. "Will you be interring, or would you prefer to keep the cremains?"

"I'll take him to go," Tina said, catching herself when she saw the look on the undertaker's face. "I mean, I'll be taking him to go to India. His spiritual homeland. Marvin wanted his ashes spread over the Ganges."

Disappointment pinched Mister Edward's lips. "Well, the Italians are doing wonderful things with urns. You can select one today, or I can give you one of our catalogues."

"Can we just do it?" Tina asked, her nineteenth gumdrop going to her head and making her skin tingly.

Unable to stop himself, Mister Edward leaped out of his seat, upsetting a bowl of malted milk balls. "Mrs. Podolsky . . . Tina . . . I have to tell you. . . ."

Tina stiffened. Was he going to jump her? Did he plan on kissing her right here, in front of the Caesars? The thought of his creepy skin coming anywhere near hers made her gorge rise. God knows what you could catch from an undertaker.

"Mrs. Podolsky," he began again, slightly hysterical, "I'm sorry, but I think you're making a terrible mistake. You are a creature of deep passions, I can see that. If you cremate your husband, I just know you'll regret it. Trust me! A funeral is the last act of love we perform for the departed. The last"—he lowered his eyes dramatically—"*act of love.* . . ."

Tina wondered if this pitch worked with other widows. She forced herself to meet his eyes, doing her best to make her gaze as sincere and longing-packed as his. Maybe she could get a discount.

"I'd like to take care of it today," she said, pulling a pair of fifties out of her purse. She'd pawned Marvin's vid cam and computer on the way down to the home. "Here's a down payment."

"But that's just not possible," said Mister Edward.

Tina almost lost it. "Why not? Look, I'm not gonna plant the guy, so give it a rest."

"Tina, *please*," said Mister Edward, "it's not that." The mortician tried to hide his shock. "We don't . . . have the body. I've been trying to think of a way to tell you."

"What are you saying?"

"The police are holding your husband. They want to do an autopsy."

"I see."

For one reeling second all Tina could think about was ground glass, how she'd explain the lightbulb salad in her husband's belly. Death by Drano was one thing, but would anybody believe Marv had committed suicide by drinking drain cleaner *and* eating a GE 40-watter?

"When will they be finished?" she asked, hoping her fear would look like grief to anybody outside her head.

"I don't know," said Mister Edward. "But a Detective Rubert called and asked you to phone him when you were through here."

The mortician handed her a piece of paper with Manny's number on it. Tina thanked him. She was almost out the door when he called her name again. "Tina, please . . ." When she turned around his eyes were wet with pleading. "Take some Jujubes. You'll feel better."

FOURTEEN

The place Tony Zank called home, a dank, cottage cheese–ceilinged railroad flat, occupied the top floor of a building that had, until years earlier, been the general headquarters and processing plant for Bundthouse Fresh-Taste Sausages. Bundthouse had once stood proudly as the region's Number Two employer, second only to Jones & Laughlin Steel. Both industries disappeared at around the same time. But, unlike the sulfurous odor of J & L, which dissipated once the mill closed, the stench of dead-pigs-walking lingered on. And no amount of air freshener could cover up the eau de sausage factory that persisted, with varying intensity, in cold weather and warm. Not that Tony bothered with air freshener. The smell seemed to live in the very walls of the Bundthouse Arms, which was one reason he picked it in the first place. Since you practically needed a gas mask to live there, the rent was dirt cheap, and there were no other tenants. For some reason, no one wanted to live in a converted slaughterhouse.

"Man, I don't know how you can hang here," whined McCardle, hunkered in front of Tony's full-length mirror. He held a Bounty paper towel–wrapped ice cube to a tiny bump on his forehead, the result of a collision between his face and the dashboard St. Christopher in Carmella's Gremlin. "I had to breathe this stink every day, I'd chop my nose off."

"You already chopped your nose off," Tony replied, knocking back his seventh Iron City. When he wasn't guzzling Colt .45, Tony liked his Iron whenever he smoked crack, which he'd been doing since the second they stumbled in. He loaded the rocks into a glass stem that'd been broken so many times it was now only an inch long and had to be held with an oven mitt. After each puff his voice came out warbly. "You threw your real nose away and glued on that Caucasian niblet instead. You say you didn't, but I know you did."

"You're obsessed," said McCardle. "You got some kinda thing about my nose. My therapist, back at Riker's, told me when you're obsessed with one thing it's usually 'cause you're really worried about something else."

"That's right." Zank sprawled on the floor in his boxers, arranging and rearranging Dee-Dee Walker's notes. "I'm worried about who to kill first, you or that bitch from Seventh Heaven who stole my goddamn photograph." He wrapped the oven mitt around the hot glass tube, sucked hard. "Oh shit!" he warbled to McCardle. "I can't close my eyes. I keep seeing that dead lady's head on the sidewalk. It's like she's *starin'* at me." His whole body gave a shudder. "I think she was even talkin' when we left. Could that *happen,* man? It couldn't, could it? I swear I heard her tell me I was gonna get *hole* cancer." He started scratching himself. "I need another Iron."

McCardle gingerly lifted the ice cube and checked his wound. "That lady's head was *dead,*" he said. "But I'd bet cash money the last thought in it was about you. And it wasn't good."

"Don't *say* that!" Tony's voice quavered, unnaturally high. "Shit, man, what are we gonna do? We don't even know for sure that chick stole the picture. There's nothin' about it in this goddamn notebook."

Tony scooped up a batch of pages and crumpled them in trembling hands. *"Nothin'!"*

"That's the rock talkin', Dog. She's not gonna come out and broadcast she got a picture of the president's genitalics. You think she wants the Secret Service all up in her face? Not everybody's stupid."

"Don't talk down," Tony panted. "I'm warning you."

"Hey," said McCardle, "it wasn't for me, you wouldn't *have* that notebook. I'm the one who did the quick thinkin'."

"My hero," said Zank. He took a shaky hit off the stunted glass dick, then crept to the window. "I hear helicopters, man. I swear! They got those new kind fly so high they're invisible to the naked eye. They can see through walls. They're *watching,* man! Oh shit, we shouldn't have done that fat bitch. . . . I shouldn't have dropped my mother out the window. . . . *I don't know what's happening!* I didn't mean to run over a priest or get that lady decapitated. *I'm not like that. . . .*" He dropped to his knees and hugged himself. "No wait, wait! Maybe it's *you,* man. Yeah! They could be FBI choppers, after *you!* You got a price on your head!"

"You're tweaking," McCardle replied nervously. "Enough of that ready-rock and you think Navy Seals are comin' out of the bathtub. Have another beer."

"Right, right," said Zank, talking fast. "Beer's good. This rock is fucked. I'm never doing this shit again. Is there any more?"

McCardle clucked his tongue and rechecked his tiny injury. "You need some kind of treatment, Tony. I'm not just saying that 'cause you're psychotic and hurt my feelings. I'm saying that for *you,* brother. I was you, I'd look into rehab."

Zank finished the bottle in one gulp and dropped it on the carpet, among the fifty or so others. He felt almost relaxed again. "Look who's talking, Shovel-killer. I got a sore poop-chute says you're not exactly nor-*male,* yourself. Nor-*male,*" he repeated, "get it?"

"I get it."

"Yeah, well, if it turns out you have the A-I-D-S, don't think I'm not gonna kill you sideways before I do myself. I don't care how I go, but I ain't goin' 'cause I got cabooosed by some black Twink with a button nose. I get so much as a herpes bump, you're toasted pumpernickel, motherfucker."

"Hey, I been tested. I should be worryin' about *you!* I seen what you stick it into. Besides, it wasn't for me we'd be fighting over grape jelly in the joint right now. You blanked out, man. Did your zombie thing. You did it in the old people's home, when your mom dissed you, and you did it again after the accident. Shit hits the fan, T-bone, you lose your nerve."

"Bullshit!" Zank countered, getting defensive. "I was concussed. It was *medical*. Look at my head! It was already banged up when I conked it again in that midget car. Fucking fat lady drivin' a Gremlin. What's up with that?"

McCardle rolled his eyes. In fact, after they'd slammed into the back of Dee-Dee Walker's Camry, after *she* slammed into a utility pole five blocks from Tina's house, Zank *had* had one of his white-outs. They'd been tailing the newspaper lady so closely, when her Toyota jumped the curb and sailed down the sidewalk for twenty yards, the Gremlin jumped the curb and skidded right behind it. When she crashed, her skull did a full Jayne Mansfield and landed on the manhole cover, looking confused. It was the worst thing either of them had ever seen. Zank zombied out until some mongrel, what looked like part beagle, part Shetland pony, scampered out of nowhere and started lapping the blood off his forehead. Zank came to with a face full of dog tongue. He hadn't been knocked out. Just stunned. Staring wide-eyed and catatonic at nothing. The horse-dog went whimpering off when Tony shoved his thumb in its eye.

"You're just lucky I stayed focused," McCardle nagged, now cleaning his minor bruise with a stray slipper-sock soaked in beer. "You never give me credit, but when you zone, you're useless, homes."

"Yeah, right. So who'd your mother fuck, anyway, Dean Martin or Prince?"

McCardle ignored him, and Tony made a show of scratching his crotch and sifting through the dozen or so pages they'd pilfered from the reporter's car. He did have a sketchy memory of Mac tugging him from behind the wheel, then propping him up in the passenger seat. He semiremembered seeing his partner scramble over to the Toyota and reach through the scrunched window, right past the smoking engine that had rammed through the dashboard. Mostly, what he recalled was the awful quiet after the crash. He'd listened to the drip and hiss of bleeding motor oil, thinking *Car sleep now.* (Zank always thought in baby talk when he zombied off. *Me sad. . . . I hope Mommy dies . . .* That kind of thing, when he was out cold with his eyes open.)

Right after the accident, Mac had snatched Dee-Dee's notebook and her purse. That's how the priest found him, bleeding from the forehead and rifling her wallet. He'd roared onto the scene in a '66 Mustang and lumbered out with an audible grunt. *"Whoa, the knees. . . ."*

Once out of his 'Stang, the man of God looked like a professional wrestler. A middle-aged wrestler, in a collar. In spite of everything, Mac couldn't help but admire the pecs and traps under the man's snug black shirt. The priest called over his shoulder as he half-ran, half-hobbled to the totaled Camry. "I'm Father Bob. What the hell happened here? And what are you doing with that purse?"

McCardle began to sweat. Did they have cop-priests? In his shock and stupor he thought he remembered a TV show called *Father Cuffs.* He seemed to recall that it starred Eddie Albert.

Mac had to think fast. "I was, uh, I was just looking for some ID on the lady here." By now he'd already slipped the notebook in his pants. He also pocketed her cash, and a corporate AmEx, which read DEE-DEE WALKER, UPPER MARILYN TRUMPET. That's when he knew they'd been following the wrong woman.

The way Father Bob kept staring at him, McCardle was convinced the wrestler-priest must have made him from *America's Most Wanted.* After he'd poked his head in the remains of the Toyota and phoned for help, the hardy man of God snatched Dee-Dee's wallet out of Mac's hand. "I'll take that," he spoke solemnly. "There's nothing we can do for her now. What happened, boy?"

All he had to hear was that "boy," and McCardle shifted instantly into his Good Negro mode. Shaking his head in simple confusion, he explained that they'd come around the corner just in time to see "that po' lady" jump the curb and hit the utility pole. They decided to pull over and help. "In all the excitement," he said, scratching his head in dumb wonder, "I guess I done run over the curb my own self. I jus' wanted to help, Father. This ol' head o' mine's all *confused.*"

"Uh-huh," said the priest, neither buying nor not buying. "What's up with your buddy there?"

"Sleepin' one off," McCardle lied again. "Fool caught his wife with the mailman. It's like some dirty joke, ain't it?"

The priest frowned. "Show me your license, boy, we got a dead lady over there. Is that what dead ladies do for you? Put you in the mood for dirty jokes?"

"No, suh!" Mac stalled. Maybe it wasn't Eddie Albert. Maybe Bill Shatner was the tough detective-priest, pre–*T. J. Hooker.* He mentally kicked himself as he shuffled his feet. Zank had been on him to get a fake driver's license. They were twenty bucks, but McCardle figured he could save some dough and make one himself. An old-timer in County showed him how. It was Mickey Mouse. All you needed was somebody else's license, a photo booth photo, and access to a laminating machine. Stone simple. Except he hadn't done it, and now Father Macho was going to nail his ass.

"Must be in the car," Mac hedged, heading for the Gremlin. If he made a run for it, he might have a chance. It would mean bailing on Tony, but he'd explain later. If Tony didn't kill him first.

The muscular padre grabbed him before he could make a move. "Hey, don't I know you? I've seen you somewhere before."

Zank chose this moment to stumble out of the Gremlin. "Musta bumped my head," he mumbled. "What happened?" Tony pretended to gasp at the sight of the dead woman and the accordianed Toyota. "Oh my God, are you here to administer the last ripes?"

The priest had peeled off his jacket and laid it over Dee-Dee's severed head. McCardle kept waiting for it to move, like a bunny under a blanket, and couldn't stop staring.

"That's last *rites,* son. This lady's already bound for eternity. The ambulance'll be here in a second to take her away." Then he turned suddenly to McCardle. "You're on TV, right?"

McCardle wanted to cry. The priest seemed to have forgotten about his driver's license, but he was still fucked—until Zank swung into action. Leaking blood from the scalp and face, he smiled big and threw up his arms. "I guess we might as well tell him, huh, Scooter?"

McCardle swallowed. "Tell him what?"

"You *know*," Zank said. "Okay, *I'll* tell him. Y'see, Father, Scooter here was a child star. Only he don't like to talk about it."

"Is that so?"

"That's right," said Zank. "Remember the old Cosby show? Scooter was one of the kids."

The priest screwed up his face. He crossed his arms at his massive chest, Mister Clean–style, and squinted hard.

"Not, you know, one of the *main* kids," Zank back-pedaled, "a neighbor kid. Only Hollywood got to him. He didn't like the, what do you call it . . . ?"

"The sin," Mac chimed in, praying another car didn't come around the corner. It was a street, like so many in Lower Marilyn, lined with dead warehouses and storefronts with cockeyed FOR LEASE signs in their grimy windows.

"The sin, exactly," Zank followed up. "There's just too much *sin* out there. Y'see, Scoot here is a real church-goer. Confession once a week, whether he touches himself or not! Just kiddin', of course. I'm his manager, Mack Mustang. Just like the car. Nice to meet you."

Zank stuck out his hand and the priest ignored it. Instead he stared at McCardle, who shuffled his feet, *aw shucks,* trying to look plantation earnest.

"As a matter of fact," Zank went on, "we're on our way to Pittsburgh now. Doing some dinner theater."

"The Dean Martin Story," McCardle blurted, feeling smart until he saw Tony's eyes. He didn't look happy.

The priest seemed incredulous. "The Dean Martin story?"

"Well, um, yeah, it's a musical. An all-*black* musical."

For a second, things were hugely silent. Nothing but clicks and hissing from the shattered cars. The sound of an approaching siren. Father Bob scrunched up his eyes. Then he smiled and showed front teeth the size of Chiclets. "I don't think so."

"You don't *think* so?" Zank returned the smile. He kept smiling as he climbed back into Carmella's car. "Let me ask you something, Father. Does being a priest make you closer to the Big Dog Upstairs?"

Father Bob rolled his shoulders as Tony tried to start the Gremlin. When it finally turned over, black smoke billowed from under the hood. The priest had to raise his voice over the coughing engine. "To answer you, Son, I believe I *am* closer, though I can't say I appreciate you referring to Our Lord as some kind of Divine Canine."

"I apologize," Zank hollered, letting his swollen, mutt-lapped face loll out the window. "The good news is, I guess you won't have as far to travel."

Tony hit the gas before Father Bob could make his reply. The Gremlin whined like a spoon in a garbage disposal and clipped the priest at the knees, sending him straight in the air, where he did a half-gainer and landed chin first on the windshield, eye level with Zank. Tony slammed into reverse, which launched the priest off again, onto the asphalt.

"My bad!" Tony hollered, but the priest didn't hear him. Collar askew, one arm curled behind him like a paper clip, the gym-bodied cleric had begun crawling toward McCardle. Fresh blood stained his mouth like sloppy lipstick.

Zank, meanwhile, had jumped out of the Gremlin and made for the Mustang. He hopped in and shouted, "Hurry up, fuckwad. He left the keys."

Father Bob groaned and grabbed for Mac's ankle. He hung on, making sounds like a deaf person trying to talk. *"Mah cacchhhh . . . Mah cacchhh!"*

McCardle didn't want to leave him. "He's a priest, Tony!"

"That's nice," said Zank, "but we hang around here, he's gonna be sprinkling your ass with holy water on death row."

Mac tried to shake the priest loose as Zank backed the Mustang into the driveway of a defunct doughnut shop and turned around. When he broke free, he jumped over the priest's head and clambered into the front seat. Once he was upright, Mac started rocking back and forth and hugging himself. "Now what?" he whimpered.

"What do you think?"

Tony touched a finger to his blood-scalloped ear. He winced and checked the powder burns on his temple, then did inventory on the twin bumps on his forehead and the comb-swipes under his nose.

"We know where she lives, don't we?"

McCardle decided now was the time to mention their little mistake. "Listen, T, there's somethin' you oughta know."

Zank took a corner wide. "What's that? You still worried about the priest? Trust me, God will provide."

"It's not the priest. It's the lady. We got the wrong one. The chick in the Camry was a reporter. Her name's Dee-Dee Walker. She musta been doing some kind of story on the real Tina, the one we're after."

Zank pounded the steering wheel. "No fucking way!"

"I saw her wallet, man. I got her notebook, too. Maybe there's something we can use."

Zank scratched the burned patch on his scalp. "Okay. We dump the car, go back to my place. Then I'll take a look at that shit." He smacked the steering wheel, down-shifted, and smiled. "I could live with these wheels, I'll tell you what. . . ."

McCardle dug up an Old Spice deodorant stick and rubbed it under his nostrils. Anything was better than breathing in musty Bundthouse sausage fumes. He wondered if that's why Tony chewed Slim Jims, so his mouth would taste even worse than his apartment smelled. Compared to jerky-breath, maybe the stench of old meat seemed minty fresh. Then the thought grabbed him, maybe it wasn't the usual apartment stench. Maybe it wasn't old meat. Maybe it wasn't jerky. Maybe it was—

"Oh *fuck!*" McCardle forgot about the deodorant. He let the green stick slip out of his hands and and looked frantically around the apartment. "Oh fuck, T, what happened to Puppy?"

"Puppy? Oh yeah!" Zank's mouth split into the snaggled, bloody slit, which, with Zank, passed for a smile. "Where is that l'il guy?"

Puppy—they'd found the spotted little thing, soaked and shivering, under the Dumpster a few days (or was it weeks?) ago, and couldn't agree on a name. Zank wanted "Killer" or "Savage," McCardle was holding out for "Malcolm." So they stuck with Puppy. For a couple of nights it was 'Puppy this," 'Puppy that," until they ran out of money, and ran out of rock, and Tony had the bright idea of staging a little breaking and entering to make things right again.

"Fuck it," Zank groaned. He slapped the notebook on his molting carpet and rubbed his eyes. "The little fucker's fine. He's in here somewhere, isn't he? We're in here and *we're* fine, so what the fuck? You got your panties up your crack over nothing!"

"What?"

Zank was always doing that: making arguments that Mac knew were insane but somehow, when he tried to get a grip on them, just kind of slipped out of his grasp. "He still has to eat!" McCardle declared finally, hearing his voice go high and getting a bad feeling in his stomach. "Maybe he's all starved and sick under a major appliance."

"He had worms," Zank answered, as if that were the solution to everything. "If he gets hungry he can eat them. Hell, I've eaten 'em. Last time I was in the joint, the bologna sandwiches had these little worm-things in them that tasted better than the damn bologna. I ate the fuckers, and I'm the only guy in the cell who didn't get crabs. The little bastards are good for you, hear what I'm sayin'?"

Before Mac could respond to this bit of logic, Tony picked up the reporter's notebook, again banged it off his forehead, and threw it across the room. "I can't read any more, y'hear me? I can't do it. This don't say squat about Mister Biobrain. Just stuff about the husband, who was some kind of swami. I still think the chick's sitting on the pictures."

"Meaning what?" Mac knew there was no point talking about Puppy anymore. Puppy would have to fend for himself, until the next time they thought about him. Being sort of an abandoned child himself, he felt extra-bad, but right now Tony was talking and he had to listen.

Zank shot Mac his how-can-you-be-such-a-moron look.

"What do you *think* I mean? I mean Tina baby's got the envelope stashed in her pad. We go over, show her we're serious, and walk out with Georgie's happy-bag and the mayor's kisser. Then we're back in business. Get me another brewski, and one for yourself."

"You know nine's my limit," McCardle said. "We've been through that."

"Then get two for me. I like to be in a good mood when I gotta get something out of a lady. That's my specialty!"

Tony belched and Mac swore he saw a little brown cloud puff out of his mouth, like Chernobyl.

FIFTEEN

Manny tapped a pair of Codeine Number Fours into his palm. He stared at them, dropped them back in the pill bottle, closed the lid, then popped it off again, tapped four into his hand, and made the mistake of catching his own eyes in the rearview mirror.

I know, I know, he sighed. *But I've got a day ahead of me. . . .*

Mornings were the worst. If he could make it through the first half hour of being awake, he could usually stay clean. Before that, staring down the barrel of another day, it seemed to make more sense to lay in some chemical buffers. He knew codeine wasn't exactly good for you, but once you've been through heroin, everything else felt like health food. Especially this morning. In the middle of a creepy dream that his penis turned into a fork as he was mounting Tina, he got the call. On one level, he was still asleep, groping for a way to tell a naked murder suspect that he was usually normal but had somehow morphed into a kitchen utensil. On another, he was listening, savoring the lavish islands of silence between rings, yet hating them, too, knowing the more peace he let himself feel, the more shattered he'd be when the little Princess rang again.

Finally, tearing himself from his fork-and-Tina dream, he answered the phone, and was drop-kicked into the sunshine of awareness with news that a honeymoon couple at the Pawnee Lodge had noticed the dread SOSO—Strange or Suspicious Odor—from the room next door. (In policeville, if somebody asked how you were, and you said "So-So," it wasn't good.)

Manny's first thought, after absorbing the notion of anybody "honeymooning" at a motel wedged between an Earl Scheib and a discount truck parts outlet, was that his chops were slipping. He'd gone to the Pawnee yesterday, straight from Mrs. Zank's hospital room, and checked it out. According to the day manager, a clammy fellow with some kind of crust on his lips, the dude with the bruises on his face and the fucked-up ear, had paid for Cottage Number Two. "So was he alone?" Manny'd asked, expecting a simple yes or no. But, as happens occasionally, his interviewee relished the chance to be part of some "real police work" and weighed in with the long-form answer.

"Was he alone? That I couldn't say, Detective. Sometimes, if they're doin' some skorkin', they keep the girly in the car when they register. Like I'm gonna ding 'em for a wedding ring," the crust-man snickered. He touched a tongue to his bearded lips and leaned his elbows on the greasy check-in desk, getting intimate. "I guess you plainclothes boys see a lotta action, huh? A lotta sex stuff?"

Manny'd assured him it was mostly paperwork, then excused himself with the duplicate key to check things out. In the room, he had found nothing more heinous than a damp copy of *Teen People* under a chair. But what did that prove? Zank was some kind of 'N Sync freak? After his minor poke-around, Manny headed back to the office to ask if the maid had cleaned the room.

"Maid?" His new pal, the Pawnee desk clerk, thought he was making a joke. "That's a good one. We got fourteen units and maybe two

customers a week. Mostly we hold off on cleaning till all the rooms are used, then we bring in some rummy from the Salvation Army to change the sheets and mop up. It ain't the Hyatt, if you get my drift."

Manny told him he did, and drove off wondering if Tony Zank was the neatest felon in history. Or if, for reasons of his own, he'd checked in, gotten cold feet, and headed elsewhere. No doubt pining for a place with free Danish and cable.

Parked in the Pawnee parking lot a day later, contemplating his co-deines and gearing up for another crime scene, Manny realized his mistake. Zank, God bless him, was a craftier thug than he'd originally made him for. After registering, he must have pocketed the key to Number Two, then discreetly picked the lock on Three, from which the night manager—Crusty the Day Man didn't show up till eight—informed him that the SOSO was emanating. Sometimes it took a week for the dead to stink, sometimes half a day. A coroner once told him it had to do with polyester and fat consumption. After that Manny stopped asking questions. The honeymooners, in any event, had cut short their dream vacation and vanished.

"Fuck it," Manny mumbled, and tossed the four tablets off the roof of his mouth. He crunched them dry, punishing his tongue with the sour, chalky crumbs of Tylenol-and-codeine as he ground them to powder. Twisting out of the Impala, he stopped to crack his back. If waking up to murder didn't justify a fistful of minor opiates, having to contort his spine behind the wheel of the Skankmobile definitely did.

There wasn't much you could do to prepare yourself for a violent crime scene. But you had to do *something*. All cops had their own rituals, and Manny's was no stranger than most. He plucked a couple of Salems from a pack he kept in the glove compartment, then snapped off the filters—recalling, in a warm and fuzzy way, Tina's peculiar habit—and plugged his nostrils with the menthol stubs. After that he slapped on headphones and tuned his Walkman to KMLD. K-MOLD, as it was known locally, catered to a demographic, he could only assume, whose average age was dead. The station featured songs of such execrable corniness it was hard to imagine anyone listening voluntarily. In a given hour, willing souls endured anything from Wayne

Newton to the Carpenters, each tune more revolting than the one before, and all announced by deejays whose sepulchral drone made them sound like they'd been buried alive before every broadcast. But what made it extra-special for Manny were the K-MOLD advertisers: a low-end collection of rib joints, keypunch academies, discount dental offices, and miracle weight-loss products that never failed to make him pause and imagine just what breed of audience the swells in charge were shooting for.

This morning, having mentholed his nostrils, covered his ears, and gulped his battery of Code Fours—the same term, strangely enough, the Upper Marilyn P.D. used for Violent Crime—Manny stepped into the room expecting the worst and knowing, from a long and checkered career, that he would not be disappointed. If nothing else, he decided, trying to look on the bright side, a dead body would take his mind off his penis-fork.

Victim heavy *Latino female. . . . Cause of death appears to be knife wound in throat. . . . No contusions, no ligatures. . . . Nothing under victim's finger-nails. . . . Bed made. . . . Victim dressed in—wait, what the fuck?*

Manny held his cell phone in one plastic-gloved hand, speaking to his answering machine as he leaned over the dead woman. Every time he put on the plastic gloves (or "meat-mitts," as the pros liked to call them), he felt like a wage slave at Burger King. Disease was rampant, but it still felt weird holding your own phone in plastic-wrapped fingers.

Chief Fayton believed your modern police-worker should dictate his reports, which was fine with Manny, except he always forgot his Radio Shack tape recorder and ended up calling himself at the station and leaving lengthy messages. Since he couldn't stand the sound of his own voice—the slight lisp that seemed to spray out of the receiver—he kept the headphones on, swinging to K-MOLD faves like Engelbert Humperdinck and Captain and Tennille, pushing the whole process to a level of excruciation that was almost cosmic.

Right now, what caught him up short was the label on the lady's capri pants: L & L, Size 22. Manny'd been staring at it, wondering idly if the initials stood for "Large and Lovely," when the obvious hit him:

The label shouldn't be on the outside. A closer look revealed that the seam was exposed. Sure enough, when he slipped a finger in the pant leg and flipped it up, the peach-colored polyblend was seamless.

Victim's, what do you call them, capri pants, inside out. . . .

That's when Manny realized that he'd met the dead woman. About two years ago. At his rape prevention class at the Y. He squelched a smile thinking about it. Beyond the paycheck, teaching rape prevention was a great way to meet women. If nothing else, they figured he wouldn't try anything. But what the fuck was her name?

Holding his breath, Manny struggled to tug down her capris. Now, for better or worse, he'd get to see how well his class worked.

Handprint on left hip, he rattled into the phone. *Where perp held on trying to tug victim's pants off? Or was he pulling them back on? Blood traces on handprint. Struggle? Consensual? Party-that-got-out-of-hand? Possible necro?*

Nice, he added, allowing himself a little editorial comment.

Manny maneuvered the body gingerly, doing his best to ease the elastic waistband down over the woman's ample hips. He'd handled enough newly dead to know the possibility of a corpse going Pearl Harbor, bladder and bowels erupting in a sudden farewell burst. As a rookie, it was his job to wrap the departed. More than once, hoisting a stiff in the bag, he'd jostled them just enough to unleash a soul-blotting storm of urine and feces. "One of the perks," Merch would chuckle, standing in the corner chewing his Cheroot. At the moment, though, Michael Bolton was trying to get soulful on "Dock of the Bay," which was even more nauseating.

No panties, Manny told his answering machine, after a couple of deep breaths. *No pubic hair, either. Jesus. . . .*

In his morning haze, Manny'd forgotten his rape kit, but to the naked eye, it did not look like anything untoward had happened to the woman's sex. Often as not, your rapists would leave bruises on the inner thigh, bite marks on the face, *that* kind of thing. But you never knew. *Inside* might be a whole different story. He'd once seen some perfectly untouched-seeming genitalia on a teenage runaway outside Pittsburgh. They'd found her wearing nothing but Mickey Mouse socks in a Wal-Mart Dumpster. Other than being dead, the girl looked fine, until the chuckling coroner plucked a crack pipe, a wad of fifties, and the key to a bus station locker out of her. "I guess," the jaded professional told Manny at the time, "the guy planned on a second date."

Still, there was enough visible weirdness without speculating on what you couldn't see. Now that he looked, the dead woman's genitalia did strike him as peculiar, though he opted not to leave that on his machine. *Can't put my finger on it,* he said to the room, entertaining no one but himself. Then he shut up. It was *too* bizarre. The left labia looked like raw steak and, unless he was hallucinating, appeared five times the size of the right, which resembled a twisted rubber band. Stranger still, the clit—*no, Jesus!*—the clit seemed less like a little man in a boat than Don King on a yacht. The departed, there was no other way to say it, sported a stubby miniature penis. With hair.

Thanks, I'll pass, Manny mumbled, feeling the codeine kick in with a grateful sigh.

Eschewing further investigation, he massaged the capri pants north again. He prayed to the Waste Angels that whatever was bubbled up inside her would stay put until he could make her decent and back off.

All right, Sir!

Thanks to the codeine rush, he was starting to feel chipper. *Optimistic!* Perky to a hugely inappropriate degree.

We've got sexual assault. Possible torture? Zank hung own mother out window. That scamp. . . .

He knew the buzz would be gone before long, and resumed his narrative with new vigor as he dropped down on one knee to peek under the bed. You never knew what might turn up. Sure enough, lodged like a fallen cruise missile in a nest of dust bunnies, he found a standard-issue plastic vibrator. For whatever reason, some guys loved to beat women with dildos and vibrators. It was Manny's theory that they were jealous. The burly marital aids made them feel inadequate.

Vibrator found at scene. Sex party?

Restless, he stepped away from the bed, seeking a new vantage point. By now his feet were tired, but when he leaned on the desk, to take a load off, he spotted the wadded towel wedged behind it.

Uh-oh.

Plucking the towel out by a corner, he unbunched the thing and tried to read it. *Brown smudges, red stains. . . .* He closed his eyes, going narcotic-philosophical. *Blood and shit—the History of Western Civilization right there. . . .*

Now Tony Orlando and Dawn seeped out of the headphones. "Tie a Yellow Ribbon." The perfect soundtrack for hell.

Manny felt a sudden urge to speak to the dead lady. He remembered how she'd hip-rolled him at the Y. How she seemed to enjoy it. . . .

The stuff on the towel, it's not yours, is it? No, they wouldn't care enough to wipe your blood off. Your blouse is soaked. You died surprised. Whoever did this to you was bleeding, too. Maybe Zank and McCardle were fighting. The Dangerous Duo, in bicker mode. Mister America's Most Wanted *and Mister Drop His Mommy Out the Rest Home Window.*

Come on, asshole, THINK! Manny yelled at himself. He stuffed the towel in a plastic bag, then dropped it. The Code Fours were floating him now. He'd entered the Opiate Zone: pure brain and rushing insight. Sailing smooth through rough-and-tumble psychic waters. He raised the cell phone and started up again.

Shit on the towel. Meaning somebody was doing somebody. Sodom and Cremora. By this desk? Did they finish and jam the towel behind it? But it wasn't you, was it, honey? No, you were on the bed, watching the show. Señora Buddha. Is that it? You were watching. Was that your thing? Watching? Or, wait, no, did they MAKE you watch? Old Tony Z and Mini-Mac. Are they THAT WAY? Little lovebirds? Maybe they'll be bunkies in Lewisburg. Up there on Section Three, the Femme Tier. Bitch City. . . .

Manny moved to the door, pacing in a straight line to the bed and back again. He tried another angle. A game he played with himself. *If I burst in, right in the middle of it, the flaming, insane middle, what do I see? Two guys, two bonehead small-time criminals, one fucking the other, and this big lady on the bed with her vibrator? What? What? WHAT? That's not right. Not these guys. Tony's a crackhead. A lapdance-and-hooker guy. McCardle, I don't know, a bodybuilder. . . . Maybe a steroid freak. Killed a gay guy with a shovel. In the Parakeet Lounge. The Parakeet bathroom. Maybe HE was the romantic.*

Maybe . . . Maybe not.

Manny stopped pacing and stared at Carmella. Her face had settled, in rictus, in a sagelike smile.

You had the gun, didn't you, Gorgeous? It was you all along. You did something. But what?

Absently, he snatched up the vibrator, which he hadn't bagged yet. He flipped it over, smacking it off his palm when—*Whoops!*—a piece of the top fell off. *What the fuck?* A curved slab of plastic and, James Bond time, inside was a little lens. And wait, wait . . . *Down at the bottom, what's this? A button.* He pressed it, heard the click of a shutter. Amazing.

Victim, he intoned into his cell, *in possession of Dildo-cam. What'll they think of next?* Tugging a sandwich bag from his pocket, he dropped in the vibrator. *For the girl who has everything.*

He was on fire now. *Did you make them do it, baby? So you could take pictures? You did, didn't you? These bastards dragged you to the motel and you turned it around. You got revenge, didn't you, Beautiful? Well good for you! You shamed the Cock Monsters. You saved your life. Until you lost it. . . .*

Manny was impressed. Tickled, even. If she were alive, he would have kissed her. Because that was it. He felt the truth in his liver, with all the other toxins.

Zank was a convict. They all carry shivs. He'd been down three times. Two years in juvey, a bit in County, thirteen months upstate. He'd know how to fight dirty. Suspected of smoking his own Daddy when he was twelve. Social workers knew something nasty happened. But mom wanted to make nice. Alibied her pride and joy. Bad move for moms. Kid grows up and uses her to prove gravity. No wonder she became a lush. . . .

K-MOLD was playing an ad for a funeral home. Martino and Sons. "We understand your needs," said a voice like rancid honey. *I'll bet you do. . . .*

Manny paced the room, eyes unfocused, muttering, thinking about McCardle's jacket. He'd read his file in the car.

Little Mac, he went on, *another freak. Small-time nothing, two-time loser turned gay-killer. A straight fruitbat. Lure some shlub who wanted chocolate cake to a dark corner, then turn around, clock him and cop his wallet. Only one time, he picked the wrong john. This one fought back. Swung a fire extinguisher. The Parakeet crowd heard screams from the Men's Room, knew they weren't the fun kind, and piled in to protect their own. McCardle, cornered, grabs the closest weapon, a shovel—there God knows why—and whacks his date in the head. Kills him dead. A fucking hate crime. Ends up with his face on* America's Most Wanted. *The poor fuck needs twenty bucks for rock and ends up buyin' himself a federal beef. Not to mention that tasty reward put up by friends of the deceased. No doubt he'd just as soon have conked an old lady for her pin money, but that's not much of a legal defense. "Your honor, I got nothin' against homosexuals, I'd mug anybody, I just needed some fuckin' green!"* McCardle had bad luck like some guys had psoriasis.

So here they are, Manny mumbled into the now-damp mouthpiece, *Mac and Tony in the Pawnee Lodge. With their hefty lady friend. . . .*

He smacked his forehead, recoiling at the feel of plastic on skin. *Stop thinking,* he hissed at himself, *"look look look look look".*

He started in the desk drawer. *Nothing.* A red Bible and crumpled condom wrapper. *Good old Trojan, choice of the working man.* Nightstand, left side. *Nothing.* Right side, *Hello hello!* A purse. Wallet still there. Flip through. Driver's license. *She wore rouge for the photo. Carmella Dendez, now I remember. Nice to see you again. Don't get up.*

More cards. . . . Price Club, Weight Watchers, credit union, Jenny Craig. Manny put them carefully back. Respect the dead. Nothing else, except—*what's this?* Slipped behind a faded picture of three husky lads and a toddler in matching Easter suits. Employee ID: Seventh Heaven Convalescent Services. *Oh shit. . . .*

He clicked off the cell. Stared at nothing. Taking shallow breaths.

She works the same place as Tina. Make that "worked. . . ."

The ice water shock of *that:* Tina killed once—that he *knew* about. The late Guru Marv. And now, *now,* a fellow rest homer found dead, cut by the guys who wanted what Tina had: the fratboy President's balls in black-and-white, the mayor's smiling face. . . .

Unless—he had to go there—they were in it together: Tina, Zank, and Mac the Shovel. Quite the little crew, until she ripped *them* off. Jesus! *Unless,* even worse, Tina had been here, too. Behind Door Number Three at the Pawnee Lodge. *Unless,* whatever the grim particulars, she was involved in more than she let on. *Unless,* there lurked some still more vile possibility that had not yet wormed its way out of his overworked cerebellum.

What was a detective's job, on a good day, but compiling an encyclopedia of worst-case scenarios?

The only certainty, and it made his own testicles tighten—minus the magic happy face—*people died young around Tina Podolsky.*

One way or another, if your paths crossed, you might wake up dead. Over the years, Manny'd encountered a few people with this lethal predilection. Gentlemen whose friends fell down elevator shafts, though the gents weren't actually to blame. Not technically. . . . Housewives whose exes all bumped into ice picks or slipped off cliffs, though the ladies, themselves, were never implicated. These things happened. . . .

Oh shit, said Manny again. And, just like that, his high was gone. Just like that, it was time for the low.

SIXTEEN

On her way home from the mortuary, Tina pulled over in a 7-Eleven parking lot to return Manny's call. She dialed the number Mister Edward gave her, and he picked up on one ring. "Tina?"

"I'm calling from a pay phone, how'd you know it was me?"

Manny told her to relax. "Cops always have a lot of cell phones. Perps leave 'em in the car. I've never used this one before so I knew it was you. Nobody else has the number."

Tina seemed to believe him, so Manny saw no need to tell her he was parked in the Pizza Hut across the street. He'd been following her since she left her house. After the Pawnee Lodge he'd decided to go to her place and sniff around, to check out any connection with the

Mac and Tony show. When he got there, Tina was just unlocking her Honda. So he cruised on by, pulled a U-ey and tailed her, two cars behind. When she hit the pawnshop, he parked up the street, watching her make two trips with Marv's computer and video equipment.

Tina didn't have a record, Manny'd already checked. But since her name might be fake, and he didn't have her maiden, that didn't mean much. He could have snagged her prints and run them, but if they came up in the system, he'd be obligated to do something. Even if they didn't, the fact that he punched them up would arouse suspicion. Fayton kept tabs. He had nothing better to do. The chief would be thrilled to catch a man in some bit of police chicanery, to uncover some L.A.–style corruption he could scam to plant his face on the front page of the Sunday *Trumpet*. Manny could already hear the chief's self-righteous harangue at the arraignment. "But I thought you said she wasn't a suspect, Detective Rubert? I thought you said she was a grieving widow?"

Fuck that. The only way to play it was to steer clear of channels and snoop around on the home front. He was tits-deep in a criminal venture—protecting Tina made him an accessory to murder—and ready to make the move with Mister Biobrain. He couldn't afford to find out after he crossed the line that his partner was hinky. Or hinky the wrong way. . . . The trick was not to con himself that she was solid if she wasn't. Tina was sex-on-a-stick, so he had to be vigilant. One wrong move and they were remaking *Double Indemnity,* with the high crime of White House nutbag blackmail added to murder. And Fayton replacing the feisty Edward G. Robinson.

"Here's what's going on," Manny said, keeping an eye on the lush swell of Tina's ass in her mourning wear as she faced the pay phone. The girl had his nose open, big-time, and he had to concentrate. "I heard today the chief is suspicious about Marv. He wants to make a canoe."

"He wants to *what?*" Tina scratched an ankle with the black high heel of her opposite foot.

"Cop-speak," he explained. "I apologize. That's what your jaded police-types call doing an autopsy. But don't worry. Just tell me if there's anything else I should know about."

"Well," said Tina, as Manny watched her fish in her purse for a cigarette. Who the fuck else under ninety-five smoked Viceroys? "If I told you you might find a bit of broken glass in his stomach, would you still, you know, want to hang with me?"

"Bad choice of words, baby. In this state it's lethal injection."

"You know what I mean." She was trying so hard to sound contrite, it was hard not to laugh. *This chick is evil,* Manny thought. He couldn't explain why this made him even crazier about her. Made her more seductive than smack. Though if she eased his mind about the late Carmella, he'd feel a whole lot better about life in general.

Manny let her stew a few more seconds, then pressed on. "As long as you tell me everything, we're cool. There's just one thing I'm still curious about."

"Which is?"

"Carmella Dendez."

"What about her?"

"She a friend of yours?"

"Not exactly. She's my supervisor at Seventh Heaven. She's all right, if you don't mind listening to fashion tips all day. Carmella thinks God made stretch pants right after He finished air and water. Which is amazing, considering what they have to stretch around when *she* wears them. Why are you asking me about Carmella anyway? You checking up on me? Gonna bust me for pilfering pillowcases?"

"Pilfering's okay. It's killing people that gets dicey. Somebody offed your boss on a motel bed."

"What?"

Manny watched Tina lean her head on the glass. After a second, she straightened up, bit the filter off her cigarette, then fired a match one-handed and lit up. She blew the smoke straight at the phone booth ceiling. He had a feeling her eyes were closed.

"What happened?" she asked, in a voice that sounded older than she was.

"I'm not sure," said Manny. "It went down at a flatback motel called the Pawnee Lodge. Ever been there?"

"No, why? What is this?" He saw her make a fist at her side. "You think *I* killed Carmella?"

"I didn't say that. I'm just saying, first a Seventh Heaven resident gets dropped out a window. Then a woman who works there turns up stabbed to death. And just to make it *really* interesting, there's you, another devoted employee, with a dead husband and a certain twisted photo you stole out of the bed of the same lady who ended up taking the shortcut from four floors up. You were me, what would *you* think?"

There was silence. Tina took a fast drag on her Viceroy. Manny watched her stub out the barely smoked cigarette on the phone booth glass, then throw it down and stomp it.

"If I were *you,*" she said levelly, "what I'd think is that I should be very fucking careful about accusing *me* of a bunch of bullshit. That's what I'd think."

Manny dug the rage. She wasn't trying to cover. "I'm not accusing, Tina, I'm asking. There's a difference. People around you seem to die a lot. If it's okay with you, I'd rather not be one of them. We're gonna partner up, it's important we trust each other."

"Is that right?" Tina clamped the receiver between her shoulder and chin. She rooted in her purse with both hands. "Well, you sure got a novel way of inspiring trust." She came up with a scrunchie and twisted it around her hair, making a ponytail. "Maybe there's something I should know about you, huh *partner?* What I've seen, you're not exactly Joe fucking Friday."

"You got me," Manny said, relaxing. "I boiled my first wife alive for shrinking my toupee. I told her not to spin-dry and she wouldn't listen. Other than that, I swear, I'm entirely wholesome."

"That's almost funny," she said. "Except I know you're lying. I've seen a picture of your wife, looking nasty, an inch from George Junior's smiling kumquats."

"Kumquats, I like that," Manny said. "Except Marge never looked nasty a day in her life. And anyway, I said my *first* wife. But never mind. Just listen, and tell me the truth. Besides the glass, is there anything else you don't want found out about how Marv died? 'Cause if there is, I'm startin' to think we gotta cremate him. Fast."

"I already did," she said, adding demurely, "that's the way he would have wanted it."

"What are you talking about?" Now Manny was stunned, and he didn't stun easily. "His body's in a drawer. I went to the morgue. I *saw* him."

"That was yesterday, sweetie. This morning he was delivered to Martino and Sons. It was a private ceremony. No family. Just Mister Edward and me. He's been very supportive."

"Supportive? Are you kidding me?"

Manny stared across the street at the woman in black. From this distance there was nothing special about her. Medium height, decent body, dirty-blond ponytail. Nothing intense but that Faye Dunaway face. Those cheekbones of death. Maybe not the girl next door, but definitely somebody the guy who dated the girl next door would love to fuck around with. If *she* wanted to. Because that's what clinched it: Tina's attitude. Like she was so tough she might let you think you could touch her; or maybe she'd even let you, for real. But it was her call, not yours. Never yours.

"You going to tell me how you did it?" he asked.

"How I *did* it?" Tina twisted the ponytail around a finger. "We've been through all that. What do you want, the receipt for the Drano?"

"I'm not talking about *that*."

Manny watched, transfixed, as Tina hung her head and grew still. Maybe she wasn't as tough as all that. Maybe, in some weird way, it was a mercy killing. Unless all the mercy was for herself. . . .

Before he could go down that road, the doors of the 7-Eleven blew open and a trio of sleazoid white guys swaggered out. Each goon clutched a forty-ouncer in a bag. Two had shaved heads, and all three wore tighty-whitey T-shirts to show off their pecs and biceps. The three plunked themselves on the hood of a beat-to-shit pickup parked directly in front of the booth. Manny could hear them from across the boulevard, talking trash. He watched them unscrew the caps, tip back their bags, and guzzle as much as they could get down without gagging. *Not good,* he thought. Maybe nothing would happen; but if something did, it would not be good.

Tina checked out the action, then turned around again, giving the boys her back. Her voice, instead of growing wary, or even concerned, grew softer, more relaxed. "What are you asking me, Manny?" It was the first time he'd heard her say his name, and it got to him.

"What I'm asking," he said, trying to sidestep the tremor in his heart, "what I'm asking is . . . are you okay?"

Then one of the mooks yelled at her, and the rest joined in. "Hey baby, forget him, whyn't you come over here?" "Yeah, you can suck on me for free." "I got somethin' in my pants you ain't gonna believe." "Yeah, 'cause it's so fuckin' small. . . ." The usual witty bullshit.

Manny could see Tina stiffen. He felt powerless, watching those assholes hassling her. There was so much sadness in her body language. The way she hung her head. Her sudden stillness. As if, on top of everything else, she'd had a lifetime full of assholes hassling her, and it made her sad to have to deal with three more of them now.

When she didn't answer, Manny plunged on with his original question.

"What I really want to know, okay, is how the fuck you got them to release Marv's body to the mortuary?"

"I didn't," she said, leaning against the door, blocking the comedy from the brown-bag party-boys. If they fucked with her, Manny knew, he'd have to go over, book all three, and hope she believed him when he said he happened to be driving by. Maybe he could tell her the 7-Eleven clerk called the cops. *Something*. . . . It was a lose-lose option. Tina had to trust him as much as he had to trust her. If she suspected he was tailing her, forget it. But he couldn't *not* go over, if the shit hit the proverbial fan. He couldn't just watch her get perped by a bunch of tanked-up skeeks.

Sighing, Manny pulled out his binocs for a better look. He recognized one of the a-holes, a terminally laid-off mill-hunk named Ranick. Ranick had more ink than Satan and thought he was dangerous. The kind of badass whose idea of a hot date was getting beer-drunk and sucker punching his girlfriend. When he had a girlfriend. When he didn't, the nearest female under fifty would do. Manny'd hauled him in for drunk-and-disorderly enough times to get him court-ordered to AA. Apparently, he left before the miracle.

"Tina," Manny hollered into the phone, more nervous than she was. She was about to get mauled, and *he* was the one shouting. "Tina, what do you mean you didn't get them to release Marvin?"

"I mean *I* didn't do it. It was Mister Edward, like I said. From the funeral home."

"*Him?* Oh, perfect. . . ."

"You know him?"

As it happened, he *did* know Edward. There'd been some trouble, years ago, after the mortician mail-ordered a Korean bride. The new spouse, a comely eighteen-year-old named Kim Sung, took one look at her crater-faced beau and decided to head back to Seoul. Edward, of course, had other ideas, and things got ugly. But Ms. Sung had watched enough American TV to know about 911. "Wait, I've got the receipt!" Edward kept yelling, after Manny and Merch swung by to pick the girl up and haul her back to the airport. *"I've got the receipt!"*

It was a grotesque and depressing spectacle: the outraged young Edward crying and waving his piece of paper on the front steps of his parents' split-level on Duquesne Street, up in Tit-ville. The boy mortician, ironically, was sporting a wifebeater. With no sleeves, you could see that even his shoulders had acne.

That shoulder acne, Manny'd suspected, is what made the terrified bride decide to hightail it back to her homeland. Keeping Edward Edward out of jail was one of the first favors a DMV-drone-turned-police-chief named Fayton ever did for the town's old money. Martino and Sons had been founded by an Upper Marilyn patriarch, the original Edward Edward, a Methodist minister who also happened to be young Edward's great-grandfather. Since much of the local populus hailed from Italy, Edward the First realized he'd get more business if folks believed their neighborhood mortuary was *paisano*-owned. So he named it after his wife's favorite crooner, Al Martino, and never looked back.

Manny stared across the street as Tina slid the elastic off and redid her ponytail, ignoring more bons mots from the yapping drunks on the truck. She seemed to be gazing at the ground. Distracted. Only one question remained. It was not strictly relevant, but it fucked him enough to ask it anyway. "Just out of morbid curiosity, Tina, why would Edward do you such a big favor?"

"He likes me," she said, and before Manny could pursue *that* line of questioning, she asked calmly if he'd mind holding on.

Manny watched, with mounting dread, as Tina pushed open the phone booth door and blew a kiss at the rowdy lugs in front of her. Through his binocs, Manny saw Ranick smirk at his buddies. He pimp-walked toward her, swigging his forty. When he was just outside the booth, Tina smiled in a way that soured his stomach. She licked her lips and slipped in a finger to deepen her cleavage.

Ranick, the idiot, leaned closer, and Tina, still smiling that *Do me* smile, whispered in his ear. There was a frozen moment—whatever she said must have meant something—then Ranick let go of his bottle, which shattered on the sidewalk as he staggered backward. He held his hands out in front of him, petrified. Even from across the street Manny could see the color drain from the young thug's face. He jumped in his pickup and started it before his buds were even off the hood. "Get in," the overgrown delinquent shouted. *"Just get in the motherfucking truck!"*

Manny did not even realize he'd been holding his breath. More amazing, Tina had yet to stop smiling. But what cinched it for Manny—what wrenched his insides with that awful, delicious mixture of fear and desire that, in his life, passed for true love—was the way Tina had kept the receiver covered the whole time. *Because she did not want him to hear.*

The truckload of brew-hogs peeled out of the parking lot and Tina settled in to resume their conversation. "Sorry, where were we?"

"Tina," was all he could manage, as he watched her tear the filter off a Viceroy and gaze benignly in his direction.

"Tina what?" she said, giving him a wave and a smile. "Is there some kind of problem, Detective?"

SEVENTEEN

Furious, Chief Fayton gazed at his Honor Wall, focusing on the framed photo of himself and Mayor Marge.

For ten minutes he'd pleaded his case, explaining till he cracked a sweat that what the city needed was a task force. The chief liked the sound of it. Task force. Which he, of course, would head up in his capacity as Whip Hand at the UMPD. (*Whip Hand*. He liked the sound of that, too.)

"Carmella Dendez and Dee-Dee Walker. Two women dead in two days!" he'd exclaimed, reading off the three-by-fives that Officer Chatlak had typed so he'd stay on point. At first the mayor didn't seem to be listening, but the chief wrote that off as typical Marge. Her Honor always did ten things at once. She was probably having her nails done and signing a law outlawing spittoons while talking to him. Marge was the original multitasker.

Knowing her tendencies, Fayton had plowed ahead with renewed determination. "Not to mention, *Mayor*, a priest has been run over and an old lady's been dropped out a window. In a rest home, damn it!"

He'd gone back and forth with "damn," but decided to throw it in, to show he meant business.

"If our citizens can't be safe *in an old age home*"—he'd underlined for extra emphasis—"where can they be safe? We're talking about the Golden Years, Your Honor!"

The chief paused, counting one-two-three, like it said in the *Orator's Handbook,* for extra emphasis, then escalated his attack.

"What we're looking at is a vicious serial killer, in our own backyard. This man Zank is a threat to every decent man, woman, and child in Upper Marilyn. We've got to act, for our loved ones, for our *constituents.*"

Fayton was especially proud of that last part. The word "constituents," he felt, was his pièce de résistance, and he sat back in his chair after he'd pronounced it, waiting for the mayor to cave. "Constituents" conjured up voters, which conjured up elections, which conjured up the fact that if she didn't act he would damn well throw his weight to her opponent. Maybe he'd even run himself. *That* would show her! Of course, the city managers had yet to decide whether or not to actually *have* elections. They raised the issue every November, and the *Trumpet* ran pro-election editorials. But when push came to shove, the bastards preferred simply reappointing Marge, as they'd been doing every two years since handpicking her for the job. Which, now that he thought about it, probably cut his legs off, rhetorically speaking.

Fayton steamed. What was the point of being police chief if you couldn't capitalize and run for higher office? He had a weird feeling Mayor Marge did not even *want* to catch Tony Zank. "For God's sake," she kept repeating, somewhat peevishly, "we don't even know for certain it's the same man."

"Maybe not," Fayton hedged. He was always nervous when he

strayed from his three-by-fives. "Dee-Dee Walker, Your Honor, was a reporter. You don't think the *Trumpet*'s going to be all over that?"

"She was their *only* reporter, so if any paper's all over it, it won't be that one. What they'll run is a nice obituary and a bunch of puff pieces full of testimonials about Dee-Dee. More important, do we even know for sure she was even murdered? No," she snorted, "we do not."

Mayor Marge let out a long I-have-more-important-things-to-deal-with sigh, then continued in a tone that made him feel like a pest.

"I'm no *police chief,* but I do think if we start alarming the public now with word there's some kind of Son of Sam running around, it'll do more harm than good. People will start to panic. Not to mention the possibility of copycats."

Copycats! he wanted to shriek. *You think other people are going to start bouncing their loved ones out of rest home windows? You think that's going to start a TREND?*

He didn't say this, however. He didn't say anything, except "Thank you for listening" and "Have a nice day" before hanging up. His authority problem was something the chief was working on. No matter how much he prepped and three-by-fived, no matter how many hours of rehearsal and mirror-work he put in before talking to someone of Mayor Marge's stature, the second he opened his mouth he heard himself doing everything but offering to wash their car to get them to like him. It was his own little Stockholm Syndrome. No matter how spunky he started out, he ended up agreeing with whoever abused him.

To calm down after his debacle with the mayor, the chief decided to review some notes for his screenplay. That's when he had another brainstorm. There was *one* way to go above Her Honor. If it worked he'd be the hero, and not just in Upper Marilyn, either. Nationwide! Rubert had said as much when they discussed McCardle and the *Most Wanted* thing. Manny'd also suggested they wait until they'd actually caught the guy before calling the show. But damn it, some things couldn't wait! Besides, how did he know Rubert wasn't going to double-cross him? Maybe phone in a tip-that-leads-to-arrest himself and snag the reward money. You couldn't put *anything* past a character like that. No, if anyone was going to look heroic, it was he, Chief Fayton, the man with a plan. And after that, who knew?

For one, lovely second, the chief let himself daydream about hob-knobbing with James Woods when they shot the movie of his life. Sure, James was older, but he had the same kind of cockiness, the same kind of *Outta-my-way, I'm-in-charge!* quality the chief liked to see in himself. Or, more accurately, that he'd like to see on-screen when somebody played him.

"Fayton—The Story of a Small-Town Lawman." Just saying it made him feel taller.

He chuckled to think about Mayor Marge's face when she saw Kathy Bates or Roseanne playing her. He'd slap that in the contract, too. Iron-clad!

Then again, if he could get his script to the networks, it might be better to go for a series. Like the *Homicide* guy. Or what's-his-name, Bill Clark, the ex-cop who got that executive consultant credit on *NYPD Blue*. That had to bring in a chunk of change. But would James Woods do TV? If he wouldn't, he decided, he'd settle for Tom Selleck. Or that young handsome guy, from the *Law and Order* reruns. Benjamin Bratt. The one who dated Julia Roberts. The chief read *TV Guide* religiously. He liked to keep up with show business, so he'd know his way around when he got there.

Fayton hit the intercom. "Chatlak, get me John Walsh!"

"You mean," asked his sluggish assistant when he shuffled in with his container of take-out potato salad, "the *America's Most Wanted* guy?" Chatlak could never get his dentures to fit and pretty much lived on potato salad, a gob of which now dotted his lower lip.

"Of course that's who I mean. And wipe your mouth! Tell Walsh it's Lyn Fayton, chief of police in the town of Upper Marilyn, in the glorious state of Pennsylvania, in the United States of Kiss My Ass!"

Oh, he was feeling Alpha Male now. It was a smart move, not mentioning Mac McCardle to Mayor Marge. He'd save the spade gay-killer for himself. To heck with Rubert! This was going to be *good!* This was going to show everybody. Oh *yeah!* Now he was cooking with gas.

Unfortunately, it took nearly an hour for Chatlak to find the *AMW* phone number and another forty minutes to get through to a human.

By this time Fayton's adrenaline had drained significantly. Once somebody from *WANTED* actually picked up, things got worse.

"John Walsh? Chief Fayton," Fayton barked into the phone when
Chatlak handed it over.

The elderly cop tried to signal *"No!"* but it was too late. The man
on the other end spoke in a tone that was beyond patronizing. "Walsh
doesn't take the eight hundred calls," he said curtly. "What is this
regarding?"

"Regarding? Oh, well, I'll tell you," Fayton sputtered, spilling his cards
in his lap. He waved for Chatlak to leave the office but the doddering
prick just stood there, stooped over and grinning his cadaverous grin.
He absolutely *had* to get the city managers to authorize a real secretary.

Damn! Fayton thought. He could feel prickly sweat in his armpits.
Somehow his perspiration smelled different when he was nervous.
Kind of like smoked salmon. He could smell himself now, loxing up.
"I'm, uh, really sorry to bother you, but, well, I'm chief of police here
in Upper Marilyn. . . ."

"Where?"

Was that a laugh? Was the man *laughing* at him? Fayton felt suddenly
tired. More than anything, he wanted to take a nap. Right there. Just
drop the phone and go fetal under the desk. Instead, curling his toes in
his brogans, he sputtered on.

"Um . . . Upper Marilyn, Sir. It's a . . . a small town here in south-
western Pennsylvania. There's a few thousand of us, and, well, uh, I
think one of your *Most Wanteds,* I guess you'd say, has been seen here in
the last day or two, so—"

"You think?" the man cut in. "You *think?* Buddy, you know how
many calls we get a day? Try fifteen hundred. You wanna be a hero?
Give us something real. Or better yet, get a real job. Upper Marilyn,
Kee-*rist!*"

Chief Fayton clutched the receiver with both hands, listening to the
dial tone after the man hung up. It was hard to believe, five minutes ago
he'd been so . . . *there.* So on top. Making *moves!* And now, some glori-
fied boiler room hack had treated him like a joke. Well, he'd take care
of that. Lyn Fayton was no quitter! He'd take care of that *fast.*

"Chatlak," he hollered defiantly, "make another call!"

"Sure thing, boss."

The ancient policeman was still smirking, and when he caught his superior's eye, he started giggling all over again. To Fayton, at this crucial juncture, Chatlak had never seemed more repulsive: crooked gray teeth, face full of gin blossoms, yellowing hair so riddled with dandruff it looked like confetti. And *he* was laughing at *him!*

"It's not funny," Fayton said, sounding schoolmarmy even to himself. "I said, it's not funny!"

Unable to stop, Chatlak waved his hand helplessly. The sickly veteran's laughs turned to wheezes. He yanked out a stained hanky, blew his nose, and tried to compose himself. But the hacking giggles persisted.

"Chatlak! Settle officer!"

While authority cowed him, the chief liked to think he *ruled* his underlings. Mayor Marge and the *America's Most Wanted* man were one thing, but Chatlak . . . Chatlak worked for *him*.

"I am not a joke!" Fayton yelled, pounding the desk, his voice going high and quivery with rage. "Chatlak, do you hear me! *I am not a joke!*"

But the old man was past hearing. He reeled in the center of the room, holding his sides, tee-heeing into his handkerchief, literally weeping, until Fayton, squeezing more police action into a single second than his previous thirteen years on the force, scooped up his cordless telephone and hurled it at him.

Two minutes later, scared out of his wits, Chief Fayton retrieved the phone. Fighting a twitch in his finger, he punched out a number.

"Ruby? It's Fayton. This is important. I need you at the station. *Now!*" He panted into the mouthpiece, saw it was dotted with blood, and wiped it off on his sleeve. "I think," he babbled on unsteadily, *"I think Officer Chatlak just had an accident."*

EIGHTEEN

At the station, Merch sat wheezing behind his desk, thumbing through a girly mag as Manny breezed past on the way to the chief's office. Merch had a thing for girly mags but preferred those published in the halcyon days before Larry Flynt came along and things went pink. The ones Merch liked had names like *Wink* and *Titter,* and featured smiling carhop types posing in leopard-skin bikinis, or tied up Betty Page–style on white leather sofas. His current mag, Manny noticed, was called *Vixen.* The cover sported a busty brunette done up in skimpy squaw-wear, holding a bow and arrow and blowing a kiss.

None of these magazines had been published since the midsixties. Merch, however, had somehow acquired a bottomless trough, and no amount of prodding would reveal his source. It was weirdly comforting, after the tense ten minutes Manny'd spent with Tina before getting Fayton's call, to walk in and see a world that was still halfway normal. As soon as he was through here, he was going back to meet her, ostensibly about their next move with the photo. But they both know the real reason was something else entirely.

The whole deal was insane, at the very least, if not completely self-destructive. *But,* Manny kept hearing himself think, *when you hate your life, what do you care about destroying it?* Especially if there's a chance you won't: A chance, if you don't end up behind bars or tied off for the lethal fix, you'll end up in bed with a bent, beautiful, edge-of-your-seat genius female who sees right through your eyeballs to the dark room in the back of your brain, the one you never let anybody into because you didn't know it was there. . . .

From Guru Marv to Carmella Dendez to Dee-Dee Walker to God knows who else, there was a stack of bodies around Tina, which made a powerful argument for steering clear of her. There was a bigger stack of reasons to bring her in for questioning, if not jail her outright. But Manny, busy as he was counting the milliseconds until he could see her again, couldn't come up with any at the moment.

"Nice of you to drop by." Merch honked, blowing his nose at the same time he talked. "There's a goddamn crime spree, in case you haven't noticed. Latest thing, a priest gets one-eighty-fived and left on the sidewalk. Goddamn *priest,* Manny. Some sick fuckos pancaked the sky pilot and left him for dead down in Butt-town. Front of the old Smooty's Donuts. Christ, I miss Smooty's, don't you? They had a choco-sprinkle-cream make you come in your pants."

The memory, apparently, was too much for Merch, who ka-banged the defecto candy machine and dug out a Chunky with a satisfied sigh.

"Don't get sentimental," Manny told him, stopping by his own desk to swipe an arm's length of memos into the trash. "Those weren't sprinkles. That was fly shit. But what about the priest?"

Manny knew about the accident from Fayton but let his old partner fill him in anyway. Virgin ears got everybody more excited. So he pretended the news was new and shocking.

"I talked to him," Merch huffed. "I like my job so much I thought I'd do yours, too." With six months to retirement, Merch was indignant about ever actually having to leave the station. It was all he could do to issue a parade permit without bitching about having to lift a pencil. "Humped all the way over to the damn hospital. And lemme tell you, that Christer looks like he crawled out of a cement mixer. Says it was two guys, a salt-and-pepper. *Entertainers,*" Merch sneered, rolling his baggy eyes. He took a bite of his candy and spit it on the floor. "*Yecch!* When'd they deliver this shit? When Nixon was president? They still even *make* Chunkies?" He slammed his snack in the basket. "Where was I?"

"The priest was run over by entertainers."

"Right, right. You'll love this. They told him they were on their way to Pittsburgh, to do dinner theater. 'I'm starring in *The Dean Martin Story.*' That's what the moolie told him. *The Dean Martin Story.* Guy's black as James Brown's asshole and he's playing Dean Martin."

"Zank and McCardle," Manny said.

Merch perked up. "Tony Zank? Guy who dropped his mommy?"

Manny nodded. "The very same." He noticed the slight palsy in his ex-partner's hands. When he'd first met him, the man had a punch that could shatter Plexiglas. One more reason not to get old.

Merch brushed a Chunky crumb off his trouser leg and whistled. "And McCardle, he's the one did a guy with a shovel, right? Some kind of sissy-fit? Got him on *America's Most Bullshit?*"

"That's him," said Manny. "These two've been busy. I make 'em for the party at Pawnee Lodge, too."

"That ties in. Carmella Dendez's car was found on the scene. A Gremlin, no less. I tell ya, there's a lot goin' on around here."

"Yeah. Good thing you're elderly, huh? You'll probably have a stroke and die before things get bad."

Merch frowned. "You take asshole lessons, or does it come natural?"

"On-the-job stress," Manny replied. "I'm not myself. So when did these bo-bos talk showbiz, before or after they ran the priest over?"

"Before, okay?"

Merch was still pissy from the stroke line. He'd been convinced he was about to die from one for as long as Manny'd known him. But delight in detailing the saga at hand blew out his anger. Next to insulting him, there's nothing a cop likes more than sharing a truly sick war story with another cop. Who the fuck else could you tell? Manny felt it would be wrong to deny his ex-partner such pleasure.

All but cackling with glee, Merch forged on. "Wait'll you hear this. Ol' Father Bob's minding his own business, rolling through town on his way to Wheeling to visit an aunt with TB or some shit, when who does he drive by but El Negro Deano, standin' there rifling the dead lady's wallet."

"What dead lady? They killed a lady before they ran the collar over? These guys must be taking their vitamins."

Merch slapped a hand on his girly mag, spanking the squaw. "If you'd stop bein' such a lop and let me finish. . . . Reason the priest stopped is 'cause there was an accident. The two clowns bashed up the Gremlin. But that's not the big news. The big news is Dee-Dee Walker."

"The reporter?"

"Yeah, that bitch. May she rest in peace. The one who nearly got me canned with her little exposé. *Graft,* she called it! What'd I take? A goddamn ham at Christmas? A fucking Thanksgiving turkey? Come on, Manny, you can't tell me that's *graft.*"

"The turkey was stuffed with twenties, way I heard it."

Merch cleared his throat. "Can we stick to the story here? Dee-Dee Walker, the *late* Dee-Dee Walker, is lying on the ground, dead, her Toyota wrapped around a utility pole. No, not true," he corrected himself. "Her *head* was on the ground. Her body was pretty much still in the Toyota. Anyhoo, she's worm bait. The Afro-American *entertainer* is cooling his heels, going through her wallet, and the white guy—Zank, I guess—is knocked out behind the wheel. Until he perks up, sees Father Bob hassling his partner, and gets the bright idea to run him over."

"Who says crackheads don't know how to have fun?"

"Yeah, right. In case he ain't suffered enough, Our Father has to lie there with two broken shoulders, half his teeth smashed, and a busted ass-bone and watch these fucks steal his ride. Apparently he's some kind of car freak."

"Who, Zank?"

"The priest! What's wrong with you? He collects classic cars, God's okay with that, so he's driving this cherry 'Sixty-six Mustang, which his new pals take off in, and nobody's seen since. Father Bob didn't say a lot more than that, on account of flying twenty feet up in the air and landing on his tongue. Did I mention that? He bit his tongue off. They had to sew it back on. So getting him to chat was no picnic. What are you doing here, anyway?"

"Fayton called. Said it was urgent. Didn't he tell you?"

"How could he? He won't come out of his office. Must be relievin' himself in a desk drawer. Haven't seen the old fart, either."

"Chatlak? I'm guessing you won't," Manny said, and headed in to see his esteemed superior.

The expression on Chief Fayton's face was so pathetic, so I'll-do-anything-to-cover-my-ass abject, Manny fought an urge to just walk up and bitch-slap him. Normally, he felt compassion for the helpless. Dalai Lama–level empathy. But not when the helpless in question had been acting like God's Own Smug Prick for the past five years. Not when it was Fayton.

"Oh Christ," whined the chief. "Oh Christ, Ruby, it's awful. He just . . . he just . . . went *crazy*. That's what happened. Really. He just went off, *attacked* me, and when I tried to protect myself, I don't know, he just kind of spun around and fell. Hit his head on the desk. See? Right in the corner. That's what happened. That's really what happened. . . . It's such a *tragedy*. I mean, I did everything I could, I swear! One minute he was standing there, the next—"

"Shut up!"

Manny'd been waiting years to say it, and the look Fayton gave him made it worth the delay. He savored the moment as he tugged a fresh pair of plastic gloves out of his jacket. He met the chief's eyes as he blew into each glove before putting it on.

Fayton was in shock. "Wh–what did you say?"

"I said 'shut up.' There's a man dead on the floor, and all you can think about is covering your ass. So yeah, you heard what I said."

Fayton tried to puff himself back up to chiefly splendor, and Manny bumped him on his way to the corpse. Chatlak lay on his back, blood-shot eyes still open. He wore the same expression he wore twenty years ago, when he knocked on Manny's door to tell his parents their son had been seen smoking "that maryjane" in the high school parking lot. The old goat had made his young life a living hell. But in retrospect, Manny realized, he'd done him a favor. Chatlak could have shipped his ass to juvey, or off to some work farm where the cons would have eaten him with a spoon. Instead he amused himself by tormenting him.

Manny kneeled down beside the body. He could never stand Chatlak, but he knew he owed him. He whispered, "Rest in peace, you bastard," and closed the old cop's eyes. Then he straightened up and turned his attention to Fayton. The chief had put on his tailored blue police coat and stood fingering his badge. The whole setup had *wrong* all over it.

The chief stepped behind his desk, sat down in his power chair, and leaned forward. "You've got a real problem with authority, Rubert."

"You think so?"

Manny dropped carefully into the metal chair opposite the desk—its legs had been sawed short two inches, so whoever sat there would be lower than the chief—and slowly pulled out his notebook and pen. With elaborate deliberation, he bit the top off the blue felt-tip and stared blandly across the desk at his boss.

The chief chewed a cuticle. "Wh-what do you think you're doing, Detective?"

"It's not about *me*," Manny said. "Guy locks himself in a room with a dead body, doesn't let anybody in, doesn't even call the paramedics, I think you'll agree, that doesn't look good, Chief."

"What are you implying? This was a police officer!"

"And you're in a police station—911's down the hall, so why the hell sit around waiting for me? Not that I'm not flattered. But, call me controversial, that smells a little like last week's haddock." Fayton had used the line on Manny frequently—it was one of his favorites—and Manny relished the chance to lob it back at him. "Quite frankly, I'm surprised, Chief. Surprised and disappointed." *Surprised-and-disappointed* was another Faytonism. This would have been fun, if it weren't for the dead old man on the floor.

The chief cringed indignantly and spoke like a slandered martyr. "I'll pretend I didn't hear that, Detective. If you're saying I wanted to bend the rules a little to protect the good name of an officer who, perhaps, crossed the line before he died, who, if the story got out, would lose that good name and, quite possibly, the benefits due his family for his years of good and faithful service, well, all right, sir! I'm, uh, I'm—" Fayton glanced quickly down to his left, to the drawer where he kept his "notes," then raised his eyes again—"guilty as charged! Book me for wanting to preserve the honor of a friend. For trying—"

Manny was out of his chair and behind the desk before Fayton could slam the drawer. He grabbed the chief's hand and plucked it, finger by finger, off the three-by-five card he was trying to cover. The man's palm felt soft as a debutante's.

"For trying," Manny read aloud, "to maintain the dignity of a man who gave his entire life to the service of his community. Who saw no shame in wearing the uniform of an officer of the law, who—Jesus Christ, Fayton, I'm impressed. You work fast. Did you just write this, or did you have it sitting around in case the old guy keeled over on his own?" Fayton gaped, red-faced, as Manny pocketed the card.

Manny couldn't help but smile. Right now, it occurred to him, Fayton was exactly what he'd always been: a man playing police chief. Badly.

He could have watched for hours. Until he noticed the blood. A red swath smudged the left sleeve of Fayton's jacket, just over the cuff. The chief, watching him, dropped his arm to his lap. Then he leaped out of his chair and faced his Honor Wall.

"All right, Rubert, if you have something to say, say it."

"What's there to say? You said Chatlak attacked you. So you *had* to do him. Self-defense. I mean, no disrespect for the dead, but I never liked the guy. He used to hassle me when I was a kid. And he wasn't exactly efficient as an assistant, right? Just between us girls, maybe you can get a real hottie in here. Get yourself some of that knee-pad dictation. Or am I out of line?"

Fayton bristled. "If you're trying to manipulate me, Detective, you're a lousier cop than I thought. In fact you're a disgrace."

"I agree," said Manny. "Really. I hate myself all over the place. Thing is, I'm not the one who killed an unarmed seventy-two-year-old in my office. 'Cause let's face it, *Chief,* your story has more holes than a bum's underwear. Even if Chatlak did come at you, which I seriously doubt, he's so fucking old, you blow on him he'd keel over."

"He fell," said Fayton. "I told you."

"Right. What was it again? Hit his head on the desk? After he attacked you?"

"That's right."

"So why'd you wipe it?"

"What?" Fayton's left eye began to twitch.

"The blood. On your cuff there, from when you wiped it up. Too bad you didn't take the time to get a tissue. It's gonna take a little more than club soda and Clorox to get that out."

Fayton stared at his sleeve, trying on expressions. He finally settled on contempt, and aimed the look at Manny. "So what?"

"So, an innocent guy isn't gonna go around wiping blood off the furniture. He's gonna call an ambulance. And if he's a cop, if he's a *real* cop, he's gonna know enough not to touch anything. So guess what, Chief, I'm gonna go out on a limb here and say you're lying right through your capped teeth. And I'll tell you something else, *Lyn*—may I call you Lyn? I mean, I feel so *close* to you right now—I write this up, get it to your friend and mine, Mayor Marge, she'll yank you out of that desk so fast you won't stop spinning till you're wearing a muumuu in County Jail. You'll be popular, too, bein' an ex–police chief and all. I bet the fellas inside'll be pretty much killin' each other to bunk with you. I might consider arresting myself, just for the chance to share a cell. Why not? A guy could get rich quick, peddlin' tickets. Even if they don't want to rape you—not *all* of them, anyway—they'd probably enjoy just fucking you up for an hour or two. What the hell, huh? I could probably make more turning you out in the joint than bein' a cop—even, like you say, a lousy one."

"I always knew you were dirty, Rubert. I could never pin anything on you, but I always knew."

"That's rich," said Manny, "coming from you. So what's it gonna be, you gonna offer me something, or do I have Merch come in here with the cuffs? Show you how an arrest is made. I'd do it myself, but I really think it'd make his day."

Fayton picked up a brass trophy, for perfect attendance at the

Department of Motor Vehicles, and clutched it to his chest. "You'll never get away with it."

Manny laughed. "*I'll* never get away with it? You got some grasp of reality. I'm not the one who just greased a senior citizen."

Still chuckling, Manny picked up the cordless and started punching out numbers. Then he stopped. He looked at the phone, then up at Fayton, then back to the phone. The mouthpiece appeared to be cracked, and a few strands of long, yellowy gray hair stuck out of the fractured plastic. Manny raised the phone to the light, turning it slightly. The sheen of fresh blood around the trapped hairs was unmistakable.

Fayton saw the blood at the same time as Manny. He placed his DMV trophy gently back on the shelf.

"Refresh my memory," Manny said, holding the phone by its rubber antenna while he dug in his jacket for an evidence baggie. "Are you pro capital punishment? 'Cause the way things are shapin' up, you might get to see it firsthand. I gotta tell ya, though, you could have avoided a whole lot of trouble if you bothered to just clean the damn phone. Or better yet, if you'd have just got ditched the fucking thing. Pitch it off a bridge, bury it in the fucking woods, throw it in a fire with your FOP pension plan. *Anything.* . . . I know you never did a lot of street time, but jeez, Chief, you only gotta watch a couple *Hawaii Five-O*s to know you don't leave evidence lying around."

"I don't watch television," said Fayton, still playing superior. "And I'm telling you, Officer Chatlak attacked me. He lost control."

"Sure he did." Manny stepped over to the corpse. He squatted down for a closer inspection, gently turning Chatlak's head. "Oh look, it's our friend Mr. Hematoma. Wound's not even that bad. You could probably skate, nobody looked too close. Makes sense a duffer like him might have a stroke and take a tumble. A jury might buy that. Unless, of course, somebody *does* look a little closer, maybe does an autopsy, finds a sliver of plastic or something embedded in his scalp. I'm only tellin' you, 'cause I know you go in for that real-life police stuff."

Manny straightened up and casually reached for the cuffs he wore hooked to his back belt loop.

His tone was soothing, even ingratiating, as he drew nearer the chief. A lot of cops were screamers or hitters. They went for intimidation. But Manny preferred to relax his perps. It was like rubbing a wild boar's belly to keep it from goring you. He'd read about hunters in Botswana who did that. Relaxing them seemed more artful. You could still club the fuckers if they got any ideas.

"I'm sure you realize," Manny went on, keeping things conversational, "as long as I have this phone, you're pretty much done. But that's okay, right? Plenty of time to work on that screenplay in jail, if that's how it goes down."

He was now only a few feet away from Fayton. This was when things happened. The Suicide Dive. The lunge for your gun so you'd have to shoot them. Or the play for the weapon they'd stashed, knowing this moment might someday come. . . .

Manny moved with exaggerated ease, speaking calmly. "I bet you can sell your script easy. A cop-killing police chief? Come on, that blows away all that penny-ante Rampart shit. You got the market cornered. But why limit yourself? Write a book, too. Bang out a tell-all, you'll be the toast of the supermarket. Maybe get on Judith Regan, by remote. You'll pull in a lot more for the movie rights with a best-seller under your belt. Guaranteed." He smiled, just to show they were still friends. "Don't even think about going for the gun, Chief. I know about the Nine taped under the drawer. Be cool."

Another step. Another. . . . Sweet and easy. Manny kept up the patter.

"Of course, the bad news is, you won't get to keep any money, on account of the Son of Sam law. Profits go to the victim's family. But what the hell. . . ."

Closer now. Arm's length. Fayton silent and tense.

"But it's not about the money anyway, is it? You want the respect. And you deserve it. You really do. That's right. That's—"

"You son of a bitch!"

Fayton jumped, but Manny saw it coming. He sidestepped, caught the chief's wrist, and spun him around. He pinned him to the desk with his head on the blotter, his right arm jammed up his back, an inch from breaking.

"Bad move," Manny hissed, close enough to lick the Chief's hairless ear. "Now let's stop dicking around. I'd love to see you go down. But there's something I want even more."

Fayton's body began to shake under Manny's. "What is it? You're breaking my arm."

"That's the idea. Justice isn't always pretty. You can put that in your memoir."

Manny let his gaze fall on Chatlak. With rigor mortis, the fingers of his right hand had curled. The same hand, no doubt, that had banged on his parents' front door to rat him out in another lifetime. Small world.

The chief began to sputter, as the first drops of urine leaked from his pant leg into his sock. "J-j-just tell me what you want!"

Manny danced out of splash range.

"For God's sake, Rubert, what do you want me to do?"

Manny jerked Fayton's arm a bit farther up his back, keeping his voice at a dead whisper. "You'll do what I tell you to do, killer."

With this he let him go, and the chief spun back around, reeling, in time to see Manny slide the baggied telephone inside his jacket.

"Call me sentimental," he said, "I'm gonna keep this as a souvenir."

NINETEEN

Well, aren't I a busy little man?

Submerged in the driver's seat of his Impala, twenty-four hours after scaring the urine out of Chief Fayton, Manny washed down a half dozen Codeine Number Fours with his 7-Eleven coffee. This morning he'd gone for Mocha Mint, which tasted like Listerine and paint thinner. Taking another slurp, he fought off the gag-reflex and glanced at the back of his gas bill, where he'd listed all the prestige activities he had to slog through that day. *Dendez, 1818 Pike* was scribbled above another notation, *Pics—Dr. Roos,* and below that, underlined three times, the single letter *T,* with a question mark.

Paperwork was the bane and backbone of police life, and Manny took great pains to ensure that his comings and goings were left out of the never ending slime trail of reports, case files, and Day Log entries maintained at the station. He'd already stopped by earlier to pick up the Pawnee Lodge report that Mindy, the Pentecostal dispatcher, had transcribed off his answering machine.

Mindy shot him her usual scowl, no doubt partly inspired by the rank nature of his Pawnee Lodge notes. (The labial details alone would have her phoning *The 700 Club*.) Mindy claimed she could type without listening, but she'd confided to Krantz, who had a crush on her, that she had to take a shower and pray after handling Manny's case reports. Mostly, Manny believed, she scowled because he'd made the mistake of buying her a Christmas present his first year on the force. Since then the freckled Christian single had been waiting, in a hot ball of resentment, for him to ask her out. Despite her faith in the Lord, Mindy was a spectacularly high-strung and angry young woman. With good reason. Among other things, it was rumored, she'd once had an affair with Chief Fayton—until he dumped her, seduced by the contact prestige of bedding down and wedding a former celebrity assistant. (Before she became Mrs. Fayton, the chief would proudly recount, his wife had gotten dry cleaning for Dr. Laura and Britney Spears's mom, respectively.)

Over the years, Manny had tried to explain to Mindy that he didn't date. It was nothing about *her,* he just wasn't a dater. But the fact that he'd bothered to show her some affection in the first place—that ill-conceived Xmas gift, a pair of macrame plant holders—made it all the worse that he'd showed her virtually none since. Still, Mindy grudgingly consented to the extra work Manny threw her. It was, he reasoned, the least he could do to help fuel her fury. Her Manny-hate, along with her faith in a Personal Savior, seemed to comprise the abiding passions in her life. Which was a fairly scary thought. But anything was better than doing his own typing, let alone listening to more than a minute of his own tape-recorded lisp.

Manny was in the station now to drop in on Fayton and make sure the chief was still in line. He had the killer cordless stashed in a safe-deposit, but it had been twenty-four hours. He knew Fayton well enough to know he had to be sat on. The chief had the metabolism of a PR-driven shark: self-promote or die. Which made the frenzy in the *Trumpet* a tad problematic. On a mission to glorify one of its own, the paper could not generate enough retro-heroics for its fallen star. In death Dee-Dee Walker was reborn an ace journalist, cut down before she could snag the Pulitzer that was her due. Nobody seemed to remember that the bulk of her copy involved pet neutering and snow removal.

Faced with Fayton's salacious love of the limelight, Manny felt compelled to brace him again. It was an odd phenomenon, but perps had a way of forgetting humiliation. Forgetting they were on borrowed time. Merch used to call it the Bad Dream Syndrome. It never failed: A day after some little dealer had been paid a visit, after he'd *agreed* to rat out the big dealer by way of saving his own ass, he would decide, in some irrational blast of optimism, that he could just—go figure—*go on with his life*. As if what happened had never happened. . . . But the Syndrome could get worse. More than once, when Manny paid a suspect who'd agreed to cooperate on Monday a visit the following Tuesday, the guy wouldn't even recognize him—so thoroughly had he blocked out his Bad Cop Dream. With Fayton, no doubt, garden-variety denial would be turbocharged with vanity and greed.

Yesterday Manny'd left the chief in a quaking puddle. Today, if he knew anything about bent psychology, the chief would be unable to resist the chance to make himself look huge by spilling tidbits to the *Trumpet* about Ms. Walker's final subject, the lonely widow, Tina Podolsky. It was the kind of thing he lived for. Visions of law enforcement glory would no doubt obliterate the nasty reality of his chat with Detective Rubert.

Manny barged into the office of the chief without knocking. Fayton peered up from his desk, a jar of silver polish in one hand, a fresh Handi Wipe in the other. His badge rested on a bed of Handi Wipes.

"Let me guess," said Manny, "you're buffing your badge."

"You could have called ahead," the chief replied testily.

"That's me, no manners." Manny kicked the door closed behind him. "So you went and got a new phone? That's good. Glad you're keeping busy. 'Cause I've got your old one on ice. Not that DNA

needs a whole lof of upkeep." He put one foot up on the chief's
Lemon Pledged desk and leaned in. "Now listen, I know from Marvin
Podolsky's widow that Dee-Dee Walker came by to talk to her before
the accident."

"Is there a reason you're telling me this?"

"Yeah, for the same reason you're shining your little star. Her editor
probably knew where she'd been before she died, and he's gonna be all
over it. Maybe they're coming to take your picture, huh? Ask you a
couple of questions. Let you act like you know what the fuck's going
on. We know how much you love that. Problem is, *Chief,* I think Mrs.
Podolsky's been through enough, so I'd appreciate if you kept any
inspiring comments to yourself."

Fayton dipped a fresh Handi Wipe in the polish, then picked up his
badge and resumed polishing. "Mrs. Podolsky," he declared, looking
put out, "works at Seventh Heaven. The same place where Tony Zank
swung his own mother out the window. The same place where
Carmella Dendez was employed as supervisor before Zank and
McCardle took her to the Pawnee Lodge and killed her. I know you
finished ninety-third out of a hundred and two at the Academy, but
surely even you can you see a connection."

Manny hated himself for wincing. "You checked my file?"

"Of course. I'm an old personnel man, remember? Since I'm going
to be answering to you, I got curious. You're even dumber than I
thought."

"That makes two of us." On impulse, Manny snatched the chief's
badge and wiped it off the bottom of his shoe, hoping he'd stepped in
something. "Not a day goes by I don't blush about my Academy rank.
It haunts my sleep. So who the fuck told you about Zank and McCardle?"

"You did, *Ruby.* Mindy showed me your case report. Very colorful."

"*Shit!*"

Fayton smiled his thin-lipped smile. "You know, you really should
go out with Mindy sometime. She's a special girl. Perhaps you could
escort her to Officer Chatlak's funeral."

Manny slapped the badge back on the desk. He wondered, for a
jagged second, if the drugs were making his brain soft. Why the fuck
was he still writing reports when he had Fayton in his pocket? *Pathetic!*

It was one more example of something he'd long suspected about himself, that deep down he wasn't a real lawbreaker. Bad didn't come natural. He had to work at it. The awful truth: Sometimes he felt like Mister Rogers playing *The Bad Lieutenant*. Unlike Tina, he thought, and smiled in spite of how pissed off he felt. You knew out of the gate that Tina could write the book on being bad.

"New rule," Manny announced. "From now on, no reports."

Fayton did not look cowed enough, so Manny cranked up the volume. He jammed his face an inch in front of his boss's. Any closer and their nose hairs would mesh.

"And one other thing, *Sir.* You ever get the bright idea you can get out of this by wearing some kind of wire, or planting a bug, you might think twice, 'cause whatever the fuck I go down for, you go down for killing a cop. You got that? You do what I fucking tell you to do."

"Which in this case," said Fayton, in the peculiar tone of ass-kissy arrogance he'd affected since Manny made off with his bloodstained telephone, "means lying to the press. Well, *I* can do that. But maybe it's not me you should be worrying about. Maybe you should be thinking about a fellow officer."

"Merch wouldn't talk. The *Trumpet* almost crucified him over his stuffed turkey."

"A dozen twenties soaked in gizzard juice? I'm not surprised. That man's a disgrace to his profession. But I'm not talking about Merch. I'm talking about Krantz. He was first on the Walker accident scene. He found a crack pipe and he's all excited."

"That's terrific. I didn't know he liked crack."

Fayton sneered. "Go ahead and laugh, he'd love to show you up. From where he's standing, you and Merch have it cushy. Plus he thinks you're a grass-eater."

"A *grass-eater?*"

The chief loved busting out cop-talk. In his mind, it made him a regular, round-the-station kind of guy, though Manny assumed he found the term in a book of police slang he'd ordered from Amazon. None of the cops Manny knew would call you a "grass-eater." They'd just call you a dirty cop.

For another minute he listened to Fayton's drone, wondering where he'd heard that same tone of mealy-mouthed threat. Finally it hit him. Peter Lorre. When he tried to be tough, the chief conjured up Peter Lorre, without the accent. Once he'd figured that out, Manny felt weirdly elated.

"Let me deal with Krantz," he said, startling the chief of police by pinching him on the cheek. "In the meantime, get yourself a hand mirror."

"Why's that?"

"So you can watch your ass."

That was how most of the cops Manny knew actually talked.

On his way out of the station, Manny ran into Krantz. The jealous cop rocker was trimming his mullet over the men's room sink. More than once, Manny'd been tempted to suggest that the kid change his style: maybe shave his head, or pierce something. That way, no matter how lame his music, at least some of the audience would think he was cool. There were a handful of young urban hipsters, even in Upper Marilyn. Manny knew because he'd busted most of them for dope and sneaked them into treatment. (Having kicked cold himself, he didn't particularly think anybody else should have to.) But Krantz, he suspected, might misinterpret his fashion tips.

When it came to the Top Forty Cop, Fayton hadn't told Manny anything he didn't suspect already. Of *course* it killed the kid that Manny got to drive around all day, doing whatever he wanted, while Merch got to sit on his ass scarfing Clark bars and ogling Eisenhowerera smut. This left Krantz with the real glamour work: chasing checkjumpers at Denny's, settling "plate-breakers" (domestic squabbles), or rousting drunks passed out on the train tracks. Who wouldn't be fucking annoyed?

Merch once told him that Krantz had even offered to tail Bad Detective Rubert to help take him down. By way of placating the Ramada guitar god—and getting him off his back—Manny had decided then and there to ask Krantz for help. It was an old snitch trick—get them to think you're humiliated, that you *need* them and you're *ashamed* about it. For that shot at superiority, lowlifes craving respect would rat out Mother Teresa. If she were still alive to rat out.

Not that Krantz was a lowlife, but the dynamic was the same, more or less. . . .

Manny pissed hugely and stepped to the sink. He scrubbed his hands while the rookie snipped away at what he called his "Sho-Lo." (Short in front, long in the back: the hep hockey player look.) Krantz played it tough and silent, but when their eyes met in the mirror Manny kicked off.

"Listen, Big-Time, next week I might be bringing down a couple of bad guys. Could be a heavy play. I was hoping I could call you to get my back. Interested?"

"Am I interested? Are you kiddin' me?"

Manny thought Krantz was going to wag his tail. The rookie slapped down his scissors and rubbed his hands together. "Dude, that is *hot!* What's the caper?"

Manny looked right and left, *the-walls-have-ears* style. "Can't tell you now. But book some range time. Get in some target practice."

"Bitchin'!"

Manny nodded, still scrubbing, and Krantz nodded back. Men being men. In the men's room. While he toweled off he watched the lunkhead guitarist pump himself up. It never failed to amaze how quickly hate turned to devotion when you gave the hater some props. Krantz was already busting his acid-washed britches. "Hey, Manny, I'm playing the Ramada Inn Lounge this Saturday, in Altoona. I could get you free drinks if you wanna come."

Manny said he'd love to, but he had a stakeout. "Police work," he said grimly, giving the rookie's shoulder a fraternal squeeze. "You know how that goes." For extra gravy, he added, "Love the Sho-Lo."

"Wow, thanks!"

As a coda to their happy exchange, Krantz fluffed his mullet and inquired, like a shy junior asking a cheerleader to the prom, whether Manny would consider "mentoring him."

"Excuse me?"

"You know," Krantz explained, even more cocker spaniel–like, "show me the ropes, the tricks of the trade. You're a great detective, dude. Maybe I could ride with you sometime. I know the chief would go for it!"

"He would, huh?"

Dying, Manny shook Krantz's hand. From a great distance, he heard himself mutter that he'd be honored. Then he fled the station wanting to slit his own throat. Clearly, the haircut remark had been a bad play. All he'd wanted was to keep the kid from tailing him. Now the bone-head was his new best friend. *Perfect!* It was just what he needed, along with Tina, Mister Biobrain, and the Zank and McCardle show: a mullet-cut puppy riding bitch in the Skankmobile.

He had just unlocked the mayo Impala when the solution came to him. It was cold—in fact it was fucking *evil*—but he could hate himself later. And it could nip his mentor duties in the bud.

The plan was simple. Krantz handled domestic abuse calls. And nothing enraged an abusee like having some male cop buddy up to her dickwad boyfriend or husband. Merch used to do it, back in the day, and Manny'd learned to walk out the door backward after an irate housewife tattooed his spine with a nine iron. Manny couldn't blame her, but Merch was old-school ignorant enough to think women deserved what they got. It was his worst quality. If Manny told Krantz to always take the guy's side, ten-to-one some enraged better half would try and put him out of commission. With any luck, he'd stay that way until Manny and Tina were free and clear.

Manny was so psyched, he relocked the Impala and jogged up the steps from the parking lot to the station two at a time. He couldn't wait to "mentor" this bit of inappropriate wisdom. When he made his way back to the men's room, happily, Krantz was still fussing with his do.

"One thing," Manny said, breathing hard from the run. "I was just thinking, Slugger, you do a lot of two-thirty-twos, right?"

"Fuck yeah I do!" Krantz whipped out a can of Hold, and Manny flinched. The rookie sprayed his scalp-mattress as he chatted. "Two times a shift, some twist calls up and says her old man's using her fore-head to pound nails. You know the drill."

"I know it all right."

They shared a laugh, and Manny actually managed to high-five the younger man. For most of his life, he was convinced he was allergic to high fives. All that guy-guy stuff at the Academy made him want to puke. But Krantz beamed, and he made himself beam back.

Manny continued, as though sharing a Masonic secret. "Listen to me, Krantz, don't be afraid to take the man's side. You hear me? A lot of women just wanna get a guy in trouble, you know what I'm saying?"

Krantz's eyes went wide. "I guess I do, but—"

"But nothin'!" Manny suppressed an urge to stop and apologize on the spot. "I learned it from Merch. A hell of a domestic abuse man in his day. Just don't tell 'im I told ya." Manny winked and clapped his new protégé on the back. "They don't teach this in human relations, buddy, but trust me. Unless it's flat-out brutality, you do better siding with your own kind. Try it next time you're out on a plate-breaker."

"Well, if you say it's okay. . . ."

Krantz looked worried, but Manny could see he'd hooked him. It was a terrible thing to do to Krantz, not to mention to any woman who dialed 911 for help. What the fuck was he turning into? He felt like a Union Carbide exec, the one who told the plant manager in Bhopal, *"Go ahead, blow off a little steam."*

Manny landed a hearty, you're-a-big-boy-now clap on Krantz's back. "Let me know how it works out. We'll have a brewski!"

"Right on!" cried the wide-eyed rookie.

Manny shot him a finger pistol and left the men's room for the second time. With any luck, the kid would be kneecapped, frying-panned, or doused with bacon grease by some righteously enraged spouse within twenty-four hours. Once that happened, Manny promised the Cop Gods, he would spend the rest of his life making amends to every wronged and battered female in the tri-state area.

Manny glanced back down at his To Do list, then checked his own face in the rearview. The Code Fours were kicking in, along with the voice of his conscience.

You're as bad as she is, it said. *You just don't know it yet. . . .*

TWENTY

Tina squatted inside the closet, sorting through Marvin's shoes. She'd forgotten how many he had, since he'd basically stopped wearing any once he went guru. She was the one who had to go to work at the old age home, bring home groceries, deal with the outside world, such as it was. Marv stayed streaming. He lived on-line, in the bedroom. Turban on his head and loincloth slipping north and south of his hairy belly button, he sat in half lotus before the vid-cam, making his money mantras. It was, she'd told him more than once, like living with a Jewish Gunga Din. *Gunga Dinberg.*

Tina'd just loaded the last pair of loafers in a Hefty bag when the phone rang. She froze. No doubt it was Mister Edward, from the mortuary, wondering where the check was. She'd promised to drop it off the day after the cremation. By the time he went to the collection agency, she figured, she'd be long gone. With or without Detective Manny.

The whole thing with Dee-Dee Walker had spooked her. Same with Carmella. One day people were there, love them or hate them, the next they were somewhere else and you didn't know where *you* were. When she was in second grade and found her mommy swinging from a noose made of pantyhose in their trailer living room, her first thought, before grief, before fear or panic or simple horror, was *Where am I?* This was not the world she thought she lived in. In that world, mommies didn't hang from their trailer ceiling. They might get high and bring home truck drivers. They might beat you with a belt or make you waffles or disappear for a day or three, but they didn't dangle in the air.

For an hour after she found her, Tina sat on the floor and sang her mommy songs. It was Christmastime so she stuck to carols. "Jingle Bells," "Silent Night." "Rudolph the Red Nosed Reindeer." Her mother was dressed in tight black jeans and a polka-dot halter. One of her high heels had fallen off and Tina couldn't get it to stay on. To Tina, she didn't look sad. Her blue-green eyes were open and her mouth was fixed in a funny O, like she was about to yodel. "*That's my one skill,*" she used to joke, when she'd put her medicine in her arm and feel happy for an hour or two, "*the boys all say I'm a hell of a yodeler.*"

Tina took a nap underneath her, on the scratchy carpet. When she woke up she got her schoolbooks and did her homework. They lived close to the highway, and every time a semi roared by the trailer shook and her mother swung a little, like she wanted to dance. Tina reheated some SpaghettiOs in the kitchenette and came back to eat. She brought in the clock radio, too, since Mommy liked to listen at night. She couldn't stand the quiet and had to sleep with the radio on. Tina never slept in her own bed, always with Mommy. Unless a truck driver was over, then she curled up on the couch, watching Christian TV. She liked how shiny the people were. Two days later, when the trailer park lady came by for the rent, she peeked in and saw the body, still hanging there, with the little bed Tina had made folded neatly underneath: Mommy's quilt and pillows, and her two stuffed puppies, Johnny and Merle.

Tina came home from school and found a policeman and police-lady sitting in the trailer. The police-lady smelled like salad dressing and had a pointy face. But the policeman was nice. He called her "Punkin." He pulled a quarter out of her ear and she asked if he was her daddy. Mommy always said Daddy would come back someday. The policeman smiled and said no, he had his own little girls. Twins. *"Maybe you can meet them. Would you like that?"*

This was another secret, an older one: Besides liking jet crashes, since that afternoon she'd liked policemen, too. No one was ever that nice to her before. After all the grown-ups finished asking her questions, the policeman took her home with him. He lived in a ranch house, with a nice yard and a big oak tree with a tire hanging from a rope tied to a branch. When he saw her staring at the rope he took her by the hand and hurried her in. Waiting by the front door, clutching her Minnie Mouse suitcase, Tina heard the policeman talking to his little girls. They were her age, but taller, better dressed, like miniature Avon ladies. *"She doesn't have a Mommy or Daddy,"* he said. *"Be nice."*

Much later, when it was very dark, Tina found herself awake. She'd never slept in pajamas before and felt hot. She took off the flannel bottoms, and then the top. The air was cool and familiar on her skin. She got out of the cot the policeman and his pretty wife had fixed next to their daughters' bunkbeds and walked down the hall. She peeped into every room—closet, bathroom, den—until she found where the policeman slept, and crawled into his bed. It was bigger than her Mommy's, the sheets so soft on her skin she fell asleep immediately. It was still dark when she heard the screams. The lights were on. And the policeman's wife, who no longer looked pretty, whose face seemed to have puffed up while her eyes had shrunk and lost their lashes so that she looked, to Tina, like some terrible white reptile, stood over her with her hands covering her breasts and her mouth wide open, staring.

"Get her out of here!" she shrieked, aiming those awful, lashless eyes at Tina, making her feel like a *thing*. "I don't want this girl in our house! Get her *out!*"

Then the policeman's daughters were in the room, giggling and whispering in each others' ears. The policeman, somehow smaller without his uniform, wrapped a blue bath towel around Tina's naked body and lifted her in his arms. His hands were smooth, not like the truckers Mommy sometimes made her cuddle. *Go ahead, Darlin', Howdy really likes little girls.* The policeman's hair was mussed and his lean face had a sad expression.

"She's just scared," he said.

But Tina did not know who he was talking to. After she got dressed, she spent the rest of the night in the policeman's car, driving to a place where he said they put children like her until they found some family to take them, or people who wanted to make them part of *their* family. He asked if she wanted him to put the cherry-top on, and she said yes. "We only do it for special passengers," he told her. So that's how they rode, with the red light flashing and Tina curled against him, her head on his shoulder, watching the white lines on the highway until she fell asleep. It was light by the time they arrived. And two weeks until Pop Lee, her nine-fingered grandpa, swooped through to take her to live with him, in a whole other nightmare.

When the phone rang again Tina snatched it on the first ring. She'd turned off the machine. She didn't want messages. It was better not to answer. But she wasn't thinking. Lost in all that history. . . . All that shit she never thought about. Her own life.

"What?" she snapped, looking around at the pile of shoes.

"Give it up, bitch."

"What?"

"Fuck you! You're already dead!"

The voice was frantic, quavery. A tweaker. When her first husband, the part-time RV salesman, got deep into freebase, he sounded the same way. She could hear fast breathing, then a worried voice in the background. "Just tell her, Tony."

The phone dropped with a clatter and she could make out the first man's garbled scream. *"Don't say my name, you fucking dink! What the fuck's wrong with you?"* The second voice said something else, and the tweaky guy came back on, panting and talking fast. "Okay, right. Shut up! We know who you are, bitch. You took something that doesn't belong to you. We're going to come and get it."

"I love company," she said, going kittenish. "Can you come over now?"

The tweaker giggled. "She's a nympho! You believe this shit!" Then he remembered he was supposed to sound heavy, and started in again. "We're coming when you don't know we're coming. And you better have what we're coming for."

"Oh, I *do*," she said. "I really do!"

There was a barking laugh, and the line went dead. She hung up and, two seconds later, another ring. She stared at a tassel loafer—when the hell had Marv bought *that?*—then picked up without saying anything.

"Tina? Tina, you there?"

"Manny? Is that you? My God—"

"What's happening? You sound, I don't know . . . what happened?"

Tina pulled herself off the floor. Took a breath. Steeling herself. "I got a call," she said, "that's all. Somebody knows where I live. Somebody wants something I have. Somebody's coming to get it. One of them's named Tony."

"It would be," said Manny, calculating. Today was Chatlak's funeral. After that he had to go to Carmella's house. To tell her family. At Manny's insistence, they'd been sitting on the news. Waiting to see who came forward, maybe filed a Missing Persons. But no one had. Normally Fayton liked to make the Hanky Calls, to represent the Force. *"We want you to know, we'll do everything we can to find the scum who did this to your mother-father-husband-daughter-wife-or-son. You know, I'm no stranger to loss myself. . . ."*

More than once, Manny'd had to sit beside him at these visits, breathing in the chief's insincerity like steam off horseshit. No doubt he'd make a speech at Chatlak's funeral, move himself to tears over the virtues of this fine, departed officer, a credit to the force, an inspiration to law enforcement everywhere, and a close, close personal friend.

"Fuck it," said Manny, making a left instead of a right on Liberty Boulevard, three blocks from the station. "I was supposed to go a funeral, but fuck it, the guy's dead anyway. I'm coming over."

"I don't need that."

"I didn't say you did."

For some reason, Tina remembered the time a long-distance hauler slapped her mother for spilling his drink. Tina stabbed him with her homework pencil, and her mother locked her out of the trailer until morning. Tina could still hear her whisper as she slammed the door: *"You little bitch, that was my medicine money. Timmy's our friend. . . ."* She was maybe seven.

"I can take care of myself," Tina said finally. "I've had a lot of practice."

"So I figured."

Manny swerved to miss a pair of dogs mating at the intersection. A collie coming in low to nail a willing schnauzer. A small crowd had gathered outside the Bentelbo to cheer. The Bent opened at six, for the wake-up boilermaker crowd. In the old days, the mill-hunks from J & L Steel used to roll in after the graveyard shift, or before heading out for the six-to-two. Now that J & L was history, they rolled in and didn't bother to roll out again. Manny waved at a pair of early-bird juicers and spoke slowly into his cell. "Tina, pay attention. Don't answer the door. Don't leave the house. And stay away from the windows. I know these guys, and they're freaks."

"Unlike most guys," she said. "Get out much?"

TWENTY-ONE

Tony Zank was crawling on all fours, nose close to the carpet, squinting for crumbs. His throat still stung from the chunk of wall plaster he'd just fired up, sucking the tainted smoke in deeply, even though he knew, right away, it wasn't actually crack he was smoking. Still, there might have been some crack on it. Maybe a molecule. He didn't want to not inhale in case he missed anything.

"Oh man," said McCardle, combing through the shag fibers beside him. "I think you just smoked a paint chip or somethin'."

"I know what I smoked," croaked Zank. "If you wouldn't have dropped the baggie we wouldn't be down here."

"I told you, Tony, it was empty."

Zank ignored him, having just found a reasonably cracklike white chunk under the couch. He held it to the light, grunted, and shoved it in the tiny pipe. "Bic me," he commanded his partner. "My thumb's too sore to flick."

"Mine, too," cried McCardle. Holding up his own shredded thumb tips, he suddenly remembered. "You seen Puppy?"

Tony slapped him. "Forget Puppy. Just fucking do it!" He leaned in close, clenching the now jagged glass stub between his teeth. By now the oven mitt was missing in action.

"I'm still worried about Puppy," Mac said, but Tony ignored him. Wincing, he flicked the lighter a few times, catching a weak flame, and held it unsteadily while Zank aimed the end of the stem into it.

"Uccch, shit!" he gagged, dropping the pipe as a waxy feather of black smoke trailed toward the ceiling. The carpet began to smolder, where the hot glass lay tangled in fiber.

"Smells like cheese," said McCardle, covering his tiny nose with his hand. "Must be parmesan, from when we had the Chef Boyardee."

"I don't care what it's from," Zank shouted. "We're out of stuff, and we need some. *Now!*"

"But Tony, man, I thought we was gonna go after the girl? To get that picture."

"We'll stop on the way there," said Zank, still combing the carpet lint. "I know a corner. Get the kit."

"You're taking your kit?"

"What are you, my mother? Yeah, as a matter of fact, I *am* takin' it. Soon as I can remember where the fuck it is."

"It's where you left it, man, in the fridge. You said you put it there so you wouldn't forget it."

"Well I didn't, so get it, ass-fucker. I'm busy here."

McCardle pouted and got to his feet. "That's really uncool, man. Ain't no need for that kind of talk."

"Read a grammar book or shut up," Zank carped. "I thought your dad was a dentist."

"He jus' *say* he was a dentist. What he *was* was a con man. Went roun' to all the different hoods with a chisel and string, pullin' out peoples' molars 'n shit. Lotta folks in them days couldn't afford nobody else. Still can't. So Daddy did 'em a service."

"That why your mama killed him?"

"Not exactly. Some of the ladies, his fingers wasn't all Daddy was puttin' in their mouf."

"*Mouf?* See that's what I mean. When you're straight you sound like Colin fucking Powell. Then you stick your lips on that glass dick and—*Yo!*—Mike Tyson's in the house. What is *wrong* with you?"

McCardle shuddered and backed toward the kitchen. "Look who's talkin'! Every time *you* smoke this shit, you go Aryan Nation on me. You get scary."

"I *am* scary, you fucking homo. Now get the kit. We're wasting time."

McCardle got five feet before he had to stop and look behind him. *There it was again!* The grinning midget. As soon as he turned his head, no matter how fast, it flitted out of sight. Around a corner, under a couch. . . . The thing was watching him now. He could hear it talking, too. He was sure. Not just talking, either. It was *laughing* at him. Making fun. That's what it was! A vicious pygmy in the shadows, calling him an asshole.

"Oh man, I am *never* doing this again! Tony, you hear me! I'm done! I never wanna *see* another chunk of cocaine. . . ."

He thought he was yelling, then realized his voice was barely over a peep. His heart pounded so hard it hurt. He felt like he'd swallowed a ringing alarm clock. The crack dwarf was back, tee-heeing in every corner.

Suddenly dizzy, McCardle clung to the door of the refrigerator as if clinging to the side of a ship, trying not to get carried off by waves. His own weight swung the appliance open. Inside, among the Iron Cities and Slim Jims—Tony liked them chilled, to bring out the bite—was a canvas plumber's bag. He made a grab for it, peeking over his shoulder for the angry munchkin, and accidentally tipped the contents onto the sticky floor.

Mac dropped to his knees, cursing. "Shit SHIT *SHIT!*" Why was it, whenever he did crack, he always ended up on hands and knees, picking at things? *Carpet-mining.* Fighting back panic, he tried to shove everything back in the bag: the two tubes of superglue, the grapefruit spoon, the thick roll of silver gaffer's tape, the eyebrow tweezers, the three pairs of pliers, the nipple clamps, the two Colt-Python .357s, the Ex-Lax, the fur-lined handcuffs, the little jug of Arm & Hammer bleach, the baling wire, the dozen packets of black pepper and hot sauce from Taco Bell, the skinny jar of plastic cocktail toothpicks, the power stapler and the rolled-up copy of *Guns & Ammo* with the "New Slim Glock .45" on the cover. He swept his fingers beneath the fridge, in case he'd missed anything, and wiped his hand on his pants as he closed the bag and dragged himself back up. Then he ran screaming into the living room.

"Tony, I just remembered something! They can find where you live, man! I saw it on *Cops*. They can check the rent computers. Everybody who rents anything, anywhere, they got 'em in a big computer!"

But Tony wasn't there. He was . . . somewhere. Mac could hear him coughing. When he called him again—"Tony? C'mon, man, this is a bad time for hide-and-seek!"—his partner replied in a harsh whisper. "Keep your voice down! I'm behind the TV."

McCardle tiptoed carefully across the room. After being awake for a week, the ground started to feel . . . soft. Like the whole world was getting as mushy as his brain. He found Tony flat on his belly, wedged in the narrow space between the television and the wall.

"Get down, you simp! They got the infrared."

"Fuck the infrared, we gotta split," cried McCardle. "Right now! I'm tellin' you, they check the rent computer, we're cooked. All's they gotta do is type in your name, then shoot over here with one of them battering rams. I seen it on *Cops,* man. They can knock down steel!"

Zank lurched forward and grabbed McCardle by the belt. Mac kneeled to keep from falling. Tony switched his grip to his shirt collar and tugged him the rest of the way down. "You think I'm stupid? Is that it? You violate my manhood and then you come in my house, and you call me stupid?"

"No, Tony, no. I wasn't—"

"Oh no? Then why you think I'd sign a lease under my own name? Huh? I'm *not* stupid. I'm De Niro. Okay? I'm fucking De Niro."

"Robert De Niro?"

Their faces were now inches apart. Both whispered, not sure who was listening—maybe the CIA, maybe NASA—but sure someone was. McCardle had caught Tony's paranoia and sploshed it on top of his own.

"*Robert* De Niro?" Zank repeated disgustedly. "*Robert* fucking De Niro?" He looked incredulous. "Only a complete moron would say they were Robert De Niro. Robert *De Niro*'s Robert De Niro. Everybody knows that. Mother *fuck!* I'm *Ed,* man. I'm not some dickhead like you. I went with Ed."

"You're *Ed* De Niro? On the lease, that's who you are?"

"Smart, right? The landlord sees Robert De Niro he's gonna know I'm bullshitting. But Ed De Niro, hey, he don't know. It could be we're related. I mean, we look alike, right?

"Uh, well, yeah. Sorta. I mean, you're both white."

McCardle stopped talking and tried to swallow. He couldn't remember the last time he'd drunk anything besides Iron City. Or the last time he'd urinated. His whole body felt seized up. *Brittle.* As though somebody'd shellacked him when he wasn't looking. Then a wedge of light through the blinds caught Tony's face and Mac had to gasp. Dried blood blotched Zank's nose and forehead, and his left ear looked like it had a bite taken out of it. His eyes glowed an unwholesome yellow-red, like a Rottweiler with distemper Mac had once seen at a bus stop.

Zoned-out, Tony raked idly at the scabs on his face, clamping and unclamping his jaw as though cracking invisible walnuts. Then the TV sparked on and they both flinched. A velvety Australian intoned: "*The ocelot is neither cruel nor kind. It is an animal, doing what animals do. When we return, we'll visit a pair of cubs abandoned at birth. . . .*"

"Sorry," said Mac. "Sat on the remote."

"No wait!" Tony whispered urgently, "he's talking to us! It's *code.* We *are* those cubs! Oh man, we gotta move. You got the torture kit?"

McCardle lifted the canvas bag, desperate to avoid looking at his friend. The blood seeping from Zank's wounds seemed to have worms in it. Tiny white worms, all swaying to the music from the Chevrolet commercial now blaring from the tube. Little worm Rockettes. McCardle could not stop staring. *"Like a rock,"* sang the TV people.

"Thanks, I *would* like a rock," Tony answered them, grabbing McCardle's arm. "What are you staring at?"

"Nothing, man. It's just . . . you're bleeding. You gotta stop picking. You always pick at yourself when you smoke too much."

"Who am I, your bitch? You fucking worried about my skin? You think my looks are goin', honey?"

"No, hey, Tony, it's not like that."

"Oh no? I think it is. You think I'm gonna put on the red dress for you, right? You think you're my daddy, huh Mac? You my jocker now, you piece of shit? I oughta chop your joint off and feed it to the dog, you fuckin' homoloid."

"Tony," pleaded McCardle. "We *talked* about this. She had a gun."

"Yeah, and you had a boner."

"You're just tweaking is all," McCardle protested weakly. "That's what's goin' on."

"Tweaking? *I'm* tweaking?" Tony twitch-hopped to his feet, pressing his palms over his ears. "Oh *FUCK!* Now see what you did? They're sendin' out brain rays, man! They catch you, they're gonna know what you are." He let go of himself and raised a hand for quiet, then broke out in a rasping whisper. "Hear that? Now they're gonna send the choppers! I can hear 'em, man! They're coming for the black Dino. Everybody seen you on *America's Most Wanted*. Shit!" Zank peered wildly around the apartment. "Grab the kit. Quick! We'll make a run for the car. Leave the TV on, so they think we're home. You remember her address, this Tina chick?"

"I know how to get there," said McCardle, careful to keep his distance.

Zank pointed a finger at him. "You better. We make one stop, load up on kibble-and-bits, then we haul ass to the bitch's house and get the picture."

"You sure she has it?"

"She either has it, or we staple her tits to her shoulders, and she tells us who does."

"Jesus, Tony."

"If Jesus smoked crack, we'd wear little pipes around our neck. Think about that. He wouldn't have touched a bite of the Last Supper."

"What?"

"Nothin'. If the tit-staples don't work, we feed her Ex-Lax, then superglue her bunghole. Saw a guy they did that to in juvey. Fucker swelled up like one of them boas with a gopher in it."

"A *gopher?*" McCardle ran a tongue over his lips. He *had* to drink something besides beer. His kidneys were killing him. The dwarf leered from behind the couch, and a thought ran through him like a shock. "How come you hate women so much, Tony?"

"Who me? What I hate," Zank snorted, "is we're out of rock. I take another hit of cheese, I'm gonna upchuck. Let's get the fuck over there, and I'll show you how much I like the ladies."

Before leaving, Tony had one of his feelings—"they're waitin' for us out front, I can *feel* it!"—so they decided to sneak out the back way and down the rusted fire escape. They made it all the way to the sidewalk before they remembered: They didn't have a car. Somehow, in the midst of all their crack-fun, this fact had escaped them. The Gremlin was toast. The priest's cherry Mustang, too hot to drive, was already dumped in the Allegheny. And Tony's regular ride, a Chrysler minivan pinched from a Wal-Mart lot, was still plunked outside Seventh Heaven, where'd they'd left it to transport Carmella in the now dead Gremlin to the Pawnee Lodge.

"I can't believe you forgot," Tony seethed, popping his fist in his palm and craning his skull left and right, as if trying to wring it off his neck.

"So did you!" Mac whined. "And stop twistin' around. It looks like you're doin' some kinda Linda Blair shit. It's creepy."

Tony didn't bother to respond. Instead, for another minute or two, he and McCardle paced in small circles in front of the Bundthouse Arms, scanning the sky for choppers and trying not to inhale dead meat fumes. (Strangely, Zank could handle them *inside*—he could *live* in them—but once *outside*, in the open air, the stink sometimes got to him.) They both noticed the spanking new Town Car across the street at the same time.

There was no reason for such a swanky vehicle in that neighborhood. But when they'd strolled around the Lincoln a couple of times—McCardle touched the hood to see if it was still warm, and it was—no one ran out waving a hand-cannon, so Tony gave the high sign. Meaning it was probably okay to steal.

"Mac," he whispered, as if agents were posted behind every phone pole, "go back to the pad. Grab my slim jim."

McCardle balked. "You hungry, after all that rock?"

"Jesus H. Piss! Not *that* kind of slim jim, you pinhead. Don't you know *anything* about crime? I'm talking about the *slim jim* slim jim, like you buy at Pep Boys, to get into your nice-ass car when you forget your keys. You're dumber than dog food, you know that?"

"You don't have to abuse me, man!" Mac sulked a few seconds, then decided he had a better idea. He ambled casually behind the shiny Town Car, pretended to kneel down and tie his shoe, and began feeling around under the back bumper. His mammoth hamstrings strained against his pants as he groped, but a second later he hopped up clutching a small black box with a magnet on the bottom and HIDE-A-KEY in white letters across the top.

"Gotcha!" he cried, sliding the top of the box sideways and plucking out the spare key. "Don't know why they call this a Hide-A-Key," he chuckled. "They oughta call it the Ride-For-Free. 'Cause that's what I'm gonna do anytime some fool be dumb enough to stick his car keys under his damn bumper. Motherfuckers might as well have a little flag on their antenna sayin' STEAL MY RIDE! I swear, the richer the White Folks, the dumber their ass. I guarantee, no brother I know's gonna leave the key to his Lincoln under the bumper. Huh-uh. Nossir. Never happen."

Zank eyed the ride suspiciously. "I don't know, man. I'm thinkin' car bomb. Get in and start 'er up."

McCardle unlocked the car door grudgingly. "I get my shit blown up, at least I'm dead," he said. "Standin' where you at, you'll probably just get maimed, have to live out your days one of them stumps they got to wheel around and feed through a mush-tube. I'll be up in heaven laughin', watchin' you tryin' to change your shit-bag with your teef."

"*Teef*," said Tony, "there you go again. Now get in and hit the ignition. But wait till I get across the street."

Car go boom, Tony heard himself think, trying to block out the stress-fueled baby talk in his brain. But McCardle didn't wait for him to cross the street. He just got in and turned the key. Tony threw himself to the ground as the Lincoln purred to life.

"Asshole," he hollered, picking himself off the sidewalk. "Shove over and let a man drive."

TWENTY-TWO

Chief Fayton, dissatisfied with the knot in his Windsor, undid his tie and tried not to think about his wife's shoulders. Lately, whenever he looked in the mirror he thought about them. He'd married Florence, way back when, because he admired her verve, her social connections, and her behind-the-scenes celeb stories. (Who knew Dr. Laura had back hair?) Mostly, though, it was because of her money. Personal assistants, it turned out, pulled down a lot more than senior DMV execs. But the years, as they say, had not been kind. Beyond the inevitable grayness, the chin sag, and the Samsonite eyelids—all, happily, repairable conditions, which Flo, just as happily, had gone to Upper Marilyn's own Dr. Roos and repaired—a yolk of suet seemed to have descended from heaven and landed on her shoulders. The yolk, he was loathe to admit, lent her upper body the approximate heft and girth of a retired nose tackle.

South of the waist, Florence remained the svelte ex–celebrity helper he'd wed. But those shoulders. . . . He sighed to think of them now while regarding his own chiseled features. (He liked the sound of this, *chiseled features,* and imagined how, once the movie of his life came out, scribes for *Vanity Fair* and *Us* would pepper their profiles with that very phrase when describing his still strong chin and prominent Roman nose.)

By and large, Fayton was happy with his wife. Flo's charity work kept her occupied. And, as top man at a police department—even a teeny one—he was understandably too busy to spend a lot of time with her. They rarely went out. When they did, it was to attend the odd political dinner, the biannual Police Department dance and fund-raiser, or, the very reason he was fiddling with his tie this very morning, a policeman's funeral.

Fayton sighed heavily as he slid the knot north on his reconfigured Windsor. Florence could hardly be expected to understand why he wouldn't want her by his side at Chatlak's burial. He'd have to think of something.

The chief slipped into his police dress jacket and snapped his freshly polished badge to the lapel. He strained his cranium trying to think of an excuse. They'd already agreed that Florence would meet him at the station, where they'd take his official black Chevrolet Caprice to the funeral, chauffeured by young Officer Krantz. Fayton was a tad miffed he didn't get to ride in the limousine. But Chatlak, apparently, had a raft of sisters in McKeesport. According to Edward Edward, the Korean bride–ordering fellow from the funeral home, the immediate family had limo dibs.

If he didn't call soon, Fayton knew, it would be too late. Flo would be on her way. But he couldn't think of how to stop her. Much as he might want to, he could not just come out and say, *"I love you, honey, I just hate being seen with you in public. . . ."* Nor, come to think of it, could he unleash the deeper truth: that he harbored a secret yen for Mayor Marge. Or worse, that he had an itch to trade up. . . .

The chief was still racking his brains when Krantz, tapping gently on his office door, stuck his head in to say that he'd just gotten a call from Ruby. "And what did *he* want?" asked the chief, wondering, as always, exactly what was going on with Krantz's haircut. Somehow, it managed to be too long and too short at the same time.

"He said he can't make the funeral," Krantz announced. "Something came up on the Pawnee Lodge case. He says he'll call when he nails it."

"I'll bet he will," Fayton scowled, giving up on his Windsor and staring at himself with the dour, defeated expression he tried to counteract every day with a hundred chin lifts. He was still staring when the door opened again and Florence pranced in, wrapped in an off-the-shoulder black Armani knockoff.

"Darling," he gushed, avoiding his own eyes in the Honor Wall mirror as she leaned in for a kiss, "you look absolutely ravishing!"

TWENTY-THREE

Manny hung up on Mullet-man Krantz and slid the Impala to a tire-over-the-curb stop in front of Tina's house. He felt slightly guilty about bailing on Chatlak's funeral, and promised himself he'd pop out to the cemetery and drop off the plastic flowers he'd bought the first chance he got. Tacky as they were in most circumstances, when it came to cemeteries, it was hard to beat phony roses. Not only did they last forever, but nobody wanted to steal them. This was the one bit of wisdom his mother had bequeathed him: Plastic flowers are okay on a grave! Manny clung to this as an absolute truth in a confused and uncertain universe.

That morning, dreading the hours ahead in the company of Fayton and Krantz—not to mention his ex-wife and the rest of what passed for Upper Marilyn officialdom—Manny'd indulged in an extra bit of medicine: a pair of plump yellow Percodan to go along with his usual Code Fours. Unfortunately, he'd neglected to eat anything, and the stew of controlled substances seemed to be working their way through his stomach like a rogue backhoe, leaving a ragged, acid-tinged divot in their wake. He'd already drunk enough Pepto-Bismol to paint a barn.

Manny made a thorough survey as he stepped onto the Podolsky property. Nothing looked out of place, except for a tipped-over garden gnome, which the paramedics had upset hauling Marvin's corpse from the front door to the ambulance. Eyeballing the fallen Hobbit, he decided to take Tina with him to the Dendez house. It might help having a woman there to hold a few hands. If she was up for it, he'd introduce her as a social worker. Families appreciated police bringing social workers along to give them bad news. It gave them one more person to scream at.

He banged on the door a few times, then gave up and hollered. "Tina? Tina it's me, Manny!" After a minute, someone tugged a curtain aside in the living room. If that was Tina, fine. If it was Zank or McCardle he'd need more than a plastic bouquet in his fist. Since he wasn't going to the funeral, he'd decided on impulse to give the faux roses to his new girl. Now he shifted them to his left hand and eased the .38 into daylight with his right.

Manny was still standing there, palm sweating on his gun-butt, when he heard a rustle behind him. He dropped to his knees, tossing the roses and bringing the gun up with both hands as he swung around.

"Freeze!"

"Nice moves," said Tina, holding a can of Diet Pepsi and sipping it through a bent straw. "I bet you were first in your class at Twister."

"Jesus," Manny sighed, "don't do that."

"Do what? Walk out of my own house?" Slurping her drink, she stooped to scoop up the fake bouquet. "These for me?"

Somehow, in her hands, the plastic flowers looked supremely cheesy. "Not really," he mumbled. "I just sort of had them on me."

He stuffed his gun back in the holster and rubbed mud off his pants. The pills had churned south, into his bowels.

"You had them on you?"

"I was actually going to a funeral, but I changed my mind, so, you know. . . ."

"So you thought you'd stiff the dead guy and lay these on the merry widow." Tina dropped the can and crunched it flat. "Don't think I'm not touched."

That was not, of course, the way Manny'd planned his entry.

"Fuck this," he said. "You call me to say two nut-jobs threatened to kill you. So I tear over here, and when I knock on the door, there's no answer. Next thing I know, I hear rustling in the bushes. You think I'm gonna just stand there so I can look cool in case it's you? Forget it." He heard himself sounding like a defensive boob, but couldn't stop. "One thing I learned on the street, you can't save your ass and your face at the same time."

"So what are you saving your ass for?" she asked, turning the knob on the front door and heading in. "Your wedding night?"

Manny pounded himself on the forehead and followed. Once inside, he tried again. "I wasn't bringing you fake roses, okay? They were sitting in the car and I grabbed 'em without thinking about it."

"No need to explain." Her smile let him know how much she was enjoying this. "Leave stuff that nice sitting in a car, you're just tempting fate."

Inside, every available inch was covered with shoes, clothes, videos, or papers. Tina cleared a space on the sofa for Manny to sit, then disappeared into the kitchen as he called after her.

"You know," he started, then caught himself before he said what he was going to say: *I can see why your fucking husband might want to swallow drain cleaner.* Instead, he declaimed, somewhat sheepishly, "If we're going to work together, you gotta stop busting my balls. We've got a lot of business to take care of before we're free and clear."

Tina returned with another Diet Pepsi and one for Manny. "I only heard up to 'balls.' I was in the fridge."

She pushed a pair of TaeBo tapes aside, sat down, and curled her legs underneath her. Manny swallowed some soda, which splashed like hydrochloric acid on his codeine divot. He wondered if he were getting an ulcer. Finding out would entail going to a doctor, which might involve someone finding out how the hole in his stomach actually got there. Which meant it was out of the question, unless he could go under an assumed name. It seemed like a lot of work just to find out he'd fucked himself up.

"You okay?" said Tina.

"Stomachache."

"Pepsis are supposed to be good for stomachaches. Pop Lee, my granddaddy, used to guzzle seventeen a day. He heard Hugh Hefner drank sixteen, so he figured if Hef was such a stud, he'd drink one more and be a bigger stud. Whenever I had a tummyache, he'd fix me one warm, mixed with milk."

"Did it work?"

"You mean did it make him a stud or did it make my stomachaches go away?"

"Both, I guess," said Manny, taking an audible gulp.

Tina flattened her black skirt over her knees and gave him a half smile. It was the first time he'd seen her look anything but all-business. "Well," she said, "Pop Lee never had much stomach trouble, and I think my tummyaches went away just 'cause of the attention. Stud-wise, the old goat used to mow the ladies down like duckpins. The only reason he didn't father more bastards was that he liked them over forty. He always used to say, 'a woman under forty is like an unripe peach.' "

"That's pretty enlightened."

"Yes and no. What he really liked were nine-year-old girls, but the over-forty thing was a pretty good front. All the ladies from church thought he was a sexy old guy. How's your stomach?"

"I'm not sure," said Manny. "That's a lot of information. Anyway, there's a couple things I want to do before we get going."

"Oh *really?*"

Manny couldn't tell if she was being seductive or mocking. Tina had, he'd discovered after knowing her three minutes, the peculiar ability to be both at once. One second he was sure they were deeply connected, the next he felt like he was wearing clown feet. It left a guy feeling off balance. But it was weirdly exciting, too. Like French kissing on a tightrope. Your partner might be in love, or she might be trying to make you splatter. . . .

On top of the painkillers, the whole Tina situation made him slightly dizzy. The more he stared at that Faye Dunaway face, the more it was all he wanted to do. He was tired of talking, so he shut his mouth, letting himself just take her in.

"So where are we going?" she asked when she realized Manny wasn't going to keep up the banter. Most guys, in her experience, would try to outtalk her, as if that were going to somehow suck her in. But Manny could meet her gaze and stay silent, which made *her* nervous. She didn't like not having control. She kind of loved it, which was even scarier.

"We're going," Manny replied finally, back in Total Cop Mode, "to meet the family of Carmella Dendez. To tell them she died. You haven't met them before, have you, at some rest home picnic or something?"

"No, but—"

"Good," Manny interrupted. "I'm going to introduce you as a social worker. You ever meet a social worker?"

"A few."

"Don't worry. If you've met one, you know. All you have to do is act kind and clueless. Hold the babies, if there are any. Tell them about survivors' benefits."

Tina finished her Pepsi and put it down on top of a stack of magazines: *Fortune, Money, Inc.,* and *American Yogi.* "So why the hell do you want to take me?"

"Couple of reasons." Manny stood and took in the piles of self-help books and sandals scattered around the living room. "For one thing, there's a couple of low-IQ killers on their way over to mutilate you. For another, I really hate going all by myself to somebody's house to tell them their mother died. It's a complete fucking drag, and I could use some company. After our 'Mommy's Dead' visit, I've got to go to a doctor's office. A plastic surgeon named Roos. Bent as they come. He developed some pictures for me, plus I think he can help us unload our friend Mister Biobrain. You got any string?"

Tina didn't question the left turn in the conversation. She was used to those. "I have guitar strings," she said. "Marvin was known to pull out his acoustic and break into "We Are the World" when he hit the catnip."

"I'll bet that was fun," said Manny. "Grab one and we'll run it a few inches off the floor across the front door, then scatter glass on the carpet. You got any lightbulbs left, or did Marv eat them all?"

Tina smiled again. "Actually, I was saving some for you."

"Terrific, we'll use those. What about shoe polish?"

"Somewhere."

"Then find that, too," said Manny. "Brown if you have it. We'll put it on the doorknobs."

"What'll that do?"

"Not much, but when they see brown shit all over their hands they're bound to get spooked. Especially if they're cracked to the gills. I want these slime to be muy paranoid. What about dolls?"

"Like Barbie and Ken?"

"Love 'em, but we have work to do. If you can't dig up any dolls, use stuffed animals."

Tina smirked. "Marv kept a family of furry bunnies. Mummy, Daddy, and Baby Marvin, for his inner child work. What do we do with those?"

"String 'em up. Believe me, a couple of crackheads roll in and see a batch of stuffed rabbits swinging from the ceiling, they'll tweak right out the window. I want these fuckers wigged-out. Jailhouse logic: If you can't be badder than the badasses, be crazier. Crazy takes bad every day of the week. You got ketchup, we can dab some around the mouth and paws before we hang 'em. Special effects."

Tina grew quiet, and Manny knew he'd crossed a line he never saw coming. "What is it?" he asked, feeling her anguish more than he ever felt his own. A slave to empathy. For one fleeting second she seemed vulnerable, capable of being hurt, which made her infinitely more real. A girl who wasn't just tough, but tough because she had to be, because something inside her wasn't tough at all. Now he really had it bad. . . .

He reached toward her, to stroke her cheek, but something checked him. His hand hung there, inches from her face. "What's wrong?"

"Nothing's wrong," said Tina. "What's wrong with you?"

She dropped her eyes to his hand, now stalled ludicrously in midair. In some dream moment, out of body, Manny continued to reach, and ran his finger along one staggering cheekbone, on a diagonal to Tina's parted lips. His heart felt like exploding butter. Neither spoke, though

Tina came close. She almost told him about her mother. About the days she'd spent alone with her body after she hanged herself. But *why?* It would either freak him out or make him feel sorry for her. Fuck it.

When Tina met Manny's eye again her gaze was hard. "Let's just take care of this spookhouse bullshit so we can get out of here."

Ten minutes later, the place was prepped with dangling bunny rabbits, trip wires, broken glass on the carpets, and—Tina's touch—WELCOME TONY! tamponed on the bedroom wall. It washes off, she said, prompting him to ask if she'd done it before.

"I used to dabble in interior decorating," she said, with a look that might have meant anything.

Their work done, the pair stepped out of the house, past the comatose garden gnome, over the tire tracks left by Krantz's black-and-white, and into Manny's Impala.

They didn't speak until Tina told him the car smelled like somebody died in it.

"Somebody did," said Manny, "and he's behind the wheel."

Tina regarded him, then slid closer on the ripped-to-hell car seat.

"The way you talk," she said, "you know how to get a girl hot."

TWENTY-FOUR

Tamping his blood-blotched face and skull with a paper towel, Tony Zank slowed the black Lincoln to a stop at Liberty Avenue. A funeral procession, led by a phalanx of motorcycle cops, was taking its time crawling by.

"Man, check out all them po-lice," McCardle said, slinking down in the seat to sample some of the rock they'd just bought from a fourteen-year-old who'd been slinging on a corner by Roberto Clemente Elementary. They'd snagged a new stem, too, since the last one had been crunched down to the length of a cashew.

"*Po*-lice," Zank repeated, still mocking Mac's part-time ghetto inflections. "You kill me. Why you ducking down like that, anyway? This baby's got tinted windows. You could wiggle your dick and stick a needle in your neck and nobody'd know the difference. Looky."

Tony hoisted the Colt 45 forty-ouncer he'd brought for the drive and chugalugged half the bottle. When he was done, he burped out a cloud of jerky vapors and grunted, "Quit hogging the merchandise."

Tony grabbed the new pipe from his partner. He fished a chip from the baggie on the seat and shoved it in. He fired up, sucking till his eyes bugged and waving the pipe at the police procession twenty feet away.

"Oh shit," he squeaked, a second later, "maybe they *can* see. Maybe they got some anti-tint radar thing. *Fuck!* We gotta turn around."

"Whoa, Tony, *no!*" Mac grabbed Zank's arm before he could spin the wheel. "There's about a thousand rollos in front of us. You're just tweakified, cuz. You smoke that much you get all paranoidal. You gotta learn to *moderate.*"

"Right, right." Tony jerked sideways and slapped at something only he could see, then jerked the other direction. "You're right. Gotta sit tight. Nothin' crazy. You got any smack? Gotta relax! This new shit is *strong.*"

"Anything's gonna seem strong when you been smokin' paint chips and cheese all day. This shit's just regular shit." Mac sat back in the plush leather seat and stretched his short, musclebound legs. "Man, this ride's nicer than my crib."

"Since when you have a crib?"

"That's what I'm sayin', if I had one, it wouldn't be this nice."

After twenty minutes stuck watching squads of Pittsburgh Police and State Troopers motor by to honor the fallen veteran, Dominick Chatlak— the last black-and-white sported a banner bearing the image of Chatlak at forty, looking Karl Malden–like—Zank couldn't take it anymore.

"See if this thing got a phone," he exploded, his voice back up to a coke-induced warble. "We oughta call that Tina twat."

McCardle, who'd just glimpsed the crack-troll grinning from the dashboard, jerked back in his seat and knocked over the malt liquor.

Zank bitch-slapped him. "The fuck you doing? You spilled all over the stuff. That's all we got, man!"

"You don't have to hit me," said Mac. "I thought I saw some-thing."

"You're gonna see a shiv in your lung you don't find somethin' to dry that shit off."

"Okay, okay!"

McCardle unsnapped the glove compartment and poked around. In front of them, a white Cadillac with the Seal of the Mayor of Upper Marilyn on the door rolled by at two miles an hour, followed by a hearse.

"Holy shit, the mayor!" McCardle cried.

"Big deal," said Tony. "She don't know it was us knocked over her pad. Don't matter if she do. Long as we got that picture of her within lickin' distance of President Happy Boy's nuggins, she not gonna do nothin' about it. She's probably more scared than you."

"I don't mean that, man."

"Then what *do* you mean? Stop fucking babbling. If the broad had any juice they'd give her a fuckin' limo. Only insurance men drive Cadillacs. You find some napkins?"

"No, but check it out." McCardle looked up from the stack of business cards he'd plucked from the glove compartment. "You're not gonna believe this."

"For fuck's sake, now what?"

Tony snatched a card out of Mac's hands. He rubbed his eyes and read, with some difficulty, LIPTON GRANT, DIRECTOR OF PRO-TO-COL, OFFICE OF THE MAYOR. Shit, this is *his* car?"

"Well why else would these be in the glove compartment?"

"Oh *fuck!*" Tony poked at the scab under his nostrils, then fumbled in the baggie and dug out a soggy rock. He managed to light up and take a weak hit before the pipe sputtered out. *"Fuck!"* He gagged after a brief coughing fit. "She musta sent this Lipton guy to scope us out." Tony dabbed blood from his ear with Lipton's business card as Mayor Marge's Caddy inched past. "She's probably seen us, too. Now we have to *kill* her! Where's my piece?"

"Are you *insane?*" McCardle twisted his buff torso on the seat and grabbed Zank's shoulders. "You can't just kill her! She's not some ho-bag, man, she's the mayor."

"Don't *touch* me," Zank erupted, and shoved him away. "Didn't I tell you before? Don't *ever* fucking touch me!"

"Okay, okay! I'm just trying to de-chill you, bro. You can't go 'round killin' mayors 'n shit. Besides, all we gotta do is get the damn photo, then trade it for green. We don't have to kill nobody." McCardle brightened suddenly and bounced in his seat. "Hey, who knows, maybe our girl already collected on the nut-shot. Did our business for us. Heck, T-bone, she done that, all we gots to do is swoop in, take her off for the cash, and get the fuck out of Dodge."

Zank eyed him for a second, then nodded grudgingly. "You know, when you're not hallucinating rock-goblins or tryin' to prang me up the butt, you're not half stupid."

McCardle, blushing, kept his eyes straight ahead.

TWENTY-FIVE

1818 Pike, the address on Carmella's driver's license, was located smack in the center of Grimston, Buttburg's perennial poverty pocket, a four-block enclave of falling-down row houses carved up into two rat-infested apartments, each holding an entire extended family or two. About half the residents were Puerto Rican, half dirt-poor hillbillies up from Appalachia. Over the years, the two had intermingled, lending the neighborhood a whole new breed of fearsome shit-kickers, known locally as "Puerto-billies."

Manny swung the Impala to a stop by a beat-to-hell house with the bottom half of a truck on its axles in the dirt patch where the yard used to be. "Ever been down here?"

"Don't ask," said Tina. "I wasn't always the glamorous rest home attendant you see before you."

The pair picked their way through the rutted mud, stepping through an obstacle course of mangled tricycles, a three-wheeled wagon, and a mysterious scattering of doll parts, mostly arms and torsos.

"This is 1818," said Manny, shouldering the door open.

Tina followed gamely. "Don't believe in doorbells?"

Manny checked out the row of name slots by the tarnished buzzers. "They're always broken. All these places are run by slumlords. Nothing works. Besides, who's gonna open up for a cop? 'Cause, believe me, they'll know I'm out here."

Tina unsnagged the sleeve of her blouse from a nail in the wall. "What's wrong with phoning?"

Manny shook his head. "Hanky calls are always in person. Official policy. You can't just phone somebody up and say, 'Hi, it's the police, we just wanted to let you know your mother was stabbed to death. Have a nice day!' " He stopped talking and looked glumly around the dark vestibule. "The trick is trying to find the right door to bang on."

Just then two small boys, one smacking the other one with a stick, both sporting shaved heads and pants so baggy they showed their butt-cracks, tore past without looking up.

"Whoa, whoa," said Manny, grabbing the stick-wielder by the scruff of his flannel shirt. "What do you think you're doing?"

The kid raised his serious brown eyes with something like pity. "Whatchu think I'm doin'? I'm beatin' his ass!"

"Terrific," Manny said.

Tina kneeled down in front of the junior perp, who made no secret of peeking at her cleavage. "You gonna smoke him or just fuck him up?"

The boy broke into a yellow-toothed grin. "Fuck him up."

They shared a wholesome laugh over that, before the kid came back at her. "You got nice titties. You the po-lice?"

Tina feigned shock. "I oughta smack your face! I'm lookin' for my cousin. Carmella Dendez?"

The boy nodded, considering. "I got fifteen cousins. Used to be sixteen. But one live in a cardboard box down by the railroad tracks. He's a poo-butt. We don't count him."

"I wouldn't either," said Tina. "So you know my cousin? Carmella?"

The boy stuck his pinkie in his mouth and started chewing, working hard around the nub of the nail. He scoped out Manny. *"You* the po-lice?"

"He's with me," Tina said, straightening the boy's collar and buttoning a button he missed.

"Well. . . ." The boy's jelly-stained mouth formed a calculating smirk. "It's maybe I do know and it's maybe I don't."

Tina winked at Manny, who pulled a short stack out of his pocket and peeled off a five. Tina took the bill and waved it in front of the junior informer. He snatched it and held it up to the watery ceiling light, just like the grown-up fourteen-year-olds when some big spender gives them a C-note for rock. The boy's older brother, L'il Pepe, had been working a corner right by his school, Clemente Elementary, for two years, and sometimes slipped him a twenty for working lookout. But he didn't mention that to the two strangers standing in his building. "Looks okay, I guess." He jammed the cash in his pants. "But I don't know no Carmella."

"You sure?" Tina showed Manny her palm and he slapped down another fin.

"My friend T. C., *his* name be Dendez," the boy confided, keeping his voice low as he grabbed the second five. "He live right up the top of the steps." He hesitated, whacking at a crumpled paper on the floor with his stick, then added, "Don't say I told you,'kay? Sometimes they give me supper."

"C'mere Shorty," said Tina, and pulled the little boy into her chest. She hugged him until Manny had to tap her shoulder.

When she let him go, the boy dawdled. "You gonna come back?"

"I might move in!"

"Cool," he cried, then scooted off down the hall.

They climbed the rotten steps and stopped at the top. Manny cast his eyes at the two apartment doors on either side of the narrow hall. One was slightly ajar. "You've got hidden skills," he said. "That little gangster's ready to go home with you."

"Yeah, well in two months he'd dump me for some other mommy. Men are all the same." Tina pointed to the unlocked door. "This one."

"How do you know?"

"They got a kid running in and out. It's too big a pain in the ass to keep locking and unlocking."

Shaking his head, Manny knocked gently, careful not to push the door open. They heard heavy footsteps. The door swung back and an overweight teenager holding a math book squinted at them through thick glasses. "Can I help you?"

Manny took a deep breath. "We're here about Carmella Dendez?"

"Who?"

Before Manny could explain further, the boy closed his oversize eyes and yelled. "There's somebody at the door!"

Manny stepped back, embarrassed, while Tina watched with amusement. A second later, a slightly older and flabbier version of the teenager pulled the door all the way open. The man looked to be in his early twenties, and had a napkin tucked in the collar of a brown work-shirt with HECTOR stitched on one pocket and ROTO-ROOTER on the other. His glasses, if anything, were thicker than the first boy's, like the Plexiglas that protected cab drivers from stray bullets.

"Yes?" he said.

"I'm Detective Rubert," said Manny, doing his best to sound official without being threatening. "And this is Mrs. Podolsky. She's a social worker. I was wondering if we could come in. It's about your mother."

"My mother?"

"Right. Is your name Dendez?"

"Yeah, but—"

"Please," said Manny, "is it all right if we come in?"

Hector shrugged a *would-it-matter-if-I-said-no?* shrug and stepped aside. The front room was tiny and neat. A threadbare brown couch and matching BarcaLounger faced a portable television with balled-up tinfoil on the antenna. An old-fashioned TV tray stood before the chair, to which the teenaged boy had returned with his homework. An Anglo Jesus, wilted palm leaf tucked in the frame, gazed dolefully down from the wall over the whole scene. Then a third man clomped in from the kitchen. Number Three was a still fatter and older variation on the first two. His pocket said LOUIE. They were fellow Roto-Rooters. Manny thought he could see some resemblance to Carmella.

"Like I was saying, I'm Detective Rubert, and this is, uh, Mrs. Podolsky. We're here because we have some news about your mother."

"How do you do?" said Tina.

The two standing brothers exchanged glances. The teenager blinked his magnified eyes from the recliner.

"Look, Detective, there must be some mistake," said Louie, the biggest Dendez. He was holding a half-eaten barbecued chicken wing, which Manny recognized as a Babe's, from Babe's Pico-Rico BBQ. Manny'd eaten maybe five hundred of those wings himself, when he was still in uniform. Merch used to have them for breakfast, washed down with Schlitz.

The portly chicken-eater gave Manny a look that was equal parts quizzical and threatening.

"Yeah, man. Gotta be a mistake," his brother Hector seconded.

"Well, that's what we're here to find out," said Manny.

Before anybody could say anything else, Tina asked if she could sit down. Hector and Louie, clearly unnerved, mumbled something that sounded like "Sex is the way," though Manny figured it must have been "Guess it's okay." He couldn't tell. He didn't really listen to the words, only how they muttered them. Something was off. It was normal to be awkward when weird, official-looking white people barged into your home. But this was different. Manny saw how both men fidgeted and stole glances at Tina. Louie took a bite of chicken and then, as if caught doing something dirty, placed the wing in an ashtray and grabbed the napkin out of his brother's shirt to cover it up.

Tina took a seat on the couch, and Manny eased himself down on the other end. With nowhere to sit unless they squeezed between them, Louie and Hector remained standing, shifting from foot to foot in their steel-toed boots.

"Well," said Manny, "we might as well get to it."

Nobody said anything, so he pulled out the snapshot of Carmella he'd taken from her wallet. In the picture, she was poured into a tight electric-green dress and spiked heels. But now that he was here, he wished he'd just brought her driver's license. With her hair piled up in that towering beehive, her lips a flaming scarlet, and her hands at her mouth as if blowing kisses to a bevy of appreciative fans, Carmella might have passed for a full-bodied but vivacious salsa legend. Either that or a burly stripper with her clothes still on. Manny stole a glance at the brothers before handing it over.

"Okay," he said, as evenly as possible. "I want you all to take a look."

"But this is *wrong!*" It was the youngest son, eyes bulging through those coke-bottle spectacles. He spoke up in a tremulous voice. "Our mother passed away, like, six years ago." He glanced nervously at Hector and Louie. "She got the female cancer right after she had T. C., my baby brother."

Manny was not sure what to say. But Tina, smiling as she had at the junior *vato* in the hall, seemed perfectly assured. She oozed concern. "I'm really sorry," she said to the boy. "What did you say your name was?"

The youngster looked at his big brothers, who nodded permission. "Enrique, but my mom always called me Gordo, 'cause I was fourteen pounds when I was born."

"Well, Gordo," said Tina, "let me tell you what we're doing. A lady named Carmella Dendez passed away a couple of days ago. Since she had this address on her driver's license, we thought she lived here. That's why we came over. We have to find out who this lady is. Do you understand?"

"I guess so."

"Good." Tina took the photo from Manny and handed it to the boy. "So this is definitely not your mother?"

Gordo stared at the picture, his eyes swelling to the size of ostrich eggs. Something clicked in his throat. His mouth began to quiver, and there was a brief, dizzying pause before he screamed. "No, no! Hector, Louie. . . . *No!*"

The youth shoved the picture back at Tina, then bolted from his chair, upsetting his TV tray. He ran from the room with his hand over his mouth. In seconds, the sound of violent retching filled the apartment. Hector, looking furious, stepped forward, snatched the picture out of Tina's hand, and held it up. *"Mother of Jesus!"* he muttered, then backed into the BarcaLounger and collapsed. His face flushed and he began breathing rapidly. Averting his eyes, he passed the photo to his older brother, who stared at it and went red.

"What is this," Louie demanded, "some kind of joke?"

A sharp spasm stabbed Manny in the gut. He realized what had happened. But it was too late. Louie was charging, and Hector jumped off the chair to hold him back. The large man's face contorted, wet with tears. Veins bulged like plump worms under his temples. Still in a headlock, Louie waved the photo in the air and shouted at them. "This is my father! My *father,* you hear me! What did you *do?*"

Before their eyes, Louie's rage gave way to fear and shame and some mutant emotion there wasn't any name for. His sobs tore out of him in great, strangling heaves, and Hector joined in. The brothers stood together, crying in each other's massive arms.

Manny knew he should say something, but what? "I'm sorry for your loss?" "Your father died a happy woman?" He sat there, mortified, trying not to dwell on why he, Manny Rubert, of all the bent and depresso cops in the world, should be the one who had to walk into this dingy apartment and tell three boys that their daddy had become their mommy and died. Not that Manny's angst mattered much to Hector, Louie, or Gordo. They'd have their own weird demons to wrestle with the rest of their lives. All Manny had to do was make it out of there and gulp some codeine. No doubt he'd feel fine in a decade or two.

"His name was Carlos," Hector managed, between weeps.

Louie nodded and swiped tears out of his eyes. "He disappeared, like, four years ago. We thought he was dead."

"It's okay," said Tina, giving the brothers a hug. "This happens more than you'd think. They have support groups."

It took a second for this to sink in, and then Hector, his voice parched and weak, asked her quietly, "How did he . . . I mean . . . how did my dad die?"

Manny started to say something, but Tina held up her hand. "It's better you hear it from us," she said. "Your father was found dead in a motel room."

Both men shuddered, and Tina paused before going on.

"I want you both to know right now, only one thing is for sure. Whatever else may have happened, he died like a man."

Before the boys could react to that, Tina led Manny out the door and down the stairs. The noises emanating from the apartment were more animal than human.

"That was insane," said Manny, fumbling for his keys on the way to the car. "I was so freaked, I forgot to tell them they have to come down and identify the body. Can you imagine what *that's* going to be like?"

"They'll deal with it," said Tina. "People can deal with anything, if they don't have a choice. I think I helped, though, don't you? They'd have killed you if you'd gone by yourself."

"I'd have deserved it. That's one of the worst things I ever had to do."

"You've led a charmed life, sailor."

Manny didn't even try to respond to that. The whole experience had left him shaky. He tapped his codeine pocket to see where he stood. Three and a half. But he didn't want to pop them in front of Tina. Not yet, anyway.

"I should have known," he said suddenly. "I mean, how fucking stupid can I be? Her vagina looked like a bad science project."

"Excuse me?"

"I'm telling you, the labia was all fucked-up. One side was like a piece of beefsteak, the other looked like a rubber Frito, all twisted up. I'm sorry, but it's not something you forget. Her clit was the size of my thumb."

"Oh, so you two dated."

"That's funny." Manny stopped on the torn-up sidewalk. "I pulled down her pants at the Pawnee Lodge. She was already dead."

Tina sighed. "I wondered what you were into. I guess that explains why you never put the moves on me."

"It was a *crime* scene, for Christ's sake! I was seeing if she'd been raped."

"Whatever, it's okay. Bad enough I did that horrible thing to my husband—*I'm still alive.* That's two strikes against me right there."

"Tina," said Manny wearily, "do me a favor?"

"What?"

"Don't fuck with my head, okay? Not now. You can do it all you want later. But right now, I can't deal."

Back in the Impala, Manny steered without seeing the street.

"Oh, Detective," Tina said after they'd been driving a few minutes, "I think you're buzzing."

"Huh? Oh yeah. . . ." He'd been thinking about the look on Gordo's face and hadn't noticed.

He grabbed the cell phone off his belt and checked the readout. "It's Dr. Roos. The guy we gotta see next."

Tina rolled her eyes. "Not now, *please*. I'm starved."

"You're *starved*? After what we just walked out of? You scare me."

Tina leveled her eyes at him. "Listen, Manny, you ever get bad news in your life? I mean, *really* bad news?"

"Nothing but."

"Hey, I'm not joking." Tina touched her hand to her mouth, as if to keep the words from escaping, then gave up and continued. "Something awful happens to you, you don't want to hear about it from some asshole, okay? That makes all the difference when you're trying to get over it. If an asshole gives you bad news, then *you* kind of feel like an asshole. But if somebody all right, somebody *decent* is the one to break it to you, whatever it is, then at least you have a chance to recover. On top of whatever nightmare your life just turned into, you don't have to feel like there's something fucked-up about you because some fucked-up, insensitive jag-off was the one who knocked on your door."

Manny stared at her. "Something tells me you've had a lot of bad news."

"Enough."

Manny started to say something else, then stopped when another thought came slamming in. Tina, catching his hesitation, said, "What?"

"You knew about Carmella, didn't you? You just never told me."

Tina rolled her eyes. "*Please*. She got a little five o'clock shadow when we worked late, but I figured it was menopause. Weird things happen to older women. I had a great-aunt whose voice got so deep, by the time she was forty-five she sounded like Barry White. Carmella never seemed particularly masculine, but it's not like I peeped up her dress. Besides, what difference does sex make when you're dead? You think they have His-and-Her restrooms in heaven? My mother always told me, angels don't sweat, they don't burp, and they never have to go to the bathroom."

"So what does that leave?"

Tina slid closer in the seat. "If you weren't such a tight-ass, you'd figure it out."

TWENTY-SIX

"Yeah, yeah, yeah, I'm gonna spend mine on a pleasure boat. Fifty, no, a hundred feet long."

"What the fuck's a pleasure boat? You mean a yacht?"

"Pleasure boat's bigger than a yacht," said McCardle. "Yacht's like a little ol' kayak compared to a pleasure boat."

"What the fuck's a kayak?"

"Forget it, okay, Tony?"

McCardle pouted and rooted in the sopping baggie, feeling for a rock that wasn't mushed from the malt liquor he'd spilled.

Once they'd waited out the cop parade without killing the mayor, Mac stopped paying attention to where they were. He kept his eyes shut until he had to open the window on account of Tony's belching. The jerky fumes were enough to curdle milk. When Mac rolled down the tinted glass, he saw the street sign with Carmichael on it and shouted. "Shit, Tony, we're here!"

"Where?"

The Lincoln swerved crazily, and Mac had to cover his eyes when a kid on a bicycle slammed into the curb and flew over his handlebars. "Careful!" he shouted.

"Don't tell me how to drive," Tony snapped. "My head feels like a bull took a dump in it. I swear, man, it even smells funny. I can tell. Lean over, sniff my head."

McCardle balked. "Naw man, no way I'm sniffin' your head. That's fucked-up. Listen—"

"*That's* fucked-up?" Tony interrupted. "*That's* fucked-up. After what you did you're givin' me that?"

"I can sniff your head later, okay? We're at the chick's house."

Tony slammed on the brakes. "You fuck! Why didn't you say so?"

McCardle flew forward, trying, and failing, to grab the crack bag before it spilled on the floor. He tried to scoop up the mess and smeared a swath of beery crack-paste over the car rug. When he straightened up, he saw they were stopped in the street. *Now what?*

"No disrespect, T," he said cautiously, "folks won't be able to get around. You either gotta park it or keep goin'."

Tony lashed out with a front-seat jab, tagging Mac on the shoulder. "You're gettin' bossy, bitch."

McCardle stepped quietly out of the car. Times like this it was better not to engage. That's what the prison therapist who helped him with his Little McCardle always told him: *Don't engage.* To Mac that meant act cool and get the motherfucker later. But he never told that to the shrink.

Tony dropped the torture kit and tried the lock, then jumped back.

"What the fuck?" he cried, holding his stained palm up to show McCardle. "Shoe polish! At least it *better* be shoe polish!"

"I see it," said McCardle, glancing nervously at the other crappedout houses up and down Carmichael. "But somebody's gonna see *us*, we don't get our asses inside."

A minute later, after fish-pinning the lock, Tony tripped over the guitar string Manny'd slung over the threshold and landed on his hands. "Ouch, *shit!*" he cried, plucking shards of lightbulb out of his palms. "It's a fucking booby trap. This chick's playing games!"

McCardle helped dust Tony off and stepped into the living room, glass crunching underfoot. Then he spotted the hanging rabbits. *"Oh Lord!"* His shriek caught in his throat. The furry creatures' eyes seemed to follow him. Their bloody bunny mouths formed winsome smiles. This was worse than the rock-goblins. This was *real*.

Tony grabbed McCardle's wrist. "Something's fucked-up," he whispered, then realized they were holding hands and quickly let go.

"Voodoo," McCardle whispered back. "Those bunnies look *fresh!* Maybe she's a priestess. This could be some kind of Marie Leveau shit."

"I don't give a fuck if it's Marie Osmond. We find the photo and we split."

Sneaking further inside, breathing hard, Mac and Zank made a tacit decision to stick together. They got as far as Tina's bedroom when something bumped Tony's forehead.

"Ahhh-*EEE . . . Get off me!*" Without thinking, Tony snatched the thing and yanked. He fell backward clutching Tina's tampon. "Take it," he squealed, tossing the tainted item to McCardle.

"Yeeech!" Mac flicked it away. "This look like some *Blair Witch* thing, man. Like them women who grow thigh hair and throw oat bran at the moon."

Tony clutched his skull. "I don't care. I can't take any more of this. You see what she did?" He bit his knuckle and pointed at the bedroom wall. *"Welcome Tony!* She wrote my fucking *name*. In *blood*. . . . This she-devil is trying to put a curse on me. I need something to drink."

"Probably wine in the kitchen," McCardle said, avoiding the welcome note on the wall. This was Manson shit, but he decided not to bring *that* up. "I had an aunt once into black magic. Them voodoo priestesses always drink wine. Sometimes chicken blood, too, so you gotta be careful."

"Fuck! Don't *tell* me that! What's wrong with you?"

"Sorry, man. I was just sayin' . . ."

Fearing that Tony was headed for a whiteout, Mac steered him gently out of the bedroom, past the dangling bunnies, over the crunching lightbulbs, and into the floral-print kitchen. It was the one room, as far as he could see, that was more or less normal—minus maybe the color snapshot of a man in a turban taped to the refrigerator. The strange thing, when Mac looked close, was that the turban guy wasn't one of those Indians. He was a white man. A redhead. You could tell from his mustache. For a second, he thought it was Ned Beatty. (*Deliverance* again!) But why would Ned Beatty wear a turban? And why would Tina stick him on her fridge? Chicks liked Tom Cruise and Ben Affleck. Kevin Costner maybe. But Ned Beatty? Topless? What kind of strange-o would want a porky redhead as a pinup?

"I got period on my hands," Tony babbled nervously. "I gotta wash."

"It's okay, the shoe polish'll kill the germs."

"You sure?"

"Absolutely," said McCardle, with no basis for the statement whatsoever. He just wanted to calm his partner before something awful happened. Something awful always happened when Tony got wound up. Mac started opening and closing cabinets, scoping out booze, while his partner talked to himself.

"*Unclean . . . unclean,*" he kept repeating, struggling futilely to wipe his hands on the dishcloth over the sink. "That's one of the Kosher Commandments, man. 'Thou shalt not touch chicks when they're packin' the pillow.' It's a Moses thing!"

"Just relax, okay? Wine's probably in the fridge."

"I'm fucking hungry, too. See if she's got any Slim Jims."

"Right," said Mac, hesitant to point out that no one ate beef jerky except for ex-cons and truckers, White Trash peckerwoods, which this lady plainly wasn't.

Before McCardle could scare up some alcohol, Tony began hopping up and down, clapping his hands in front of what looked like a brass cookie jar.

"You find it?" Mac asked cautiously. He hoped Zank hadn't flipped out altogether. "You find Mister Biobrain?"

"Fuck that, Judah Macabee! We got rock, baby. This bitch got *beau-coup* rockaloo."

By way of demonstrating, Tony plunged a hand in the urn, sifting a fistful of off-white chunks—what looked, to McCardle, like albino granola.

"I don't know, T. That's a stupid lot of crack, if that's what it is."

"What *else* could it be? Maybe that's why she's into so much freaky shit. I had this much coke in my crib, I'd be hangin' bunnies from the ceiling, too. Fuck, *I'd* be hangin' from the ceiling. I'd be all-the-way buggin'!"

Zank cackled and sniffed a knuckle-sized chunk, then brought it to his mouth for a quick lick. "Oh yeah! It's payday, man! We keep half this shit and sell the other half, we're fartin' in silk! We'll be high *and* money! All we gotta do's go out and get us some vials, and we're in business."

McCardle tried to catch Zank's excitement but didn't feel it. "That's cool, but we still gotta—"

"Gotta what?" Tony was on a mission. "Don't you get it? A chick lives in this dump, with this kind of weight—what's that tell you?" He made a fist and knocked on McCardle's head. "Hello? Anybody home? What that tells you, my short nigger amigo, is that she already unloaded the fucking photograph. She made a ton of cash and she spent it on rockareeno." He rubbed his groin and leered. "Tell you the truth, I wish the slit would come back now. I'd love to blow some of this candy and go Rick James on her ass. Get freaky with the freak-ette. You got the pipe? I'm gettin' hard as Jesus' forehead just thinkin' about it."

"Yeah," McCardle said, "I got it, but I don't know. . . . If we're not gonna look for the picture, we should probably just book."

"Chill out. Load some up, I wanna try this stuff."

"All right, man, but this feels kind of fucked-up."

Halfheartedly, McCardle tugged the pipe out of his pocket and wodged in a whitish crumb. Before he could raise it to his mouth, Zank snatched it away. "I found it, I get the first taste. Beam me up, Scotty!"

Sighing, McCardle sparked the Bic and held the flame to the stem while Tony sucked for all he was worth. Finally a thin spindle of smoke billowed in the glass and he crashed against the counter, eyes popping out of his head.

"Fuck," Tony sputtered and exhaled a small puff of smoke. *"Strong."* Mac had a feeling it was pipe residue, not the pallid nugget he'd fired up. But he knew better than to cross Tony when he was enthusiastic.

"Bag it," Tony chirped. "Sooner we get it bottled up and hit the street, the sooner we get some cash money."

"But *Tony,*" McCardle tried not to whine. "What about the photo?"

"We'll get it. You gotta be flexible, man. That's the key to bein' successful in business. Opportunity knocks, you don't slam the door on its fingers. Read Og Mandino. *Greatest Salesman in the World.*"

While Mac was busy bagging the contents of the urn, Zank had another idea. He rifled the kitchen drawers until he found a hammer, then plucked a choice morsel out of the urn and placed it on the counter. With a happy whoop, he brought the hammer down, then brought it down again, until he'd reduced the solid nugget to a batch of chalky powder.

Using his shiv, Tony worked the mound into four straight lines, then leaned down and rhinoed two enormous snorts.

"Oh yeah," he said, pinching his nose when he'd horned up the deuce. "This shit's off the hook! We got *tootonium* here. I left a bump for you."

"Not right now."

McCardle hoisted the four stuffed sandwich bags. Tony grabbed one and hooted. "All *righty!* Let's make tracks. We sell this shit fast, we can come back in time to torture the broad before dinner. Find out what she did with the happy-balls. Two fortunes in one day, not too shabby."

"No, it's not," Mac admitted, though, deep down, he had a feeling shabbiness was going to be the least of their problems.

TWENTY-SEVEN

It had been over an hour since they'd left Chez Dendez, and Manny was still smarting. But not, for better or worse, because of what happened with Carmella's sons. Heinous as it was, that kind of weirdness tended to dissipate once you left the scene. On an average day, a cop saw more lives ruined than saved. Saved was the exception.

By comparison to some of the shattered worlds Manny'd walked in and out of, what Louie, Hector, and Gordo had to deal with was relatively benign. True, the trio might be psychologically shattered—especially when they got details of the murder. (Bad enough their dad was a woman; now they'd start wondering if maybe she was some kind of slut.) But still, nobody was bleeding brown from their liver, nobody picking brains out of the playpen. He'd witnessed both and wished he hadn't.

Not for the first time, Manny realized that what constituted tragedy, in his mind, was a few notches beyond what most souls would consider endurable. Except, of course, when it came to his own feelings, tender waifs that they were. In spite of all the plates he had spinning—the Zank and McCardle show and Fayton and Krantz, Dr. Roos and the wrath of Mayor Marge, not to mention George W. and his smiling testicles—the only thing Manny could think about was Tina calling him a tight-ass. That hurt. He knew he was overreacting, but each time he recalled her words, he had to bite the insides of his cheeks to create a pain big enough to blot out his anguish.

He assumed that his current moodiness was due to drugs. Or lack thereof. Not that knowing helped. It was Newton's Law of Applied Narcotics: The higher you got, the lower you fell. And he'd gotten pretty blitzed, what with the Percodan he'd added to his usual breakfast of codeine and coffee. Whenever he started jonesing, he tended to get emotional. That was the first phase. Which was fine, if you were home alone and weeping at a Volvo commercial. But here he was, with the first woman who'd stopped his heart since forever, and he was acting like a twelve-year-old girl who'd been cut from the pep squad.

"Pathetic," he muttered, before he realized Tina would hear him talking to himself. He tried to play it off by squeezing the wheel and setting his jaw in a manly fashion, but Tina wouldn't let it pass.

"What's pathetic?" she asked, clearly glad to be speaking after his sulky lull. "That you've been taking every back alley in Butt-burg at eighty miles an hour? Or that I'm riding around with a guy who pulls down dead she-male's underpants? Not that I'm criticizing. I'm a live-and-let-live kind of girl."

Manny stole a glance at her, and she met his eyes as if daring him. But daring him to what?

"Lighten up, cowboy. You want to do strong and silent, that's fine. Girls love that. Some girls. Me being newly widowed and all, I wouldn't say no to a little social intercourse. But hey, it's your car. You wanna go all broody and mumble 'Pathetic!' every couple of minutes, knock yourself out. My house is being overtaken by killer crackheads. It's not like I can throw a snit and say 'Take me home!' "

"Look," said Manny. "I know I'm being weird."

Tina smiled. "It's okay. I was you, knocking around with a hot chick who probably offed her husband, I'd get the clam-ups, too. Who wouldn't?" She looked at him thoughtfully. "You're conflicted. Your right brain says, 'I really like her.' The left is like, 'What are you, insane? She made the last guy gargle glass!' So where are we going again?"

"What?" Manny glanced over just in time for Tina to dive sideways and turn the wheel a foot before they rammed an oncoming mail-truck.

"That was exciting," she said.

"Sorry."

"It's all right. I have great reflexes. I've heard cops were lousy drivers."

"I don't mean that," said Manny, feeling retarded but forging on, in the grips of some narcotically deprived need to express himself, a stress-fueled combo of terror, lust, and all-purpose emotional confusion. Even as he spoke, he knew he'd probably regret it, but regret not saying anything even more. Every thought in his head was like a fork in a toaster. "I mean, I'm not used to this."

"To what?"

"To feeling anything. Okay? I *feel* something for you. You know how unfucking likely that is? Most of the time I don't feel. I don't want to. The life I live, it's better not to. But now, I mean, looking at you. . . . From the minute I walked into your kitchen, it's like, I don't know, I won the lottery and forgot how to cash a check."

He went back to watching the road and felt his whole face burn. Tina's silence was crushing. Air whistled through the back window that never closed all the way. He steered blindly, seeing but not seeing: warehouse, stop sign, bar; vacant lot, gas station, red light, church. . . . His grip was slick on the steering wheel. He more or less knew the way to Dr. Roos's office and trusted his car to get him there.

After what seemed like months, Tina spoke. "Give me your hand."

"My hand?"

"Your hand. Give it to me."

He reached over and she took it, her own fingers warm around his. She studied both sides intently, following the groove of his knuckles with her fingertip, the play of dead veins leading down from his wrist.

He used to shoot there, in his fun-filled youth, and his sclerosed vessels had never forgiven him. The effect was tantalizing and clinical at once.

"What are you," he asked finally, slowing as the light went yellow to red. "A palm reader?"

"More of a palm taster. You can find out a lot about a person with your mouth. Ask any hooker. You must know a few, in your line of work. Screwing is one thing. Even giving head—but that doesn't count. That's the job. But kissing, going mouth-to-mouth—no way. That's way too intimate."

As if to emphasize her point, she gave his palm a teasing lick.

Manny shivered. The sensation was so dizzying, he had to speak to keep from driving into a tree. "Tell you the truth, I never had anybody lick my hand. Is that a Guru Marv thing?"

She dropped his hand and glared. *"Fuck you!"*

"Sorry! I was just trying to make conversation."

"Forget it."

Manny stared at the road, sensing the creature beside him moving away as surely as if she'd boarded a train going the opposite direction. Suddenly he understood. *This is as hard for her as it is for me. . . .*

Maybe that's what love was: damage loving damage, and in the process turning itself into something else, something—he heard the word in his mind and fought to keep from choking—something *beautiful.* Something—again his mind recoiled—something *pure.* Which felt like dying.

That was the truth. Despite the teasing, despite the sharp mouth and the swagger and the attitude for days, Tina was struggling the same way he was, trying to violate the bone-deep rule she'd made for herself to survive what she'd had to survive: Don't let anybody in.

She had opened the door, against all that life had taught her, and he had stood in the doorway, babbling.

In that instant, Manny knew, he had to make a move or lose her. And he made it, without knowing he was going to, just as the light changed to green. He reached for her, loving the feel of his hand on the back of her neck as he pulled her toward him. *Finally.* Her skin was so soft it startled him. A hard-ass with soft skin. . . .

The first car started honking as soon as his lips found hers. He kept
one foot on the brake. The harder he pressed down, the deeper he

kissed her. It was rougher than he intended. He had meant to seduce, and instead he pounced. Tina didn't resist, but she didn't burst into passion, either. It was as if, he somehow understood, she was waiting to see if she felt anything—or maybe to see what the fuck he'd do next.

Shouting began to accompany the horns, but the noise sounded far away. The part of his mind that considered odds and consequence had shut down entirely, snuffed by the sheer adrenal rush of holding her, falling together onto the Impala's sunken upholstery. He took her face in his hands as he kissed her, wanting to just get it right, to stamp the moment, to blunt the thunder of fear pounding in his skull as the rest of him succumbed to a sensation beyond pleasure, a kind of twisted relief that he'd macheted all his moorings, that whatever happened now would happen because he'd said "Fuck it" to everything that had rendered him, for more years than he could count, a soul-dead, heart-numbed misfit staggering from pill to pill just to get through the dull risk of his own existence.

Tina tasted like honey and cigarettes. The flavor lingered as he slid south over her throat. She undid her blouse and he kissed her nipples, accidentally biting the left, feeling it harden between his lips as she cried out. He raised his face, just to see her. Then he plunged under her skirt, up along her damp thighs where her panties had soaked through to the wet heart of her sex, like some small, throbbing animal waiting to be born on his tongue.

Tina began to murmur and Manny recognized a language he thought he'd lost forever. *"Anything,"* she whispered, as he breathed her in. *"Anything. . . ."* He knew her words had nothing to do with him, which made him want her more. In some strange way, they sounded like prayer.

Tina was almost there. *Almost.* Until, in a lightning flash of unwelcome awareness, Manny pushed off her, bolted upright, and blinked until he knew where he was. He looked down and saw Tina's eyes shining with the same wild excitement he felt himself. She met his gaze, then let loose the most crazed laugh he had ever heard.

Manny watched her, stunned—he realized he'd never heard her laugh—and when he saw that she was looking past him he raised his gaze to the faces looming outside all four of the Impala's windows. A pair of grinning old geezers, an outraged African-American lady in a flowered hat, some giggling punkettes wielding Cherry Big Gulps, and a pack of squealing, freckled boys mashing their faces against the glass on the driver's side. It was like *Night of the Living Dead,* with live people from Upper Marilyn, all watching him emerge, dazed and sticky-lipped, from beneath Tina's rumpled skirt.

"Jesus," Manny heard himself mutter. He hadn't noticed that he'd popped out of his pants, which only made Tina howl more insanely.

"Oh God, I'm going to pee," she stammered, hugging herself, until she saw Manny's expression and touched his lips. "Relax, Detective, they can't arrest you. You're a cop."

He was still absorbing this when, out of nowhere, he heard a voice he recognized but couldn't place. That's when he saw Krantz, mullet tucked safely under his police hat, tapping on the window, mouthing "Open up!"

TWENTY-EIGHT

Dr. Willard Roos poured his protein-and-hormone shake into a sixteen-ounce 7-Eleven Slurpy cup and checked his breasts in the mirror. A stoop-shouldered, mousy fellow who wore his hair in a Giuliani sweep, Roos favored lab coats and short-sleeve white shirts from Penneys.

He didn't particularly want breasts, but as a money-maker, Tits-in-a-Cup—that was his private name for the powder, which he planned to market as Fem-Fem—could be just the thing to bring in the cash he needed to hire a top lawyer or, if necessary, disappear and start his practice all over again in South Africa or Rio. So far nobody'd connected him to the Carmella Dendez thing, but if they did, he had his bag packed. In the lop-job business, you didn't rustproof a scalpel until you had an escape plan and an attorney on retainer.

It was Chooch, the day man at Pawnee Lodge, who'd called to inform him that the police had found Carmella's body. The surgeon had helped him with a stubborn goiter, and Chooch owed him a favor. Roos could guess what happened, but decided not to think about it. He focused instead on measuring the slight increase in nipple girth and fat content around his aureole. At this point he had the budding mammaries of a pubescent thirteen-year-old girl. When they grew in all the way, he planned on reversing the procedure with equivalent doses of testosterone. He knew it was risky—one wrong move and he'd end up with big breasts *and* extra chest hair—but he was confident he could pull it off. If not, he told himself bitterly, he could join a carnival or try for an Internet start-up: Hairy Men with Tits dot Com . . . "Products for the Man Who Has Everything."

Buttoning up, he padded to his desk and leafed through his appointment book. Business, as usual, was slow. A bride-to-be from Pittsburgh in at two for a tattoo removal. (The IBM exec she was marrying might not want to see CRIPS BITCH on her posterior.) Mayor Marge coming in for her monthly Botox. And Mrs. Fayton, the police chief's wife, who'd decided her ears were saggy and wanted a tuck. There was also a new patient, who gave his name as "Smith"—they all gave their name as "Smith"—stopping in for a transgender consultation. Roos had a dream of some day making Upper Marilyn as tranny-friendly as Trinidad, Colorado, which the legendary Dr. Biber had single-handedly built into the Sex Change Capital of the World. If only this Carmella thing hadn't happened. . . . Should word get out, it would put the kibosh on his dreams of Genital Reconstruction Glory.

Right now, Roos still had to develop the film Detective Rubert dropped off the last time he'd popped in for codeine scrips. Which was another thing. The prescription situation was starting to get worrisome. Though he had to admit, Manny had taken his share of risks for *him*. When he was caught shopping those she-male pix on the Net, it was Manny who convinced the FBI that he'd shut down his operations and disappeared.

Roos was still going by Dr. Mayo in those days. (If a patient asked, he'd say, "Yes, as a matter of fact, my great-grandfather *did* start the Mayo Clinic!") By way of saving his bacon, Manny led the team of feds to an abandoned doctor's office downtown to show them that the man they were after had vanished. An Air Guatemala schedule "discovered" under a phone book convinced the investigators their quarry would be too expensive to track down. Resources, apparently, were scarce. So Manny assured the agents he'd stay on the case for them: He even confided that he had a personal stake, since the butcher they were after had given a girlfriend a breast enhancement that left her with mismatched Santa hats.

Since quashing the investigation, however, Manny had been demanding favor after favor. There were the painkillers, of course, and the fake affidavit claiming that some flake named Marvin Podolsky had come in for "throat reconstruction"—as if there were such a thing— after swallowing drain cleaner on four separate occasions. Manny never explained why he needed it, and even after Roos read about Marvin's suicide, he still didn't know why Manny needed the false report. Not that it mattered. He was in no position to balk at the detective's requests.

Roos flipped on the lights in his outer office and sighed. He slept on a gurney in his examining room, just off the tiny reception area, and lately he'd been waking up every hour on the hour to take a stress pee. No doubt the estrogen had something to do with it. And Manny's mounting demands weren't helping, either. But what could he do? As long as his friend the detective was sitting on evidence that could put him away, he had to go along.

To his credit, Manny never asked for a penny. Sometimes Roos almost wished he would. Straight extortion might be easier. The doctor blushed to recall the time he protested having to write so many prescriptions. When he complained that he could lose his license, Manny had smiled and reminded him that he didn't *have* a license, so why worry about it? Until then, Roos hadn't realized Manny knew he'd been asked to leave med school in Granada after the unpleasant indigent incident. (Roos had tried some practice sex-change surgery on a comatose homeless man. How was he supposed to know the fellow would wake up, three days later, and have a coronary when he saw a vagina between his legs?)

That was the thing about Detective Rubert: He never let you know how much he knew, so you were always anxious that he knew more than he let on.

Dragging himself into the darkroom, Roos massaged his tiny breasts and checked on the photos soaking in the tray. He'd just set the timer for five minutes and slipped back to the examining room to stash his pajamas when he heard the office door open, and the unmistakable voice of the savior who was making his life hell.

"Willard, where are you?" Manny called. "We have business."

"Coming," Roos called back, shutting the darkroom door behind him. That was another thing about Detective Rubert. He didn't like to knock, and he seemed to have a key to everything.

"Dr. Roos, this is Tina. She's working with me," Manny announced, introducing a striking creature with the best cheekbones Roos had ever seen.

"Amazing bone structure," he said. "I'd love to make a mold of your face."

"I've had stranger propositions," Tina replied, taking in the dismal reception area and the nerdy little man in the lab coat who stood rubbing his rib cage before them. Some kind of very old vegetable soup stained the carpet—at least she hoped it was vegetable soup—and what had to be a pound of moth carcasses were visible in the light fixtures overhead. The only magazines on the filthy glass table were *Modern Brides.* By way of decoration, the doctor had taped up calendar pictures of frolicking kittens. But somehow, in this context, even kittens looked sleazy.

"I guess you know why I'm here," said Manny, noting the doctor's exceptional squirreliness. Roos was always the jumpy type, but now he looked like he'd shot up strychnine.

"I . . . I didn't know this would happen," Roos blurted. "After the first operation, I realized I used too much erectile tissue to construct the outer lips. That was a mistake, I admit. Whenever Carmella got aroused, her labia got hard. It was . . . embarrassing. She came in for her appointment very upset, and I don't blame her."

Roos wiped his forehead with the tail of his lab coat.

"Go on," Manny said.

"Well, naturally, I told her I'd do the reconstructive surgery for free. I removed the tissue and performed an ileum loop. I've done them before. You take a piece of intestine, leaving it attached to the blood supply, and divert it to make a vagina. It's fairly routine. But something went wrong. The patch of intestine continued to digest food, which meant that it secreted enzymes. At first it was just a matter of smell."

"Oh my God," said Tina, covering her mouth while Manny remained silent. Expressionless. Roos was confessing to something. Stomach-churning as it was, whatever he let slip could be used to squeeze him later.

"The odds of something like this happening are one in a million," Roos blabbed on, wiping his face with his coat again. "But it happened. She began to experience some leakage."

Tina groaned. "Leakage?" It was like listening to Don Knotts channel Joseph Mengele. But Manny held up his hand to quiet her, to let Roos talk.

"Feces," the doctor explained shakily. "Not a *lot*. But, of course, she was very concerned."

"Concerned?" Tina rolled her eyes. "I'm surprised she didn't come back and cut *yours* off!" Manny had to signal her a second time to stop interrupting.

"I brought the lady in for a third operation. No charge," Roos wanted them to know. He rubbed himself nervously. "This time I gave her a temporary shunt, to make sure there was no chance of peritonitis, then I went back to my original tissue construction. But one side of her vagina developed swelling. Toughening. So the final result was more . . . *uneven* than we would have liked. There were also some hair issues. Though, I assure you, when all was said and done, Carmella Dendez could perform like a woman."

"You're sure about that?"

"Absolutely!" Roos directed his appeal to Tina, unable to face Manny's ungiving stare. "Many females are naturally asymmetric. Among the Maori, it's actually considered a sign of beauty. And I think, at least I *pray*, by the end, even Carmella was satisfied."

"Who told you she died?" Manny asked casually. He'd bullied Fayton into keeping her death out of the paper for a day, so the news had to come from elsewhere. It was important that Roos keep squirming under the belief that he'd botched the surgery. That he'd killed her.

"Who told me? A friend, at the motel. He said you found her body."

"Right. And do you know how she died?"

The doctor pawed at his chest, his gaze shifting back and forth from Tina to Manny. "Well, aren't you here to . . . I mean, I just assumed there were complications. I often send patients to the Pawnee Lodge to recuperate. So when I heard, I naturally thought. . . ." He began kneading his chest more vigorously, with both hands, then caught himself and stopped.

"You have to believe me! She never even called. I swear to you, I would have been there to help out!"

"Sounds like you helped her plenty. I found your phone number in her hand," Manny lied, "and I don't think it's 'cause you were selling her Special K."

"You know I got out of that," Roos injected, his skin jellied with perspiration.

"Whatever. You're just lucky I got to the motel first, so I can cover your ass. You owe me big-time, Willard. Even more than before. More than you even know. Just one more question."

Roos touched his chest. *"What?"*

"Are my pictures ready?"

The doctor wilted. "Oh God. . . . They should be. If you wait here, I'll check."

"That's all right, I'll come with you. Be right back," he said to Tina and started off behind the stunned surgeon. Manny knew he had to stay with him, in case he decided to try something drastic. Nobody was more dangerous than a coward in a corner. And Roos had that trapped mouse look in his eyes.

Alone in the waiting room, Tina leafed through a *Modern Bride*. She was trying to block out the visuals of what happened to Carmella and let her eyes rest on a splashy ad. Beneath a full-page spread of some Doris Day blond in the arms of a doltish hunk, the caption read "Honeymoon jitters? Don't let menstrual cramps spoil your stay in paradise!" Could this be what Roos's customers thought they were getting when they bought vaginas? A life where the biggest romantic worry was whether or not Captain Blood was in town? Then again, ex-men probably didn't menstruate, so they wouldn't *have* to worry about it. Or did they? Maybe for an extra thousand, the twisted little sawbones could make them bleed.

No doubt the doctor had his own reasons for restricting his waiting room reading to bridal magazines. The whole subject made Tina want to spray her brain with Lysol. And yet, on some level, she understood the torment that drove a person to endure what Carmella endured. Her late husband had a theory that capitalism instilled humans with the sense that they weren't enough, that there was somebody else they were supposed to be. If they didn't believe this, according to Marvin, they'd never buy anything and the economy would disintegrate. The world would be overrun with happy, liberated idiots and chaos would ensue. The reason for advertising, in Marv's view, was to keep people feeling so creepy about themselves that they spent all their money on items which, deep down in their psyches, they believed could transform them into divine versions of who they really were. "We don't *need* shoes," he used to say, "we only wear them because we want god-feet." No doubt, if he were still around, her husband would tell her that a faux vagina was the ultimate consumer good, right up there with Lexus, Rolex, and a top-of-the-line Sony PlayStation.

Tina threw the magazine on the table, convinced all over again that, even if it was half an accident, things had gone the right way with Marv. "Things happen for a reason," he used to say. Wherever he was, she hoped he still felt that way. In any event, she'd no longer have to listen to his endless theorizing, which was almost as unendurable as his nose hums. Still, in this case, his notion of people wanting to be other people sounded on the money. Carlos needed to be someone else so badly he paid to get gelded and become Carmella. Now *that* was desperation. . . .

The scary thing was, Tina could relate to it. She just didn't know what she was desperate *for*. Although, after a hot five minutes in the Impala with Manny, she had a pretty good idea. Any man who'd keep one foot on the brake in the middle of an intersection while he kissed her all the way to her panties was amazing enough. What was more amazing—and she sighed just remembering—was that he was so into it, it never occurred to him to just pull over. Which meant, she supposed, he was either mentally challenged or the most passionate bastard in captivity.

Before she could chew on that, Manny himself slammed back in the room waving a stack of still wet photographs and grinning.

"Check these out," he said, slapping the eight-by-ten glossies on top of her *Modern Bride*.

Tina leaned in to take a look and blanched. "Romantic," was all she could think to say. She picked the first one up by the edge to take in the details: a black man built like a midget wrestler sodomizing a rangy white guy bent over a desk chair. The black guy bore an incredible resemblance to Dean Martin, and the white guy, when she squinted, looked like a pissed-off knucklehead version of the batty Mrs. Zank from Seventh Heaven. The same beady eyes and sour mouth. He also looked like he'd chewed through a plate glass window.

"So who are these lovebirds?" she asked.

"Nobody special," said Manny, taking the photographs back. "Just the two psychos who are trying to kill you. This picture might be exactly what we need to get 'em off your back."

Tina shook her head. "You know, until I met you, I thought this town was normal."

"It is. That's the funny part. You ready to go?"

Manny helped her out of the dirty vinyl chair, then stopped and snapped his fingers. "I almost forgot." He turned just as Dr. Roos, looking, if possible, even clammier than he had earlier, shuffled into the reception room. "Oh, Doctor, I have something I want to show you. I want to know what I can get for it on the Internet."

Manny reached in his jacket and pulled out the manila envelope, the one Tina'd yanked from under Dolly Zank's mattress. He carefully removed the photograph and showed it to Roos. The shock brought the sex doctor back to life. "Is that who I think it is?"

"If you mean, is that the president of our fine nation and our own Mayor Marge," said Manny, "the answer's yes. You've made some cash putting up extreme-o stuff, so what do you think?"

Roos rubbed his hands together. "I think it's way too hot for the Web." He hesitated, gently massaging himself, and gave Manny a sidelong glance. "Something like this, you want to stick to major media. I

know a guy—well, he's only a guy for another month or so—but he's very connected. Did a lot of Monica work. I can't tell you his name, but I bet he'd pay pretty heavy. But he'd probably want to shop it himself."

"How much is pretty heavy?"

"I can't say without speaking to him. But if you'd like to leave it. . . ."

"*Leave it?* Did someone stitch MORON on my forehead? I'm not going to fucking leave this with you! Talk to your guy and see what he offers."

"How do I know you're not going to bust him?"

"I didn't bust you, did I?"

"You need me," Roos said.

Manny narrowed his eyes. "I *use* you. Don't confuse the two." With that he snatched the photo back and slid it in the envelope. "I want an answer by tomorrow or I'll nail you for Carlos Dendez. After a jury hears what you did between his thighs, you'll be lucky to operate on queens in the joint for Q-Tips and pruno."

Roos's chin began to quiver and Manny clapped him on the back. "Now you're making me feel bad, Willard. I'll tell you what, you get me decent bank, I'll split it eighty-twenty. And I promise I won't tell the police chief's wife you gave her a face-lift without a license."

TWENTY-NINE

Mayor Marge took a nibble of Balance Bar—ginkgo-yogurt-berry—and rolled onto her back. She knew Lamb hated when she ate during massages, but she couldn't help it. She was tense. Bad enough Lipton doesn't show up for Chatlak's funeral. Then she spots his car at an intersection on the way to the cemetery. This after he actually had the gall to call and say he had a dentist's appointment. Nobody owned worse teeth than Lipton. It was part of his British charm. Mayor Marge had been to England, and the one lasting impression she took home was the unbelievably gross state of British dental care. The richer they were, the worse it was. Having crooked, yellow teeth, she concluded, was some kind of badge of honor. If you were a true aristocrat, you could flaunt your status by boasting canines that looked transplanted from a cocker spaniel. And don't get her going on British hygiene. . . . Much as she loved and admired Margaret Thatcher, there was no excusing the sorry truth about Great Britain's gums. But maybe, to be fair, the dental decline took place after Maggie left office.

"Spleen-verk!" Lamb barked as she began to knead away at the bottom left of Mayor Marge's stomach. The beefy German girl pounded extra hard—or so Marge felt—as punishment for noshing and talking on her cell phone during bodywork. Well, screw her! For $200 an hour, she could damn well send faxes, balance her checkbook, and eat an entire meatloaf, if she still ate meat.

The problem was, Mayor Marge already felt queasy, and the deep tissue work wasn't helping. The nausea had started at Chatlak's service, when Chief Fayton whispered in her ear that she looked "delicious."

Lyn Fayton! That pompous lunatic who got his picture taken every time somebody in Upper Marilyn got a parking ticket. For the funeral, the police chief had pinned on so many medals, badges, and stars he looked like a blue Christmas tree. To make matters worse, as they lowered the casket and the minister intoned the Twenty-third Psalm, Fayton leaned over again and told her that he found her "irresistible." *Yuk!* Not only had he suggested they "reconnoiter" after the ceremony, but, this was the kicker, he even told her that the two of them could be *really good* together: "Like Bill and Hillary, without that whole Lewinsky thing. . . ."

The really creepy part, beyond the fact that the chief was completely delusional, was that, even as he was speaking, it sounded like he was reading the words off cue cards. The man could not be spontaneous if he stubbed his toe and said, "Ouch."

"Ze eating compromizes ze prozess," Lamb complained, doing something with her knuckles on Marge's kidneys that had her writhing. Her Honor crunched another bite of Balance Bar and considered her options. She could call up her ex, that low-life son of a bitch, and ask him to tail Lipton, to bring him to ground. But how would she explain it? "Well, you see, Manuel"—she could never bring herself to say "Manny," which sounded so ethnic—"I think my assistant may be going off the deep end, and I need him for a special assignment I can't really talk about, since it involves a photograph of me and the presi-

dent's privates. Oh, and did I mention the smiley-face? Please don't ask questions!"

A sudden thought jolted Marge upright. She nearly banged heads with Lamb, who stepped back furiously.

"Vot is the meaning of zis?"

"I have to make a phone call. Take five."

The masseuse, a large-pored, perpetually scowling bottle-blond who'd come to America to compete in bodybuilding, glowered as if someone had insulted her family. Marge ignored her. Being mayor meant not having to be liked by people who didn't matter. She didn't think Lipton would have the nerve to rip her off. But still, he was the one who'd told her that somebody had broken into the mansion and made off with Mister Biobrain. Temptation was temptation. Other stuff was missing, but what did *that* mean? He could have taken the watches and jewels, to make it look like garden-variety burglary. Or he could be in cahoots with some rough trade who did it for him. Nobody looked more elegant than Lipton: perfect hair, male model lips, a glamorous bearing, and confident stride. The man would have come off suave in sackcloth and ashes. Everything about him spelled class, except for those teeth, and on him, even *they* somehow worked. But so what? That didn't mean he didn't know people capable of a little light breaking-and-entering. Especially when he had keys to the house.

After the crime was discovered, Lipton assured her he could get the photograph back himself. She could still hear him, sounding almost cocky. "Leave it to me, ma'am. I'm the resourceful type." How could she let herself fall for that *Upstairs, Downstairs* crap?

The more she kicked it around, the more likely it seemed. Lipton had been with her forever, but who knew what he did on his weekends off? Or what went on in that dentally challenged head of his. No doubt he harbored his own mammoth ambitions. Ambitions that required money. The payoff potential of something as explosive as her Bush party-picture was pretty much unlimited.

Just to make the scenario more chilling, Lipton had been there every step of the way. Which meant he knew her contacts. Her *Republicans*. He even knew their phone numbers, because *he* dialed the phone. Damn! Perhaps she *should* have cut him in for something. . . .

Marge closed her eyes. Part of her wanted to just get up, to tear back to the mansion and start rifling Lipton's quarters. But it would take a while to get there, and God knew how long to go through his stuff. She wasn't sure she even *wanted* to touch anything of Lipton's. Plus which, what was she really looking for? A check stub? A scribbled fax number? Maybe a business card: B&E'S ARE US. . . . Not likely.

The problem was, there were too many variables. And time was crucial. Mayor Marge knew she had to make a decision now. If it turned out that she was wrong, that Lipton had some legitimate reason for disappearing, then she could clear her tracks later—come up with a lovely and feasible explanation for doing what she was about to do. What else was politics but fucking people over and making them believe that you did it for them? Or better yet, that they weren't being fucked at all. That, thanks to you, they were actually being *helped*.

Exactly! No doubt her personal assistant would be less than delighted to hear that she'd sicced a detective on him. But she would explain. She would say that she thought something had happened to him. When he didn't turn up at the funeral, or answer his phone, she grew *concerned*. She was *afraid* he may have been in some kind of *danger*, and she wanted to *help*. That sounded convincing enough. *I did it because I care.* . . .

Decided. She'd call her ex, the low-end detective. He'd be suspicious, but that prick was always suspicious. She could live with the ex-husbandy snide remarks. As long as he didn't suspect anything about W.'s genitals—and why would he?—she wouldn't hesitate to let him think she and Lipton were having an affair. She knew how his mind worked. She'd have the last laugh later. That's all that counted.

Ignoring Lamb's furious sighs, Mayor Marge reached for her Star-TAC and poked out Manny's number. She got his voice mail ("Talk if you have to") and spoke in as even a manner as she could under the circumstances: "This is the mayor. I've got a problem. My assistant, Lipton, is missing and I need you to find him." She paused a second, then added, "I'm not certain, but I'm afraid something may have happened to him. As soon as you know anything, call." She slammed the phone shut, then quickly snapped it open again and hit Redial. "And Manuel," she added, "I do not want this going through Fayton. Report directly to me."

Mayor Marge tossed the phone in her bag and laid down again, determined to relax if it killed her. Nothing happened. When she opened her eyes Lamb was standing above her, arms crossed, glaring down.

"*I vill not be treated like zis! I am pro-vessional.*"

Mayor Marge eyed her evenly. She didn't enjoy the pummelings Lamb gave her, but she always felt better afterward. Without bothering to sit up, the mayor asked about the state of Lamb's green card application. More than once, Lamb had complained that she couldn't compete on the women's bodybuilding circuit until she got her card. Marge had promised to look into it, though she certainly hadn't strained herself doing so. Making promises was just another part of being mayor.

"*Iz not good,*" Lamb replied, her defiant posture suddenly sagging. "*Iz not good at all.*"

"Well," said Marge, settling herself more comfortably on the massage table, "I think I've found somebody who can help. Of course, I can't guarantee anything, but I think we can get your application on the fast track."

Lamb nodded, a flush of scarlet darkening her extra-large pores. "*Zis iz true, ja?*"

"Like I say, I can't guarantee," Marge said, closing her eyes and anticipating another forty minutes of therapeutic kneading. "But I'll put in another call after we finish."

Lamb grabbed a squeeze bottle of massage oil and squirted a puddle in her meaty hands.

"*Very good,*" she announced. "*Now ve attack ze rump!*"

THIRTY

It was Zank's idea to peddle the stolen crack to L'il Pepe, the fourteen-year-old who worked the corner across from Clemente Elementary. Tony copped from L'il Pepe all the time, so he naturally figured the slinger would be bitch-happy one of his best customers had some stuff for him. At a discount. Unfortunately, L'il Pepe took one look at the chunk Tony handed him and threw it back in his face. "Yo, you think I'm a dumb ass, you Anglo motherfucker? You think 'cause I'm part Rican, I'm some retardo punk?"

L'il Pepe was short for his age, with a voice like a little girl and the dead eyes of a con who'd walked the yard for a decade. McCardle was sure Tony was going to kill him. Instead, he just froze, and Mac nearly scorched his shorts when the boy yanked a sawed-off out of his pant leg and stuck it in the Lincoln's window.

"Wanna piece of this?" L'il Pepe asked in that little girl voice. It was like being jacked up by Alfalfa, if Alfalfa sold crack and packed a hog-leg. The youngster kept taunting him. "Huh, Zank? You tore-up, loco *maricón*. Come over here and diss *me* with your fuckin' bone chips? Tryin' to sell *me* a chopped-up kneecap or some shit? You gotta be out your fucking *mind,* homes!"

Somewhere a boom box blasted Snoop Doggy Dogg. *"You don't wanna step to me. . . ."* McCardle got worse heebie-jeebies when he saw a boy-gangster even smaller than L'il Pepe mad-dog him. He might have been the crack dwarf's brown-skinned cousin. The tiny banger, who was maybe six, seven tops, leaned on a graffitied garbage can smoking a heater. He sported a shaved head and what must have been size five children's Nikes. Mac heard him brag to the thug-in-training beside him that he was making twenty bucks working look-out, and that a white lady showed him her tits in the lobby of his building. "Way she hug me, I know she be wantin' my ass. She wantin' it *bad.*"

Clemente Elementary, McCardle had read in the *Trumpet,* had just installed a metal detector, and he suspected these boys might have been the reason. They didn't look like honor roll material. It was as if he and Tony had been air-dropped onto the Planet of Pee-Wee Gang-bangers. Mac felt righteous anger, watching them front. Where were their parents? *The middle of the goddamn day!* If he had any say, these young men would be chained to their desks, memorizing state capitals. He was a big believer in education and discipline. That's what made good citizens! He just wished they could finish the crack deal and get the fuck out of there.

McCardle sighed and glanced at the sky, often a source of solace in high-stress situations. He glanced down again to a gaggle of killer pre-pubes that had somehow cropped up alongside the Lincoln. They weren't surrounding the car, but they were definitely within banging distance. He had a twitchy vision of being set upon by an army of shrieking seven-year-olds, ripped apart by dirty fingernails and milk teeth. *Lord of the Flies* with Puerto-billies.

At that moment, a stoop-shouldered white man in a plaid sportcoat strolled to the Clemente playground fence. His face registered what was going on across the street. Mac made him for a teacher by the way he backed away and ran. A civilian would have wanted to *do* something—L'il Pepe wasn't exactly trying to hide the shotgun. But a teacher would *know.* You didn't fuck with armed prepubescents. This was America.

Meanwhile, Tony, no longer frozen, kept staring at the full-to-bursting baggies on the front seat. He looked like a man who'd won a suitcase full of fifties and found out they were counterfeit. McCardle was shocked when his friend began to sniffle. "I thought we had it made. . . ." He punctuated the words with vicious little dashboard punches. *"I thought this stuff was good. . . ."* Mac had only seen him like this when they ran out of crack with no alcohol to cut the crash.

"You thought it was *good?*" Li'l Pepe poked him in the jaw with his sawed-off. "Now you *really* gettin' on my jock."

Mac wondered if he should do something. But what? Tony's .357 was still in the torture kit. He couldn't very well start groping around for it. When Tony finally raised his eyes to the grade school gangster, they were brimming with tears. Pepe hitched up his pants and glared in disbelief. "Mang! You really *is* a pussy!"

The boy was still sneering when Zank snapped. He whacked the sawed-off aside, clamped a hand around the muzzle, and made a play for the bulk in the baby dealer's pocket. L'il Pepe spun sideways, trying to wrestle the shotgun back. But Tony was too strong. Man and boy grunted in an impromptu tug-of-war. Terrified Pepe was going to fire, McCardle dropped facedown on the car rug. He didn't want to get maimed by a seventh grader and could all but feel the hot metal searing through his massive lats.

L'il Pepe screamed for Tony to let go, and Tony pulled harder. He twisted his fingers in the pocket of Pepe's Tommy Hilfigers, clawing and growling until he hooked the stash: a dozen or so vials crammed in a knotted baggie. Tony let out a cackle and said, *"Fuckin' beautiful!"* That's when L'il Pepe pulled the trigger. An ear-crunching boom split the air, followed by an evil hiss, like an expiring Gila monster. The car lurched left and down onto the curb. L'il Pepe had shot out the front tire.

After the blast, Mac's eardrums felt like they'd been poked with knitting needles. L'il Pepe, impervious, saw his chance and snatched the crack back out of Zank's lap, then slammed the still-smoking muzzle across his jaw. Tony crumbled and spit out a tooth. L'il Pepe laughed. He and his little pals thought this was hysterical. To cap the fun, the boy worked up a hock, grinned, and spit a goober the size of a chicken head onto Tony's cheek.

"Teach you to come 'round my turf tryin' to sell me bones 'n shit."

Tony didn't bother to wipe his face. Instead he grinned back, lips peeled to show the fresh gap on the lower left. Then he waved to L'il Pepe and his sneering crew, and started the car. Now all of them were spitting. Tony gunned the engine for a few more seconds. Then he blew Pepe a kiss, slammed into Drive, and threw open the door at the exact instant the Lincoln launched from zero to forty. The black metal slab caught the dealer and a taller boy in a bandanna. Bandanna hit the sidewalk. But L'il Pepe got dragged, his ankle caught between car door and concrete. He screamed horribly, his high voice going even higher. Tony smirked and pressed his shoulder to the door, wedging the kid's leg to the curb as the Lincoln churned forward.

"Tony, NO!" McCardle shouted. But Zank just chuckled. Pepe's shrieks seemed to tickle him. "Teach that banger to diss Tony Z!" he hooted, slapping his free hand on the steering wheel. "That's the trouble with this damn country. Kids got no respect for their elders!"

Pepe's Hilfigers tore away, and the sight of the stick-thin brown calf underneath made McCardle shiver. He screamed *"Stop!"* and Tony cackled louder, keeping the gas pedal jammed to the floor. L'il Pepe bumped along the curb for another few feet, then the car gave a lurch and, as if shaking its anchor, veered off and clattered up to speed. McCardle craned around to see the crowd. A dozen people hunched over the boy's body, and a dozen more were tearing up the street after the Lincoln. "Hoo-wee, looky," Zank chortled. "A parade!"

As they rounded the corner, Zank's laughter grew manic. Which is when McCardle saw the little foot wedged in the door. The bottom of the boy's Nike was remarkably clean. It occurred to Mac, in the middle of everything, that L'il Pepe had probably just taken the shoe out of the box that day.

When he saw McCardle gawking, Tony giggled. He reached down and grabbed the shoe. The ankle stump protruded from the top, ragged muscle and skin around shattered bone, trailing blood on the uphol-stery. The laces were still neatly tied.

"Footloose," Tony hooted, waving the stuffed tennis shoe in McCardle's face.

Mac slapped him away, and the Nike landed in the seat between them. He snatched it up without thinking, surprised how heavy it was. *Same thing with Cornish hens,* he thought, idiotically, until he felt the worm-warmth of blood wriggling down his wrist and tossed the thing. The foot plopped onto Tony's crotch, and the Lincoln swerved across the double line and screeched to a stop on the wrong side of the road. A green Jeep honked as it swerved to miss them and Zank waggled Pepe's foot out the window. "Honk on this, asshole!"

Tony swung back across the double line without looking and parked. "I'm fucked," he shouted, working a grubby finger in the hole where his tooth had been. He mumbled furiously around the digit, "Mac, slide over. Take the goddamn wheel!"

"You know I can't drive," McCardle protested. "I got a *phobia.*"

Tony foot-whopped him in the chest, then pointed the toe of the shoe at his own bloody mouth. "You see what that little prick did to me? You think my tooth is gonna grow back? Shut up and fucking drive!"

McCardle sulked, trying not to look directly at Tony's smeary face. "Okay. But we go into a ditch, don't say I didn't warn you."

There followed an awkward moment when, to get by, Mac had to kind of shimmy over Tony's lap—"I ain't no tail gunner, Dark Meat, so keep movin'!"—but after that Tony just slumped in the corner, wiping his wounds with his sleeve. The air seemed to have gone out of him. The instant McCardle saw him close his eyes, he snatched Pepe's foot by the toe and tossed it out the window. There was probably some dog out there who would have a happy dinner. It was important to be kind to animals. Plus which, he didn't know much about search and seizure, but he figured if the cops peeked in and saw a torn-off foot in your car, they probably had the right to rifle it without a warrant. Which could not lead to anything good.

Half blind with terror, McCardle twice steered the Lincoln over a curb, upending a mailbox and a bus bench advertising some funeral home. Driving on four wheels was hard enough. Trying to steer on three and an axle was making him sweat. The Lincoln kept listing left, and the shotgunned tire made an obscene flapping noise, a sort of *thwoppeta-thwoppeta* as McCardle alternately lurched forward and slammed on the brakes.

Mac stressed out loud about getting pulled over. But Tony, nursing his newest wound, insisted the cops wouldn't be stopping anybody— they were too busy getting shitfaced on account of planting one of their own. "It's a union thing," he explained, still probing the fresh hole in his gums, "police funerals and Christmas they're allowed to booze all day. You wanna knock over a pharmacy? Rob a bank? Wait till they're sinkin' a cop, you get a guaranteed Pasadena."

For another five minutes, McCardle clattered through sleepy side streets, gradually getting the hang of the whole steering and stopping thing. If he'd been driving on four tires, he might even have enjoyed himself. But when he saw a red light up ahead, feeding into Liberty Boulevard, he started to worry.

"Hey, T, I gotta know where we're goin', man! People are startin' to stare. . . . We gotta make a decision."

"Like what?"

"Like either we kick it at your place. Or we double back, check for the photo again at that chick Tina's."

Mention of Tina got Zank fired up all over again. "Bitch tricked us, you know that?" The missing tooth didn't impede his speech, but it made him spray when he spoke, forcing Mac to shrink back in his seat. "She planted the fake rock just to cluster-fuck us. Same with those dead bunnies, and that goddamn bloodsicle on a string. You know why she's even *alive?*"

"I don't," said McCardle.

"To *fuck* us, that's why." Zank gave a meaningful nod. "Somebody in hell paid Satan to send her up here to fuck us."

"So," said Mac, after what he thought was a pause appropriate to Zank's last pronouncement, "you wanna go back and get the picture?"

"What the fuck you think? I'm a cunthair away from pulling a Steubenville."

McCardle did not bother asking what that meant. He didn't want to know. When Zank was amping out like this, it was better not to.

Tony angled into the rearview, tugging back his bloody lip to get a better view inside his mouth. "Least it's not my front teeth," he sprayed. "The little spic knocks out one of my front teeth, I'm not just ripping his foot off, I'm goin' for the burrito platter."

"He was only a kid," McCardle ventured. "He could bleed to death, man. That's not right. That's just . . . *wrong!*"

"Fuck him," Tony spat. "He was old enough to diss me, wasn't he? And what about my tooth? Think they grow on trees? I don't think so. I'm gonna have to pay for a new one. Only place they give you free teeth is in jail. And I ain't goin' back to County for that."

Just then, they noticed the car full of punk types watching them from a blue Saab parked across the street.

"*Wave* to 'em," Tony ordered, slinking down in the seat.

"What?"

"Wave to 'em. My face is too fucked-up. It'll freak 'em out. Pull over, then walk over and ask what they're lookin' for."

"Why?"

"Why do you think?" Zank spritzed red when he yelled. "We got four bags full of dick-knuckle sittin' here. Tell 'em we're havin' the sale of the century."

After a minute, Mac returned to the Lincoln and leaned in the window.

"They say they're in a band. Told me they wanted fish-scales. It took me a minute to figure out that meant crack."

"They got money?"

"I told 'em five hundred a bag."

"They went for that?"

"Not really. I'm gettin' seventy-five for two. You wanna keep two for us, right?"

Tony shifted in his seat. "Whatever." When Mac reached in for the crack bags, Tony grabbed his hand. "I'm going to count to fifty, then I'm gonna roll up on you." Tony eased the .357 from under a thigh.

McCardle jerked back. "What are you doing?"

"Don't fucking worry about it. Just give 'em the shit and get the money. When you hear me say Limp Bizkit get outta the way."

"Limp Bizkit?"

"Wake up and smell the MTV. They love that shit. Get going."

McCardle went, wondering if Tony had *meant* to point the gun at him, or if he'd only imagined it. When he got a foot or two from the blue Saab, he flashed the baggies and said, "Show me the dough. Real slow like."

The kid behind the wheel, a sweating, sucked-up tweaker with bushy muttonchops spilling out under his FUCT cap, nodded like he understood. He looked at the pimply girl beside him and another skinny kid with a shaved head and—unless Mac was hallucinating—the Incredible Hulk tattooed on his scalp.

The sweating driver reached for the bag and Mac pulled it away. "Huh-uh. Show me the money."

"How do we know it's good?"

Mac caught the wad of twenties in the driver's fist. "How do you know it's *good?*" He was about to drop some jive when he heard the footsteps behind him.

"Limp Bizkit!" Tony hollered, rushing the car, and Mac jerked out of the way

"Limp Bizkit?" came the girl's voice. "Are you lame or what?"

Tony bent down to let all three enjoy his face. By now, it looked like he'd scrubbed it with a cheese grater. There wasn't a square inch that wasn't swollen, scabbed-up, black and blue, or still bleeding. Tony's face was all FUCT Hat needed to see. He went for the ignition and Tony jammed the gun in his muttonchop.

"I know what you're thinking," he said, as pleasant as Mac had ever heard him. "You're thinking, 'Oh, here's another badass with a .357. BFD—*Big Fucking Deal.*' One on every corner, right?"

The trio gaped in silence. Tony rubbed the muzzle around the boy's temple, then snatched off his FUCT cap and tried it on. "Well, guess what, Young America. This is not just another .357. For your information, this happens to be a Colt Python .357 Magnum with a modified four-inch barrel. What's special about that? Well, I'm glad you asked. What's special is, it takes a heavy bullet. Am I pitching over your head here? I drop a heavy bullet in this death-dog, it's gonna generate six hundred foot pounds with every—fuck, maybe I *am* going too fast. . . ."

Tony thrust himself half in the car and grabbed the shaved-skull boy by his nose ring, twisting until he curled in the seat and squealed. A siren sounded somewhere behind them. "The Incredible Hulk," Tony cried, when he made out his scalp ink. "I bet that drives the girls crazy, huh? Bet they just cream up when they see Lou Ferrigno on your head." He wrenched the nose ring some more and the Hulk-head began to cry.

"Maybe," Zank continued, keeping the tone conversational, "being musicians and all, you didn't take physics. That's cool. I'll make it real simple." He held up the .357, checked the load, and wrist-snapped the cylinder back in place. "A bullet from this motherfucker can punch through a truck. I mean it. Right through the engine block. Like it was made of paper towels. You wanna think about what that could do to your dangerous haircuts, or you wanna gimme your fucking money?"

Quickly, the rock 'n' rollers began thrashing around for cash.

"Right on," said Tony. "Now take off your fucking clothes and throw 'em out the window. Start at the bottom and work up. Do it!"

Boots, socks, and pants came flying out of the Saab. Followed by jackets, T-shirts, and a black lace bra. Zank elbowed McCardle and leered. "Panties, too, Ellie May. Hand 'em over. And you studs peel off your undies. Hurry up, I'm clothin' the homeless."

When he was holding three sets of underwear and three wallets with chains attached, Zank tried to open the door, but it was locked. He sniffed the girl's leopard-skin panties and made a face.

"*Somebody's* bakin' brownies." He balled up the panties and shoved them in the driver's mouth. "You wanna play games, Iggy Pop? I'll play fuckin' games. You must be a real brainiac, lockin' the door and leavin' the window open."

Tony inscribed a tight circle on the driver's cheek with the gun barrel. The kid nodded frantically, still biting the leopard-skin, and the autolock made a satisfying crunch as the doors unlocked.

"That's better." Tony made his voice coplike. *"Now step away from the vehicle."*

During this performance, McCardle kept glancing up and down the street. Citizens driving by either didn't see them or didn't want to. Zank had that effect on people. Still, Mac was worried. "Tony, man, somebody's gonna call the police." He knew it would piss Tony off, but he couldn't help himself.

Sure enough, Zank glared. "Be a black man, McCardle. *Fuck the po-lice!*"

Mac stopped talking after that. He wrung his hands while Tony marched up and down beside the Saab, smiling and bleeding like a depraved valet as the naked driver slid out of the car and handed him the keys. The naked girl followed, her arms over her breasts and a giant red squid tattooed over her ass. Wavy blue tentacles extended down-ward, embracing the word **PRODUCT** in Gothic script. Tony leered at her, tongue poking through the hole where his tooth had been. "How'd you know I love seafood, beautiful? If we didn't have business, I'd take you with. I don't care what anybody says, I like little tits. How 'bout it?"

Zank puckered up, and even McCardle had to cringe. The girl shuddered and crouched behind the driver as Hulk-skull, cupping his bleeding nose, joined them on the street.

"You're right," Tony sighed, "business before torture. But tell you what, just to show I'm a stand-up guy, you can keep the crack. Fuck it, I'll even throw in the keys to the Lincoln. All she needs is some axle work. And a new tire. But hey, you can't argue with the price."

Two blocks later, Mac couldn't hold his mud anymore. "Man, we can't just drive around. We gotta *go* somewhere."

"Who's drivin' around," Tony said. "I'm just getting the feel of this cage. I never rode Swede before."

"I just want to know what we're doing."

Tony grumbled. "Back to Plan A, okay? We swing back and tor-ment the bitch 'til she tells us where the photo's at. She has it, we grab it. She doesn't, we rip off whatever she's got, then find out where it is."

"What if she *gave* the picture to somebody? You know, to help unload it." If it were *him* stuck with Mister Biobrain, Mac figured he'd hook up with a fence who knew what to do with the thing and split it fifty-fifty.

"If she gave it to somebody, then we got no choice."

"Meaning what?"

"Meaning we fuck her 'till she goes bald, then sell her for parts.

Anybody dumb enough to give somethin' worth a million bucks to somebody else *deserves* a dirt nap. We'd be doing her a favor."

Tony produced a Slim Jim and belched as he shoved it in his mouth. His jerky burps blended with the scented pine tree dangling from the rearview, perfuming the Saab with a peculiar, woody halitosis odor, a pungent, piney-beef combo that nearly burned the skin.

McCardle, blinking tears from his eyes, realized they were driving right by Tina's front yard. "Tony, pull up. This is it!"

"This is shit," Tony hollered back, without slowing down. "We go in there and do her, I wanna be smoked up."

"Where we gonna get it?"

"Fucking Pepe can't run too fast on one foot. We head on over and take off his corner, then we come back and party with the pretty thief."

Tony gunned the Swedish engine. McCardle closed his eyes and prayed.

THIRTY-ONE

"Mustard or dry?"

"Mustard. Lots."

Stuey the Hunchback plucked a pretzel out of his oven and went to work. He'd parked his cart in the mini-mall parking lot between Dr. Roos's office and the Ross Dress for Less next door. Tina and Manny ran into him after leaving the squirrelly plastic surgeon, and Manny insisted on stopping. The pretzel vendor, an Upper Marilyn institution, was a surprisingly vigorous eighty. His claim to fame was having been an extra in *On the Waterfront*. By way of nostalgia—and proof—he kept a photo of Brando taped to the side of his cart, signed "To Mike, from your friend Marlon Brando." When anybody asked why the actor signed the picture to somebody else, the hunchback would tug up the collar of the pea coat he wore year-round—in the manner of a fifties stevedore—and explain defensively, "If Marlon liked you, he called you Mike."

Stuey slathered French's like a cake artist on the jumbo pretzel, and winked at Tina. "I know you ladies like 'em wet."

"Aren't you cute?" Tina accepted the the hot bow of salted dough and aimed a smile at Manny. "Pretzels, plastic flowers, boy-boy pictures—I've said it before, Detective, you know how to make a girl feel special."

"Nut-cruncher," said Stuey, slamming the lid on his oven. "Eva Marie Saint was the same way. Used to tease Marlon somethin' awful. Kept tellin' 'im Mickey Rooney was better in the sack. Give 'im credit, though, Marlon never popped her. Strangled a pigeon once, during the rooftop scene, but he never smacked Eva Marie, even when she was beggin' for it."

Stuey rolled off, still muttering, and Manny pulled out his cell phone. Tina grabbed his arm. "Hang on. You want to tell me what that was all about? Starting with Pretzel-man?"

Manny lowered the phone. "Stuey's got ears. Sometimes he tells me stuff."

"He's a snitch?"

"I prefer 'information facilitator.' He fences, too. You want a Game Boy, a CD player, some videos, he's got a regular small appliance store in that oven. Kids rip the radio out of a Beamer, they know Stuey's good for a dime bag."

"He deals, too?"

"It's called multitasking. C'mon, I have to check my messages."

He lifted the phone, and Tina stopped him again.

"If he's an informant, why didn't you ask him about Zank and McCardle? And how did he know you'd be here?"

Manny sighed. "Stuey moves around. He probably saw my car. There aren't a lot of mayo Impalas on the streets these days."

"So ask him if knows anything about those freaks."

The look Manny gave her was almost sad. "I ask him about somebody, I know he's gonna tell whoever I asked about that I was asking. Sometimes that's okay. Sometimes that's the idea. But right now, the best thing we got going is that Zank and McCardle don't know we're onto them. I mention them to Stuey, that could change. You never know."

Tina nibbled the hot pretzel, slow-licking mustard off the top while Manny tried to concentrate on calling his answering machine. Since he'd never read the manual, he hadn't put himself on speed dial. But the buttons on his cell phone were so tiny, he felt stump-fingered. He looked up and Tina was still licking. "Must be fun," she said, "being a dick."

"Not now, okay?"

Manny aimed his eyes somewhere else. How could anybody make eating a jumbo pretzel nasty? His machine sounded like it was in Greenland, and he had to cover his free ear to hear. When he was done he snatched the pretzel from Tina, took a bite, and said, "Strange."

"What's strange?"

He handed the pretzel back. "I got two calls. One from my ex-wife's assistant, this Brit named Lipton. Gay guy. Very cool. He tells me his car's been stolen, but not to say anything to my ex-wife. Then I get a call from my ex, telling me Lipton's *missing*, would I please find him, and by the way don't say anything to Chief Fayton."

"It's nice you two keep in touch."

"Me and Fayton?"

"You and the ex. It's heartwarming."

Manny ignored the sarcasm. "Actually, this is the first time she's called since we were divorced. She didn't even call *before* we were divorced. I'm telling you, if Mayor Marge is picking up the phone and calling *me*, she must be sweating. And our mayor doesn't sweat easy."

"I guess you'd know. So what are you going to do?"

"Let her sweat, what else?"

"That's what I like," said Tina, "a man of action. What about this Lipton guy?"

"DWIL."

"What?"

"Deal-With-It-Later. Right now you and I have some business."

Manny took her roughly by the arm and led her toward the car.

"Ooh, police brutality. Maybe later you can show me your cuffs."

"Please, if anyone's watching, I want 'em to think I'm arresting you."

"Oh wow. Most guys just say, 'C'mon baby, you know you want it.' "

"So you're not a virgin?"

"No, but I'm sure your pal Roos could make me one. I'd probably end up shitting out of my armpit, but what the hell, it'd be worth it to feel nine again."

"You," said Manny, "are a very unique girl."

"You want unique? We had a virgin once at Seventh Heaven. Seventy-seven and never been kissed. Her name was Phoebe. One time I asked her why she never tried it and she said, 'Darlin', I just didn't want none of them female problems.' The old men used to give her ten bucks to show them her hymen. It looked like a big pink fang."

"Oh, man. . . ."

"No wait. You'll like this. There were six old goats who paid for a peek every Sunday. You should've seen them, bulging their diapers and dragging their IVs back to their rooms before they lost their inspiration. *Dignity in the Twilight Years.* That's what it says in the brochure."

"This is really fascinating," said Manny, "but we better get back to your house. See if the psycho-twins have been to visit. I have a plan."

"You wanna make God laugh, make a plan," said Tina.

"Guys like Zank running around, He could probably *use* a laugh."

Manny held open the Impala's dented passenger door. "But even if it just pisses God off, you're gonna like it. It's a little sick." With this he pushed her into the car and leaned in to sneak a bite of her mouth.

Tina returned his kiss, then pulled back. *"Smooth."*

THIRTY-TWO

Lipton scuttled on hands and knees beneath the window, trying to hold his breath and not sneeze. The whole neighborhood smelled as if it had been built on top of rotting carcasses. In his near delirium, Lipton imagined that some giant muskrat, Three Mile Islanded, had spawned a Buick-sized brood who scooted south to this corner of Upper Marilyn, then slunk underground and died. The sour must off Zank's shag did battle with the dead animal fumes. This close to the magenta fibers, breathing Zank's personal odor, Lipton felt weirdly intimate with the man who'd ripped him off. *I'm sick in the head*, that odor said. *I never change my clothes. I smoke crack and stay up for months.* It was horrifying.

"I am such a dunce," Lipton thought bitterly. Of course a crook like Tony Zank would double-cross him!

He'd been dumb enough to hire him to burgle his own home—the mayor's mansion, in which Lipton occupied a room on the top floor—so why wouldn't Zank think he could get away with screwing him? Who was he going to call, the police? "Why not just wear a sign around my neck," Lipton muttered, in a tizzy of self-recrimination, "I'm a complete boob, please steal from me!"

He pounded the floor, then peeked under the sofa to see if maybe the photos were under there. His Armani jacket was already stained from the garbage-and-beer-soiled carpet, so he stopped worrying about it.

Demoralized, Lipton recalled the neat little map he'd made for Tony, all those ruler-straight arrows to the jewelry drawers and the nightstand where Mayor Marge kept her twin Cartier watches. He jammed a fist in his mouth to keep from screaming.

If they show that map in court, I'm dead. . . .

DON'T THINK ABOUT IT!

Oh God, please help me. . . .

Lipton felt the panic attack coming on. What was he thinking when he trusted Tony Zank? Well, he knew what he was thinking. . . . It was his eighth day on Wellbutrin, and he'd had a sudden burst of world-changing confidence. Everything was going to be okay! He had energy. He felt charged-up, capable of great things. So he went to the Parakeet Lounge, the only gay bar in Upper Marilyn, to celebrate. And got arrested.

Look where you met him, he derided himself, *in the holding tank!*

This was *after* the unfortunate morning he'd found himself swooped up in the backroom of the Parakeet. It happened during the Church Hour. Sunday morning at ten, when Tiny the bartender gave you every third drink free. Nobody was there but Lipton and a couple of regulars, along with Tiny himself, watching Siegfried & Roy. Tiny had a major Siegfried thing. Somebody in Vegas shipped him show-tapes twice a month.

Anyway, Lipton was happily sipping banana daiquiris, watching Roy kiss a tiger on the lips, when, out of nowhere, there's this fat cop, Officer Merch, smirking behind him. "Hands on the bar, ladies."

Next thing you know, Lipton, still cashmere elegant, is in the slam. And Tony Zank is asking him to trade shoes. Well, not *asking* exactly. . . . Lipton handed over his square-toed Prada loafers, and Tony tossed him his own pair of damp, filthy, hole-in-the-bottom generic tennis shoes with the laces missing in return. After that they were friends.

Riding his daiquiri-laced Wellbutrin buzz, just *bursting* with fellow feeling, Lipton chattered away to his cellmate about his job: how much he *adored* living at the mansion, and how much stress was involved, *like you wouldn't believe,* trying to keep Mayor Marge stocked with L'eggs panty hose, her absolute *fave,* or running to the airport to pick up visiting venture capitalists.

Somehow, by the time he was sprung—Merch wanted $300 for tearing up the arrest report and driving him back to his car in the Parakeet lot—Lipton had drawn Zank a map of the mansion's treasures, told him where he could find a key, and given him special instructions on how to find A Certain Photograph. Hating himself, he remembered Tony's grin when he'd explained his one condition: "I keep the photograph, Tony, you can keep everything else."

"Don't worry," Tony had said, running his fingers through Lipton's pompadour. "You have real power hair. I'd rather have hair like that than all the money in the world."

Lipton found himself running his own fingers through his pomp when he thought about it. No doubt Zank, in his criminal fashion, was toying with him. Only he'd been too naïve to see it.

Ricocheting between panic and despair, Lipton plucked a fist-size dust-kitten off his nostril and swept his arm under the couch. *"Oh please,"* he pleaded, appealing to the Divine Being he imagined ruled the universe, a sympathetic, slightly crazed diva, like Judy Garland in her tranq-plagued later years, *"I deserve it!"* The problem was, he didn't just want money, he *needed* it. And the person he needed to give it to needed it as much as he did.

Lipton's thoughts whirled in frantic circles. If he could only *find* it, he had no doubt he could parlay the close-up of those puffed-out, illustrated presidential testicles into boatloads of cash. For days, after the mansion was burgled, he'd plotted his Biobrain moves: whom to contact first for possible purchase, where to set up his offshore accounts, even what new items to add to his wardrobe—starting with some replacement Prada loafers, since the first had taken three months to save up for—once the payoff came in. All the while, what he was really doing was trying not to go crazy while waiting for Tony to phone. And waiting some more. And a little more. Until, in a heap of 4:00 A.M. Wellbutrin sweat, he had to face the fact that his brand-new friend had fucked him.

Now here I am, thought Lipton, trying to block out the reek of molting dishes and buried muskrat fumes. He dragged a magazine called *Labe Happy* from under the couch and peeked at a photo spread. The glurping vulva made him think of open-heart surgery and he had to close it. How did straight men keep their lunch down?

Every time he moved, he heard the crackle of glass vials, discarded jerky wrappers, and God knows what else. *The horror!* In a sudden fit of sense memory, he reexperienced the greasy slide of Zank's hand on his blond pompadour and began to shake. That awful, brutal, cold-eyed man!

Mmmmmm . . .

STOP IT!

Giving up, he crouched behind the sofa and punched out Manny Rubert's number. He remembered it, because it spelled HUNKY 11. *Dreamy!* He'd heard rumors—

Never mind! Manny would know what to do. That's what mattered. He would tell the detective everything.

"Come on," Lipton chanted. *"Pick up pick up pick up pick up!"*

His shaking had progressed to a full-body quiver. He had to hold the cell phone with both hands. Knee-walking back to the window while Manny's phone rang, Lipton perched his chin on the sill and peeked outside.

"Jesus, Mother and Mary!"

Forgetting his sanitation concerns, he pressed his face against the filthy glass. As if that would give him a better view of the street . . . the sidewalk . . . the now empty patch of asphalt where he'd parked the Lincoln.

Just then Manny's machine picked up.

"Someone stole my car!" Lipton screeched, jumping up to see further down the street, as if maybe the Town Car had decided to move, on its own, to a better spot. Catching himself, he skittered away from the window. He was in Tony Zank's apartment. *What was he thinking?*

"Can you hear me, Manny? They stole my car, and I'm *trapped,*" he whispered hoarsely. How many Wellbutrin had he taken? If you took more antidepressant, why didn't you get more antidepressed?

He squealed into the phone, "Please, please, *call back!*" Then he crawled on his belly across the malodorous carpet, counting inches until he got to a closet. He just wanted to hide. To curl up in the dark. He needed safety. Wombness. He made it to Tony's bedroom, which somehow smelled even worse than the rest of the apartment, and found a closet there.

"Oh Judy, *help!*" The second he scurried inside the bedroom closet the odor was staggering. He had to slide the door open to let in some air. When he did, a shaft of light landed on a shoe box. His heart leaped. Maybe this was it! Where Tony hid the photo! *Yes!*

Spirits soaring, Lipton opened the box, saw the cute little face, the maggots teeming in the hollows of Puppy's eye-sockets, and crumpled to the floor.

THIRTY-THREE

They'd been inside Tina's house two minutes when Manny heard the scream from the kitchen. He was still in the doorway, checking the knob. Someone had rubbed off a swath of shoe polish.

"What is it?" he called, catching his foot on the trip wire and tumbling knee-first onto broken bulb-shards. The glass ripped his pants. He cursed himself for not unmanning the booby trap, then fumbled for his gun and ran into the kitchen.

Tina stood beside the fridge, holding what looked like a brass cookie jar over the Formica counter. She wore an expression somewhere between shock and hilarity. Manny recognized that look. People got it when they came home and found the hamster microwaved, or walked in on their spouse kneeling in front of the UPS man. It was the look that said, *"If this weren't the worst thing that ever happened to me, it would be fucking hysterical."*

Manny stepped closer. He saw the two lines of grayish white powder and crumbs beside a broken crack pipe on the Formica. "Okay, so they were here. We knew that was gonna happen."

"It's not that," she said, her voice catching slightly. "It's Marvin. I think they snorted him."

"What?"

Tina lifted the urn and Manny spotted the embossed logo: *MAR-TINO AND SONS*. She turned it over and a few chunks of what looked like kitty litter hit the counter. Tina picked one up, then picked up the pipe and showed Manny. An identical grayish-white nugget was jammed in the tip.

"See? They probably tried to smoke him, and after that, they said 'Hey, let's smash him up a little, see how he snorts.' One way or the other, they figured he was drugs." She paused, and Manny couldn't decipher the expression on her face. "Talk about bad karma. My husband died and came back as *crack*."

Manny was careful not to react. Some jokes it was better not to laugh at. "Well," he said evenly, "my guess is, they'll be back."

"Why?"

"Well. . . ." Manny struggled for a way to word it delicately. There wasn't one. "If Marv got 'em high, they'll wanna head back and scarf around for more. If they think he's bunk—no knock on your husband, I'm sure he was a great guy—they'll wanna head back here and get *you*. By pipehead logic, you ripped them off. Either way, they're coming."

Manny tramped out of the kitchen, moving quickly through the house and calling behind him. He ducked into the tiny bathroom and popped five more codeine, washed down with a slurp from the sink.

After he swallowed his bad vitamins, Manny studied himself in the mirror, then said what he always said to his own face. *"Don't look at me that way, it's still better than heroin. . . ."* After that, he dashed back into the bedroom and yelled. "They didn't do anything else that I can see." He walked face-first into a dangling string and yelled again. "Check that. They took the tampon down. God knows what they did with it."

"What?" came a return yell from the kitchen.

"Nothing," Manny answered. "They must've just found the shit—

I'm sorry, the ashes—and forgotten about the photo. A guy like Zank would figure it's easier to move primo rock than a hot scrote-shot. I'll tell you what, though. They realize how much money they're not gonna get for Marv's ashes, they're gonna want the picture twice as bad."

"What are you saying?"

Tina stepped in from the kitchen. She seemed composed, but you never knew. Manny tried to keep things matter-of-fact.

"I'm saying, when they come back, they're going to come back mad."

"This is insane. So what do we do?"

"You got a camera?"

"Marv had a Polaroid. And a couple of disposables."

"How about one of those fax-copier deals?"

"We have one, but—"

"Magic Marker?"

"Yeah. All that stuff."

"Perfect." Manny unbuckled his belt and took Tina's arm. "Get the camera and marker and bring 'em to the bathroom. The light'll be better there. We gotta work fast."

Tina glanced at that blood-scrawled WELCOME TONY on the wall and looked away. That's when she noticed Manny's condition. "What's up with your pants? You trying to get me hot?"

"That's optional," Manny said, unsnapping his trousers as he headed for the bathroom. Once there, he closed the door, reached in his underpants, and squeezed. He wanted to work up some heft before she came back. This may have been work, but a man still wanted to look his best. . . .

When Tina returned, Manny was down to socks and jockeys. He'd propped the original photo on top of the hamper. George Junior, he now realized, had cupped himself in such a way that the main event was hidden. All eggs and no sausage. Which was easy enough. The tricky part was attaining Biobrain. To get that full-on Mister B. bulge, you had to really *swell* your testicles. This, he discovered, involved making an O with thumb and forefinger, and squeezing at the root. He tried a couple of practice squeezes, until he pretty much mastered the technique. But he didn't want to just whip himself out and go Bio before telling Tina what was up. She might get the wrong idea.

Tina set down the Magic Marker and two cameras—an old Polaroid and a Thrifty disposable—on the furry toilet seat. The seat cover was the same saffron shade as Marvin's loincloth. *What a special man,* she thought, at the exact moment she took in the photo on the hamper and the sight of Manny in his skivvies. *And here's another one. . . .*

"You want to tell me what we're doing here?" she asked.

There was no attitude in the query. No snarky undertone. She'd just lost her husband, for the second time, but she wasn't whining about it. For Manny, this made her even more incredible. Almost heroic. He tried to sound halfway together as he spoke. "My plan, remember? This is it. We make a duplicate of the Bush photo. Develop that. Then we let Zank steal it. Leave it under the sink, in the towel drawer, somewhere he's gonna think he's a smart guy for finding it."

"He finds the fake, so what?"

"So while he's busy trying to break into the White House to make Bush a blackmail offer, or whatever genius move he thinks he's gonna pull off, we unload the genuine article."

"Who's gonna know the difference?"

"What do you mean who's gonna know?"

"Say somebody showed W. a fake Biobrain, you think he'd know?"

"Of course."

"Guys recognize their own balls?"

"Definitely. They spend a lot of time looking at them."

"Why?"

"To make sure they're still there. . . . C'mon, we gotta get started."

Manny was determined not to make this into sex. This wasn't sex. If it was sex, it wasn't the kind of sex he'd imagined when he imagined sex with Tina. When he thought about sex, with Tina, he thought—

"Manny, you're mumbling again."

"Sorry."

"Stage fright?"

"What? No," he said. "It's just, this made sense when I came up with it, but I didn't think about the reality. This just feels kind of . . . strange."

"It was *your* idea. Think of it as an icebreaker."

"Thank you."

Manny felt the same way he did before he went to the beach with his brother as a kid. Stanley always plunged right in the water. But Manny was a toe-dipper. He'd stand there, thinking about how cold it was going to be, how *wet,* until he drove himself blue and goose-pimpled before even hitting the water. That was the trick. Work yourself up to such a state of agitation, whatever you were originally agitated about starts to seem like relief compared to the hell of *dreading* it.

"Okay," said Manny, cranked up to his take-the-plunge head. "Okay!"

Keeping his eyes on the photo, he quickly tugged off his underpants. He caught them on his right foot and kicked them into the air, snagging them with his left hand. It was something he'd been doing since he was three, and when he realized he'd done it in front of Tina, he was mortified. But Tina didn't say a word. He made himself look at her, and saw her staring. Of course.

"What?" He knew this was going to happen. It always did.

"Sorry," she said, "I mean, not for nothing, but did Roos make you that big?"

"I'm afraid that's the original package."

"You're afraid? Most guys would be passing out cards."

"Trust me, the kind of women who think this means anything are the kind I don't need."

"I don't mean to be crude," she said. "But I don't think there *are* any other kind. When you popped out in the car before, I thought that was all of you. I didn't realize it was a preview. You're too humble."

"So what? Now you're all hot? 'Cause I'm party-size?"

Tina laughed in his face. "I know, where are my manners? And who said I was hot? I'm just wondering why you're a cop when you could have been a porn star. *Officer Wadd.* How cool is that? See Manny Wadd, Johnny's long lost son, starring in *The Naked Detective.* Or maybe *The Naked Dick.* Or, no, wait . . . how about *Plainclothes Naked?* That's got a feel. What do you think?" Tina stopped and crossed her arms. "I'm pissing you off, aren't I?"

Normally, Manny would have played it off. Made a joke about moonlighting at bachelorette parties. But the codeine, whooshing into his brain for that hour of bliss before he felt like dogshit again, made him want to be real. To tell her the truth, because that was the hotter move. Scarier but hotter: Show her who he really was, and if she still wanted him, he'd know that she was the *One*. That somehow, after a lifetime of fractured relationships, everything he'd been feeling but afraid to believe would be proved genuine.

"I want to tell you my darkest secret," he blurted.

"You don't have to."

"I want to. You ready?"

"Don't tell me, you have a *problem*."

"Not the one you think. Mine is, I have to care. I can't just point and shoot."

"That's a problem?"

"Depends. It's probably kept me out of a lot of trouble. On the other hand, I've probably missed a busload of great fucks."

"Not that you haven't. . . ."

"Had my share? Sure. Enough so I can't remember when I stopped remembering. But at some point sex turned into New Year's Eve. The night you're supposed to have fun, so having fun feels like work. Pathetic, but there it is. In my old age, I have to trust a woman before I can do anything. Before I want to, anyway."

"That's not pathetic," she said. "Just dangerous."

"So you know what I mean?"

"Sure. The trick, for me, is not to *have* to trust anybody. To enjoy them but not need them."

"And you can do that?"

"No, but it sounds good."

"Exactly." Manny couldn't believe that she *got it*. That turned him on, more than anything, to have found a mind so in alignment with his. A mind in Tina's body. With Tina's face. . . .

He felt super-buzzed, as if he'd stumbled into some pocket of psycho-emotional ether, where the air was so pure it made you giddy because your heart missed all the usual pollution. "If you know who I am—who I *really* am—and you don't freak, then I can screw you till your eyes bleed. But I have to be able to connect. And how the fuck often does that happen?"

Tina shot him a cryptic smile. "I've scared a few off myself."

"So you see what I'm saying."

Manny couldn't tell if he was talking himself into a relationship or out of sex. If *he'd* had to listen to someone jabber this way, he might have been out the door. He had never articulated any of this, and wasn't sure why he was doing it now, of all the insane occasions. But he'd gone this far. . . .

"I know it sounds lame, but I have to dig the way you think. And I have to feel like you *get* me. My whole fucking life, I pretended I could relate to chicks so I could get in their pants. Then once I got in, all I wanted was out again."

For a second or two, Tina was silent. When she spoke he couldn't tell if she was amused or annoyed.

"Listen, Sensitive Guy, I'd want you even if you were hung like a nipple. But I'm not going to lie to you. This"—she hefted his semi-erect penis—"is not something a woman can ignore."

Tina wrapped her fingers around his cock, but the way she did it, so *naturally,* felt more reassuring than erotic. Like she was saying, with that casual grip, *It's all right, Junior, you can relax. I won't make you play the piano.* . . . Which was, to Manny's own surprise, the most weirdly erotic thing of all.

"You know," she continued, "this is the first time I've gotten post-coital without getting coital."

"Same here. I just needed to say something."

"Then I need to say something, too. I'm afraid I'll get hurt."

"That's the other dirty little secret." Manny gave a resigned shrug. "Some women, when we try to do it, it doesn't work. I don't fit. For them it's painful. For me, it's like taking a bath with my feet out of the water. The bane of my existence."

"You big jerk," she said, "I don't mean hurt *that* way. I mean in *here.*" She tapped her heart. "I'm wired the same as you. For it to be good, I have to give a shit about the person I'm with. But I don't *want* to give a shit, because that's when it can hurt."

"So you never let yourself care. It's too painful."

"How'd you guess?"

At that moment, they both looked down. Manny's organ had begun to stiffen, expanding until Tina's middle finger barely touched the tip of her thumb. She smiled. "Honesty, the thinking man's fore-play."

"Something like that." With willpower he wished he didn't have, Manny placed his hand on top of hers and removed it. "A little risk is exciting, but this isn't screwing in a dressing room at the Gap. Those two psycho-freaks burst in, we got a real situation. I shouldn't have started blabbing."

"Never apologize," she said.

"I won't. But now we have to take the picture and get the fuck out."

"This still seems crazy."

"Maybe," said Manny. "But it's the only way to buy some time till we get rid of the original photo—or figure out how to get rid of Zank and McCardle. We've got the shots of them fucking at the motel, but there's no way to use them without meeting face-to-face. And that's too risky. If we stage a fake Biobrain, we can take the film to Roos and have pictures in an hour. Then all we have to do is plant them."

"If that's all, then we should get going. Assume the position."

With Nurse Ratched efficiency, Tina scooped up the Magic Marker and bit the top off. Then she moved the cameras and sat down on the furry toilet seat. Manny went in and out of feeling freakish. Naked from the waist down, while Tina still had her clothes on, made him feel twice as naked. But he couldn't think about it. This was crunch time. As he'd rehearsed, he flattened his penis against his belly, keeping it out of sight under his left hand. Biting his lip, he squinched his balls with his right and squeezed at the root until they bulbed out in veiny approximation of a human brain.

When he was set, they both scrutinized his swollen orb, then looked over at the picture on the hamper and back at each other. *Shit!* There was a problem. Two problems. But size could be fudged. Being furrier than George required more drastic measures.

"Maybe he shaves his nuts," said Manny.

"Either that," said Tina, "or that's what they mean by Skull and Bones. Anyway, you're going to need a trim."

"What did Marvin shave with?"

"Marv was a disposable man. Gillette Good News. But this is too delicate."

"So what are you thinking?"

"Well, I did two semesters of beauty school."

"I don't want a permanent. I just need to be defuzzed."

"I know. But to get the diploma, you had to shave a balloon. The instructor lathered it up, then we had to shave it clean with a straight razor. Without breaking it."

"And you did that?"

"It's not so hard. I got it on my third try."

"*Terrific. . . .*"

Manny gulped as Tina rooted through her purse. When she produced the straight razor, he could have fainted. She flicked it open and smiled up from the toilet seat. It had a pearl handle, engraved with a bucking bronco like a prop from *Gunsmoke.*

Maybe it's an heirloom, Manny thought. *Or maybe she comes from a family of slashers.* Once again, he had to confront the niggling fact that she'd offed her husband. That he'd walked in while the corpse was still warm on his kitchen floor. The image sent his mind into overdrive: *Maybe she likes to kill. . . . Maybe she hates men. . . . Maybe mine is a punishing God and she's my destiny. . . .* The possibilities dropped like little weights tied around the cloud of his codeine buzz, bringing him down. *And yet. . . .*

When Tina turned to open the medicine cabinet, he didn't even think about changing his mind. Or running. Instead, he found himself wearing a weird grin. *Details,* he told himself.

Manny tried to relax as Tina unearthed a can of Barbisol. She plunked it on the sink, then filled a glass with water that came out milky. She set the glass down and snatched a blue washcloth from the shower rod. Manny wondered if it had been Marvin's, and briefly obsessed on the implications of being washed by a dead man's washrag. *A dead husband's.* He couldn't think of any right off, but still. . . .

Tina ran more hot water. When steam started rising out of the tap, she plunged the washrag underneath. She kept it there for as long as she could stand. Then, pinching the scalding cloth between thumb and forefinger, she flipped it out of the sink and over Manny's balls as if she'd been shaving them for decades. He juked backward and yowled. "Careful!"

"Sorry. Heat softens the follicles."

Before he could cool, she plucked the washrag off, threw it in the sink, and squirted some shaving cream on her hand. She slapped it on gently, until his scrotum looked like a snowball.

"I don't know about this," said Manny, his voice not quite normal.

"Steady, Detective. Police business."

"It's like John Wayne Bobbitt, except I'm awake."

"I know. Kind of a dream come true. . . ."

With this, Tina raised the blade beside her head, Tony Perkins–style, and started in. Manny was still waiting for the pain when he opened his eyes and realized she was already shaving him. In two minutes he was smooth. Tina toweled him off and grabbed the Magic Marker. Taking stock, she shot her gaze back and forth from Manny to the original. And then, with an ease and certitude that bordered on Zen, she kneeled down and drew a perfect Smiley Face.

Manny compared his happy balls to George Junior's and nodded. "Amazing job."

"Thanks. I lied about the balloon, by the way. I popped it every time. Let's see how we look on film."

Before Manny could react, Tina started firing off Polaroids. They examined each alongside the stolen photo, making adjustment after adjustment until they'd managed to make Manny's look all but identical to W.'s more wispy, Waspish golf bag. After they nailed *that* down, Manny picked up on another problem: In the original, the backdrop was white. The walls in the Podolsky bathroom were green. To cheat, Tina tossed a white sheet over the towel rack and posed him in front of it. Once that was rigged, and the Polaroids looked okay, she ran off a roll on the disposable.

"Done," she announced, dropping the camera in her purse and giving his tingling testicles a friendly squeeze. "How are Abbott and Costello holding up?"

"They feel kind of raw."

"Hang on, I have something that can help."

Tina grabbed a fresh towel and wiped her straight razor lovingly, then snapped it shut. Manny'd known a couple of cops, and a few criminals, who handled their weapons with the same kind of affection. They were always the ones who knew how to use them.

She placed the razor daintily on the hamper, beside the real Mister Biobrain and the Polaroid forgeries, and laid a dry towel over them. Then she opened the medicine cabinet.

"Here's what *I* use," she said, retrieving an ugly yellow jar. Seeing it, Manny had a retroactive flash. He realized what was different about Tina back in the Impala. When he'd plunged in, she'd been smooth. Shaved. Up, down, and sideways. Just like Carlos/Carmella. If there was a connection, he didn't want to think about it. Maybe all the ladies were going baby these days.

"A lot of people knock Vaseline," Tina declaimed, in the manner of a TV spokesperson. "But, for this little lady, nothing works like petroleum jelly on those pubic razor bumps. You can find fancier products, but nothing better."

Done with her pitch, she dropped back to her knees in front of him. She'd just sunk two fingers in the Vaseline, ready to swab, when they heard the crash in the living room. Without thinking, Manny scooped up his underwear. Before he could pull them on, Zank was in the doorway, his face like a blood-spattered moon, twirling one of the lynched rabbits on a string and pointing his custom .357.

For a long time, nobody spoke. Then Zank piped up like it was natural. "Wanna know my favorite thing in the world?"

His tone was creepily familiar, *neighborly,* as if they were chatting at a supermarket check stand, basket to basket. "It's this gun. Really. Colt Python .357 Magnum, with the heavy bullets. That's the secret. I had it modified for heavy bullets."

He dangled the stuffed animal in Tina's face while Manny watched, still covering his cock with his jockeys.

"Let's say I shoot this bunny. When I do, its bunny cousin's gonna die in the house next door. Magic bullets, man. These fuckers'll go through walls, through bricks, through your *neighbor's* walls, right into his fat ass if he's sittin' in front of the big screen watchin' gay S & M. Which is *exactly* what he's doin,'cause I had a peep on the way in. When I get tweaked up, I like to do me a little peepin'."

Seeing Zank, Manny was struck by a peculiar truth: The truly dangerous guys were not always the scariest. He'd met hitmen who looked like department store Santas. And here was Tony Zank. . . . Almost clownish. Drug-muddled and babbling, with a face, at this point, like something scraped off an emergency room floor. Zank blasted a thousand dirty watts from both eyes. He was the kind of man who'd make you cringe if you saw him within twenty feet of a child. Manny watched him lift his gun to his lips and lick the barrel. He French kissed it, putting his tongue right in the hole. Manny watched, and thought: *Killing us would be fun.* Tony was definitely a unique case: He managed to look ludicrous *and* scary. For Zank, a situation like this was champagne brunch.

Manny took a long, slow breath and repeated his personal mantra for handling psychotics. *When facing the unhinged, stay hinged.* With psychopaths, it was all theater. If you didn't know your lines, you were dead.

Neither Manny nor Tina moved as a skittish black man, built like a miniature bodybuilder, stepped timidly behind Zank. Tina couldn't help staring. In the flesh, the miniature hunk bore an even stronger resemblance to Dean Martin. She'd seen *Robin and the Seven Hoods* three nights ago on AMC. They were having a Rat Pack festival. Beyond the obvious difference in size and pigment, he was Dean to a T. Except, Tina noted with fascination, for that adorable little nose. And the expression of terror on his handsome face. McCardle, the shrunk-and-dyed Dino, came off as traumatized as his partner did crazy.

Tony wrapped his nongun hand around McCardle's shoulders. "My best friend. He'll kill me for sayin' this, but he's a peeper, too. Ain't that right, little buddy? 'Course Mac here, he's more your bathroom type. A specialist." Zank cupped his free hand to his mouth and continued, in a mock-whisper. "More *toilet*-oriented."

Tony giggled and wiped away a bubble of blood from his lips. "Mac likes to see ladies wiping themselves. Big ladies. Not Number Two, though. He's no sicko. Just pee-pee. He likes the way ladies tamp. Don't you Mac? You done some tampin' yourself, huh, slugger?"

McCardle retreated, pleading. "C'mon, Tony. Don't play me like this."

Zank guffawed. "What do you got to be shy about? You think that Vaseline they got there is for diaper rash? She's about to go *Last Tango* on his ass. We walked in on a hemorrhoid massage."

He cackled and snatched Manny's underpants, revealing the rest of him. *"Whoa!"* Zank stopped laughing and whistled respectfully. Then he dropped the jockeys and elbowed McCardle. "Nice bone for a white man, huh Mac? The guy's a credit to his race. Which is more than I can say for you."

He grinned at Tina and Manny, like they were all in on the joke.

"Mac got hit by the teeny stick. Right, Dog? But that ain't the funniest. Tell everybody about your auntie, the one you had to 'tidy up.' You told *me* enough fucking times. It's Auntie Big'n, right? Tell the story. Why not bless somebody else's world?"

"Come on, Tony," McCardle said again. Then his eyes met Manny's and Manny knew he'd been made. Tony was the maniac; McCardle was scared. The scared guys were always smarter. Mac smelled cop, Manny could see it. By not saying anything to Zank, he was sending a message. Letting Manny know: If he had the chance, he'd cross his partner in a hot minute and cut a deal.

Manny gave McCardle a faint nod. He recalled, with reluctant wonder, the photo Roos had produced this afternoon. The buff black guy pranging the rangy white psycho over the Pawnee Lodge dresser. Here were the two players, in the flesh. Mac McCardle and Tony Zank.

Tina sat down on the furry toilet seat and Tony leered happily. He held the Python steady, aimed in the general direction of Manny's newly smooth genitals. With his free hand, he scratched at a gash in his forehead, then fingered the scabs dotting his nostrils. "You must feel pretty lucky, gorgeous, landing a hunk of lumber like him. I respect a slit who knows what she wants."

Tina didn't answer, and Manny was impressed, all over again, at the way she handled herself. A beautiful woman who knew how to keep it together with a .357 on her. Now *that* was special. It occurred to him, then and there, if he ever composed a personal ad, he'd include *Must be cool at gunpoint* as a key qualification. It would weed out the dinner-and-a-movie types.

"Dag nab it," Tony chuckled, "I think we came at a bad time! Tell you what, why don't you crazy kids go ahead? Might as well party down before I paint the ceiling with your brains."

He stuck out his thumb and forefinger, went "pow-pow!" then

grabbed Mac in a headlock and gave him a gun-butt noogie. After he let him go he shot Manny a demented wink.

"Here's a fun fact. Did you know people relieve themselves when they die? Sometimes I trip on that. Guys gettin' the chair, they gotta walk that last mile in Depends. Reason I know, a celly I had in Lewisburg, he had a brother did hard time down in Texas. Worked in the infirmary. After they fried a guy, they'd wheel the body down and my buddy's brother's job was to unload him. You imagine that? Your gig is to take the diapers offa dead fried guys? But he actually *liked* doin' it. Know why?"

Zank stuck a finger in the hole where his tooth used to be, as if checking to see if it had grown back, then resumed chatting.

"It's kinda sweet. See, a condemned man gets a visit from his old lady the night before his execution. That's the law. My man's bro makes some arrangements, gets her paid ahead of time to slip the dude a big balloon of dope. All he's gotta do is gulp it, and when my buddy's brother gets his body the next day, after he's state-sautéed—voila!—he just plucks the stuff out of his diaper. Nature does all the work. Neat, huh? The dope comes out precooked. Ready to shoot."

"Dead Man Packing," said Tina, from her spot on the toilet seat, and Tony slapped his knee. Everybody juked, but Tony didn't notice. He just hustled his balls and started chatting again.

"Funny lady," he said. "I like that. I used to jerk off to Lucille Ball when I was a kid. Ever check out the *mouth* on her? Suck-a-licious! But wait!"

Zank took another lick off the gun barrel, the oil staining the blood on his lips a greasy purple.

"You're probably thinking, 'If he's gonna fry anyway, what's to keep some condemned motherfucker from pullin' a rip job? The fuck's he care?' Well, this is the genius part. The guy knows, if my buddy's bro don't find that dope in his diaper, then his old lady, and his sister, and his mom, and his grandma, and all his fucking kids and babies are gonna get dicked and slit. Somebody's gonna fuck 'em and cut their throats and they're gonna do it *slow*. No motherfucker in the world wants to get strapped down with *that* on his mind." Zank paused to pluck a pulpy scab off his forehead and grinned. "It's what they call a win-win situation."

Done with his happy saga, Zank dropped to his haunches, a posture he'd no doubt struck on the yard, and snapped his fingers over his head. Tina and Manny stole a glance at each other, and Manny tried to convey a message with his eyes. *It's okay. . . . We're not going to die.*

"Mac-a-dino, pipe me," Zank sang. "I need to beam up. Party-time." Then he giggled. "Are you guys into the *Lifestyle?* Is that it? This some kinky-swappy thing?" He brushed a bead of sweat off Manny's brow with that extra-wide barrel. "Tell me the truth. You got some hot blond tied to a washer-dryer in the basement? I read a thing on it in *Maxim.* Goddamn it, McCardle, gimme that glass dick!"

Mac slipped the pipe he'd plucked from the torture kit into Zank's hand, and Manny again picked up the fear in the tiny man's eyes. In private, if Carmella's candids were any indication, McCardle got to be the top; Zank was the bitch. But the bitch got to play shot-caller in public. Which meant what?

Manny's gut was that McCardle was not as submissive as he came off. That if it came down to it, Mac would put a slug in Zank's back as soon as anybody else's. Maybe sooner. The sodomy thing might just be a hobby.

After McCardle lit him up, Tony sucked in a lung-numbing hit— there was some gunky resin lodged in the bottom—and bashed himself against the bathroom wall. His eyes rolled north and he gave a diseased shiver. Waving the .357 wildly, he exhaled a cloud of chemical smoke and, grunting with effort, tugged down his zipper.

Nobody moved when Tony exposed himself. Compared to Manny, his member looked like a boiled shrimp. This, Manny knew from experience, was not good. In any kind of naked situation—it could be a sauna, a locker room, a sex club—packing what Manny packed was like being the biggest guy in a bar: a walking provocation to every non–big boy on the premises. They wanted to fuck you up, to make themselves *feel* bigger. Which might mean giving you shit. Or kicking your ass. Or—in Tony Zank-land—raping your girlfriend before blowing your brains out.

Zank nudged Manny in the stomach with his gun. "Don't be a hero, donkey-cock. This isn't *my* fault. I don't *want* to dry-fuck your bitch up the ass and make her call me Daddy. I'm actually gentle. *Peace Brother!*" He flashed a hippie V as he staggered to his feet. "But I'm gonna have to get my freak on till she tells me where she put a certain very important something that she stole from my mother's bed. *My mother's bed!*" he repeated, in tones of self-righteous shock, as if no one knew he'd dropped the old woman out a window. "You got that? She ripped me off!"

Tony concluded his rant by placing his hand on Tina's head. He stroked her hair with the Python's barrel, then pulled her face close to his. Tina tried to avoid his breath, which stuck to her face like malathion. As a child, she'd been caught outside in an EPA pilot program near Wheeling. There weren't any medflies in West Virginia, but that didn't stop army helicopters from buzzing overhead and unloading a ton of sticky insecticide on her third birthday party. They thought they'd spray hillbillies and see what happened before they tried it in L.A. But Mommy didn't want to waste the Kool-Aid, and dumped in more sugar to hide the taste. Only it didn't work. That Kool-Aid stank just like Zank's up-forever-on-crack-and-jerky breath.

"How you doin', baby?" Tony asked her, and Tina managed a smile. The same one Manny'd seen her give Ranick in the 7-Eleven parking lot. Which reminded him. On the odd chance they lived, he'd have to ask what she whispered to the guy. . . .

It was impossible to know what was going on in Tina's head. From experience, she'd learned to let her mind off the leash in these situations. (*Honey, you just let Big Earl kiss your tummy. Mommy'll be right here.*) Zoning out could get you through. Until you came back, and things were worse. That was the problem. Reality was like a teenage delinquent: It did what it wanted, but got pissed off if you ignored it for too long.

When Tina tuned back to Here-and-Nowsville, Tony Zank was planted in front of her, milking his rubbery organ. Fresh blood dappled his fingers, from shoving them in and out of his mouth. He craned his head back to Manny and chuckled. "I'm letting you watch, Hoss, but you gotta behave yourself. If you're nice I'll let my friend here grease your keister. Once you go black, you never go back."

Tina fought off nausea as Tony shmushed his fish-white, sagging member against her lips. He began to play with her hair, grabbing her ponytail and twisting. But Tina didn't unclamp her mouth. She wouldn't, even when he wrist-snapped the .357 and tapped it off her eyelids.

"Come on, doll-face, I'm no monster. I'm just trying to cut you a break here. Let you get my petey wet. Dry *hurts,* I know! Just gimme a dribble. C'mon, Precious, kiss Tony's tubesteak so he don't have to go in dry."

Tina pressed her lips tighter, not breathing. Zank's genitals had the consistency of bleu cheese.

Fuck it. . . . Manny took a step forward. Tony caught the movement and swung the gun from Tina's skull, level with his belly. "You want some, Foot-long, keep movin'. I don't give a shit. I'm just tryin' to show the bitch some respect here. Do her a solid. I got contacts, see? I get what I'm lookin' for, I'll know what to do with it. Tony boy knows how to bank the Franklins. She plays nice, maybe I'll kick her down some."

Manny stayed where he was. Tony shrugged and turned back to Tina. "Tell you what, Mary Poppins, I'll give you a fighting chance."

He waggled his eyebrows and, as all three gasped, plunged the barrel of the .357 in his mouth. Then he bit down hard and let go. The gun dangled from his blood-caked face, locked in his choppers.

It was a freak show. Tony planted his hands on his hips and began to wiggle. He danced like a syphilitic hula boy, force-fed methedrine. Ropy veins the size of pencils ran down his forearms. He looked drug-skinny, made from the same beef jerky he consumed by the case.

Tony was still doing the hula, gun-biting, when Manny made his move. He feinted left, then lunged low the opposite direction. But Zank was faster. He opened his mouth, dropped the gun, caught it on the pivot, and jammed it in Manny's chest.

"Check my moves, y'all!" Tony milked himself some more, keeping that four-inch barrel in Manny's solar plexus, and again lifted his saggy manhood to Tina's lips. "I used to practice in my cell, with a hairbrush," he bragged. "That's the kind of shit you get good at. But hey, we're all friends here. I don't want a kill-party. That's not *me!* I just want to find Mister Biobrain. If we have some yucks along the way, what the heck! Does that make me a bad person?"

Not being hard didn't seem to bother Zank. He was beyond shame.

Tina cringed and Manny tried to breathe lightly. The thick barrel poked him harder on the inhale.

Grinning happily while McCardle fidgeted beside the door, Zank swung the gun back to Tina's head and tried stuffing his putrid organ in her clamped-shut mouth. He used his finger, *pushing,* and Manny forced back emotions he couldn't name.

"Come on," he taunted Zank, figuring to piss him off, maybe make him get sloppy. "You can't even get it up. Eat some fucking Viagra or put it away."

Zank remained unfazed. "Listen, Jumbo, you think she wants you just 'cause you got that piano leg? I think she kind of digs *me.* Don't you, beautiful? Sure you do. C'mon baby, say *Ahhh!* Your boyfriend's gonna enjoy this. Hey, we should grab a photographer. One of those guys from *Swing World.* You ever read that? You can only buy it at truck stops. They got them crazy personals. Man, there's a lot of lonely freakoritas out there. Mac, gimme another hit, I'm gettin' *drove!"*

McCardle extended his stubby, ballooning arm. He seemed to have learned how to reach and flex at the same time. No doubt to impress the pretty things at the gym. He slid the pipe in Tony's lips and fired it up. Tony sucked until his eyes bulged.

Manny breathed slowly, calculating the odds. Poke him in the throat when he's holding his breath, he's out for thirty seconds. Maybe fifty with coughing and gagging. Trip him and step on his windpipe, he's yours. All possibilities. But he let the moment pass. He had to. Zank's gun was pointed at Tina's brain. Even knocked out cold, he could squeeze the trigger on the way to the floor.

Then Tina let out a cry, "Yeee-*ecccch!"* and shoved Tony away. Still soft, the bloodied killer had started to ejaculate, moaning *"Shit! Shit! Shit!"* and pounding himself in the head. He squirted on his own thigh and groaned. "You fucking *cunt! That never happens!"*

Zank rubbed splooge off his leg with the back of his gun hand. Then he grabbed the towel from the top of the hamper. He wiped off, and Manny felt his heart skid sideways. Beneath the towel was the original Mister Biobrain and a stack of Polaroids. Beside them was Tina's straight razor.

But Zank was too distracted to notice. "You hear me? *This never happens!* Tell 'em, Mac. I can fuck. I'm a *good* fuck. Remember that redhead from Hooter's, the one with the twitch? She said I was an artist. A goddamn fuck-artist! That's what she said. Tell 'em, Mac!"

McCardle spoke up. "That's right, Tony. You're a stud. All the strawberries say so."

"Damn straight. And not just strawberries, either. I fucked some normal chicks, too. Plenty."

Mac fired another rock in the pipe. He took a courtesy suck, then handed it to Zank, who pulled in a king-hell hit, exhaled fast, and whipped his head toward the window behind him. "Oh SHIT! You hear the helicopters? You hear 'em?"

His eyes darted wildly around the bathroom. Tina pretended to sneeze, knocking the original photo behind the hamper.

"What was that?" Tony cried. "I saw that! What was it?"

He spotted the blade and, stiff-arming Tina, lunged for it. But Tina grabbed it as she fell sideways. She flipped the razor open back-hand and swung. A high shriek escaped Tony's lips. He fired the gun, which blasted the bathtub, shattering one side to dust and blowing a hole the size of a bicycle seat through the wall opposite. A cloud of plaster dust floated past the shattered tiles.

"Jesus fuck, I'm *cut!*" Tony let go of the gun and spun around on the throw rug, clutching his penis. Blood leaked through his fist. He wailed in disbelief, *"You cut me! You bitch, you cut me down there!"*

Tony rechecked his organ, saw that only his finger was bleeding—the tip of his pinkie—and clamped his hands together at his chest. *"Oh thank you, God!"* He raised his eyes and threw back his head. *"Thank you thank you thank you thankyouthankyouthankyou."*

Moving fast, Manny took advantage of Zank's gratitude to scoop the Python off the bathroom rug. Surprised at the heft of it, he checked the clip and pointed it at Zank and McCardle. "Police, freeze!"

"Police? Are you *kidding* me?" Zank hopped up and down and shouted at McCardle. Blood spritzed out of his mouth when he yelled. "Grab the other gat, man. Come on! Shoot the mother-fucker!"

McCardle didn't move. "It's in the car, Tony. My bad."

"Thanks a lot, Soul Brother!"

Zank took Tina by the hair and swung her in front of him. Then he tried pinning her arms at her sides, but she managed to jerk one hand free. Still clutching the straight razor, she jammed the blade straight up, slicing the lobe off his good ear, the one Mac hadn't shot half off in the Pawnee Lodge. The pad of flesh plopped onto the toilet seat, where Tony regarded it. "Doesn't hurt," he said quietly, as if having a mystical experience.

Manny prepared to squeeze the trigger, but Zank kept himself behind Tina. When he noticed the Polaroids, a sickening grin split his face.

Manny followed Zank's eyes to the pictures scattered on the floor. Close-ups of Manny's own shaved balls, freshly happy-faced.

"Ka-ching," Zank warbled, back to tugging his shiny-wet penis. By now it looked like a rubber dog toy. "You sex-freaks were holdin' out on me!" He tugged faster, examining the first Polaroid. "Look at this, Mac. The fucking sicko *likes* puffing his nuts out. Fuckin' Georgie-boy's a *kink!*" His tone was commiserating. "Rich kids! They can do this shit, right? Nothin' better to do than play with their peters and count their ducats. Pop's got them CIA connects, a billion in the bank. Hey, he can buy Junior the party jobs, like ownin' a base-ball team or bein' President. Ever notice that little nut-puffer's eyes? Nobody can tell me Daddy's boy ain't sucked the glass dick. That fucker's eyes are *glittery.*"

Still grinning around his tooth-hole, Zank turned to Manny. His ear poured blood, and his whole face seemed stained by gummy wine. He was enjoying himself.

"Thought you could get over on Tony Zank, huh? You thought Tony Z wouldn't find these? Well, I guess you blew it, moose-cock." He fingered a scab over his eye. "You know what you see when you look at me?"

"A dead crackhead," said Manny. But Tony let it pass.

"What you see here is a professional criminal, my friend."

Manny faked a yawn. "I'm impressed."

"You fucking oughta be." Zank waved the Polaroids over Tina's shoulder. "Winner take all, copper. Y'hear me? I'm taking all of 'em!"

It was all Tina could do to keep from laughing. So she pretended to cry. Zank hadn't bothered to tuck himself in his pants. He backed toward the door with Tina still shielding him, his boiled shrimp mushed against her spine. When he got alongside McCardle, he shoved her into Manny and shouted. "Come on, Mac Daddy, I'll start the car!"

Zank tore out of the bathroom. But McCardle froze. Manny met his eyes and pulled the trigger. The sink blew off the wall. A gusher streamed out of the shattered pipe. Through the spray, Manny nodded toward McCardle, who nodded back and dropped to the puddled floor, screaming. "Tony, he's gonna kill me, man!"

They could hear Zank crunching across the living room. He stopped and yelled from the front door. "I *told* you you didn't know shit about crime. You fucked yourself, Dino!"

Then the door slammed and, seconds later, Tina found the valve and turned the water off. They heard a car start and Tony Zank roar off with a peal of rubber.

"I didn't hit you, did I?" Manny asked McCardle.

"No, no . . . I'm fine."

"That's more than I can say about my bathroom," Tina said. "It looks like fucking Bosnia in here."

"You think we could have this discussion later?"

"Suit yourself, Kojak."

"Thank you." Manny turned his back to McCardle. The shaken mini-lifter put his hands up, though nobody'd asked him to. Manny fished around in his jacket, now a soaking heap on the floor, and dug out his badge. This was the first arrest he'd made with no pants on. He flashed the shield and announced, in a flat voice, "You're under arrest. You know the drill, right?"

"I guess so."

"You heard of plainclothes cops?" Tina asked him. "Manny's no-clothes. It's a whole new branch."

Manny eyed her balefully. "Do you mind?"

"You just destroyed my house. You want a thank-you note?"

"Let's just do this, okay?"

Manny put the badge back and gathered up his pants and underwear. He tried to wring them out, gave up, and dug a pair of plastic cuffs out of the pocket. McCardle held out his wrists, looking grateful.

"Okay, then. You have the right to remain silent. Everything you say can and will be used against you in a court of law. You have the right to an attorney, *et cetera, et cetera.* . . . Fuck with me and I'll shoot you in the head and get rich."

THIRTY-FOUR

Fayton hunkered over his desk, examining fabric samples. He'd thought, once the *America's Most Wanted* money came in, that he would just repaint his office, maybe lay in one of those aircraft-carrier-size CEO desks, the kind the big boys always posed behind with their arms crossed in *Fortune* photos. The chief had tried out the CEO pose, but it blocked out the medals on his chest. Fabric walls, though, that was a bold move. The kind of move that said *innovator*. That said *visionary*. That said *Leader of Men*.

Well, maybe he was getting carried away. But not completely. His wife had introduced him to fabric walls when they'd decided to redo the den. Even with those beefy shoulders, Florence could give Martha Stewart a run for her money. She got into decorating in her personal assistant days. Apparently, Dr. Laura liked to unwind reading wall-paper catalogues, and Florence picked up the habit.

Fayton had set the missus up in business, when he first made chief. But, no doubt fearing an aesthetic clash with the spouse of a police legend, clients were few and far between. In fact, there were no clients at all. Poor Flo. She just didn't have the spunk. The pizzazz. Not like Mayor Marge—that power-mad tease! He couldn't wait to tell Her Honor that he'd captured McCardle. Which reminded him—how could he forget?—he had to line up a photographer before Manny got back with the prize. Chatlak used to take pictures of the chief making major arrests. Or, if you wanted to split hairs, of him standing next to major guys who'd been arrested. Often as not by Manny Rubert. That arrogant . . . *hot dog!*

Fayton smiled to himself. Wouldn't Manny be surprised that he even *knew* he was bringing in "the Black Menace?" ("The Black Menace" is what the chief had decided to call McCardle in the screenplay of his memoirs. He loved the sound of it, and had already worked it into a dramatic voiceover: "Evil comes in all colors, but in this case it came in black . . . the Black Menace." Now *that* was the kind of line that spelled Oscar!)

But back to Manny. God forbid he should keep his superior officer informed! No, Fayton had to tap Officers Merch and Krantz's phones to get the skinny. Not that Krantz ever had anything worth hearing, beyond spats with club owners who refused to pay him because he sucked. Of course, it might not be strictly legal. It might upset your ACL-*JEW* types. But he'd be willing to bet his pension he wasn't the only chief who indulged in a bit of not-quite-constitutional telephonic surveillance.

Fayton checked his imitation Rolex. It had been ten minutes since he'd "overheard" the call. Manny had told Merch to ready the interrogation room. Which meant moving out the stacks of paper towels and toilet paper, and moving in table and chairs. It wasn't like they did a whole lot of interrogating in Upper Marilyn. When they did, it was an event.

Manny Rubert had a rep as some hot-shit interrogator. Well, we'll see about *that*, Fayton huffed to himself. We'll just see who wrestled a confession out of "the Menace." It would feel so good to call that patronizing gob at *America's Most Wanted* and let him know that Lyn Fayton, police chief of Upper by God Marilyn, had captured one of the most wanted *Wanteds*. Or so Fayton fancied. Doubtless the crumb who'd mocked him on the 800-line was lolling around some swanky office, cackling on his network-padded behind about the rube down in Hicksville, Pennsylvania, who thought he could reel in a big one. Well *hah!* Fayton said out loud. *Hah* and *Hah* and *Hah!*

Returning to his chief's chair—which squeaked, now that Chatlak wasn't around to oil it—Fayton spun around a few times then buzzed Merch. "Oh, Officer," he said, "would you please tell me the second Ruby gets back here with McCardle? I want to be there for the inter-rogation."

There was a beat at the other end. He heard crumpling paper, then a loud crunch—Merch unwrapping and chomping a candy bar before bothering to respond. "Guess you heard it on the tap, huh Chief?"

"Never mind how I heard about it. It's my business to hear what goes on around here!" Fayton pounded his desk, imagining that James Woods, in *Lawman,* would pound the desk exactly the same way. "My business, understand? That's why I'm chief and you're, um . . ." Fayton fumbled for words. It was tough, without the cue cards. "And you're—"

"A real cop?" Merch offered helpfully between crunches.

"That's just about enough," Fayton snarled. But he hadn't mastered the snarling thing, and it just sounded like he had a bone in his throat.

"Whatever you say," said Merch. "You want me to alert the press?"

"Just do what you're supposed to do. Think you can handle that?"

"Maybe."

"Well, then—"

Fayton was still trying to come up with a really mean, really power-ful response when Merch hung up. For a second the chief glared at his new cordless. (After the mishap with his last telephone, he decided to trade up. He'd selected a white Panasonic that picked up the Weather Channel.) Fayton was still glaring, as if it were the phone's fault he couldn't think of an insult, when inspiration struck. "Charles Durn-ing," he said out loud. *Charles Fucking Durning.*

Fayton swelled with manly ire and fantasized the conversation he'd have with his bloated subordinate. "You wanna mess with me, Merch?

Fine. I've got two words for you. *Charles Durning*. That's who's gonna play *you,* Tubby. I bet *that* will impress your friends, if you have any. I won't even change your name. I'll hire an old, fat actor and I'll call him *Merch.*"

The chief was still tittering when the actual Merch rang back to tell him Elvis was in the building.

THIRTY-FIVE

After planting the docile McCardle on the living room couch, Manny decided to check his messages. Tina was busy hauling in dry clothes from Marvin's closet, since Manny's own shirt and pants had been soaked in the sink explosion.

"Pick something you like," she said, holding aloft an armful of Marv-wear. Everything the dead man owned pretty much fell into the saffron category. Riffling through his options, Manny settled on an orangey-saffron turtleneck and matching drawstring pants with Sanskrit symbols on each leg.

"Any idea what this says?"

"Marvin told me it meant *Yin and Yang*." said Tina. "But for all I know it means *White Shmuck With Scrib-*

ble on His Thighs. Your Third World sweatshop worker has to have a laugh, too, don't you think?"

Manny started to say something, then noticed that McCardle was going into spasms on the sofa. Manny bent over him cautiously and shook his shoulder. "Hey Mac, you feeling okay?"

"Just crashing," McCardle replied, his voice far away. "Been up for a week. Maybe three, I don't know. I can't close my eyes 'cause I see bats."

Manny nodded and backed away. "Well, think happy thoughts. I have to make some calls, then we go down to the station. You don't think your partner's gonna stage some Steven Seagal rescue thing, do you?"

"Tony? Help somebody else?" McCardle laughed sourly, and Manny was struck all over again by how much his insouciant grin evoked the prime-of-life Martin, Dino in his Celebrity Roast days. "Not fucking likely."

"Just making sure."

Unless he was driving, Manny could not stay seated and talk on the telephone. He was a terminal pacer. As he dialed his answering machine, he crunched back and forth over the broken glass in a pair of Marvin's open-toe sandals. Tina marched by with an armful of broken sink, shaking her head, and Manny gave her an apologetic shrug. She stopped on the way back, listening to the shouts coming out of the receiver.

"Who the hell is that?"

"Mayor Marge."

"Doesn't *she* sound happy."

"Very. She called eleven times."

"Wow." Tina stooped to tie the drawstrings dangling around his waist. "She must miss you huh?" She pulled the drawstring extra tight.

"*Ooof. . . .*"

"Too snug?"

"Kind of."

Manny found it oddly arousing, but decided not to broadcast it.

For her part, Tina had to smile, taking in the vision of Manny Rubert, cockmonster and sensitive detective, decked out in orange yoga-wear. "You know," she said, "you shave your head, grow a pigtail,

I'm guessing you could mop up at airports. There aren't a whole lot of badass Hare Krishnas."

Not sure how to take this, Manny held up the cell phone to show he was busy. "You don't mind, I've got some stuff to deal with. You can insult me later. Why don't you go off and cry a little? Get your eyes red."

"Excuse me?"

"You should at least *look* like a grieving widow. Now please. . . ."

But Tina didn't move. "Oh, gosh, am I in the way? You can come over and destroy my home, but don't let me bother you when you're making a phone call. For your information, fucker, I'm grieving on the inside."

Even as Tina spoke, part of her was thinking: *I must love this guy, it's so much fun giving him shit.* Still, she saw the strained expression on Manny's face and lightened up. "I'm not as cold-blooded as you think, okay? This is how I do sadness, I get sarcastic." She thought about giving him a hug, but decided against it. Not with McCardle on the couch. "So Mayor Marge has some problems, huh?"

"Two, as a matter of fact." By now Manny was fighting for breath, and clawed at the knotted drawstrings. It felt like he was trapped in a napkin ring. "Her personal assistant, Lipton," he gasped, "the guy she called about earlier, he's still missing. Only now she's—*man, I can hardly breathe!*—she's frantic. She's called, like, nine times."

Tina pushed his hands away and had a go at the drawstring. The knot untied instantly. "What's her other problem?"

Manny took a gulp of air. "I never call her back."

They both turned when McCardle, who'd been more or less dozing, jumped to his feet and began swatting the air in front of him. "Bats . . . *Yeesh!* . . . SHOO! **SHOO**!!" Then he fell back on the couch in a tense hunch, exhausted. In another second he was snoring.

Tina beamed. "It's so cute, the way his little feet don't even touch the floor. Anything else happening in cop-land?"

"Well, that's the bizarre part." Manny stuffed the cell phone in his jacket pocket. "I actually got another call from Lipton."

"The missing link. What's he want?"

"I don't know, but he sounds hysterical. We have to split. We should be getting down to the station. Wake up mini-Dean."

"I'm not asleep," McCardle called from the couch. "I'm restin' my nerves."

"My mistake."

Tina grabbed Manny's arm. "Wait a second. You want *me* to come? To the *police* station?"

"As my *guest*. You think I'd let you stay here alone? You saw Zank. He's psychotic *and* he's hyper. That's a bad combo."

"He's more stupid than anything. Did you catch the way he jumped on those Polaroids?"

Manny held a finger to his lips. He nodded toward McCardle, who was now drooling. He didn't appear to be listening, but you never knew.

"That's the thing about making plans," said Manny, keeping his voice low. "A guy as wrong as Zank comes along and fucks 'em up, and they end up working out even better. It's almost cosmic."

"It is," said Tina. "God's probably just a bored five-year-old with A.D.D."

"That explains everything. Anyway, this saves us having to run back to Roos to develop the disposable. Tony probably won't come back here, but you never know. What he's probably doing is running around tryin' to sell pictures of my nuts."

"I'd buy one, if you signed it."

"Nasty is as nasty does," said Manny

"You make that up?"

"No, my grandfather used to say it."

"Huh. My granddaddy was a little different. He used to say, 'Lift up your dress, Candy-pants. Show Pap-Pap some of that pink sugar.' "

"Jesus. . . ."

Tina sighed, and Manny wondered if he was supposed to share some monstrous confidence of his own. He'd have said anything to make her feel better. "My mother made me cuddle nude till I was twelve. . . . In seventh grade, I let a priest slap himself in the face with my penis for twenty dollars. . . ." But when he finally got the gumption to meet her eyes, she seemed fine, apparently free of fallout from her remembered trauma. Which made him wonder: Did it mean anything that the first woman he felt he could actually love was some kind of serious sexual abuse victim? No doubt this accounted for the alternating currents of tenderness and anger that seemed to sizzle through her, so you never knew if she was going to snuggle up or say something that made you feel like an idiot. And yet. . . . The truth was, he felt more comfortable knowing Tina'd survived some supremely horrific shit. It meant he would not have to hide the supremely horrific shit he'd been through himself. Penile priest-slapping was the least of it. . . .

Beyond all that, Manny could not stop obsessing on the word *candypants.* Just thinking it set off little pleasure bombs in his head, and he fought a guilty urge to make her say it again.

Get a grip, he told himself, and pointed at McCardle. "Be careful waking up His Nibs. Guy coming off a monstro crack binge, he's bound to be a tad cranky."

Tina ripped the filter off a fresh Viceroy and nodded. "Gotcha."

Taking no chances, she went into the kitchen and returned with a vacuum cleaner. Planting herself halfway across the living room, she poked him in chest with the lint attachment.

"Hey Mr. Universe, up and at 'em."

McCardle blinked, as if he wasn't sure where he was but knew he didn't want to be there. Tina held him at vacuum length while Manny yelled into his phone. "I said, *WHERE ARE YOU, LIPTON?* You sound like you're in a closet . . . You *are* in a closet? Fine, that helps, but I need an address. There are a lot of closets in this town, that's the crazy thing about it."

Manny covered the mouthpiece and rolled his eyes. "The poor guy's in shock." Then he went back to shouting. "Lipton? LIPTON! You still there? Good. Listen to me, I need a street where the car was stolen. Gimme a store, an apartment building, anything. . . . The what? The Bundthouse Arms? That's where you are? *What?* Calm down. I said calm down, damn it! I'll be there." Manny began to yell even louder. "*What?* I don't know. As soon as I can. . . . Lipton? LIPTON! *Shit.*"

Manny snapped the phone shut. Tina raised an eyebrow. "So?"

"So he's out of his mind, in the Stink District, where the slaughterhouses used to be. Great part of town if you own a gas mask."

"If it's such a shithole, why would the mayor's assistant be there?"

"I have no idea, but I hope he's comfy, 'cause it's gonna be a while till the cavalry arrives. We gotta get to the station." He turned to their de facto prisoner. "Ready, Mac? The cuffs okay?"

Shocked out of his stupor, McCardle simply stared, his mouth making abortive attempts at speech. His tongue skidded over his lower lip, as if struggling for traction.

"For Christ's sake, Mac. . . ."

Manny and Tina ran to the sofa and helped him up. Wedged between them, the addled weight lifter moved in a dazed, splay-footed shuffle toward the door and continued sputtering.

"Spit it out," Manny told him. "We don't have much time."

But McCardle only gaped, his eyes darting and frantic. *"Zank's,"* he finally managed.

"What's Zank's?" Tina asked, but Manny was losing patience.

"Forget it, he's tweaking."

Manny handed her the keys. "Unlock the car. I'll bring Crack-man in a second."

"Does this mean I've been deputized?"

"I'm not sure that's what I'd call it," Manny replied. Then McCardle started babbling again and Tina stayed to watch.

"Zank's," he ranted, slamming his cuffed hands off his forehead, hopping around in a way that reminded Manny of Rumpelstiltskin. They were about the same size. "Where Zank is, *where Zank is!*"

"Where Zank is, huh?" Manny'd booked a zillion pipeheads. The harder they tweaked, the steadier you needed to be to deal with them. "I don't know where Zank is. Probably out crippling the weak. Just relax, okay? You'll be all right as long as you shut up. You want, I can hit you in the head with something, knock you out. Might make the ride easier. Your call."

"No, no, *no!*" cried McCardle, emerging into something like coherence. "You don't understand!"

Manny grabbed him by both shoulders. "I understand fine, okay? I understand if you don't calm down, it's 'cause you want me to take a blunt object to your skull. It's not the kind of thing I like to do, but if it makes you happy, I'll go along. But only 'cause I like you."

McCardle lapsed into stunned silence. Tina killed her cigarette.

"You can be a cold son of a bitch," she said, without sounding particularly upset about it.

After Tina finally headed to the car, Manny hung back with McCardle, who'd started to spasm again. His teeth sounded like cuff links in a spin dryer. Manny dug in the side pocket of his yoga pants, unearthed the pair of soggy pills he'd retrieved from his soaking trousers, and offered them to the crack-damaged felon.

"Codeine," Manny told him. "It's still good, just a little mushy. Takes the edge off."

Offended, McCardle frowned at the drugs and raised his eyes. "No way, man. That shit's *addictive!*"

THIRTY-SIX

The idea came to Manny as they passed the Parakeet Lounge. McCardle, who'd been bouncing on the seat since Manny'd locked him in, seized up at the sight of the place.

"Scene of the crime, huh, buddy?"

This perked up Tina. "What's that supposed to mean?"

"You don't watch TV? Macky here's a celeb. Got that Hollywood mug on *America's Most Wanted.* Am I right?"

McCardle slunk lower in his seat as Manny slowed beside the bar, a powder-blue storefront with a yellow-and-green neon parakeet, dead in the daytime, perched over the entrance.

Tina wiped a porthole in the unwashed passenger window and peered out. "Isn't that a gay bar?"

"Only one in town. But we don't judge," said Manny. "The Skank-mobile is a judgment-free vehicle. Whatever goes on between consenting pervs is okay by me."

They watched a pair of pigeons roost on the neon parakeet, and Manny smiled over his shoulder. "Of course, I don't know if the boy Mac here wanged with a shovel actually consented. But who knows? Maybe he begged for it. Maybe he was one of those crazy shovel-freaks, and things got out of hand."

"Go ahead, make fun," McCardle whined, scratching his nose with his plasti-cuffs. "It's not your keister about to get fried. Bad enough I gotta go through what I'm about to go through, I gotta have some white sumbitch with a pompadour on the TV talkin' about it. No offense."

"None taken," said Manny, steering away from the bar. "Sometimes I'm ashamed to be a white man myself. Thing is, Mac, there's a way you could get your ass out of this shit."

"Which part of this shit you talkin' 'bout my ass gettin' out of?"

"The getting-on-TV part, for starters. But I wouldn't be surprised if you walked. Period."

McCardle sighed. "Your gratuitous barbarity is uncalled for." Then he slammed back in the seat and pouted. "Why you wanna do me like 'at?"

Manny met his eyes in the rearview. "Is it me, Mac, or are you some kind of a schiz? Half the time you sound straight outta Compton, the other half I'm thinking, 'This guy majored in humanities at Dartmouth and he's keeping it under his hat.'"

"Now you be talkin' just like Zank. Maybe I got dual citizenship."

"Nicely put," said Manny, switching lanes. "I'm no stranger to identity crisis. I'm a cop, and I don't like cops. But because I'm a cop, people who aren't cops don't like *me*. It's no picnic." Manny cleared his throat. "But enough about my little problems. What I'm saying is, you don't necessarily have to end up on national TV. Not if you don't want to. Though what I hear, once you make it onto *AMW,* you're a big man in the joint."

"That's great," sneered McCardle. "Problem is, people in *law enforcement,* all them DAs, are so down with that show, they'll jack up your sentence just to kiss John Walsh's balls. Some no-name do what I do, maybe he gets twelve to life, gets sprung in eight and change. But they flash your face on *America's Most Wanted,* don't matter *what* you did, they'll give you five lifes consecutive. Shit, they'll give you the goddamn chair, just so's that dude can get on TV and *brag* on your dead ass."

Manny laughed. "Call me a party-poop, you did kill a guy. But like I say, in this car we don't judge. I'm just telling you, pal, you wanna go for it, I'm giving you a way to improve your situation."

"Uh-huh. You're gonna do that, with the reward they got hangin' over my dusky butt."

"Well technically, no. Only the chief can let you go. He's the one hung up on the reward. Though personally, I think the whole thing's bunk."

McCardle rehurled himself against the seatback. "See, there you go. *Fuckin'* with me. This whole time, gettin' my hopes up, talkin' 'bout 'maybe this, maybe that,' this whole damn time, you just *fuckin'* with me."

"McCardle, I'm not fucking with you. You do me one favor"— Manny snapped his fingers—"I can make it all go away."

"Oh yeah? And what *I* gotta do? Maybe I did smoke somebody, which I *didn't,* that don't mean I meant to. And it sure as shit don't mean I'm gonna smoke somebody for you. You wanna hit, you come to the wrong nigger. You wanna play that way, talk to Zank. He'd shoot a motherfucker just to see which way he bleed." Mac banged his bound hands off his knees for emphasis. "That man is plain *amoral.*"

Manny caught Tina's eye and winked. He wasn't usually a winker, but lately it seemed called for. He cocked his finger for Mac to lean forward, then whispered in his ear. McCardle let out a gasp and shrunk to a far corner of the backseat. "No way, man! No *way* I'm gonna do that!"

"Come on, just one kiss," Manny said, catching the prisoner's eyes in the rearview. "How bad can that be? I'm sure you've done worse for less. I know *I* have."

McCardle lowered his eyes, going for his "pleading-Dino" look, and Manny ignored him. He picked up the phone and punched out a number. "Fayton? It's Rubert. I'm coming in with McCardle. . . . Hey, spare me the faux-surprise, I know about the tap. That's not why I'm calling. I just want to make sure you remember the deal. . . . No! No, no, *no!* We talked about this. No press. Nada. . . . *Because I fucking say so, that's why!*"

Manny threw the phone down on the Impala's floor and grinned happily. Tina had to ask. "Isn't Fayton the chief of police?"

"That's what it says on his door."

"And that's how you talk to him?"

"We have an understanding. So what's it gonna be, Mac?"

McCardle scrunched up his gigolo's face, conflicted. "A thing like that could ruin a man's reputation."

"Is that right?" Manny hit the brakes so suddenly Tina fell forward and McCardle, who wasn't wearing his belt, was thrown face-first into the back of the front seat. Ignoring him, Manny opened the glove compartment, selected one of the eight-by-tens Roos developed from the dildo-cam, and tossed it over his shoulder.

"While you're thinking, Macho Man, take a peek at this."

"Shee-it," said McCardle theatrically, acting put out until he picked the glossy off the floor. Then he shrieked. "Oh man, this is . . . this is *inappropriate!*" He began to breathe rapidly, switched to sniffly weeping, and worked his way up to full-blown sobs before Tina dabbed his tiny nose with a Kleenex. "We didn't wanna do this," McCardle blubbered. "She made us. That big lady, from the home. The one with the beehive. *Carmella.* She pulled out a gun and said I had to do Tony or she'd blow my *pinga* off."

"Your what?"

"What do you *think?* My *bone* phone . . . my *love*-thang . . . my manhood, okay? She had a gun on it. Lord, I didn't even *see* no camera! Musta been somebody under the bed." His sobs grew plaintive. "You gotta believe me!"

"Whatever." Manny smiled sympathetically into the rearview. "*I* believe you, Mac. But that's just me. Once this picture starts showing up places, who knows? What I hear, a lot of your finer homosexual magazines pay top dollar for a shot like this. You bein' such a beefcake and all. . . . Of course, the worst thing would probably be if copies of this got in the joint when you were in there. Imagine if the fellas on the yard had a chance to check it out. . . . Now *that* could fuck up a man's reputation. But hey, no pressure, brother. You do what you gotta do."

THIRTY-SEVEN

Massive shoulders hunched, a copy of *Mademoiselle* raised in front of his face, McCardle did the perp walk from Manny's Impala to the sliding doors of the police station. The *Mademoiselle* was Manny's idea, and they'd stopped at a 7-Eleven on the way down to pick one up.

"Keep 'em guessing," he explained, when McCardle asked why he couldn't go with *Muscle and Fitness*.

"But *Mademoiselle*'s not me," he protested, and Manny had to launch into his my-way-or-the-highway rap all over again.

Tina walked behind them, ready with the story Manny'd supplied in case Fayton asked what the hell she was doing there. "Get teary," Manny'd told her in the car. "Get all new widowy and distraught. Tell him you're so grief-stricken about Marv you were gonna do yourself, then you found my card and I swung by to pick you up, get you into some grief counseling down at U. M. General. But we had to make a stop."

Chief Fayton, meanwhile, waited just inside, hopping from foot to foot like a nine-year-old who had to to go the bathroom. Merch was theoretically desk sergeant but rarely bothered to man the fortresslike desk that flanked the entrance, preferring to hang out in back by the candy machine. It wasn't like the station did a lot of business. Whole days went by with no more than the odd bar-thug or bus-flasher. Seeing Fayton in such high dither, however, brought Merch up front. Krantz, too, had rolled in to check out the action.

These were the moments the chief lived for, and Fayton intercepted Manny the second he came through the door. After glaring at his outfit—somehow, the yoga-wear seemed more *orange* under police station fluorescents—he edged in front of Manny, next to the suspect.

"This him?"

Fayton grabbed McCardle by the arm. He loved to get tough with perpetrators. To show what he was made of. Manny noticed a photographer from the *Trumpet*. He leaned in close to the chief and whispered.

"I told you, no pictures."

"Officer, I don't think—"

"You don't think what? You wanna fuck everything up?"

"Well no, but . . . but can we at least *call* now?" Fayton could not keep the greed out of his voice. "Ruby, we don't want to lose that reward."

Tina sized up the situation and pulled her Viceroys out of her purse. Fayton stopped pleading long enough to nail her. "This station is a smoke-free zone, young lady."

"Fine with me," she said, announcing to anyone who cared. "I'd rather catch cancer outside anyway."

She planted a smooch on Manny's cheek and sauntered off with an extra twitch in her walk. Fayton and Manny both watched her move, McCardle hovering uncomfortably between them. His huge bicep had begun to tire from holding up the magazine. It was the Fall Fashion Issue, and it was bulky. He switched hands as Krantz, Merch, Mindy the

Dispatcher, and a moody ex-con named Melvin who delivered sandwiches crowded in for a peek.

"Very nice, bringing a date to an interrogation," the chief huffed. "You've got some explaining to do, Detective."

Manny stepped past McCardle, so close to Fayton he barely had to whisper. "My days of explaining anything to you are over. You wanna pretend you're the Man to the rest of the world, fine. I *know* what you are."

Fayton glowered. "Very well. But I still think we should lock up that reward money before it's too late."

"You call now," Manny lectured him, "they're gonna take all the credit. You want that? No! What you want is for everybody to know it was Chief Lyn Fayton's superior police work that snagged this guy. You want the money *and* the props. You want it all, or am I wrong?"

"No, no," said Fayton. "You're right."

"Good. I'm glad we agree. So do the right thing for once. The *smart* thing."

Manny gave the chief's arm a knowing squeeze, amazed all over again at the power of greed and ego to render a human stupid. In fact, he knew exactly what would happen if the chief called the *AMW* people. They'd send down a crew, do an interview, have the chief swear that it was seeing the killer's face on *America's Most Wanted* that led to his capture, and make Fayton famous for a week. The downside, of course: It would fuck up Manny's personal plans.

Fayton grumbled but had to concede; when it came to scheming, nobody could outdo Rubert. The bastard had him licking his boots in his own station. All because he'd bumped off Chatlak, who was nothing but a dandruff factory anyway. He'd done the old guy a favor. It was all so unfair. So *unenlightened!* A person could only take so much. . . .

Catching Manny before he could step back to the prisoner, Fayton stammered sotto voce, "There's no harm in a couple of photographs!"

Manny pretended to scowl. "I'm telling you, don't do it!"

The chief ignored him and waved the shutterbug over, and Manny gave McCardle the nod. They'd rehearsed it all on the ride over. The photographer swooped forward and assumed a crouch. Fayton shoe-horned himself beside McCardle, fixing his face in a crime-fighting scowl. The five-four felon glanced in panic at Manny, who nodded again. *Now.*

The photographer pressed his eye to the camera, finger poised to shoot, and McCardle jumped forward, thrusting his puckered lips toward the chief. He kissed Fayton hard on the lips at the exact instant the shutter clicked.

"You big stud, I've missed you *so much!*" Mac cried, before Fayton could react. "But sometimes you make me so *jealous!* You *know* you're the only man for me! Have you told your wife yet?"

Fayton's face collapsed in terror and McCardle moved in. He kissed him again, and the chief tried to slap him away.

"What the—? *Stop!* Stop the pictures! *Stop the fucking pictures!*"

But the photographer, sensing that this was his Ruby-shoots-Oswald moment, ignored him. He snapped away as Mac launched himself upward for another smooch, catching the chief square on the mouth.

Krantz and Merch were both snickering, until Mindy, who'd refound Jesus after a brief lapse, thrust the wooden cross she wore around her neck toward the chief and let him have it. "Abomination!" she exclaimed. "Adam and *Eve,* not Adam and *Steve!*"

"Shut *up!*" Fayton shouted, turning in desperation to his nearest underlings. "Goddamnit Krantz, get this pervert off me! He's insane! Merch, use your stun gun!"

Shocked as they were, neither policeman could find the will to move. Finally Manny came to his boss's aide.

"I told you not to bring in photographers," he whispered. "I was trying to *protect* you."

Manny faux-struggled to peel McCardle off Fayton, but the diminutive criminal continued shrieking, arms flailing as Manny tugged at him. "I love you, Poopy. I'll always love you! I just want to feel your arms around me again! *Please!* I want to be your chocolate love-toy! How can you pretend you don't know me, after all those nights of ecstasy? Lyn, please! You said you loved me! You said we were going to find a Unitarian minister and get married! You promised me a *gown!*"

Fayton's face had gone ashen. For one bad second Manny thought he was going to pull a Cheney, have a heart attack on the spot. "Get this man down to interrogation," he ordered Krantz. The Mullet was eager to please after the dressing-down Manny'd given him for barging in when he caught Manny with his face between Tina's thighs. ("Lesson One, Rookie: No matter what it looks like, never question another officer's tactics. It could mean the difference between life and death!")

Manny, guiding the still-stunned Fayton down the hall, called over his shoulder to Merch. "Do me a favor, get the photographer out of here." Then he leaned back in to the chief. "We're just going down to question the suspect. It's going to be okay. Trust me."

In the tiny Interrogation Room, Manny and Fayton watched through adjoining peepholes as Krantz unfolded a metal chair and shoved McCardle into it. They'd ordered a two-way mirror years ago, but it was installed backward and shattered when Merch cracked it with his forehead trying to get it out of the wall. He claimed shrapnel from the Tet Offensive made him pitch forward occasionally, but the city managers thought he'd been drinking and refused to reorder. So they'd gone with peepholes.

"I want you to know, I'm not judging you," Manny whispered, keeping a supporting hand on the chief's back. "I *understand*."

Fayton blanched. "What are you talking about? This is some fabrication! He's deranged!"

"Of course he is." Manny put on his most soothing voice. "And I'll do my best to try and keep Mayor Marge from hearing about it."

"Mayor Marge?" Of the myriad hellacious consequences inflaming his brain, this was one Fayton hadn't considered. "Why does Mayor Marge have to hear about it?"

"She doesn't. And I'll do everything I can to make sure nobody leaks it to her. I know how bad that would be for you."

"But it's all *lies!* I've never seen this man, except on TV. He's making it all up!"

"You know it, and I know it. But you have to admit, it doesn't look good."

"*What?*"

"Think of the headlines: POLICE CHIEF'S SECRET TRYST WITH EX-

CON HOMO-KILLER! How do *you* think it sounds? This thing goes national, I don't even want to *think* about it. . . ."

Fayton sputtered as if his oxygen had been cut off. His eyes seemed to swim in his head.

"Gentlemen, we're ready," Krantz called from the Interrogation Room.

"Hold that thought," Manny told the chief. "Let's see if we can poke some holes in lover boy's story. Why don't you take a Valium or something?"

"I don't take drugs."

"Maybe you should start," said Manny, laying on another supportive back-pat before ducking into Interrogation.

McCardle sat at the small wooden table, his large head in his hands in front of a sandwich-size Radio Shack tape recorder. Krantz lingered behind him, holding the door as Manny swept in.

"Coffee, Sir?"

"Coffee? Somebody oughta bring this piece of shit a jug of dog-piss! You read his jacket?"

Krantz patted his hair-pad. "Uh, no, I—"

"Don't bother," said Manny. "It's bullshit. *Candy-ass* this, *candy-ass* that." He swung around and slapped his palm on the table in front of McCardle's face. "Two-time loser? Full-time loser's more like it. This clown gives criminals a bad name. Then he ups and brains some butt-rustler in a goddamn boy bar." Manny hoped he sounded convincing. "It's *disgusting!*"

"I want a lawyer," McCardle squeaked.

"You're not under arrest. You're here as our guest."

Manny dropped into a folding chair across from Mac and clamped his hands in prayer at his chest. He took a deep, dramatic breath and closed his eyes. When he opened them, he went into his best Jimmy Swaggart. Jimmy when he's apologizing for impure deeds, for masturbating in motel rooms with overweight prostitutes.

"I'm sorry, Mr. McCardle. I got carried away. I'm a little upset, that's all. You see, that's my boss you're slandering. That's my *friend*. A man I *admire*. Can you understand that? You have people you admire, don't you, Mac? You don't mind if I call you Mac, do you?"

Manny didn't wait for an answer. He crooked his finger for Krantz.

"Officer, maybe you had a good idea there. Bring this fellow a cup of coffee. Bring cream, sugar, half-and-half. No! What am I thinking? Our man's a weight lifter, Krantz. Body like a baby Schwarzenegger. Bring him some skim. I'll take mine white and creamy. Who cares if *I* get a spare tire? *I'm* not the Hercules at this clambake. And close the door on the way out."

Krantz balked. "I don't know, Manny. Maybe I ought to stay, get your back. I mean, he killed a guy."

"Hey," said Manny, "do your job. I lost my temper, and I apologized. He'll be fine. Right, Mac? The butt-rustler crack, I didn't mean it, okay? That was crude. It was ignorant. I was upset. That wasn't *me* talking. Some of my best friends are gay. Maybe *I'm* gay. Who knows? I'm all fucked up here. It's a bad day. This thing on?" Manny tapped the recorder. "Krantz, before you go, can you help me out here? I'm the worst with machines." He raised his hands, miming helplessness, and shook his head to McCardle. "I know, I know. I'm a virile guy, I should be handy. But that's me. I need a week of night school to plug in a fucking hot plate."

Krantz pressed RECORD and Manny waved him off again. "Coffee. Go!"

When they were alone, Manny dragged his chair around the table, until he was almost rubbing knees with McCardle. He spoke very softly, with what sounded like affection.

"Let's just kind of wade in here, okay? Full name?"

"Mac Donald McCardle."

"Old MacDonald, huh? Nice touch. Mom into drugs?"

"I don't have to talk about my momma."

"Of course you don't. God knows I hate talking about mine. That lying *cunt!*"

McCardle winced, and Manny held up his hands.

"Sorry, thought I was alone. . . . I know your mom's doing time. Gets out in 2039, right? I know everything. But we have to start with this stuff. Police policy. It's a formality. How about place of employment?"

McCardle straightened in his chair. "Self-employed."

"I'm sniffing an entrepreneur," said Manny. "Home address?"

"I've been stayin' with friends."

"Friends? How nice. I guess that's where they send your tax state-ments, huh? You being self-employed and all. They just send stuff to your *friends'* house."

Manny rubbed his stomach and groaned. "*Mmmff.* . . . I'd strangle a nun for a Bromo right now. I got one of those bellyaches, feels like I'm about to give birth to a piece of *pig iron.* Now you wanna tell me what really went down? Start at the Parakeet."

McCardle lowered his eyes and shook his outsize, immaculate head. They'd rehearsed on the way over. *Make it look like I'm goading you,* Manny'd told him. *Like I'm pushing your buttons.*

McCardle began to pant, his mammoth trapezoids heaving beneath his shirt.

"I . . . I *can't.*"

Manny wasn't sure if he was acting or not. He'd done beautifully so far, but you never knew. . . .

"Listen to me, Mac, you're looking at a world of shit. You give us something we can use, maybe we can work with you. I know you weren't out there alone. And I know your little shovel party isn't the only thing on the menu. You've been a busy little bee. Nobody likes a snitch, but come on—you think Tony Z would think twice about sell-ing *your* pert behind down the river?"

McCardle sniffled, and Manny backed off.

"Now, the Parakeet. If that's too personal to kick off with, fine. Give us something on the Pawnee Lodge. Or Seventh Heaven. Or Dee-Dee Walker. Or maybe that holy man you guys banged up, huh? I gotta say, you and your road dog, Zank, you fellas were on a real spree. Old ladies, middle-aged nurses, a priest . . . I mean, step aside John Dillinger! I'm surprised you didn't knock off any schoolkids. Oh wait—my mistake!—*you did!* Though technically, I don't know if L'il Pepe was enrolled at the time of his demise."

Manny gave McCardle's shoulders a friendly rub.

"Thing is, Mr. McCardle, I don't see you as the heavy in this stuff. Call me a cockeyed optimist, I'm thinkin', y'know, maybe you hooked up with Zank in the joint. You both did jolts upstate. Maybe when you got out you decided to team up. Butch and Sundance on crack. But it didn't play. Guy may be King Shit inside, out on the street he's just another psycho with artillery. But you can't shake him,'cause after you pull a couple jobs, you know too much. You try to split, he'll ice you, right? Plus which, all that ridin' around, lookin' for people to fuck up, you two do a lot of talking. Almost like being cellies. He knows where you hang, where your girlfriends live, where your grandma goes to church, every little thing. You try to bail—*huh-uh*—a crackhead like Tony's gonna get paranoid. Gonna think you're gamin' him, maybe cuttin' a deal. Next thing you know he tracks down Granny and makes her deep-throat his chicken bone. Or beats her with the phone book. Who knows what a freak like that is capable of? The bottom line, you don't have a choice. You gotta hang in. So what happens? 'Cause you're tryin' to do the right thing, to protect your loved ones from this maniac, you end up an accomplice to all kinds of shit you never wanted any part of. I mean, *come on,* we both know the score. Tony's not the kind of guy takes no for an answer."

Manny crossed his arms behind his head and leaned back.

"But, fuck me! I been doing all the talking. It's your face, I gotta admit. You're so damn elegant, the way you work that whole Dino thing. Makes me a real chatterbox. But just between us girls, that's not exactly an asset on Death Row. You've been down, Mac. You know how it is. Pretty as you are, those fellas ain't gonna be after you for beauty tips. . . . It's lonely in there!"

Tears welled in McCardle's eyes. He bit down hard on his lip, his fine-honed nostrils beginning to quiver.

"Krantz," Manny yelled, "where's that fucking coffee!"

On cue, the young officer popped back in, setting Styrofoam cups on the table, along with a quart of skim milk and a fistful of Sweet'n Lows.

Manny grabbed a cup. He poked a hole in the plastic lid and slurped. A few drops of coffee splashed onto his yoga pants and he slapped himself. "Oh *perfect!* Now it's gonna look like I dribbled. I hate that! It's like, you see some hot chick, then she notices your pants are wet and gives you that *look.* You know the look I'm talking about. You want to say, 'Hey, it's not what you think. It's coffee. Really!' But you can't. You have to stand there while she makes you for your some loser who *drips*. Or worse, she's gonna think you just pulled your pud. I'm telling you, sometimes life is a fucking nightmare. . . ."

McCardle regarded him with confusion, and Manny waved his hands.

"I'm sorry. Ignore me. Bad day, I told you. Let's get back to the Parakeet. You give up Tony on the other stuff, we can work with you."

Manny took another slurp, then fixed a coffee for Mac. "Just a splash, right? I made you for a skim man right off. You health nuts! Go on, I'll shut up. Lay it out for me, Adonis. Take your time."

McCardle continued to stare in sullen silence. Until Manny tugged his right earlobe—that was the signal, in honor of the slice Tina took out of Zank—and Mac hurled himself out of his chair as if propelled.

"He messed with my *man!*" the tiny fireplug exploded. "He tried to move in on my sweet policeman. I couldn't have that, y'hear me? I wouldn't stand for some toilet-trick tryin' to get between me and the man I love!"

"Whoa, whoa, back up," said Manny. "*Who* tried to move in? And who'd they try to move in on? This some kind of love triangle?"

Manny stole a quick glance at the peephole to the left, where he knew Fayton would be watching, and gave a *hell-if-I-know!* shrug.

McCardle banged the table. "That boy at the Parakeet. He be goin' around sayin' how him and my sweet chief had a *thang*. He say my man tell him he gonna make *him* his special girl. But that ain't true. That ain't *never* gonna be true. 'Cause Poopy love me. I *know* he do! He even tell me 'bout his wife. Lady *Florence*. He say she used to be sexy but now she packin' on shoulder-fat. He say she pumped so much Botox in her fo'head, she always look surprised. He even 'fraid to kiss her, in case some of that swine hormone leak out, 'cause that stuff be *poison*. Uh-huh. Poopy don't just buy me presents. He *tell* me stuff."

Manny threw up his hands. "You lost me on that curve. Who's Poopy?"

"*Chief Fayton!* Thass his *love*-name."

The little strong man's shoulders worked up and down like pistons as he sobbed. "He all the time sayin' no one know his love-name but me. And I believed him. I *still* believe him. But then that pony boy in the bar be sayin' Poopy like him better! I knew he had to be lyin'. . . .

Oh God," wailed McCardle, his voice visiting the higher registers. *"Poopy please! Poopy, you said we should never be 'shamed of who we are!"*

On the other side of the peephole, Fayton closed his eyes. He saw fabric, great swaths of it. The lovely, fleur-de-lis pattern danced before him and he knew, in that moment, that he'd never see his office redone in the magisterial style to which he aspired.

The chief had never fired a gun outside the range—and even that was only twice, since the Academy didn't push marksmanship on fellows flagged for administration. Coming from his post at the DMV, nobody expected Fayton to actually go out and fight crime. But he had a weapon, a Beretta nine-millimeter—standard issue of the L.A.P.D., according to the brochure that came with it—which he kept in the hand-tooled ankle holster he'd ordered off Cop.com.

Fayton suffered another bad moment trying to figure out the clip, and when he got it in he said the Lord's Prayer to steady his nerves. Keeping the Nine in front of him, he pressed his eye grimly to the peephole, observing this insane young Negro who harbored some deep-seated delusion that he'd been romantically involved with the chief of police. *Had to happen,* Fayton consoled himself. *Your weak sister types are drawn to powerful men. They can't help it. . . .*

Meanwhile, Manny forged on, his voice simultaneously incredulous and soothing. "Let me get this straight, you're saying that you and Chief Fayton were *engaged?* You were going to be married, but then you found out he was seeing this other fellow, this . . . Armand Putella? And *that's* why you cracked Putella's skull open with a shovel?"

McCardle buried his face in his hands. "It was a crime of *passion.*"

Manny whistled, then picked up the tape recorder to make sure it was still on. He didn't even see Fayton enter the Interrogation Room until he was already on top of McCardle.

"Chief? What are you—"

"Interview's over," Fayton said. And before Manny could stop him, the chief leveled the L.A.P.D.'s favorite hardware at McCardle's head, closed his eyes, and pulled the trigger.

·   ·   ·

When he realized he wasn't dead, McCardle climbed cautiously off the floor. He checked himself like someone stumbling out of a bombed building to see if anything was missing. Discovering he was still in one piece, he stared in stunned horror at his attacker.

Chief Fayton, at point-blank range, had managed to miss his target and blast a hole in the table. The report from the Beretta still echoed in the room. Manny extended his hand and asked the chief for his weapon. *"Nice and easy."*

Krantz, who'd heard the Nine's report from his post by the coffee machine, had dashed in with his own gun drawn. But Manny waved him away. "Stand down, Krantz!"

The young officer reluctantly holstered his weapon and stalked off. Manny turned back to Fayton. The chief loomed over McCardle, unmoving except for a tic in his cheek, gazing at him with an expression that said, *"Why?"*

Manny eased Fayton into a folding chair. "Come on, Tiger," he said, as if speaking to an errant eleven-year-old. "Violence won't solve anything." Then he cupped his hand to the chief's ear and whispered, "This makes it look like you have something to hide. Why don't you go back upstairs?"

"You mean, you're not going to arrest me?"

"I don't think that will be necessary," said Manny. "Not unless Mac here wants to press charges."

Still dazed from the blast, McCardle just stared at the two men. "See," Manny said, "he's not going to do that."

"And you won't. . . ." The chief raised his face to Manny, his eyes haunted.

"Tell?" Manny gave his commanding officer's arm a manly squeeze. "Of course not." He seemed, of late, to be in the manly squeeze–dispensing business. But what the hell? He felt strangely tender toward the two stricken characters before him. He'd induced them both to behave exactly as he'd wished. And the best part was, nobody got hurt. Not physically, anyway. Fayton *did* have that haunted look in his eye. But that only made sense. Adding to the chief's shame at being in the center of a sordid, nonhetero sex crime, he was now exposed as a cop who couldn't hit a stationary target ten inches away in perfect light. Which had to hurt.

Fayton kept staring at his own hand as if it belonged to somebody else. It was his hand that had picked up the gun and pulled the trigger, not him. . . . But Manny's real concern was for McCardle. Young Mac, God bless him, had played his part beautifully. Beyond his Dean-alike charisma, he was an absolute natural as an actor. When things settled down, Manny planned on encouraging the young man to pursue a career on-screen. Of course, the height thing might work against him, but lots of big stars were tiny guys. Tom Cruise wasn't exactly strapping. And it hadn't slowed down Hoffmann or Pacino over the years, either.

"I want him out of here," Fayton declared, speaking in a shell-shocked monotone. "Let him go. Now."

Manny blinked back from his tiny superstar reverie. "Can't do that," he said.

"Why not?"

"For one thing, Armand Putella isn't the only treat on the table. There's the little matter of Carmella Dendez, and the priest. Plus, even though the evidence is still circumstantial, I'd make him for the Dee-Dee Walker thing, too. And let's not even get into Felipe Garcia. Better known to friends and customers as L'il Pepe. That one bled to death after his foot was ripped off. Crack brings out the best in everybody, don't you think? He was fourteen."

McCardle jumped. "I didn't do *none* of those!"

"Any," Manny corrected. "Don't go homey on me. And I didn't say you did. But you were there with Zank. Even if you weren't actually stabbing, driving, or foot-ripping, it wouldn't take Clarence fucking Darrow to prove you were an accomplice."

"Clarence who?"

"Forget it."

As if no one else had spoken, Fayton set his jaw and repeated himself. "I said, I want him out of here."

Manny aimed his gaze at the water-stained ceiling. A dozen of the dirty beige soundproof tiles were either missing or curled partly off.

"Okay, listen, both of you. If Tony Zank sees his partner walk the same day he was brought in, he's going to think one thing. You understand me?" Manny turned to McCardle. "He's going to think he's been snitched off. No way in hell Mac hits the street without giving something up. And the only thing he got to give is him. You with me?"

McCardle wilted in his chair, and Manny shifted to Fayton. He spoke slowly, to make sure what he had to say sunk in.

"If you want to release this man, on the condition he stops talking about your—" Manny feigned discomfort, just to see the chief squirm—"about your alleged *relationship*, that can happen. But we have to make it look good. We gotta hold McCardle for at least a week. It'll be our little secret."

Hearing this, Mac began to sniffle, as though he'd just been sent to Attica for forty years to break rocks.

"Look on the bright side," said Manny. "Three hots and a cot. All you have to do is tell us where he is."

"You *know* where he is. Your boy Lipton gave you the address. I heard you and the lady talking about it."

Manny balked. "Why didn't you tell me?"

"I *tried* to," McCardle whined. "Check out the Bundthouse Arms. Number Three. That's Tony's place. He ain't hard to find 'cause he's the only one living there. He's the only one who can stand the smell."

THIRTY-EIGHT

The hooker took one look at Tony Zank's blood-pulped face and backed away from the door. She was a whip-thin, sloe-eyed brunette in six-inch heels. Her fishnet stockings sagged under her red leather microskirt, but the cutoff Metallica T-shirt she wore under her chinchilla jacket was so tight her nipples stood out like knuckles. A tiny heart dangled out of her pierced belly button, which looked infected.

"What the hell happened to you?" she shrieked, clutching her car keys to her chest.

"What do you think happened?" Zank had found her number in the Yellow Pages, under Escorts, and when he called up she asked if he was a police officer. Tony'd ordered up before. He knew that only pros asked if you were a cop when you gave them your address. "I was in a bus accident," he told her. "On my way to work. Fucking bus driver drove into a phone pole when a possum ran across the road. You believe that? He saves a goddamn possum, now *I* got a mug like road-kill."

"You lie," said the girl.

"Hey," he shrugged. "You don't gotta touch me above the neck."

Zank glanced over the girl's shoulder to see if anyone was looking. He wasn't officially checked in, if you wanted to get technical. But he liked the Pawnee Lodge, despite what happened there with Carmella and McCardle. More important, he still had the key to Number Two, the room he never used.

Zank pulled the girl inside. "Just come in and we'll talk about it. It's uncool standing here. You don't exactly look like a Jehovah's Witness."

"You should talk," said the girl, eyeballing the room where Tony'd made himself at home. Clumps of Chore Boy dotted the dresser top, scattered around his glass pipe, some empty vials, and the five rocks he still had left. Zank didn't know for sure whether McCardle had ratted him out. But he knew enough to know he might be taking a risk going home. Which was a drag, for all kinds of reasons. Not the least of which being that Mac had dug up the phone numbers of some big-timey Republicans, party stalwarts who'd be willing to pay plenty for snaps of W.'s bubble, to put the kibosh on a potential scandal. "First we tell 'em we have the nut-shots," McCardle'd explained, in one of his rare take-charge moments. "Then we tell 'em there's a happy face painted on them, *then* we tell 'em they're superbloated two inches from the mayor of Upper Marilyn's mouth. Once that sinks in, all we gotta do is make sure the money's in cash."

Assuming McCardle could still move his lips, Zank had to figure he'd already fingered him. Which meant they'd have his apartment scoped, if they hadn't already tossed it. No, Tony had to come up with something on his own. Which was why he decided to call *Time*. He was hitting the pipe and thinking about what to do next when a rock popped out on the carpet. Thrashing around for it, he'd discovered the old news magazine under the bed. Bill Gates was on the cover, looking very NAMBLA. Tony took this as a sign. It was *Time*! But when he tried calling their office in New York, the snotbag who answered the phone hung up when he told him his business.

What kind of dude worked as a telephone operator, anyway? Had to be some kind of pud-monkey. "Time Warner," the operator'd said, "how may I direct your call?" "Well," Tony explained, "I'm sittin' here looking at some Polaroids of President Bush's testiculars, and that's not all. He drew a smiley face on 'em, in Magic Marker. Guy must have a lotta free time. Who do *you* think I should talk to?" There was a long silence after that, before the puffwad just clicked off. Tony called right back, and this time got a friendly lady who connected him to the photo department, where he tried a different tack with a young-sounding girl who said she was the assistant photo editor. "This is your lucky day!" Tony told her, trying to come on upbeat and professional right out of the chute, "I have pictures of George Bush Junior's genitalia." "I'm sorry?" the girl said. "Don't be," Tony continued, "you'll probably get a raise. This is the type of thing your editor in chief is going to want, especially when you see what they're doing." "What who are doing?" the girl asked, in a tone Tony couldn't quite get a bead on. "The president's testicles," Tony said. "I didn't know they *could* do anything," the girl giggled. "Well," Tony persisted, *"that's* why you need to see these pictures."

He was proud of himself for the editor in chief angle, but in the end it didn't matter. At least the assistant photo editor said good-bye before slamming the phone down. . . .

Metallica Girl snapped her fingers in his face. "You gonna stand there or you wanna do something? I got my kid in the car."

"Okay! Keep your tits on."

Ignoring his guest, Tony tamped at the filthy Band-Aid flopping off his earlobe, then stretched out his upper lip and stuck his finger in his mouth. He poked around until he found what he wanted, a loose chunk of gum flesh that had been driving him crazy since Pepe pistol-whipped him. He ripped out the bloody morsel and smeared it on his pants. His missing tooth hurt like fuck, but he was amazed how little pain his sliced-up ear caused. The blade must have missed his lobe nerves.

"That's better," Tony said, having finished his little surgery. He plopped down on the bed and patted the spot beside him. "So how much?"

The girl hung back, playing with the tiny heart in her belly button.

"Twenty-five."

"For what?"

"Blowjob."

"What if I want somethin' else?"

"You should've thought about that before you stuck your face in a fan."

Tony smiled. "I am having one fucked-up day," he said, spreading his knees wide over the side of the bed. "Pull down my zipper and say hi to Mister Rogers."

"Money first."

"Come on, I'm just tryin' to get some love here!"

He tried to reach under her leather skirt and she smacked his hand. "No cash, no gash."

Tony tugged a crumpled twenty out of his pocket. "That's all I got."

"Bigshot." The girl snatched the bill and squeezed it into a crumpled ball. "Okay, unpack."

Sighing—he didn't want trouble, just some honest relief—Tony laid back and fished himself out of his pants. The girl's scream jerked him up again.

"What?" he yelled, fumbling for the gun under the pillow.

"You're *bleeding!* No way am I gonna do you."

Tony checked himself. Sure enough, his wrinkled organ was dabbed with blood, and clumps of his patchy pubic hair were dyed bright red.

"Relax," he said, "it's not dick-blood. I must have touched myself."

"Excuse me?"

"You know, I probably rubbed my face or something, then held my doggy when I went to the bathroom. It's no thing."

"It's blood," said the girl. "I knew you were a sick shit the second I saw you. Fucking crackhead!"

She turned to go, and Tony caught her hand. "What's your hurry? I don't even know your name."

The girl glared at him. "If it's Tuesday I'm Cherry. But I don't know if it's Tuesday, okay?"

"You took my money, you can't walk out now."

The girl bounced the balled-up twenty off his forehead. "Keep your money, cock-breath. It's probably diseased anyway. Now lemme the fuck go!"

Tony wrestled her close, keeping one hand on her throat and shoving the other between her skinny legs. She went for his eyes and missed. He tried to jam a finger inside her—sometimes that got girls hot—but it was no go. "How come you're dry?" he said hoarsely. "You some kind of dyke?"

Tony yanked her hair, and the girl whipped something out of her coat. It looked like a skinny deodorant can, and for one happy second he thought, *Nice, she wants to freshen up. . . .* But when she raised the can to his face and pressed the nozzle, his skin exploded in scalding pain. His eyeballs felt scorched in their sockets. Tony yelped and ran for water. But his pants were around his knees. He made two steps and tripped. Picking himself off the carpet, he began to crawl, gasping up at her. *"You peppered me, you bitch! I'm on fire . . . ! I'M ON FUCKING FIRE!"*

The hooker drove a stiletto heel in his ribs as Tony struggled to tug his pants over his shoes. It was like some demented IQ test. When he finally managed to get his pants on and stand, he staggered straight into a wall. Feeling his way to the bathroom, he found the sink and started to splash water on his face. When suddenly—*What the fuck?*—there was a hand on his ass cheeks. She was spreading him.

"Hey, Hey! No! Cut that out! Hey, NO—"

Screams tore out of him as she pepper-sprayed his sphincter. It felt like he'd shit a barbecued chicken.

Tony spun around to grab her but she tripped him. He crashed hard off the toilet. Brain-dizzy, he pushed himself up. All he could think of were glaciers. If he could just get to Alaska and sit on a glacier. Then something banged—it all happened fast—and she shoved him forward, down, crunching his throat on the rim of the bowl. She slammed the seat on the back of his head and his face hit liquid. *Fuck!* From now on he'd flush.

Zank's anus felt napalmed, his face sautéed, but in spite of the agony at both ends, he smiled into the rust-stained bowl. He mouthed words underwater, chuckling bubbles. *Just leave my coke, bitch, I'll only rape you a little before I suck your eyes out and fuck the holes. . . .*

. . .

When Tony came to, he realized he was alone and dragged himself out of the commode. His eyes still burned. He blinked a few times and made out the blurry forms of the sink, the door, the wastebasket. *Not blind.*

He lurched out of the bathroom to the dresser and checked his supplies. He shoved a rock in the pipe, fired up, smoked it wet-lipped, and staggered to the bed. Lifted the pillow. The .357 was still there.

Zank collapsed on the mattress, exhaled, and let the jagged rush overtake him. His nerves were screaming in Siamese. He sped back to the bathroom, stood over the toilet, and flushed. That echoey *WHOOSH* always calmed him, like Niagara Falls in Sensurround.

There was no way he could stay in the Pawnee Lodge. Not now! This was a bad idea to begin with. He'd killed a lady in the next room. *What was he thinking?* Sometimes he didn't know what his brain was saying until he smoked some crack and it started yelling at him.

"Okay," he said, trying not to piss himself off. "Okay, be quiet, I'm *leaving.* Shut the fuck *UP!*"

He spun back to the dresser and squooshed all the rocks back into vials. Before a run, he liked to handle his shit. After the crack was stashed, he slid the pipe in his sock, retrieved the .357, and scooped up the keys to the Saab. He rushed to the door, opened it a sliver, and checked the room one last time. That's when he realized he had no pants on.

"Close call," he muttered, and moved jerkily back inside. The pants weren't anywhere he could see, so he looked under the bed. *No.* Maybe she'd thrown them in the closet. *No.* Maybe the bathroom. *No.*

Did he already check under the bed?

No! *No, No, No, NO NO NO NO!*

Naked from socks to navel—he hated underpants, they chafed— Zank paced in tight circles in the center of the room. He squeezed his hands into fists, mashed them into his pan-fried eyeballs, and moaned. Then he opened his eyes again, to see if he was still in hell.

"Stole your pants," a voice from the TV giggled.

Tony looked over his shoulder. The TV wasn't on.

"Stole your pants," screeched the tube again. *"Bitch stole your pants."*

"Shut *UP!*"

Tony hoisted the .357 and blew the screen to a thousand pieces. A puff of tinkling smoke filled the motel room.

"Teach you to mess with me!" he said.

Fuck the pants. It wasn't like he needed to stop for anything. He had his big-ass Colt Python and a batch of crack. What else did he need?

He just had to make it back to his pad and call some big-time Republicans, and the future was his.

THIRTY-NINE

Manny found Tina outside the station, chatting with Stuey the Hunchback and nibbling a pretzel. She had one arm slung over the deformed mound of his shoulder.

"Stuey used to double-date with Brando," Tina said, while the vendor beamed up at her.

"We did a lot of bowling," Stuey crowed, swiping a rag over the top of his cart. "Lotta people don't know this, but Marlon coulda gone pro."

"Tough call," said Manny. "Do I go with the greatest-actor-of-my-generation thing, or do I stick with the ten-pins?"

"Manny does nothing but mock," Stuey told her sadly. He threw down the rag and began pumping French's mustard from a jumbo tub into a plastic squeeze bottle. "A man hates himself, he can't be nice to nobody else. You got such nice kaboolies, whyn't you forget him and let me take care of you?"

Tina dropped the pretzel in the trash and smiled. "Only if I get my own cart."

The Impala was across the street, and Manny had to kick the passenger door to get it open. "You know," Tina said as she got in, "I can't decide if we're *Bonnie and Clyde* or *Starsky and Hutch*."

"Probably *Bonnie and Hutch*," he said. "One more stop, then we unload the goods and get comfy."

"So should I ask how it went with Mac and the police chief?"

"It was pretty much what you'd imagine."

Tina watched Manny reach under the seat for his prescription bottle. He tapped out three pills, crunched them dry, then popped three more. He saw her looking as he shoved the bottle back under the seat. "When this is over, I'm gonna cut this stuff out."

"You talking to me or you?"

Manny didn't answer. He slammed into DRIVE and skidded into traffic.

"You don't mind my saying so," Tina continued, "for a guy who's supposed to be a cop, you seem to pretty much do what you want."

"It's a dirty job, but somebody's gotta fuck it up. Anyway, I don't see you doing much nursing."

"Personal leave. You want, I can put on the uniform. What I hear, a lot of guys like that. So where we going?"

Ahead of them, a line of cars stopped at an intersection. Manny made a quick left into an alley and floored the Impala, dodging potholes and garbage cans. "*I'm* going to Tony Zank's. Our pal McCardle was nice enough to tell me where it is, and it turns out that's where Lipton's been calling from. But I can drop you anywhere. I just want you off the streets while Tony's on the warpath. By now he's gonna know McCardle gave him up, so he has to figure we know his moves. Where he lives, and all the rest of it."

"The guy didn't strike me as the logical type."

"There's logic and there's logic." Manny reached in the back for a thick sheaf of papers, stapled at the top, and tossed it on the seat between them. "I grabbed the guy's jacket. Often as he's been popped, there's not a whole lot anybody could make stick. He did a jolt for burglary, assault, minor possession. But none of the people he really tore up—I mean the ones who weren't dead—ever wanted to show up in court and talk about it."

"How surprising."

Manny took a left wide and Tina was thrown against him. She stayed with her hand on his thigh an extra second, then straightened up.

"To go around that crazy, you gotta be smart," Manny said. "A cat like Zank learns young. Far as anybody can tell he killed his old man, but the only person who could testify against him was his mother, and she gave him his alibi."

"And he *still* throws her out a window. Whatever happened to gratitude?"

"Right. You want me to leave you anywhere special?"

"And let you keep those swanky yoga pants? I don't think so."

Manny contemplated her before speaking. "Tina, let's cut the bullshit, okay? If Lipton's in Zank's pad, then he's in it as deep as anybody. But if we're gonna make a move with Mister Biobrain, we need to know the back story. Lipton's the missing piece."

"Yeah, and?"

"And something seriously bad could go down, that's all. Zank is a major piper. He hears voices telling him to buy a steak knife and X out pretty white girls, it could be a shitstorm. I don't want you in it."

Tina beheaded another Viceroy and flipped the cigarette to her lips. Manny lit her up. She exhaled a slow train of smoke and stared out the passenger window. In spite of himself, Manny felt a pang of desire. If there was anything sexier in the known universe than Tina smoking a Viceroy, he hadn't seen it yet. He had to force himself to watch the road.

"I can't leave you," she said at last, tossing the lipsticked cigarette out of the car half smoked. "Somebody has to make sure you don't blow up another sink. You've got to be stopped."

"Tina," Manny began, then let his voice trail off. He made the turnoff toward the river and drove in silence. The Impala crawled past blocks of abandoned meat-processing plants toward the unlikely apartment building. By the time they were close enough to see the faded letters spelling BUNDTHOUSE ARMS, the stench had penetrated the closed windows. He parked a hundred feet past the door, killed the engine, and turned to her again. "I'm gonna give you the car keys, okay? Take off. I'm not asking. If I need a ride, I'll call you."

"What if you need a ride in a hurry?"

"I'll dial fast."

Something in his eyes told her not to argue and she held out her hand. Manny dropped the keys in her palm, then folded his own hand over hers. The codeine was kicking back in and he felt that opiated itch to get intimate. Though maybe it wasn't the codeine. "This isn't my style," he confided, "but I want to tell you something."

Tina met his gaze. "Go ahead."

"Okay, listen. The reason I don't want you going up there with me? I've got this total fear of being shot in the spine and ending up some kind of dead-from-the-neck-down hump in a wheelchair." He cleared his throat. "What I'm saying is, if that happens, I'll need you alive. I don't want anybody giving me baths but you."

Tina grabbed the keys. "Is that your idea of romantic? You fucking asshole, get out of the car before I cripple you myself."

She slid behind the wheel while he gathered himself on the side-walk. "Just remember. If you do end up paraplegic, I'll use your face as a seat cushion."

"Promise?"

"Definitely," she said sweetly, "but only when I have company."

Manny watched her roar off down the street, in love all over again.

FORTY

Once, at the flaming height of indian summer, Manny'd stumbled on two half-decayed bodies in a Tit-ville garage. It was a double suicide, weeks old, and the stench hit him like a fist. He had to shove mud up his nose to keep from throwing up. Thirty seconds in Zank's apartment and the suicide garage seemed like a happy memory, meadow fresh compared to the rank miasma that made every breath in Chez Zank as gut-churning as a gulp of sewage.

The smell was so stupefying, he didn't even notice Lipton's cries. He was overcome. Then he heard them, faintly at first, then louder. The model-handsome may-oral assistant was keening.

Manny's head cleared, and he swam his way deeper into the apartment, into the bedroom. He found

Lipton in the closet, fully fetal under an army blanket, his peroxide-blond hair pasted to his head. His Armani jacket was badly stained and his crisp white shirt had wilted. When Manny pulled him out, he could barely stand.

"Lipton, Jesus, what the fuck are *you* doing here?"

"I broke in," Lipton sobbed. "And then, oh God, I got trapped with a dead puppy. He's got a really cute, really dead puppy in there!"

Manny gripped his shoulder. "Try not to lose it, okay?"

The bedroom was no more than a mattress dumped on a molting carpet, strewn with sex mags. Most, as far as Manny could tell, featured "anal" in the title. *Anal Antics, Asian Anal, Anal Cheerleaders.* Even *Senior Anal,* which he first misread as *Señor.*

"Would you listen to me?" Lipton pleaded. "He's got a deceased pet in the *closet!*"

Before Manny could tear his eyes away from the Anals, Lipton let out a cry and threw a shoe box at his feet. Manny'd never seen him like this. As long as he'd known him, the Brit had never appeared anything less than debonair. He patterned himself as a kind of peroxide Tony Randall. Mannered, suave, impeccably attired. Lipton was the perfect complement to Mayor Marge's iron blandness. Now here he was, rocking back and forth on the floor of Tony Zank's meat-stink bedroom, hugging himself and babbling.

Manny kicked the lid off the shoe box. There was indeed a cuddly puppy corpse jammed inside teeming with maggots. Lipton let out a hysterical giggle.

"What are you doing here?" Manny asked quietly, dropping the lid back on the box and kicking it aside. There was no point in even *attempting* to deal with this right now. Not with Lipton still giggling and sobbing. In movies, the hero slapped hysterical characters across the face. In Manny's experience, all a slap did was make them mad *and* hysterical. What he liked to do was scream in their ears. Which is what he did, squatting beside Lipton, leaning close, and shouting "CALM DOWN!" at the top of his lungs.

This did the trick. Manny led the shaken assistant into what passed for the living room: a scarred coffee table and green-plaid couch so riddled with burn holes it looked like it had been strafed by machine gun fire.

"Sit down," said Manny, and Lipton dutifully lowered himself to the one good cushion, stopping long enough to wrinkle his nose and remove a pair of burnt bottlecaps and a furry pizza slice. Manny wondered if furniture could grow gangrene.

"I can't believe this," Lipton sniffed. "How does he live?"

"Doesn't matter how he lives. It's his house," said Manny. "Ever hear of breaking and entering?"

"But Tony's a thief!"

"Thieves have rights, too. This is America. You wanna tell me what you're doing here or you wanna go downtown? I'm sure Mayor Marge would be happy to provide you with a lawyer."

"Mayor Marge!" Lipton grabbed Manny's hand.

"Is there a problem?"

Manny freed himself and picked his way through the empty Iron Cities and KFC buckets to the window. He tried to wrench it open, and nearly threw his back out before giving up.

"Painted shut," he said, hopscotching through the carpet rot back to the couch. "You still haven't answered me."

Lipton played with his hair, trying to shape it in approximation of its former splendor. "Tony stole something of Marge's."

"I don't remember her filing a report."

"It's not that kind of something."

"What's that supposed to mean?"

"Tony stole a photograph that belonged to her, all right?" Lipton smoothed down his shirt, rubbing at a fresh brown stain over the pocket. "She sent me to get it back."

"She did, huh? It wouldn't be anything like a picture of our beloved President smiling at his own balls, which happen to have a happy face drawn on them, would it? With Mayor Marge down in the right-hand corner rooting him on?"

Lipton clamped his hand over his mouth. "You *know?*"

Manny stared at him, expressionless, until Lipton couldn't take it and started babbling.

"Okay, don't look at me like that! You probably know all this already. There's a congressional seat opening up because of redistricting, and Marge wants it."

"So?"

"So, the Heinz family gave a quarter million dollars to the Republican party. They wanted to get one of H. J.'s heirs, some character named Melton, out of the ketchup business, which he's apparently running into the ground. So they thought they'd put him in Congress. For their 'contribution,' the party will back him, supply endorsements, even fly in a couple of trophy Republicans, like William Bennett, to talk about his character. There's not even going to be a Democrat opponent. Maybe the Heinz people bought *them* off, too. I don't understand the American system."

"What's that have to do with my ex-wife?"

"Oh come *on!* If your President Bush makes a call and says 'I want Marge Beeman,' the Heinz boy will have to find another seat to buy. Maybe *he* can be mayor. Scandal trumps money, that's what Marge says." Lipton seemed to go in and out of hysteria. One second his voice was screechily high, the next it dropped to an urgent monotone. "She's already made high-level inquiries, to some of Dick Cheney's team." Here he sighed dramatically. "Don't you *adore* that man? He's so buttery and ruthless!"

Lipton closed his eyes, in the grip of some private, vice-presidential swoon, and Manny had to tap him. "Keep going."

"Okay, okay! These were Deep Politics People. That's what she called them. *Deep Politics People.*" Lipton giggled. "It sounds like one of those tribes in New Guinea, doesn't it? Where they practice *manhood rituals!*"

"Maybe I've banged my head off the wall too many times," Manny interrupted, "but am I missing something? Marge is *in* these photos, right?"

"*Exactement!* And if the President doesn't give her what she wants, she has a *very juicy* story about how she got there. Believe me, that photograph is more than enough to get our girl in Congress. Assuming George doesn't ask Daddy to send some old hand from the CIA to make *wet work* out of her. Washington, D.C.," he concluded dreamily. "Dupont Circle. . . ."

"Aren't you getting a little ahead of yourself?"

"Right, right," said Lipton, racing from chirpy to morose and back again. "Did you find my car? God, this odor is like a *living thing* on my skin. Do you think we could catch ebola? We are both going to have to get *steam*-cleaned!"

Something in Lipton's frenzy set off a buzzer in Manny's brain. The last thing he wanted to do was hang around Zank's apartment. If Tony was fucked-in-the-head enough to come back, it would be a catastrophe. But he did not want to walk out without the whole story. Especially the part that Lipton, unless Manny was losing his touch, was holding back. The part that had the traumatized personal assistant jumping out of his skin.

"How come you got so freaked-out?" Manny asked, trying and failing to speak without breathing. "You were in that closet for what, an hour? Two hours?"

Lipton's mid-Atlantic grin looked depraved. "I lost my nerve. Like those blokes who try to rock climb, then get paralyzed with fear halfway up the cliff. They have to be snatched by your Park Service rescue copters."

"And I'm your rescue copter?"

"Yes!" Lipton went tittery. Pleased with himself.

"Well, what would happen if I called Mayor Marge right now?"

"What?" Lipton fell back on the couch as if struck and plunged his face in his hands. Manny pulled them away.

"She didn't send you, did she?"

"No." Lipton whimpered. "Oh damn! I knew I shouldn't have done it. *I knew it!"*

"Done what, Lipton? Help Tony Zank rip off the mayor's mansion?"

"I only gave him the *key!"* Lipton bellowed. "I told him I wanted the photo. He could keep everything else. But he had to get greedy! After he did it, I never even heard from him. I mean, I waited. I called. I even wrote him a letter. Not a word! Finally I decided to come here. What else could I do? But then it all went wrong. Somebody took my *car.* Only it's not my car, it belongs to the mayor's office. *Oh God!* It was so easy to get in here. The door wasn't even locked! But once I was inside, I suddenly realized, *I could be killed!"*

Lipton tried to compose himself, and his tone changed again. Now he sounded like a BBC commentator.

"One doesn't generally think about violence. All we see is the eleven o'clock news kind. The kind that happens to someone else. But, once I walked in, the reality began to just *wash over me.* I realized, it could be *me* on the news! I could be one of those bodies they carry off in the bag, before they interview the neighbors who say what a jolly nice fellow I was."

Suddenly his voice veered back to squealy terror.

"*I'm going to die!* That's what I kept thinking. I could not stop imagining what would happen if Tony Zank, that *criminal,* that *beast,* that . . . *disreputable person,* just barged in while I was sneaking around his apartment. I realized, *coming here was crazy!* But what could I do? I was stuck. I was too scared to stay and too scared to leave. I simply *could not move!*"

Lipton fussed desperately with his hair. Manny let him rave.

"I started to freak out, and next thing I knew I was in the closet. In a full-blown panic attack. Have you ever had one? My God, it's like bad LSD. I used to dabble, at university. But a panic attack is even worse, because you know you're not *on* acid. It's just *you!* The walls close in. The floor starts to wobble like a teeter-totter. I went absolutely *catatonic.* This dreadful stench . . . the danger . . . the *sheer stupidity* of what I'd done! I just kept thinking, I am going to *die* in this *cesspool!*"

Lipton punctuated his soliloquy with a quick sob.

"So you called me?"

"I . . . I . . . called you. Was that wrong?"

"Not particularly." Manny arranged his face in a bored smile. "I can get you out of here. There's just one thing."

"What?"

"How'd my ex-wife get the photo in the first place?"

Lipton clucked. "Oh *God!* There's a story and a half."

"I'm listening."

Lipton sat back on the mildewed couch and crossed his legs. "San Diego,' Ninety-six. The Republican Convention. Marge was a delegate, you know."

"I haven't kept up."

"Well, she was. And, *apparently,* she and George Junior met up after some kind of platform committee thingy. I don't know, I suppose he wasn't having much fun. It was all about Bob Dole. And Jack Kemp. Remember him? The footballer. A bad time to be a Bush."

"Fuck the political landscape. Tell me how she got the picture."

"All *right!*" Lipton raised his hands in front of him, palms out, as though warding off a blow. "Look, I am *not* going to say cocaine and single malt scotch were involved. I'm paid to be discreet. Let's just say George and Marge hit it off. They became very . . . *relaxed.* Very . . . *uninhibited.*"

Lipton pursed his lips in what Manny supposed was his "knowing" look.

"One thing led to another, and they ended up in Marge's suite at the Four Seasons. You figure it out."

Something skittered across the carpet, mouse or rat, and Manny gave a start, surprised that even vermin could stand the odor.

"You still haven't told me. Who took the picture?"

Lipton blushed all the way down to his GQ jaw. Then he looked away and admitted, in a tone shot through with embarrassment, *"I did."*

There was a tense silence. Manny sat with it. He fancied himself a connoisseur of awkward pauses. Verbal discomfort was a powerful tool. (Rubert's Law Number One: When grilling suspects, do not react. The more provocative the admission, the more not-reacting you did. Which generally drove them to admit more, because of Rubert's Law Number Two: All perps crave a reaction. It didn't matter if they were hard-core felons or shoplifting trophy wives. Nine times out of ten, they'd tell you more than you asked, just to get you to say "Wow!")

Manny waited a beat, then marched out his most ho-hum demeanor. "You want to tell me what happened?"

Lipton nodded rapidly. "They were, I don't know, getting kind of silly. Marge started it. She asked if he wanted to play Abraham Lincoln."

"What's that?"

"That's what W. wanted to know. So Marge showed him. First she took off her blouse and painted eyebrows over her nipples with Magic Marker. Then she drew a nose under her cleavage and painted a lipstick mouth just under her belly button."

"And then what?"

Lipton appeared near tears. "Then she pulled down her panties and said *'Look! Here's Abe's beard!'*"

"Thank God there's no picture of that."

"The light wasn't right," said Lipton, missing the irony. "But they were both so loopy by then, *he* pulled down *his* pants and said, 'Okay Marge, now I've got somebody I'd like *you* to meet!'"

"Mister Biobrain?"

"Not yet." Lipton shot his cuffs. "Before he drew the smiley face, he painted a pair of eyeballs on his stomach, with Groucho brows, then he pretended his penis was a sort of long nose. 'Look at my big honker, I'm Rabbi Dickstein!' That's what he said. 'I'm Rabbi Dickstein! Have some matzoh!' I suppose it's some kind of fraternity gag. After that, I don't know where he got the idea, he just started squeezing his, pardon my French, his *man-bag,* until it absolutely *bulged,* and then he sketched on that preposterous face. When he told her its name was 'Mister Bio-brain,' Marge laughed so hard they both nearly fell off the loveseat. That's when she said, 'I must get a picture of this!' I don't know if she was thinking about blackmail, but I am certain that Mister Bush—he's rather scrumpy in person—would not have agreed if he hadn't been, as the saying goes, *feeling very little pain. . . .*"

The contrast between Lipton's mannered enunciation and the subject at hand, not to mention the gamy flavor of their surroundings, was enough to induce some kind of psychic bends. And the codeine didn't help. He kicked himself for not bringing a tape recorder.

"So you were there the whole time?" he asked.

"In the next room," Lipton let out sheepishly. "Marge and I had adjoining suites. But, well, the door *was* open a crack. Anyway, she didn't invite me in until she wanted the picture. So of course, I came in with the camera and I . . . I took the picture. That's the whole story."

"Except for the menage-à-trois, right?"

"Don't even *joke,*" said Lipton.

By now, Manny's leg had gone to sleep. He shook it and saw that a viscous divot, some kind of green carpet-mold, clung to the bottom of his shoe. He prayed it was guacamole, but the stuff wouldn't budge. He had to pry it off with his fingers and wipe them on the couch.

"Let's hear the rest," Manny said matter-of-factly.

"What do you mean?"

Manny massaged his calf. "C'mon, you ripped off your boss. You wanted her to think some burglar had the photo, so you could pretend to buy it back and pocket the cash. Or else you were gonna double-cross her and sell it yourself. That was it, wasn't it? Only Zank double-crossed you first. He kept the picture, so you decided you'd steal it back."

Lipton hung his head. He looked stricken. "It's true."

Manny felt a rush of sympathy. "You're no criminal. Why the hell would you do something like this?"

"I need money." For the first time, Lipton's voice sounded unaffected. "And the man I needed to give the money *to* needs money."

"Somebody's squeezing you?"

As if forces within him were waging war for his soul, Lipton raised his head, then looked down again, then turned back to Manny, jutting his Ken doll–perfect chin defiantly. "The money is for Dr. Roos," he declared. "So that he can make me the woman I am."

FORTY-ONE

Tina was halfway back to her house—she had to clean up sometime—when she got the tingle. She'd been getting it since childhood. That prickly sensation, like a cool, rough hand on the back of her neck. Letting her know. . . .

She'd had it, for the first time, on the way home from school, the day she found her mother hanging from the trailer ceiling. And she had it now, imagining Manny in Zank's apartment. It was nothing specific. A kind of cellular dread, a whisper across the skin: *You're here, but you should be there.*

Ignoring the vituperative honks of the blueberry SUV behind her, Tina slammed on the brakes, pulled a Richard Petty 180 in the middle of Liberty Boulevard, and aimed the rattling Impala back toward slaughterhouse row.

Dreading something awful without knowing what, she screeched to a stop before the Bundthouse Arms. Leaving the car a foot from the curb, she scrambled out and made for the entrance. She was nearly there before she sensed him.

Zank.

She knew that stink. Even in the waft of long-dead pork that clogged the air, it dominated. The rank scent of crack-sweat, of flesh gone off. Shuddering, she recalled his tongue, that puff of corpse gas and malathion when he opened his mouth to kiss her. And the worst, *the worst:* that diseased slug of a penis, sliming her lips.

Tina stopped on the sidewalk, senses on alert. She reached in her purse and touched the straight razor. She couldn't see him, but she knew. *Any second.* Stiff-legged, she remained still, torn between running back to the car or into the building to warn Manny. She needed another cigarette. Fumbled in her purse for pack and lighter.

And then—"Miss me, Tina?"

The voice like curdled syrup.

Tina cracked off the filter, finished lighting her Viceroy, and exhaled with exaggerated leisure. She turned slowly. He wasn't there. She turned again. Nobody. Then, from behind the Dumpster fronting the rutted alley that ran beside the building, a figure stepped toward her. Draped in a Pawnee Lodge bedspread, Tony's face was shadowed, his coke-psychosis eyes blasting affable madness.

"Ready to party?"

Tina spotted the muzzle at the same time she noticed his bare knees. When Tony raised the .357, the bedspread parted, revealing his bloody thighs and sex. It was hard not to gag. But her fear was not about his lack of pants. It was about the gun. The blue-steel twin of the Magnum Manny'd snagged in her bathroom.

Zank waggled the Python's fat barrel toward the entrance and Tina marched in front of him, her hand working around the blade in her purse.

Mistaking the gesture, Tony came alive. "Don't pull out the picture here," he said, nudging her with the weapon. "Wait'll we get upstairs."

Then he pressed his cracked lips to her ear. Conspiratorial. That same insecticide breath.

"They got midgets under the sidewalk," he whispered, "with the infrared. Same guys who used to flush Cong out of their tunnels, in Nam. Now they're FBI. They got that infrared, so they can see up. Through lead, if they want to. They're watching us now but it's okay. I'm demagnetized. Did it myself. Go ahead, just open the door. Walk in normal."

In the vestibule, where tenants would buzz people in if people ever came, if there were any tenants besides Tony Zank, Tina poised to make her move. She had her fingers around the straight razor, when he surprised her.

"I felt it right away," he announced giddily. "Didn't you?"

"Didn't I what?"

She turned, morbidly curious, keeping her grip on the blade and trying to aim her eyes somewhere besides Zank's car accident of a face. She didn't want to look down, either—he still hadn't washed, and the dried blood made his penis look like a rusty doorbell. This left her staring at the ceiling, where yellow paint was peeling off in great, curling sheets.

Tony appeared to be pulsating. "Didn't you *feel* it?"

"Feel what?"

"The *thing*. The magic! The *LOVE* that this was meant to be from the beginning of time."

He gestured with the .357, tapping his chest.

"It's undeniable, right? The vibe. Between you and me."

Tony's body broke into twitchy quiver, almost a seizure, and he made what he thought were goo-goo eyes. From somewhere, he pulled out a crack pipe, clamped it in his bloodstained teeth, and lit up with a purple Bic, all the while keeping the gun fixed at her breasts. He sucked wolfishly, exhaled, and squeezed his exposed organ.

"Wanna hit? It's life-changing."

"I'm good," Tina said.

"Have a hit," Tony said again. "I'm not asking."

He shoved the pipe in her mouth and right off she could taste him. His sticky, toxic saliva. The dead-animal tang. He ran a flame along the bottom of the crusty glass.

"Come on. You'll thank me later."

Tina wanted to fake it, but that gun was huge. He might know, and then what? She wrapped her lips around the hot tube and sucked, willing her mind against the dirty rush. She'd done crack, but never enthu-siastically. Her mother's best girlfriend, Curly, used to bring over a few rocks when she came to baby-sit. Curly thought it was cute the way Tina got scared and began to dance after she gave her a hit. Tina hated how she felt after she did it, but she hated how she felt it before she did it, too, which is why she always went along. If she hesitated, Curly would promise her candy. But once she took a hit, Tina always forgot about the Clark Bar Curly didn't have anyway. Right away, her heart would start banging on her chest like a child trapped in a coffin. Like it was banging now.

After Zank slipped the pipe out of her mouth, he zoomed his face up to hers, until their lashes touched, and then he laughed. Tina felt the inside of her head turn to glass. She could not move or she would shat-ter. She held still as the bells gonged behind her eyeballs. That's what she remembered: how noise got scary. Blood roaring through your veins. An airplane ten miles away screaming like a chainsaw between her ears. She fought the drug, but the drug won.

When the volume faded, she saw Zank leering at her. He'd jammed the pipe back in his own mouth and loaded another rock. He flicked the Bic and sucked, until thick white smoke swirled inside the tube before flooding out his gory nostrils.

Zank spoke through the acrid cloud. "I knew you wanted me, but you couldn't say anything, right? Maybe the cop's got something on you. But it's okay. I can take care of him. We can be together. When I get the money for that photograph, we can go away. Just you and your Tony. The Bahamas are nice, but I'm thinking Israel."

Insane, Tina thought. Her two-minute ride had skidded to a stop, and her entire skull throbbed. Crack cocaine, when you didn't want it, was like brain-rape. She lit up a cigarette just to do something.

Tony cupped his sex nervously. "Israel's the *shit!* They got great beaches there. The Dead fucking Sea. Ever heard of it? We make skunky love, head down to the Dead Sea. Float our asses off. I read all about it. You can pass out and nothin' happens. Jesus peed in there, so the water's got, like, healing powers. It's beautiful."

"But Israel," Tina repeated. "Are you . . . ?"

"Jewish? Damn straight. Proud member of the tribe. My daddy was actually Moe Zankberg. He changed his name 'cause he sold used farm equipment. Who's gonna buy a John Deere from a Yid, right? Not that Moe was so hot, either. That's why he named me Tony. 'People like Tonies,' that's what he used to say. The stupid fucker." Tony pounded himself with the gun. "Jew-genes, through and through. I got Hebrew DNA. So what do you say? Honeymoon on the Negev?"

The cocaine had left Tina hyperaware. She shrank from Zank involuntarily, but he kept crowding her, reeking, full-frontal naked, his features a bloody mask of scabs and damage.

Tony smiled in a way he no doubt thought seductive. That was the creepiest: He believed they had some kind of relationship. To keep from looking at him, she focused on the dusting of grime over the wound where she'd cut his earlobe off, the filthy bandage on his other ear, the ugly bruise across his throat. She tried to imagine what could have caught him under the Adam's apple.

"You don't have to answer now," he teased, doing a thing with his eyebrows. Then he stuck out his cankered tongue and wiggled it. "Maybe a kissy-poo will help you make up your mind. You took my drugs, you gotta at least French me."

He puckered up, and that was it. Tina made her move. Viceroy dangling from her mouth, she whipped out the razor, flipped it open, and brought her knee up in his exposed balls as she slashed. Tony hooted and juked backward. She'd sliced the bedspread, opening a gap from Tony's foul shirt down to his fish-white thighs.

"Shit!"

She swung again, and caught his hip this time. The flesh opened like a wet pair of lips, but Tony only giggled. He fondled the wound and licked his fingers.

"My soulmate." He panted happily. "We're gonna have crazy fun."

Grabbing her knife hand, he flipped the .357 in the air, caught it by the barrel, and swung the butt at her head. Tina ducked and, without thinking, jammed her cigarette in his pubic hair. The curls burned with a savage hiss.

"Mmmm, *yeah*. . . ." Tony moaned. "I can't wait for the wedding. I wanna go Animal Channel. I wanna fuck you in the neck. I wanna eat your pink ass like a hyena."

Still squeezing her wrist, he pointed the oily muzzle in her face and jammed her into a wall of mailboxes. He pressed himself into her, then stepped back, letting the bedspread fall away like the canvas at an unveiling.

"Daddy needs some squinky love," Zank warbled, breaking into a barefoot soft-shoe. "You're my kinda gal. Wanna do it on the floor? Nobody lives in this palace but me. They say it stinks. But all I smell is your love-juice. I smell you wantin' me like a trailer park geisha."

With an awful pang, Tony remembered that ho at the motel, and the memory made him jam his hand into Tina, right through her dress. He wasn't going to let Tina play him that way. Tina was different. Tina *wanted* him.

Zank busted his kiss-move, but she fought back, afraid of those black scabs on his lips, the fresh blood smeared on top of them. She raked her fingernails over his eyes, then knuckle-punched him, crunching the blue bruise over his Adam's apple. Zank coughed and she hit him again. He fell back a step, and she ripped the filthy bandage off his ear.

"What'sa matter," Tony howled, "you anti-Semitic? We are going to have some *times!* I like a girl who plays hard to get. Makes me know you're *hot* for it." A car passed by and he dropped to a crouch. "Cover me, I'm going in!"

Zank kicked open the lobby door and shoved Tina through ahead of him. She checked for exits. Nothing but filthy linoleum and scuffed walls. An OUT OF SERVICE sign slung on a chain across an open elevator shaft. Tony scratched at his scorched pubes with the gun. He crooked his head to the right, where a broad stairway littered with old newspapers and Iron City bottles mounted to watery light.

"Up the stairs, party girl. I do you out there, some mau-mau's gonna roll by and want a taste, then I got *that* to deal with. What I been through, I can't handle a confrontation. I just want a little peace and quiet. . . ."

FORTY-TWO

Lipton had finally gotten his sea legs.

"I feel so foolish," he kept saying, clearly appealing to Manny to tell him it was okay, that it happened to everybody. "I just completely broke down. I came apart."

"You came to your senses," Manny reassured him. Anything to keep the nervous Brit together until they could get out of here. He considered slipping Lipton a codeine, but had a feeling he'd tell Marge. "You're okay, that's the important thing. What we've got to do now is get you out of here."

Lipton nodded too quickly, eyes bright with fear. "You're right. The picture's not even here. I know that now. I knew it as soon I came through the door." He lowered his gaze and, unless Manny was hallucinating,

kissed his own wrist. "I just needed to know I could do it. I'm a bit of
a ninny, aren't I? But, if you don't mind me asking, are those *yoga*
pants?"

"It's a long story."

Manny managed a smile and cast one last glance around Zank's slice
of heaven. He took a breath of fetid air and realized, to his own surprise, that he felt all right. Now that he knew how Mayor Marge came
by Mister Biobrain, he could relax a little. He had W. for flashing—not
to mention adultery, drugs, and scrotal doodling—and now he had
Marge for setting him up.

Mission accomplished, he thought, ready to take it home, then he
heard the noise outside. And knew at once: He'd just been worst-case
scenarioed. He'd relaxed too soon.

"This place is *transitional!"*

Zank's grating bellow echoed through the flimsy walls. He was rav-
ing in the hall outside the apartment.

"That's why I haven't decorated! Once we move in together, I'll
trade up. What I want is a bear rug! And a fireplace! They got bears in
Israel. Lotta people don't know that. *Jew-bears.* They're kinda sickly. I
learned that. I got my GED in jail. Even went to junior college.
There's lots of stuff you don't know about me, Tina."

Manny felt his blood turn to antifreeze. He held up a hand to Lipton, who'd gone green, and put a finger to his lips. He pointed to the
couch, and Lipton skittered behind it.

Once the Brit was out of sight, Manny tiptoed to the wall by the
door, on the hinge side. He figured he'd count to five, wait till Zank
was in all the way, then stick the gun in the back of his neck. It was
scarier when metal touched flesh. If he tried something, Manny would
have him cold. As long as Tina dove out of the way, the bullet wouldn't
catch her coming out of Zank's throat. At least that was the general
idea.

"I never lock it," Zank boomed, just on the other side of the door.
"It's reverse paranoia. Some junkie wants to boost the TV and sees the
door's unlocked, he's gonna know something's on. Like, what kind of
person's so ass-bad they don't even lock their door? Think about that.

He has to figure, he's gonna walk in on somebody *evil*. I don't even lock it when I'm home. I'd *love* for some scrunge to try robbin' the place, just so I could fuck him up legal. I'd dick-shoot the guy. After *you*."

Manny held his breath as the knob started to turn. He could hear his pulse. He was listening to it, hard, when—*Jesus Christ!*—the phone rang. His own.

Motherfucker! He always forgot to switch it to vibrate. He fumbled to get the thing out of his pocket and flipped it open out of habit.

He kept the phone jammed in his ear and his shooting arm flat against the wall. The ranting outside had stopped.

"Goddamn it, I know you're there," Fayton shouted on the other end. "It's Krantz. He's been shot and he says it's your fault."

Manny cursed and stepped back from the door. He had to get rid of Fayton. But he'd just been accused of murder.

"It was a domestic," Fayton quacked on importantly. "The girl-friend got him in the back. Her old man was beating on her with a Dust Buster 'cause he wanted to watch pro wrestling and she wouldn't stop cleaning. When Krantz got there, he told the lady it was her fault, she oughta be more understanding. He says you told him to say that. She got him in the ribs with a .22. Just missed his kidneys. Did you tell him that, Ruby? Well?"

Manny wanted to smash the phone off the wall. "I'm hanging up," he whispered furiously. "I'm in the middle of something."

"And I'm still the chief. I intend to conduct an investigation."

"Good. Dig up Chatlak and ask *him*," Manny hissed, ready to tear his hair out. That's what he needed right now, threats. "You bring me up on charges, Chatlak's corpse is gonna be beside me in court, holding your cordless. We can have two investigations at once, save the tax payers some money."

"This isn't over, Detective," Fayton warned him, doing his best to sound ominous. He was still trying when Manny pounded END.

By now Lipton's ragged pompadour had popped up behind the couch. Manny signaled him to stay down, but Lipton ignored him, waving his hand like a prissy fifth-grader dying to get called on.

"What?"

Lipton made his face contrite. "I just need to know, was that Marge? Am I in trouble?"

"Just stay out of sight," Manny implored him. What the fuck else could happen?

Manny took a deep breath and heard the click. The one you don't want to hear. Two seconds later, the door blew off its hinges in a blast of wood and plaster that left him sprawled on the floor. The shot set Lipton off on a shriek-fit.

Zank fired again and the sofa exploded, burying the Brit beneath a mound of dust and plywood and chunks of foam with green plaid still attached. The shrieking stopped. Manny opened his eyes and blinked through the smoke at a pair of naked legs, the left one slashed at the hip on a diagonal. He rolled sideways just in time to miss the blast Tony aimed at his head. The floor went away beside him, leaving a splintered hole, and Manny saw a room below, its walls refrigerator white, criss-crossed with shelves stacked with dusty cartons. Some had burst, spilling lumpen mold. Others were intact, bearing the unmistakable Smiling Sausage logo of Bundthouse Farms. *That's the smell,* he thought, in the middle of everything. Whoever converted the Bundt-house plant into an apartment building had skipped the meatlocker, leaving a lifetime supply of links and patties to rot in their boxes.

Tony's manic warble brought Manny back. "I'm a little teapot!" he sang, rubbing his exposed gonads as he raised his fat-barreled weapon. Manny snatched up a dead Iron City and threw it, distracting him long enough to jerk left and get off a shot on the fly. The bullet caught Zank high on the hip and spun him around. The impact shattered the bone and sheared off a chunk of flesh, so it looked like something had started to gnaw his buttock and changed its mind after it got a taste.

Tony gave a howl that sounded more joyous than painful. He fired as his legs went and Manny felt something gouge his hand. He looked down and saw a raw chicken leg on the carpet. Then he saw the ragged wound at his wrist and realized the chicken leg was his thumb. Manny clamped his good hand over the gushing nub, protecting it from sausage germs. Then he scooped his thumb off the foul carpet and stuffed it in his jacket pocket.

Somewhere Lipton was wailing again. Zank screamed "Round and stout!" and got off another shot. This one knocked Manny onto his back. His head dangled over the splintered hole in the floor. His right side felt basted in liquid warmth. He couldn't breathe. The stench from the sausage vault was mind-altering. It seemed to rise up in a solid waft.

"*Meatlocker of Death,*" Manny muttered. To stay calm, inside moments of bad savagery, he sometimes pretended he was in a movie, that whatever he was trying to live through without losing his shit was not even real. He'd close his eyes and repeat, like a minor prayer, "*I can go home whenever I want.*" Sometimes that worked, but not now. Not when he was thumbless and gut-shot. When five feet away, dragging his shattered limb like a foreign object, Zank was crawling toward him, cackling as he dug the muzzle of his Colt Python .357 into the carpet for traction.

"Tina bo bina," Zank giggled. "Where you want me to shoot your boyfriend? I'm takin' requests."

Manny clung to the hope that Tina wasn't even there. That Zank was so tweaked he was babbling to phantoms. He discovered he couldn't stand and tried to push himself off the carpet, to free his gun. But the pain in his stomach glued him to the floor. He couldn't roll off his own weapon. Even crawling was impossible. He watched, with a kind of detached wonder, as the man who was going to kill him dragged himself closer, his eyes like balls of rotten jelly, forming what could only be kisses with his purple lips. His sing-song taunts sounded at the end of a long tunnel.

"*Say good night, donkey-dong. . . . Ass-fuck an angel for me!*"

Zank tottered a foot away. Near enough for his sticky breath to stain Manny's face. He grunted happily and walked the .357 in front of him, like a mountaineer planting a spike. When he got close enough, he raised the gun off the carpet. A trio of muzzles fluttered before Manny's eyes, circling each other. Pain was making him see triple. Or maybe it was blood loss. If he looked down, he could see the brown puddle spreading underneath his middle. Brown meant liver. That much he knew. But he didn't feel it if he stayed still. What really hurt, insanely, was the thumb in his pocket.

"Baby, come here! Look at his face," Zank cried, his voice a giddy rasp. "This here's a brave cowboy." He smiled through his spoiled tomato mouth. "Tina, where are you, baby? I'm gonna count to three."

That's when Manny saw her, stepping silently through the door, cuffed at the wrists, her straight razor open in front of her.

"*One!*"

Manny forced his eyes straight ahead. If Zank noticed him looking, the next bullet might be Tina's.

"*Two!*"

"Hey Tony," Manny called, though the effort seemed to press some pain lever in his middle. "Hey Tony, I know about the Boy Scouts."

Tony's smile froze. He held the gun where it was. "You what?"

"I saw your juvenile file." Every word was a fist in his viscera, but he had to keep talking, to keep Zank from turning around. "I—*shit*—I know it's illegal, but I got a friend who works at the court. That's"—*keep fucking going*—"that's really a shame about what happened." If he could talk without breathing, he'd be okay. "Your daddy being the Scout leader and all, that had to be embarrassing, huh? What were you—*fuck!*—ten or eleven?"

"Shut up!" Tony hollered. "*Shut the fuck up!*"

Tina was across the room, moving closer.

Manny made his interrogation face: the wrinkled brow, the faux concern. "That's why you killed him, right? You were embarrassed? I don't blame you. My daddy was a weeny-wagger and a pedophile I'd probably do the same as you. I—" Manny gasped once, fighting the pain buzz-sawing his guts—"I mean, that had to fuck up summer camp, huh?"

Zank flinched. Manny willed the words out of his mouth.

"It's okay, man. It's not genetic. You're a normal guy! It's not like your dad getting caught trying to fuck one of your little scout friends means *you're* messed up. Even if he fucked *you* once in a while, you're totally cool, right? You"—*hang the fuck on*—"you worked it through, right?"

Zank ripped a ripe scab off his earlobe. A dozen expressions careened over his features simultaneously. Two steps behind him, Tina raised the straight razor, clutched in her cuffed hands. She dropped to a crouch and her eyes met Manny's over Zank's head. She bit her lip, ready to strike, when suddenly, like a peroxide jack-in-the-box, Lipton popped up screaming from under the exploded sofa.

"You lied to me, Tony! We had a deal!"

Zank was so stunned he barely moved, even when Lipton produced the tiny derringer.

"You were never going to call about the picture, were you? *Were you?* You were just making carnival with me!"

Lipton closed his eyes to squeeze off a shot, and Tony watched like it was happening on TV. After the bang, a small flower of blood appeared on his shoulder. He regarded it with mild curiosity, then plucked out the bullet and flicked it away like a dead fly.

Lipton struggled to reload, his hands shaking violently. With a weary sigh, Zank hoisted the muscular Colt Python and waved it at his wanna-be assassin. He called to him in a pleasant voice, just a couple of friends talking death over the back fence.

"I'll tell you a secret, Lipton. Some people fuck, some people get fucked. It's just nature, buddy. Nothin' personal."

Lipton lifted his eyes in time to catch Zank fire the shot that splattered his face off the window behind him. For one wobbly second he continued to stand, spraying blood from the neck, as though no one had let his body know it was dead. Then his left arm twitched north, in reflexive good-bye. His knees folded beneath him and his torso tumbled forward onto the floor.

"Twenty-two," Zank said, to no one in particular, "I pick my *teeth* with a fucking twenty-two."

"You're a sick piece of shit," Tina said quietly.

A grisly smile lit up Tony's face. "Sweetheart, you came back!" He swung around, delighted, and the girl of his dreams dissected his Adam's apple. Tony's throat opened into a pink yawn, and before the blood started to gush she slashed him again. Tony made a sound like a guffaw. He lifted his gaze to hers with something that might have been love, might have been relief, then looked at the gun as it fell from his hand onto the spongy carpet.

Zank angled himself back toward Manny, coughing out a wad of tarry scarlet as he tried to speak. "*Pipe . . . pocket . . . one hit. . . .*"

Manny and Tony locked eyes, and Manny understood. Or thought he did. The killer knew he was dead and wanted to go out with a rush.

Deep down, Manny knew, if someone had a gun to his head, and offered him the chance for world peace or a bang of heroin before he pulled the trigger, he'd probably go for the heroin. Staring down the barrel, all bets were off. . . . Strip everything away, and that's what this moment came down to: one dope fiend cadging a high off another one.

While Zank gurgled, Manny turned to Tina. Her face was a blank, whether from shock or anger he couldn't tell. So he went ahead.

With the four fingers of his mangled hand, Manny tapped Zank's chest, plucked the glass pipe out of his pocket, and worked it between the killer's trembling lips. Then he reached back down for the lighter. With no thumb, it was tricky. But after three tries he got a flame. He lifted it to the tip of the pipe, where a rock was already planted. Which proved, in retrospect, to be the single most stupid act of his entire life.

Zank sucked hard, and a puff of smoke escaped the bloody little mouth Tina'd made in his throat. That's what Manny was staring at— that puff of throat-smoke—when Tony, mustering the last strength he owned to have some fun on the planet, launched himself forward and jammed the hot tip of the pipe in Manny's right eye.

Manny screamed, then Zank's head hit the carpet and he expired, face-first, his crack pipe still jammed between his bloody teeth.

After that things got foggy. Tina seemed to loom over him, looking more Faye Dunaway-ish than ever, and Manny thought he heard her call him an asshole before he passed out in her arms.

FORTY-THREE

BONDAGE.

That's the first thing he thought when he came to. I've gone to hell, and it turns out Satan's into S & M.

When he was alive, he never told anybody he believed in Satan. But now that he was dead, it didn't matter. Manny felt the restraints: the straps on his ankles, the clamp at his throat, what seemed like steel claws over his wrists and a manacle all the way around his waist, and knew he'd either been drop-kicked into hell or Maximum Security. Maybe there wasn't any difference. He'd seen the Devil once, staring out of his own eyes in the rearview mirror of the car he was living in when he kicked heroin. It occurred to him that he needed to tell Tina about that. Not only because it would explain the codeine—instead of hitting himself in the head with a sledgehammer, he'd switched to a rubber mallet—but because it could help explain life as a cop.

Darkness pressed down on Manny's eyes like damp cotton, and he realized that he'd never seen the Big Picture until now. Until waking up dead, in this bondage parlor, stinking of starch and disinfectant, and waiting for the blanket of narcotics to lift and let him feel the screaming pain he knew, in some grim corner of his psyche, was roiling underneath it.

Now it all seemed obvious. The only world more hellish and revolting than a heroin addict's was a policeman's. The difference was, as a junkie, hell was your home address. As a cop, you occupied other people's nightmares. Which made your own reality—the desolation and solitude, in Manny's case, he'd been hanging on to with white knuckles since crawling off the hard stuff—more endurable by comparison. That was the beauty part: The policeman was his own perp. On permanent lockdown in the Big House of fear-driven weirdness and gainful employment. With the key rotting in his pocket. . . .

It took getting gut-shot and mangled, half-blinded and burned, to make him remember who he was. In the aftermath, a single thought ricocheted off the back of his eyeballs: *I am too fucking scared to be alive.* The truth was mortifying.

ENOUGH! he moaned. All these words lodged like metal shards in the pulp of his brain. And all he wanted was something to rip them out.

A cool hand brushed Manny's brow and he wondered if he'd been talking out loud. Then the hand moved down, and he heard the sound of tape being ripped off skin before he realized the skin was his. His left eye blinked through the blur. The hand dabbed at it gently. In a few seconds the fuzziness cleared, and she was there. Her hair pinned up and her lithe body poured into a white nurse's uniform.

"*Tina.* . . ."

"That's Nurse Tina to you."

"How long have you. . . ." He let his voice trail off and she smiled.

"I decided I needed a new job after you were admitted. Just a coincidence. You've been in the hospital a week. They kept the patch on your good eye until they did what they could for the other one."

"So then?"

"So the doctor said they do wonders with glass. But, personally, I think you'll look hotter than shit in a black patch."

"Jesus!"

He managed to raise his head, and saw that he hadn't dreamt the restraints. He was strapped to the bed frame by his bandaged left hand and his healthy right. What felt like a fat gauze belt bound his stomach, and his ankles were strapped with the same worn leather as his hands. One tube ran somewhere under the blanket he didn't want to think about. Another drained from his chest.

Tina let him take in his shattered body, then said, matter-of-factly, "It could have been worse. They've got your thumb on ice. You totaled some ribs. And a gang of bone slivers lodged in your lungs."

"Tell me later. . . . What's with the restraints? Is this the prison wing?"

"Not yet. You were throwing yourself around a lot, which wasn't good. Bad dreams. You have to stay still or you'll never heal."

He looked down at his middle, then back up at her, afraid to ask.

"Relax," said Tina. "Your new liver is taking nicely."

"My WHAT?"

"You lucked out. They had a nice fresh one when you got here. In the same ambulance, as a matter of fact."

"Zank?" he made himself ask.

"They considered it, but with his you'd have come out of postop like a big crack baby."

"Don't tell me. . . ."

"You guessed it. The late Mr. Lipton. Turns out you two were very compatible."

"Jesus," he croaked again. His vocabulary seemed to have been sapped along with his strength. He wasn't exactly loaded, just numb in a comfortably toxic way. But all the special effects were back: the basso squawk his voice took on on smack, the itch in his nose, the glaze of putrid sweat. . . . But mostly, he felt so chewed up it was hard to tell nausea from intoxication. "What am I on?"

"Demerol. But your last shot was hours ago, so it's probably faded. You can have your codeine back tomorrow."

"I don't want it," he said, surprising himself, and instantly regretted the statement. Who was he kidding?

Tina watched him squirm. Pleased. She smiled in a way he hadn't seen before and unbuttoned the top button of her uniform.

"Maybe we'll find you a better drug."

She undid two more buttons, then pulled a prescription bottle out of her pocket and dropped it on the night table.

"What's that?" he said, gripped with equal parts dread and excitement.

"Toradol, handsome. Nonnarcotic painkiller. Kills the pain without the euphoria. Strong as the real stuff. Just no fun."

"And that's the better drug?"

Manny felt something cave in his chest. He already had that steel-wool-on-the-nerve-ends feeling. In a few hours the air would sting his skin. His hair would hurt. There were a couple of years on junk and a decade on codeine before the little taste of Demerol.

"I didn't say *that* was the drug," said Tina, and stepped out of her uniform. This was the first time he'd seen her naked, and the sight made him religious. She watched him watch her for a minute, her expression hard to read. He one-eyed her breasts, the aureoles purple-red half dollars around nipples already erect. Then his gaze fell to her belly and he realized what she was waiting for him to see. A lavish scar, the same shade as her nipples. As thick around as the cord on a vacuum cleaner. It ran at a smooth diagonal from her left hipbone to her navel, then dog-legged down and curved around her right side, where it stopped.

"First time I saw a straight razor," she said, with a shrug that contained a lifetime.

Manny wanted to let her talk, but she said nothing else. Her eyes were inside his.

"One of Mommy's boyfriends?"

"The one I married," she said. "Don't ask. I was fifteen and a half."

Then she turned around to lock the door, and showed him her other surprise. On her back, in brilliant reds and blues, was a tattoo of a nine-armed goddess. It looked a little like Betty Page, in full lotus and bare-breasted, hurling diamonds, arrows, snakes, and hearts in a fan pattern that converged on the cleft of her teardrop ass.

"Kali?"

"I'm impressed," she said.

"Don't be. I eat in front of the Learning Channel."

"Whatever. It was Marv's idea. Sometimes I like it, sometimes I feel like the cover of a menu in an Indian restaurant. Mostly I don't think about it." Tina plucked her nurse-wear off the floor and tossed it over the visitor's chair. "But we can talk later," she said, when she turned off the bedside lamp.

"Okay," said Manny, suddenly wracked with the sense that one eye was not enough to absorb the vision before him. He felt strain in ocular muscles he never knew he had. His eye wandered over her breasts, moved south to her sweetly shaved pussy, then traveled upward, returning to the thick cord of scar tissue. It was the scar that obsessed him, at once beautiful and tragic, startling and exotic, and erotic in a way he could not explain. Everything, in short, that he felt about the woman who bore it.

He didn't know he was choked up until he spoke. "The bastard must have gutted you."

"Actually, he gave me guts, baby. Now don't move. And don't peek, either."

Manny closed his eye and she stepped out of her shoes. Then she eased the blankets all the way down to his ankles. A drainage tube ran from under the gauze cummerbund at his middle. She eased it sideways and reached beneath it.

"The nurses were all impressed," she said huskily. "The one who trimmed your pubes took a Polaroid."

"I don't want to hear anything about Polaroids."

"Live by the sword, et cetera," she said, and took him in her hand. "I hear the doctor dropped his scalpel when he saw you."

Manny talked with his eye shut. "I thought they kept the patient covered up."

"They do. You got an erection during the operation. Nearly poked his eye out."

"He can have my glass one," Manny said, and gave himself over to the sensation. Tina leaned down and let her breasts drift across his face. He parted his lids and she slapped him, lightly.

"I said no peeking."

His eye went wide then shut obligingly. After she kissed him, she ran her tongue over his face, down his bruised-blue chest. She unpinned her hair, let it fall over his skin, and repositioned herself on the south side of that giant bandage. When she licked his inner thigh, the stirring in his penis was a relief. He'd heard about guys, after major surgery, who couldn't get it up without a pump. But by the time she'd run her tongue to the base of his shaft, that particular doubt was allayed. She licked him gingerly, working her way to the head, then took him in her mouth, taking her time about it. He felt the urge to thrust and panicked, imagining what that would do. He pushed once, from the hips, and the pain was like a vampire's teeth in his spinal cord.

"Oww, shit. . . . Hey Tina, can we do this?"

"*I* can," she said, kissing the now swollen head of his cock. "You can't move. Can you take it?"

"What do you mean?"

He stared up at her, saw the smoky softness clouding her eyes. She raised her face reluctantly. "God, it's like a taffy apple."

Manny squirmed. "What did you mean, can I take it?"

"It means I can fuck you, but you can't fuck me. Can you deal with that?"

"So I wasn't just having bad dreams. You tied me up when I was asleep, so you could do me like this."

"If you have a question or complaint about medical procedure, the patients' advocate is in the nurses' station every morning from nine to ten-thirty."

His left hand was a solid gauze paw. He opened and closed his right one, working his wrist inside its taut canvas strap. "Tell me straight, is this you, or is it the doctor?"

"As nurse, I have authority and responsibility for the comfort of my patients."

"In other words, you did it."

He tried to glare at her, but she ignored him. "I thought I told you to close your eyes. I mean, *eye*."

Manny kept it open, staring up at her as she climbed on the bed. Gripping his IV bar for balance, she squatted no more than an inch or two over his face, straddling him.

"You're going to have to be very careful," she whispered, easing herself down until her wet lips just grazed his mouth. "Any violent movement could rip your stitches."

Manny breathed her in, then extended his tongue, and she let him taste her. He tried to crane upward, and she placed a firm hand on his forehead.

"What did I say about your stitches? Listen to your nurse, Detective. No straining."

She lowered herself again, gauging pressure, so that she could rock gently backward and forward on his face, all the while holding the IV arm with one hand and making sure he didn't try to crane upward with the other.

"Oh, baby, this must be so hard for you."

"*Mmmmmppphhh. . . .*"

She eased herself up, out of licking distance, and ran her finger over her sex. Her voice was a breathy whisper. "A man like you wants to be in control. That's what being a cop's all about, right? Control's just another drug you can't give up. *You* can't give it up, can you, Manny? But you *want* to. You *know* you want to. . . ."

Manny stared up at her, transfixed. His thumb began to throb.

"Are you going to torture me?"

"Is that a request or a question?"

Tina laughed and eased herself backward, careful not to touch him above the waist, where he'd been shot, where his ribs were wrapped tight, where the late Lipton's liver rested in its home away from home. Then she leaned down and kissed him, still talking softly. "Is this torture, Manny?"

She slipped her tongue in his mouth and planted one hand on his shoulder, reaching back to angle his cock between her legs. She threw back her head and shivered as she took him inside her.

"Come on, tell me" she murmured, digging her nails into his collarbone. "Is this torture? Huh, Manny? Is this torture, you big bad cop. . . ."

"You fucking bitch," he hissed through the sweat already running down his face. His kick was coming on by the second, the pain mounting even as the groaning pleasure ignited his psyche. The words poured out of him in a mindless rush, "I want to fuck you until I die . . . *I fucking love you. . . .*"

But Tina kept teasing. She pushed herself steadily up and down, never letting him all the way in. She stopped before her ass collided with his thighs, at once careful and reckless, driving him crazy by her own control. She'd push him to the brink, then slide back up, shimmying from side to side, all the while keeping her two eyes locked on his one.

"Is *this* torture," she kept repeating, timing each languid murmur to her downward thrusts. "Is *this* torture?"

Until, losing himself in the rhythm, in brute mortality, Manny forgot where he was. He abandoned all awareness of fresh stitches and drainage tubes and wounds still suppurating under gauze. He gave in and plunged upward, gone, until he opened a seam of flesh over his liver and cried out—*"FUCK!"*—and stopped completely, paralyzed by the blade of white-hot pain that impaled him like a jailhouse shank.

"Be careful," Tina whispered, and held still, only her beautiful small breasts rising and falling as she breathed. Manny wanted to run his tongue over the sheen of sweat on her body. He wanted to roll her over, to pin her down, *to be the man*. But he was helpless. She'd made him that way.

Tina lowered her face to his, so close he could see the flecks of blue and copper that shimmered in her green irises. "I know what you want, but you can't have it right now, baby. Right now *I* am fucking *you*," she chanted, "*I* am fucking *you*. . . ."

She repeated until she lost herself, and slammed down all the way, filling herself with every inch of him, and Manny let out a scream that made her clamp her hand over his mouth, come back to earth, and whisper, "I'm sorry. . . ."

But it wasn't pain that sent him out. It was something else. Something darker. The delicious, guilty, counter-to-everything-he-thought-he-knew-on-the-planet pleasure of surrendering control. This was, he knew beneath all consciousness, more dangerous than any narcotic. If he let go, like this, then surely the world would fall away. The earth would crack open and swallow him. It was that wrong. *And he no longer cared*. He gave up and savored the long, slow fall into the wet unknown. . . .

When he jerked back to consciousness Tina was riding him. *And there was nothing he could do.* Tears streamed down his face from his one good eye. The pain was a family of blood-red rats strangling on barbed wire under his skin.

"*You . . . can . . . kill . . . me,*" he heard himself cry, through clenched teeth, and something in the way he said it touched her in a place she'd never allowed anyone to touch. It was as if they'd left sex behind. Gone beneath it. The same delirium drove them both: love broken down to naked need, to jagged symmetry, the perfect insanity of passion between a woman like Tina and a man like him. . . .

Then Tina cried out his name, and she came with a kind of shuddering, perfectly still, drawn inward by a climax so strong as to paralyze her. She bit her lip until it bled, and released a long, low "*Yes-s-s-s. . . .*" Manny watched her, some desperate question stamped on his face. He fucked through the pain, toward the one thing that could consume it. Until Tina kissed him, let him lick the blood off her lips, and held his face so she could see it when he arched his back and shot whatever he had left of himself inside her.

"*My . . . whole . . . life,*" Manny muttered when it was over, breathing so hard his bandages popped apart.

Tina laughed, taped him back up, and slid sideways onto the hospital sheets. Careful not to press his wounds, she stretched beside him, nuzzling as close as she could, her lips pressed against his throat.

"Christ, I need a cigarette."

"You don't wanna know what I need," Manny replied, and looked miserably at his gauze girdle. "Hell on earth doesn't begin to describe what's going on down there."

"All right then," said Tina, swinging into professional nurse mode. "Take a couple of those Toradols. I'm also authorized to give you Chlonodine, as required."

She stood up, pulled open the nightstand drawer, and removed a mini–Dixie cup containing three chalk-white tablets.

"I hate Chlonodine."

"In that case you should take some. It lowers your blood pressure."

"I know what the shit does."

"You're an expert, I forgot. So you should know that when you lower your blood pressure, you reduce the discomfort of withdrawal. I'll leave some Xanax, too."

"I can't stand Xanax."

"Perfect, I'll leave three of those. And, in case you convulse, there's Tegretol."

"Are there any shitty drugs you're forgetting? Why not throw in whippets and airplane glue, and we can have a party?"

"Fine."

Tina'd pinned her hair back up, and was already stepping into her nurse's uniform. "If you OD it's no problem, the ICU's one floor down. We can make you a happy cabbage."

"Right," said Manny. "Speaking of human vegetables, if I don't get out of these restraints, I'm gonna need a diaper."

"Actually, you had one until yesterday."

Manny cringed, and Tina patted his hand. "Don't worry. It only makes me love you more. See you later."

She headed for the door and Manny called to her. "Tina, come on!" He tried to keep the pleading out of his voice. "You're not just going to leave me strapped down like this?"

She paused and made a show of considering. "Doctor would be very mad."

"I'm sure," he said miserably. "Would you just fucking get over here?"

"So much for postcoital glow." Tina took her time undoing the leather restraints at his hands and ankles. "I may never see you so lovable again."

"I don't know," said Manny weakly, when he could move his limbs, "that was amazing. I never . . . I mean, I've always been the fucker."

"Trust me, honey, you still are."

Manny waited until Tina closed the door, then shut his eye. He felt dizzy, ready to throw up, and completely in love. His own good luck scared him.

EPILOGUE

Manny's last morning in the hospital. Tina, pushing an empty wheelchair (the hospital's insurance required all departing patients be rolled to the curb), walked into his room just as a pink-faced, Jerry Falwell—looking fellow was walking out with a manila envelope.

Manny stood by the window, idly fingering the gouge under his eye patch where Zank's crack pipe had burned out a hollow of flesh.

"Time to go," Tina called, breaking his reverie with a bite on the back of his neck. "You're a free man."

Manny turned. No matter how many times he saw her in her nurse's uniform, the sight scorched him.

"I hate to leave," he said. "I was starting to dig the place."

"Checkout time's eleven, Stud. Who was your visitor?"

Manny hadn't decided whether to tell her, but one look and he knew there'd never been any question. He just had to lay it out.

"A guy from the RNC. The Republican National Committee."

"Right. . . . What did he want?"

"What do you think?" Manny paused, felt for the fresh scar on his belly, and started up again. "You know, I never realized, but when you really look at Mister Biobrain, up close, Bush is totally leering at his own equipment. Marge has a weird expression, too, like she's being goosed from the other end. 'It looks like an odd party.' That's what this guy said when I showed it to him. I don't know if that's Republican for 'perverted,' or if that's just how guys who went to Andover and Yale and work in 'deep politics' talk."

"Deep politics?" Tina didn't look happy.

"That's who Marge was dealing with. He's some kind of operator. And he was fucking sharp. I thought I recognized him from CNN, maybe MSNBC, but I didn't ask. Anyway, he said the smiley-face might have been drawn on the photo, not on George. 'We can bring people in to prove his testicles were undecorated.' He actually said that, like we were already in an impeachment hearing. You would have loved listening to him. 'We can show the photo was tampered with, but that doesn't buy us much. It's still the President's genitals, eye-level with a lady who's not his wife. One wrong move and we're looking at Scrotum-gate. That's the last thing our country needs. We had just about enough of that from Mr. Clinton, thank you.' "

Manny rubbed his one good eye, which throbbed from all its new responsibility.

"Did you tell him?" Tina asked.

"Tell him what? That that 'lady' used to be my wife? He probably knew anyway. He had all the angles." Manny imitated the man's genteel delivery. " 'If it turns out he did draw the little face on himself, that's a different kind of trouble. Then we're into abnormal behavior. Like Dick Morris and the toe thing. Or else it just looks juvenile, and we're back to the frat boy issue. . . . ' "

Tina squinted at him. If he was pinned, she'd spot it. Codeine would teeny up the pupils every bit as much as heroin.

"You haven't relapsed, have you? You seem a little chatty. You're doing voices."

"Give me a piss-test, Sweetheart. I'm eight days off everything but Advil and ginger ale. Did you know they bring twelve-step meetings to the liver ward? N.A. or the highway." He massaged his temples. "I'm kind of in shock that it's finally over. The guy came here to deal. So I made a deal."

Tina tried to read his face but couldn't. Since the morning he rolled out of surgery, they'd spent hours together every day. They'd made love whenever they could. Talked about everything in the world. The only secret left between them was the future.

Manny suddenly took her by the shoulders.

"Listen, Tina, they offered money."

"And?"

"I said no."

"You said *NO*?"

After all the times she'd fucked with his head, she wondered if now he was fucking with hers. Either that or he was going Marvin on her.

"Look," he went on, "I've thought about it. If I wanted cash, I could have sold the photo through Roos's buddy, to the highest bidder. But it's too messy. Once that picture hits, everybody's going to try and trace it back. Like Deep Throat. Besides, there's more important things than money."

"I wouldn't know," Tina replied. "I've never had any."

"Well, you could."

"What do you mean?"

"What I mean," Manny said, "is how would you like to be the wife of a Congressman?"

"WHAT?"

"I need to explain? Marge was planning to use Mister Biobrain to get into Congress. There's going to be a new seat from Upper Marilyn County. Some redistricting bullshit. And thanks to some backroom deal between parties, the Republicans own it."

"Manny—"

"Just listen." He moved a hand to her face, ran a finger over those cheekbones that still made his mouth dry. "Turns out Marge already let the big boys know she had a picture that would fuck their world. God love her, she told W.'s pals that unless they put her in Congress, she'd tell stories about her and the leader of the free world that would make Bill and Monica look like Fred and Ethel. Her bad luck, when I let the heavies know that I had the picture, well . . . let's just say they trust me more 'cause I'm a man. And I wear a badge." His grin was ambiguous. "Anyway, now she's fucked, and I'm in."

Tina started to speak, and Manny pressed a finger to her lips. "Before you say anything, there's something else. As part of the deal, I can't fix any of this."

He pointed to that pocket of seared flesh under his eye, then tapped his eye patch. He finished by raising his still bandaged fist, Black Power–style.

"It's sick," he said, but not unhappily. "They had their way, they'd chop off the rest of my hand and fit me with a hook. They want to play up the 'personal sacrifice' angle. *NOBLE COP WHO GOT MAIMED IN THE LINE OF DUTY.* Do the John McCain thing. The more I've sacrificed, the more people will love me. 'There aren't a lot of heroes, Detective Rubert, but you're one of them.' The guy actually said that. He also said they'd keep my thumb on ice—they can do that—and pay for any kind of surgery later, after I'm established. They'll put the money on account with whatever doctor I want."

Manny knew how this must sound. But he wanted her to know everything good, bad, and unconscionable.

"If it's okay with you, I'm gonna lay my surgical gift certificate on McCardle, let him get a new face. Maybe he can turn over a new leaf and go for Sammy Davis this time. I'll give the business to Roos. I owe both of 'em. Anyway, the Democrats aren't even going to field a candidate, so it's a lock. In a couple of years, a Senate seat comes available. Who knows? In a decade or two, we could be banging in Lincoln's bedroom. . . . Of course, if you say yes, you'll be married to a mutant. But what the hell."

For a long moment, Tina didn't say anything, then she smiled and slipped her hand between his legs.

"I can handle the mutant part, baby, but I never had you pegged as a Republican."

Manny shrugged. "Life's a compromise," he said, and dropped into the wheelchair for the long ride out.